THIRTEEN HEAVENS

GUERNICA WORLD EDITIONS 26

THIRTEEN HEAVENS

Mark Fishman

GUERNICA
World
EDITIONS

TORONTO—CHICAGO—BUFFALO—LANCASTER (U.K.)
2020

Michael Mirolla, general editor
Julie Roorda, editor
Cover design: Allen Jomoc Jr.
Interior layout: Jill Ronsley, suneditwrite.com
Guernica Editions Inc.
287 Templemead Drive, Hamilton (ON), Canada L8W 2W4
2250 Military Road, Tonawanda, N.Y. 14150-6000 U.S.A.
www.guernicaeditions.com

Distributors:
Independent Publishers Group (IPG)
600 North Pulaski Road, Chicago IL 60624
University of Toronto Press Distribution,
5201 Dufferin Street, Toronto (ON), Canada M3H 5T8
Gazelle Book Services, White Cross Mills
High Town, Lancaster LA1 4XS U.K.

First edition.
Printed in Canada.

Legal Deposit—First Quarter
Library of Congress Catalog Card Number: 2019947117
Library and Archives Canada Cataloguing in Publication
Title: Thirteen heavens / Mark Fishman.
Names: Fishman, Mark, 1954- author.
Description: Series statement: Guernica world editions ; 26
Identifiers: Canadiana (print) 20190163453 | Canadiana (ebook)
20190163461 | ISBN 9781771835282
(softcover) | ISBN 9781771835299 (EPUB) | ISBN 9781771835305 (Kindle)
Classification: LCC PS3606.I835 T47 2020 | DDC 813/.6—dc23

Come now, let us reason together, says the Lord:
though your sins are like scarlet,
they shall be as white as snow;
though they are red like crimson,
they shall become like wool.
—Isaiah 1:18

Forgiveness is for small things, not for sins.
—Mohammed Mrabet, *"Qrira"*

ubén "Rocket" Arenal, standing in front of the plate glass window of a bridal gown store, La Popular, and its wood-paneled shop floor, raising one leg then the other, a cramp, calves sore from running, a kind of stitch in his side, the muscles of his legs aching, never out of breath, and the sun hanging by a cable above Chihuahua in a blue sky streaked with clouds, a city in the north of Mexico, south of New Mexico and west of Texas, the sun pouring its heat on the tapped inhabitants, bled of energy, people walking the grid-patterned city, moving here and there, not such a big city after all, or just sitting down fanning themselves in the high temperature of midday, in the central Plaza de Armas, or Plaza Hidalgo, but Rubén Arenal, feet firmly planted on the sidewalk, looking at a woman's tall, slender figure in a bridal gown, *La Pascualita,* or Little Pascuala, veined hands, wide-set sparkling glass eyes, eerie smile, real hair and blushing skin tones, she even had varicose veins on her legs, Rubén Arenal rubbing the calluses on the palm of his right hand with his right thumb, a habit when he was nervous, a tic without moving a muscle of his face, he didn't raise his eyebrows, no surprise, he was frozen there, a fixed gaze resting on a woman standing behind glass in a shop window, a mannequin first installed there on March 25th, 1930, dressed that morning in a spring-season gown, they still put curtains up in the shop window to preserve the dummy's modesty, March 25th, 1930, a Tuesday under the sign of Aries without a cloud in the sky, and now, Rubén Arenal, faster than a speeding bullet, stopping to look at her three times a week, or more, a destination after making his way through the city, a population of a little more than 800,000, and Rocket, what year is it? I don't remember, and who cares, Rubén Arenal concentrating on other things, recognizing a trait in the face of the dummy, a distinguishing characteristic, not the daughter of Pascuala Esparza, a striking resemblance to a girl he'd seen, and Rocket, you'll remember, take your time take your time, giving her more than a once-over, I *am* taking my time, Rubén Arenal answering no one, each day thinking the same thing, remembering a story, a sort of rumor that the figure wasn't a dummy, a mannequin resembling Pascuala Esparza, the shop's owner at the time, looking a lot like her, it was the perfectly preserved corpse of Pascuala Esparza's daughter, she didn't have a name, or if she did no one remembered it, *La Pascualita,* who died from the bite of a female black widow spider—*araña capulina, chintatlahua,* or from the Nahuatl, *tzintlatlauhqui,* meaning "the red one"—on her wedding day.

Rubén Arenal admiring her, a well-preserved corpse, *La Pascualita,* and the other passersby, turning away from the bright reflection of the sun on the pavement, passersby casting their reflection in the window of La Popular, a few of them gathering around the shop window, lighting votive candles, leaving flowers, white dahlias, and already there were bright orange zinnias with yellow stamens, the purple flowers of the cane cholla, a cactus with a cylindrical stem, and a handful of pink sand verbenas, a prostrate perennial with thick, succulent leaves and pink-colored flowers with white centers, and Rocket, they must've come from far away, but from where? Rubén Arenal, fond of plants and flowers, appreciating them, and Rocket, Chihuahua's name in the Uto-Aztecan language, Nahuatl, maybe it's rooted in the word *xicuahua,* meaning "dry and sandy place," the pink sand verbenas might've come from someone's garden, Rubén Arenal watching the flickering light of five votive candles, a light lost in the painful brightness of daylight, and there was a quiet respect from everyone standing there looking at Little Pascuala, no words, a stillness, and a little veil of curiosity, Rubén Arenal counting the faces, one two three four five, and then they dispersed, went on their way, but another arrived, then another, and a few people who just turned their heads, looking left and right, looking at the window display of Casa Meouchi S.A., Victoria number 805, *artículos del hogar,* household articles, shiny pots and pans, or a building for rent half a block away, who could say, but now Rubén Arenal was the only one standing in front of the shop window, rubbing the calluses on the palm of his right hand, the synovial palmar carpal tendinous sheath, then folding his arms, turning his head to look up at the sky, his thoughts evaporating in the heat of the sun.

Rubén Arenal turned away from the window, the weight of long minutes of concentration lifting from him, shoulders light as feathers, but right away he missed the absent weight, as if he'd lost something that had always belonged to him, but another day, another visit, Rubén Arenal facing Avenida Ocampo, blinking in the sunlight, his eyes looking away from the heat waves shimmering along the street, now gazing up at the red banner of Zapaterías Irlanda, Coyote Joe boots, then across the street at Rodeo City, Rubén Arenal turning right and walking down Calle Libertad, approaching Plaza Merino on his left, Calle 4a and the Catedral de Chihuahua ahead of him, the skies in his head as clear as they'd been while he was running, with circulating blood carrying loads of oxygen, no *La Pascualita* to get in the way, a mind free of questions, but his taste buds opening their eyes, an appetite after physical and mental exertions, Rubén Arenal thinking of Shiwawita on Calle Victoria, his favorite grocery store, scratching his head, and Rocket, so why take Calle Libertad, you oughta be heading straight for Shiwawita, taking Calle Victoria, spending a little money on *chabacanos,* apricots, and a bag of *mango enchilado,* mango with chile, or *pinole,* roasted maize-flour so I can mix it with cold water, cinnamon and sugar, make a couple of glasses when I get home, and the discomfort of the day with its glaring light ready to kill, Rubén Arenal wanting a cigarette, reaching for a pack of Faros in his shirt pocket, nothing there, it was empty, no rice-paper cigarettes, not a pack of Delicados or Fiesta, no white and green and black pack of Aros, he'd have to wait, maybe a piece of chewing gum, he put a Chiclets in his mouth, and Rocket, from the Nahuatl, *tziktli*, or *tzictli*, check the dictionary, shutting his eyes against the light, listening to his footfalls, under his lids images flickering, then slowing down to snapshots, a part of the stock of Shiwawita at his fingertips, jars of salsa, walnut jelly, crisp tortillas, cheese, dried meat, walnut, almond and pine eggnog cream, fig honey-drop candies, and he saw his hand reach for more than a few *paletas*, a handful of popsicles, *plátano, cereza, mamey, y limón*, banana, cherry, mammee apple, and lemon to cool him off.

A scissor-tailed flycatcher, *tirano tijereta rosado*, bluish-gray with salmon-pink flanks extending to under-wing patches, red-orange sides, blackish wings with an elongated, deeply-forked black tail with white edges, a *tirano tijereta rosado* standing on a bench, not resting there, but alert and watching and ready to shoot like a star into the overly bright sky, Rubén Arenal approaching it—he didn't see a thing, blind as a bat with his eyes shut—and the bird stood its ground, the bench, a scissor-tailed flycatcher, *Tyrannus forficatus*, waiting for him to get nearer, and the flycatcher, Ernesto Cisneros, a bird's whisper as accurate as a dart, hitting Rubén Arenal right between the eyes, the name of his best friend, he could count his close friends on one hand, Ernesto Cisneros Fuentes, named after the football midfielder, a happy coincidence provided by Ernesto's father's first *apellido*, Rubén Arenal hearing the bird without seeing it, recognizing its voice, his eyes still closed, but he saw Ernesto and himself projected on his eyelids, it was a long time ago, a memory, and in the memory he was talking to Ernesto, and Rocket, you're intelligent, Esto, we both are, we're advanced for our age, Rubén Arenal and Ernesto, the same age, around nine years old, and Rocket, you're better with words than I am, *mi amigo*, I'm good with my hands, but I can't draw you something right here right now without my pencils, so say something! a few words, don't be shy, Ernesto lowering his eyes to hide his emotions, Rubén Arenal ribbing his friend, giving him a light punch on the shoulder, Ernesto giving him a playful shove back, and Rocket, that's right, you can say we're learning to read and write, so we're deserving students, how about a few *paletas,* popsicles or ice cream, what do you say? I'm buying, my allowance is a little pocket money that'll give us both a treat, Ernesto's expression brightened, but his lips were still sealed, Rubén Arenal opening his eyes, focusing on the flycatcher in front of him, and Rocket, here I am now and not then, but look how one thought leads to another, with my two feet in the present, I'm going to take a step back to yesterday, or it was the day before, what difference does it make, when friends are friends it doesn't matter which day it is, it's the content that counts, but it really wasn't long ago, earlier this very week, just a few days, or only two, and weighed down by the heat of the midday sun, standing in front of Ernesto's house, having a heart-to-heart, but there were tears this time, crying, because there's no good-natured teasing in a tragedy, Rubén Arenal with his arm around Ernesto's shoulder, comforting a friend because his friend's son, Coyuco Cisneros Muñoz, a student at the Raúl Isidro Burgos Normal Rural School of Ayotzinapa in Tixtla, was missing, disappeared, Rubén Arenal squeezing Ernesto's shoulder in a firm grip, and Rocket, I know you've got to go, don't explain a thing, but it's a long drive in that rust bucket of yours, your Renault 8, *mi amigo,* almost a thousand miles by car, so you better take my Ford F-150, the Lobo pickup, you know the wolf, you've driven it, a proud animal and relible machine, Rubén Arenal, a mind like a steel trap, shutting his eyes again, his voice repeating from memory while his fingers drew a map, and Rocket, let's see, Esto, you'll be heading out on Mexico 45/ Carretera Jiménez-Chihuahua to Mexico 45D, and then Mexico 49D/Carretera Gómez Palacio-Jiménez and Durango, merging onto Mexico 40D/Carretera Durango-Gómez Palacio to

Mexico 49/Carretera Entronque La Chicharrona-Cuencamé and Zacatecas, continuing on Mexico 49/Carretera San Luis Potosí-Entronque Arcinas and San Luis Potosí to Mexico 57/ Carretera Querétaro-San Luis Potosí and Querétaro de Arteaga, Mexico 57D and Mexico, Mexico 95D toward Taxco Cuota/Iguala Cuota and Guerrero, then Mexico 95/Carretera Taxco-Iguala into Iguala, and what the fuck! what happened, and why on earth? *¡Madre de Dios!* and *¡Dios mío!* Rubén Arenal retching without bringing anything up, thinking to himself, plunging into a canyon of no hope, and Rocket, it doesn't really matter where or when, disappeared or dead, we'll never see him again, it's a country of ghosts, *mi México,* and I'd bet 7,754 pesos, a sum I haven't got, but if I sold two dozen *hidrias,* two sets of bowls, plates, tea and coffee cups, and don't forget the price of gas to fill up the Ford, I'd bet that Coyuco was killed in Pueblo Viejo, fifteen inhabitants, not even a village in the middle of nowhere, near Iguala, Iguala de la Independencia, on Federal Highway 95, around sixty-seven miles from Chilpancingo, the capital city of the state of Guerrero.

Rubén Arenal, opening his eyes, almost colliding with another pedestrian, a fat woman eating peanuts without looking where she was going, tears in the corners of his eyes, a memory's as good as it feels right now, a big sadness stuck to the soles of his shoes making him drag his feet, perspiration under his arms, the damp fabric of his shirt sticking to the skin on his back, chewing his mint gum, a fresh flavor, Rubén Arenal shaking his head to throw off a despairing thought of Ernesto, and of Coyuco, Rubén Arenal looking at his hands, fingernails with clay residue beneath the nails, long hours throwing pots, a ball of clay placed on the wheel head, shaping it, then another, and another, firing the clay, making pots with narrow spouts, mugs for *posol,* bowls, plates, a *hidria,* a jar or pitcher for water, cups for tea, mugs for coffee, a vase for flowers, Rubén Arenal making pottery with fettling knives, fluting tools, wires, paddles, ribs and scrappers, a few things he'd brought from Mata Ortiz, a *ejido,* a small land-grant village with adobe dwellings, a village four and a half hours south and west of El Paso in the high plains of northern Chihuahua, between the mountains of the Sierra Madre and the desert, along the banks of the Palanganas River, it was a long time ago, learning how to make pottery, not hitting the books, but hands on, studying not far from the ruins of Casas Grandes, and the city Nuevo Casas Grandes, Rubén Arenal learning to use the coil method, and scraping pots with a hacksaw blade to shape them, using an inverted flowerpot sagger covered in cottonwood bark, or manure, and then setting it on fire, the Mata Ortiz way, then Rubén Arenal returning to his home in Chihuahua, refining his technique, a curious amalgam of the traditional and the modern, and Rocket, but I owe an enormous debt to Mata Ortiz, forever and ever and each day after, Rubén Arenal using as many methods as he could put together in his head and hands and eyes, using a potter's wheel, not always, but most of the time, they didn't use a potter's wheel in Mata Ortiz, and now and then, a few pots with the bottom molded, the upper part created by the coil method, just to keep his hand in, Rubén Arenal, blushing, wiped the tears from his eyes.

Rubén Arenal kept on walking, cruising on automatic pilot, and Rocket, you've got to follow the feet, brother, they're taking you somewhere, and you've got to have the confidence that even though you think you don't know where you're going they'll get you there, and in this case, a hint, a nudge in the ribs to say to yourself, I know where I'm going, I'm headed straight for the cathedral, going there with *La Pascualita* and my memories, *La Pascualita* and my daydreams, *La Pascualita* and my nightmares, my fears, and the un-equivocal sorrow of Coyuco's disappearance, and then a voice in his head, a reply he wasn't expecting, knowing he was already talking to himself, a voice saying, so you're going to see the judge? that's a new departure, and Rocket, what're you talking about? and why are you bothering me with questions? it's a cathedral, and in a cathedral there's God, not a judge, Rubén Arenal at first feeling a warm caress in the palm of his hand, it felt like a feather had dropped there, Rubén Arenal turning his head sharply to the left, something or someone brushing against him, he was sure of it, and now it was like a hand grasping his, but there was no one there, nothing, an empty sidewalk in the heat from the sun that burned like the bite of a rabid dog, an insensitive sun beating down on pedestrians, cars, trucks, lampposts and traffic lights, Rubén Arenal wiping his forehead with a handkerchief, the other hand occupied by a warm hand he couldn't see, and a sudden thirst, desperate even, mouth parched, harking back to a childhood memory, and Rocket, a few *paletas,* that's what I want, my sister's got them in the freezer, popsicles and three children, Avelina, Perla, Cirilo, my nieces and a nephew, one thing—or three, in this case—goes with the other, I won't buy anything now, I'll go to my sister's, with a stop on the way, Rubén Arenal tightening his grip on the hand that wasn't there, exhaling, not a breath of fresh air, some pollution, and Rocket, but really, it's warm, and using the handkerchief again, the hand holding his was squeezing back, but Rubén Arenal, focused on what was in front of him, he'd got to where he was going, Plaza de Armas, looking at the Catedral de Chihuahua, and Rocket, it's no time for shamanism, or maybe so, but I haven't got the patience for someone with access to and influence in the world of good and evil spirits—how I remember a definition when I read one!—prayer's what it takes, and he went into the Metropolitan Cathedral of Chihuahua, heading straight for the side altar on the northern side of the chancel and the statue of Our Lady of Sorrows to make the sign of the cross.

A recording of Mariachi Coculense, lead by Cirilo Marmolejo on guitarrón, Pedro Casillas and Casimiro Contreras on violin, Jesús Briseño and Pedro Alaniz on guitar, José and Juan Marmolejo on vihuela, Mariachi Coculense playing "La Pulquera," "The Pulque Vendor," a bright and mournful *canción*:

Pensando en que me querías
me pasaba yo los días
rasguñando la pared.
Al tiempo en que despertaba
la tristeza me agobiaba
y volvía yo a beber.
Buscando en otras mujeres,
en el vino, en los placeres
un consuelo a mi dolor;
allá donde me dormía
de mi mente renacía
un consuelo embriagador.

Al santo señor de Chalma
yo le pido con el alma
que te deje de querer;
porque esta vida que llevo
si no fuera porque bebo
no la habría de merecer.
Recuerda de aquella madrugada
en la pila colorada
con otro hombre te encontré;
sentí que ya no eras mía,
luego, allá en la pulquería,
solito me consolé.

Chaparra yo te maldigo
pues cuando vivías conmigo
me juraste un amor;
Mas nunca me comprendiste
no supiste lo que hiciste
sólo fui tu diversión.
Al fin, la vereda andamos

si algún día nos encontramos
para ti no habrá perdón:
¡ingrata mujer perjura
le robaste la ternura
a mi pobre corazón!

But Coyuco wasn't drunk or drinking, enjoying the song playing in his head, thinking of Irma Payno Cruzado, his fiancée, named by her parents after the singer and actress, Irma Serrano, La Tigresa, Coyuco riding in a bus, Costa Line 2513, traveling down the road beneath a sky like any other evening sky at this time of year, a passenger together with eight others from the Raúl Isidro Burgos Normal Rural School of Ayotzinapa, a group of nine students, Coyuco, and half a dozen regular passengers in a bus they commandeered outside of Huitzuco, now heading for Iguala, nineteen miles and less than twenty minutes away, the driver wanting to drop his passengers off in Iguala before taking the students back to Ayotzinapa, and the students agreeing to it, ok, nothing unusual, it's better not to mention it, we do it all the time, and the two buses they'd taken on the road from the Raúl Isidro Burgos Normal Rural School, expropriated from Chilpancingo in the middle of the month, to get them to just outside Huitzuco in the hopes of getting their hands on other buses, those two buses somewhere back there outside of Huitzuco, and Coyuco, that makes three altogether, we can't see them now but we know they're there.

The students of Raúl Isidro Burgos Normal Rural School intending to use all the buses they seized to take them to Mexico City on October 2nd, in seven days, to attend a march commemorating the army and police massacre in 1968 of hundreds of university and high school students in Mexico City, the *Battalón Olympia* starting the shooting, that's what everyone said, Díaz Ordaz Bolaños was president then, and the police and army firing into a crowd outside the Chihuahua Building in La Plaza de las Tres Culturas, tanks

bulldozing the plaza, the Tlatelolco massacre, Tlatelolco, from the
Nahuatl, meaning "little hill of land," an area in the Cuauhtémoc
borough of Mexico City, the stain of Tlatelolco, a dishonor with everyone watching—I don't *want* to be dead because I can't forget what
they did, those who aren't afraid of God—and now, Coyuco, and at
least eight other students, the regular passengers getting off in less
than fifteen minutes, they were all traveling in a bus *normalistas* had
commandeered outside of Huitzuco, Coyuco hearing the song, "Las
cuatro milpas," "Four Little Cornfields," another *canción,* and still
Mariachi Coculense, or "El Gavilancillo," "The Young Hawk," a *son
mexicano* to give him courage, but he didn't really need it, he had
plenty of courage, Coyuco knowing their songs by heart, his mind
interrupting him, hey, what's wrong, why are you so distracted? but
the music wasn't trespassing on anybody's land, instead, it was a
kind of fuel, a propellant driving him forward, and without knowing it, Coyuco was heading down the highway toward Iguala and
nothing that looked like the grace of a good death.

Nobody but the police or the army could smell blood at any distance, except the mayor of Iguala and his wife, who had a reputation
for smelling the liquid that circulates in the bodies of humans in advance of those who only saw it once it was spilling out on the street
and running down the gutter cut for carrying off rainwater, so no
one had a clue about what was going to happen after nine o'clock that
night, maybe a *cuervo llanero,* if it'd been daylight, a Chihuahuan
raven could've told them, calling a high-pitched *a-a-rk,* a bird with
surprising talents, sending out a warning, an alert to anyone who'd
listen, but it was night, the birds were asleep, or busy, so there was no
one to tell anyone to watch out, keep your eyes peeled, life's treacherous, it's not just the mayor, José Luis Alacrán, it's the government on
a bigger scale, the Center for Command, Control, Communications
and Computer Systems, C-4, in Chilpancingo, in Iguala, the clues
are everywhere, don't be naive, and the police, with something up
their sleeve, plan ahead, that's our motto, the local police waiting for

the students of the Raúl Isidro Burgos Normal Rural School, a kind of ambush, a surprise attack, or a gift for improvisation, performing spontaneously or without preparation, and nearby, the political big shots of Iguala were gathered in the Civic Plaza for the second annual report from a regional development agency—the National System for Integral Family Development's Iguala office—with four thousand *acarreados,* people bused in to fill the event, a rally in the plaza that was a thinly veiled pre-campaign party for the mayor's wife, a woman hoping to succeed her husband once he'd left office, the first lady and the Queen of Iguala, but they were in the Civic Plaza, while a couple of second-year students at the Raúl Isidro Burgos Normal Rural School, Fernando Marín and Bernardo Flórez, a.k.a. Cochiloco, were coordinating a majority of first-year students on one of their *actividades,* an action—they'd got their hands on the first two buses in mid-September in Chilpancingo, Estrella de Oro 1568 and 1531, keeping them at the school, the drivers, too, with meals provided—an action that brought them out tonight to take possession of a few more buses because there weren't enough of them at the Raúl Isidro Burgos Normal Rural School to get them all to Mexico City on October 2nd, a total now of about a hundred students on an *actividad* led by student teachers, second-year and first-year students that'd left the all-male Raúl Isidro Burgos Normal Rural School of Ayotzinapa, a *Escuela Normal,* at around five-thirty in the afternoon with the idea of getting their hands on as many buses as they could find around Iguala, not Chilpo, where they usually went to do their activities, it was too dangerous, second-year students and the mostly first-year students, all of them *normalistas,* were heading for the bus station in Iguala de la Independencia.

And now, José Ángel, or Tío Tripa, a *normalista,* a married man with two daughters, seated in front of Coyuco, it was José Ángel, a rallying voice, a voice of experience because of his age, thirty-three, the bus pulling off the road, and the driver, sounding his horn to clear the way, arriving at the station, it was twelve minutes after nine, Coyuco looking at his watch, and the driver, opening the door to let the regular passengers off, turning his head, looking back at Coyuco and the nine students still sitting on the bus, the driver fixing an eye on José Ángel, and the driver, hang on a minute, I'll have to get permission to head back to Ayotzinapa, if that's where you're going, I'll take you there, no problem, Coyuco hearing every word, José Ángel nodding his head, Coyuco grinding his teeth when he heard the words no problem, and Coyuco Cisneros, there're some words I just can't stand, Coyuco and José Ángel and seven other pairs of eyes watching the driver get down off the bus, eighteen impatient eyes following the driver, or seventeen, Miguel Alfonso's bad eye didn't know, he himself couldn't see much, not blind but blurry, and the driver walking to where a couple of station security guards were posted in order to get the permission he was looking for.

And José Ángel, a voice in his head, it might be a delay tactic, I don't like it, but Coyuco, hearing Los Alegres de Terán playing "Prefiero sufrir," "I'd Rather Suffer," still another *canción,* a little *música norteña,* with Tomás Ortíz, vocals and bajo sexto, Eugenio Abrego, vocals and accordion, and Spiros "Pete" Arfanos on bass, Coyuco, keeping his mind on the street, but relaxed, not watching the driver speaking to two security guards, he was looking at the passersby, but José Ángel, eyes fixed on the driver who looked at his watch, tapping the watch's face with a couple of fingers, the driver giving the impression he was listening to what the security guards had to say, nodding, okay, but they weren't saying much, and a guard, you did your duty, now we're going to make a couple of calls, and the driver, looking up at the sky, a feather of light from the sunset lingering there, but the sun had already fallen off the edge of the earth, a fiery feather of light hanging like a thread of smoke in the air, the driver scanning the horizon, shooting a glance at the bus, and a few blocks away the political elite, including a colonel from the 27th Infantry Battalion, and four thousand *acarreados,* peasants bused in to listen to speeches, future voters if the politicians played their cards right, together, they were listening to speeches, an enthusiastic crowd, a burst of applause, a little whistling, but right here, not far from Civic Plaza, the bus driver, talking again with a security guard, the other taking a couple of steps away, speaking into a radio, the driver trying to hear what he was saying, but the station guard standing in front of him, a voice burnt by tobacco and pulque, and the station guard, don't bother, it's got nothing to do with you, friend, if you know what's good for you you'll mind your own business, and then bringing his phone to his ear, an official on the other end of the line, his superior, the driver kept on listening, each conversation stumbling over the other, mixing words, the driver trying to look like he wasn't paying attention to anything, a lousy actor, José Ángel watching him, the guard acting like a pro, like he'd been on the stage, confidence and authority, the voices muffled or there was too much noise floating around to hear more than a phrase or two hanging in the air, then words falling to the hard surface at the driver's feet, he couldn't gather much out of what he was hearing, the guards rattling off information, one into a phone, the other into a radio, José Ángel, waiting and restless, Coyuco, wide awake and wary, and he wasn't hearing anything but the loud throbbing and constant pulsating in his blood vessels, his skin beginning to itch, José Ángel and Coyuco, and eight other students were more than anxious that the driver wasn't going to get back on the bus, and the doors were locked.

José Ángel holding his phone in his hand, Coyuco, all sound except the voices around him fading in his ears, nobody was jittery but on the alert, a collective spark, a small fiery particle thrown off from a fire igniting the explosive mixture in the bus, here we are! and José Ángel, to himself, you can wait for only so long before waiting isn't worth the time you spend, and a couple of other students, reaching for their phones, and José Ángel, we've got to do it, and now's the time, *mis amigos,* or never—just as real events are forgotten, some that never were, that didn't exist, can be in our memories as if they'd happened, and this situation, the one we're in now, is as real as the sweat on our skin and the hairs in our nose, you can believe me, *aquin achtopa iztlacati ayecmo occepa moneltoca,* he who lies once, is not to be believed twice, José Ángel turning to Coyuco, and José Ángel, fuck it, we're going to take more buses when the others get here and let us out, shouting to the eight other students, when you get hold of the others tell them to get what they can off the street, fill their pockets and hands with rocks, anything, we've got to defend ourselves, *mis amigos,* and tell them to get the fuck over here right now, José Ángel thinking, danger's heading toward us like spilled blood, and a little panic in his voice, *¡Órale que no tenemos todo el día!* we don't have all day! and all of them on the phone, trying to reach the *normalistas* on the two buses still outside of Huitzuco, Estrella de Oro 1531 and 1568, buses they'd grabbed at the Chilpancingo bus station ten days earlier, and when they'd reached them, José Ángel, Coyuco, the eight other students, telling them what was going on, and their voices, together, just in case, you'd better pick up rocks, sun-dried bricks, anything you can throw with your bare hands, a little courage in your hearts, a living flame in your balls, so the students still outside of Huitzuco, or they were already on the highway and had to pull over, almost tripping over each other as they clambered out of the buses, each in a fury, loyal figures leaving crimson streaks of light in their wake like they'd swallowed habañeros, running here and there, left and right, collecting rocks of all sizes and shapes, a couple of broken branches, finding a bent wheel rim, a dented hubcap, a thick piece of tire tread, stockpiling them, as many as they could carry and lay at their feet on the floor in the buses next to their seats, and the *normalistas,* student teachers, and the first- and second-year students, okay, let's go, the two buses pulling out onto the highway, two vehicles moving as fast as the two drivers could make them go, each with a foot pressing the accelerator to the floor, heading for Iguala and the central bus station.

Rubén Arenal returning home from the Metropolitan Cathedral of Chihuahua, and the statue of Our Lady of Sorrows, having comforted his broken heart, it was only slightly torn when it came to Little Pascuala, *la sombra de la mujer amada,* the shadow of the beloved woman, but it was completely shattered when it came to Coyuco, and Our Lady of Sorrows, a statue in the altar on the northern side of the chancel, he'd made the sign of the cross in front of her, bearing a truly broken heart—one thing was vulnerable love, the other the end of Coyuco's life, Rubén Arenal marking the difference in the degree of his suffering by counting his heartbeats— Rubén Arenal making the sign of the cross and offering a prayer for Ernesto, Guadalupe, he'd almost forgotten about her until he found himself standing in front of the statue, and a prayer for their son, faith in the palms of his hands, and now, as he opened the door of his ground-floor apartment, a simple home, and his pottery studio, Rubén Arenal pulling his shirt over his head, the sweat on his back making it stick to his skin, Rubén Arenal leaving the shirt hanging over the back of a chair, and a song sung by Dueto Río Bravo, Eva Gurrola Castellanos and María de la Luz Pulgarin Gurrola, a melancholy song, "Llorando a mares," "In a Flood of Tears," written by Rogelio González, "Llorando a mares" was playing in his head, Rubén Arenal wanting to take a bath, stripping off his clothes, laying his trousers neatly on his bed, and Rocket, it's time to wash away the sadness stuck to me like paste, or wedged clay, Rubén Arenal, his untidy long hair falling onto his rounded cheeks, his languid, sad eyes, and the marked signs of good health, in contrast with his mood, he turned on the tap and let the water slowly fill the bathtub, at first a bit rusty, or brownish in color, and later, in the bath, another song, Dueto Río Bravo, "Vengan jilgueros," a *canción* about goldfinches, written by Ricardo Domínguez, Rubén Arenal scrubbing himself with a sponge made of a sponge gourd, its coarse fibers removing dirt and dead cells from his skin, and a few of his worries, while the window in the ceiling above him threw afternoon light in the shape of a lozenge on the surface of the bath water.

La Pascualita, or Little Pascuala, veined hands, wide-set sparkling eyes, and an eerie smile, most of the time and almost every day, *La Pascualita'*s face and figure, as attractive to him as an ordinary world of daydreams, Little Pascuala appearing in Rubén Arenal's mind, standing before him just as she looked standing in the window of La Popular, but living and breathing, and Rocket, yes, she's alive! Rubén Arenal wondering if she really was Pascuala Esparza's daughter, knowing that he'd seen her before, not once but many times, and it wasn't in the shop window but on the street at night, walking in Chihuahua, although he couldn't be sure, he might've been imagining it, because he never really saw her face, not in full light, a streetlight behind her throwing a shadow on her head, a woman accompanied by her mother in the street at night, arm in arm, a couple of dignified women, maybe Little Pascuala, maybe not, but Rubén Arenal swearing he'd seen someone who looked a lot like her, swearing under his breath so no one would hear him, and Rocket, otherwise they'll drive me out twenty miles southwest of Juárez, on the northern edge of the state, and leave me at Visión en Accion—that's the place, Vision in Action, an asylum in the desert—in the hands of José Antonio Galván, *El Pastor,* a charismatic man, a kind of saint, wearing black trousers and a black blazer, it was José Antonio Galván who built it, Visión en Accion, somewhere for people with problems to go for help, drugs and prison, or a faulty brain, Rubén Arenal, rubbing the calluses on the palm of his right hand, the ulnar bursa, and Rocket, I don't want to be there, *en serio,* okay, so it's like a home or family, but I'm not crazy, not yet, I'm pretty sure of what I've seen, Little Pascuala's got a dead ringer who isn't standing in a shop window, and a question, is it you? yes, it's you, but Rubén Arenal shaking his head, wet strands of long hair sticking to his face, he wasn't quite certain, doubting himself except when it came to throwing pots, a ball of clay placed on the wheel head, shaping it, then another, and another, Rubén Arenal looking closely at his face in the bathroom mirror, wrapped in a towel, leaving wet footprints on the floor, searching his studio, picking out clean clothes, getting ready to visit his sister, Luz Elena, Rubén Arenal putting on a T-shirt and a pair of jeans, no socks, combing his hair, looking forward to seeing Avelina, Perla and Cirilo, his nieces and a nephew, and a freezer full of *paletas,* ice pops, creamy milk-based and fruity water-based flavors, as many as he could eat, he was dying of thirst, as dry as the desert, so it's his sister, Luz Elena, and her three children, Rubén Arenal already tasting popsicles, freezing his tongue, and a longing for a glass of something cold to drink, a thought for Ernesto, Guadalupe, and Coyuco, Rubén Arenal changing course, heading for *La Pascualita,* a gleam in his eye, always Little Pascuala, and Rocket, it had to be last night, with the burning heat of the day still playing in the dark, Rubén Arenal and the last time he saw the woman who looked like a double for Little Pascuala, *esa mujer celestial,* that heavenly woman, who's existence seemed not to belong to this world, but a higher region, *La Pascualita,* or her look-alike, dressed in black, walking next to her mother, also dressed in black, a *rebozo* draped over her shoulders, her mother's shoulders not *La Pascualita*'s, and the woman who was a double for Little Pascuala, opening her lips, a few remarks to her mother about the heat, the wind, the night, he didn't really hear what she said, just the sound of her voice, but her words echoing in his ears, her alabaster fingers pushing a few strands of hair away from her face, but still in shadow, he couldn't see her eyes, a veined hand, he couldn't say because there wasn't enough light, the double for Little Pascuala, graceful, her mother with a *rebozo* covering her shoulders, black and deep-blue with knotted fringe, a shawl from Pátzcuaro in Michoacán, mother and daughter, ever-shifting, together, walking unhurriedly, taking a stroll, getting some fresh air on a night radiating with heat like a furnace, they rounded a corner and disappeared.

Five painted plaster mariachi figurines, dressed in elegant black suits trimmed with white, gold belt buckles, ties the color of the Mexican flag, and sombreros, not the old-style mariachis, white pants and shirts and huaraches, but plaster figurines with skulls for faces, each playing an instrument, except the singer, his arms at his sides, Rubén Arenal thinking of Mariachi Tapatío when he'd bought them, Mexico's premiere mariachi, the mid-1930s to the mid-1940s, from Tecolotlán in Jalisco, to the south, with the leader José Marmolejo Ramírez, *El hombre de la eterna sonrisa*, "The man of the perpetual smile," playing vihuela, a five-string guitar, and the others, certainly Jesús Salazar, trumpet, Gabriel Arias, after a drinking binge, sober and playing guitarrón, and Amador Santiago on violin, and there were still others in Mariachi Tapatío, a musician playing Spanish guitar, another playing a second violin, and a guitarra de golpe virtuoso, but in his collection, with their skeleton's faces, there weren't enough figurines, standing in a semi-circle on a low table, to make up all of Mariachi Tapatío, so it couldn't have been them, but Rubén Arenal hearing Mariachi Tapatío, and it wasn't his figurines, now a couple of singers' voices, always a singer to carry him away, it was Mariachi Tapatío, Rubén Arenal imagining the music, but it was really playing, he could hear it, a song drifting in through the open window, radio station XEB or XEQ, he wasn't paying attention to what day, month, or year it was, or it was his heart playing it back to him, and Rocket, they're singing a *canción tapatía*, "De mañana en adelante," "From Tomorrow Onward," it's my song for right now, but music changes like the hours, I can count on it, Rubén Arenal shutting his eyes, a wave of sadness, he was in love but couldn't find her, obstructed in his search for a woman resembling *La Pascualita*, hoping one day she might find him, and then another kind of sadness, and anger, too, his friend's son, Coyuco, missing, probably dead, and Rocket, to himself, dead and buried you can bet on it, it's a fact sure as I'm standing here right now, and with his eyes still shut, Rubén Arenal, knowing his way from memory, no blind fingers reaching for the corner of a table jutting out, a wayward chair or lamp, walking straight to one of two wooden chairs with wicker seats, not as comfortable now as they'd been when he bought them, sagging wicker seats, loose strands, but his eyes didn't notice, they were still closed, and his body weighed so much from sorrow that he was afraid the chair he'd sat on wouldn't support him, tapping his fingers to the rhythm of "De mañana en adelante" on his knees, licking his lips without saliva to moisten them, remembering a *chayote* in his tiny refrigerator, opening his eyes, a little hope for Rubén Arenal as long as he didn't think of *La Pascualita*, or Ernesto, Guadalupe, Coyuco, and Rocket, at least not until I've quenched my thirst with a *chayote*, a pear-shaped tropical fruit tasting like cucumber sitting in his refrigerator in the company of some jalapeños, cheese and butter, Rubén Arenal opening the refrigerator door, taking out the fruit and weighing it in his hand, still full of plenty of liquid inside, a hand reaching for a knife, peeling a *chayote*, seasoning it with salt, the heat from the sun having forced him to sweat almost all the salt out of his body, and a thirst, Rubén Arenal was as thirsty as the earth in a drought, and he ate the flavorful cucumber-like fruit with delight.

Rubén Arenal, slices of *chayote* melting in his mouth, resting his back against the edge of the table, a rough wooden table in the center of the kitchen area, part of his studio, Rubén Arenal facing the refrigerator, and a few shelves with spices and canned soup, and Rocket, time to think, not time to dream, wondering if Ernesto, sitting in the Ford F-150 pickup he'd lent him—Rubén Arenal, always a mind like a steel trap, and a voice in his head repeating from memory because he'd got the directions down pat—Rubén Arenal wondering if Ernesto had already merged onto Mexico 40D/Carretera Durango-Gómez Palacio to Mexico 49/Carretera Entronque La Chicharrona-Cuencamé and Zacatecas, continuing on Mexico 49/Carretera San Luis Potosí-Entronque Arcinas and San Luis Potosí, heading toward Mexico 57/Carretera Querétaro-San Luis Potosí and Querétaro de Arteaga, and there was still Mexico 57D and Mexico ahead of him, then Mexico 95D toward Taxco Cuota/Iguala Cuota and Guerrero, Ernesto was taking Mexico 95/Carretera Taxco-Iguala into Iguala, and Rocket, not arriving in Iguala now but before nightfall, at least an eighteen-hour drive if he isn't speeding, and more if he stops on the way, but he's in my Ford Lobo, not that rustbucket, the Renault 8, my pickup'll get him there in one piece, and at the same time and in two different places, Rubén Arenal and Ernesto, the two of them hearing "Hay un momento," a song by José Alfredo Jiménez Sandoval, he was singing with Mariachi Tacalitlán, the RCA recording, "Hay un momento," "There Is A Time," Rubén Arenal believing in this correspondence in nature, or in time of occurrence, listening with his best friend to "Hay un momento," far from each other, but a synchronous listening, and Rocket, a lucky moment, we need it, Rubén Arenal and Ernesto, two faithful friends with the same song at the same time, and Rocket, no matter how you may resist believing it at first, and Ernesto Cisneros, sitting behind the wheel, *por más de lo que de pronto se le resista creerlo,* as much as he's reluctant to believe it, Rubén Arenal and his best friend, another sentence, together, said in different places at the same instant, and Rocket, my heart is tired of suffering, and Ernesto Cisneros, *mi corazón cansado de sufrir,* both of them listening to a song by José Alfredo Jiménez, the road was a long one no matter where they were taking it, a man driving a pickup, a Ford F-150 Lobo, the other, leaning against a long sturdy table serving as work bench and dining table, the last slice of *chayote* melting in his mouth, Rubén Arenal rinsing his hands under the flow of water in the sink, while the shade of *La Pascualita* strolled through his mind just as he'd seen her walking with her mother at night in a neighborhood not far away from his own.

E rnesto Cisneros Fuentes, named after Ernesto Cisneros Salcedo, the football midfielder born in Guadalajara in 1940, Ernesto and a happy coincidence provided by Ernesto's father's first *apellido,* a kind of wonder, a local reaction of interest and excitement, and Ernesto Cisneros, a man to be proud of, both of them, Ernesto driving Rubén Arenal's truck on the way to Iguala, a knot in his stomach, looking at vehicles moving on a public highway with eyes that were empty, no tears, a blank stare at the ribbon of the road, Ernesto heading for Iguala de la Independencia, cruising on Federal Highway 95, almost sixty-seven miles from Chilpancingo, the capital city of the state of Guerrero, and while he was driving, as if his mind had a mind of its own, Ernesto and Rubén Arenal, together, at the same time but in different places, hearing "Hay un momento," one here one there, Rubén Arenal, his back against the edge of a rough wooden table in the kitchen of his studio, while Ernesto was gripping the wheel of the Ford F-150 Lobo, Ernesto and Rubén Arenal, together, listening to a song by José Alfredo Jiménez Sandoval, who was singing with Mariachi Tacalitlán, the RCA recording, "Hay un momento," "There Is A Time," Ernesto believing in this correspondence in nature, or in time of occurrence, listening with his best friend to "Hay un momento," a bit of synchronous listening, he was sure of it, even though they were far from each other, and Ernesto Cisneros, how we hear what we hear is a mystery, but that's a pleasant riddle, and then Coyuco, about my son, that's another thing, damned life, right now life's an open sore, and I'll keep seeing his face in the faces of others if I don't find him, and Lupita, too, I had to leave her at home because there's nothing she can do right now but cry, and weeping won't get us any closer to knowing anything, only wrenching our guts, that's all, just take a look at these hands holding the steering wheel, they'd be trembling if I didn't have to keep the truck on the road, and it isn't my Ford Lobo, so much the better, or I'd drive it straight into an abutment, or a tree, because this life, like I said, right now this life's an open sore, an agonizing wound, you can't see it, it's here—Ernesto taking a hand off the steering wheel and tapping his chest with an index finger—at least the life we've got, me and my wife, we're two, man and woman, and in this, a fucking nightmare, we're two but we're one, if you get what I'm saying, the thing that's happened to Coyuco's ripped a hole in both of us big enough to drive this truck through, it's a hole you can't see, like I was saying, but it's right where it counts, tearing us in two, even though we're one, Lupita and me, and there's Rubén Arenal, I call him Rocket, because he's faster than a speeding bullet, mind and body, so let me tell you something, as his sister, Luz Elena, would say, with respect to the pottery he makes, a skilled pair of hands, studying near Paquimé, or Casas Grandes, a fourteenth- to fifteenth-century prehistoric settlement, a big deal in the Sierra Madre Occidental, and the Paquimé culture, beginning around the year 700, people living in small semi-subterranean houses built on the banks of the Piedras Verdes River, San Pedro, and San Miguel, each joining Río Casas Grandes, you can see it on a map, and Paquimé, now a ruin 350 kilometers northwest of Chihuahua, Paquimé, a pre-Hispanic settlement with a population of about three thousand five hundred, you can count them on dozens of hands, shaman-priests in the driver's seat in Paquimé, and their pottery, the pottery of Paquimé, shamanic spiritual journeys portrayed on Chihuahuan polychrome vessels, that's what they're called, Chihuahuan polychromes, red-and-black-painted ceramics on a light tan-to-brown paste or slip, vessels from the Medio period, AD 1200-1450, like an Escondida Polychrome jar with light tan yellow paste, meandering red elements, black design elements, a jar with a low rounded shoulder and sub-conoidal neck tapering to a direct rim, black on white and red decorations featuring a meander band, a kind of decorative border, like those found on Tonto Polychrome, it's a pottery type, yes, Tonto, I know it's hard to believe, that's what I thought when I first read it, somebody's got a sense of humor and it isn't me, not now, never again, because as I see it, shamans travel between the spirit world and the world of the mundane, they're liminal people, "at the thresholds of form, forever betwixt and between," in the words of Barbara Myerhoff, and they speak with the supernatural through ritual and ecstatic trances, so now I'm on the road to Iguala to find my son, our son, Lupita's and mine, our Coyuco, but I can't afford a trance, I'm driving, and it's a journey between the living and the dead, too—God forgive me— we're on one side, he's on the other, the earthly world, material, temporal, and the spirit world, who's speaking to who in Iguala de la Independencia? and how? a megaphone won't get you there, but

I'd never tell Lupita a thing like that, not now, not ever, because there's always a chance we'll find him, and find him alive, that's why Rocket, giving me the keys to his F-150, he's given us a little hope in a hopeless situation, and not using my Renault 8, a car he calls a rust bucket, but it's our car, Lupita's and mine, she drives it whenever she wants, I don't care where she's going, not a long distance, okay, Rocket's right, I don't think it'd hold up, it's a rust bucket, but it's our rust bucket, and we drive it whenever we've got somewhere to go, not too far, but within a certain radius, a specified distance from a center in all directions, and now a voice, I can hear it, a voice asking, and you, where are you going? that voice's logic speaking, and I don't want to answer, sorry, nobody's home, and back to Paquimé, or Casas Grandes, with Rocket's skilled pair of hands, studying not far from the ruins of Casas Grandes, you don't know him, but he's my friend, Rocket learning to use the coil method, and scraping pots with a hacksaw blade to shape them, an inverted flowerpot sagger covered in cottonwood bark, then setting it on fire, the Mata Ortiz way, that's what he told me when he got back to Chihuahua, more than eight hundred thousand souls, our city in the north of Mexico, south of New Mexico and west of Texas, and there, you can always find someone if you're looking for him, me and Rocket, Rocket and me, we never lost touch, not since we were kids, and that's what I'm praying for, Coyuco and me, me and Coyuco, finding each other, bringing him home, and me not finding a corpse, either, but our son, alive and in one piece, not chopped up and burned on a grill like a steak, or locked up somewhere without food or water, our son, Lupita's and mine, our Coyuco, and take a look at this *cuervo tamaulipeco*, a Tamaulipas crow, he's flown over from Matamoros in Tamaulipas just to be with me, a companion, or he's from General Bravo, a town of around five thousand in the state of Nuevo León, northeast of the city of General Terán, General Bravo, it used to be called Rancho del Toro in the late eighteenth century, well, my *cuervo tamaulipeco*, wherever you've come from you're welcome, take a seat, there's plenty of room, and now back in

Paquimé, its polychrome vessels, illustrated by likenesses of humans, male and female, and owls, badgers, snakes, fish, lizards, and other creatures, too, shamans throwing off their clothes, getting rid of their facial markings, disconnecting from the worldly world, shaking it off to begin their journey, a journey starting in the everyday, run-of-the-mill—you can imagine how it was by knowing how it is today—because that's where they lived, where we all live, our routines, the here and now, you might say, and off they go to an ethereal, mystical place, nothing I've ever known, shamans kneeling and smoking a pipe, tobacco laced with datura or peyote, losing their identity with the shedding of their clothes, transforming into supernatural beings, horned and wearing a headdress, macaw-headed, and flying shamans, birds are common guardian animals among shamans—magic is as magic does—plenty of bird imagery, and tobacco, I guess they were getting high, a physiological and biochemical reaction from nicotine intoxication, and narcotic alkaloids, loaded on pipes, cigarettes and cigars, in a trance, making them see flashes of movement they interpreted as birds, tiny shooting stars the size of fists, the birds and the horned and plumed serpents guiding the shaman through his journey, helping him bring back critical information—I wouldn't mind a little critical information on Coyuco's whereabouts—the outward expression of interior inspiration, the dreamer reciting his dreams, helping the shaman perform tasks while in the spirit world, a whole landscape of voluptuous peaks fills my eyes as I speak, maybe you think I'm talking to myself, my *cuervo tamaulipeco,* but you're listening, too, my warm-blooded tutelary friend, you're no shrimp, how big are you? not a *pajarito,* fourteen inches long? I don't have a tape measure on me, sleek, handsome, with glossy dark, bluish plumage, a slender and black beak, black legs and feet—arm candy if I could get you to stand on my arm—and you're croaking like a frog, a Tamaulipas crow, a few things to say, balancing on the edge of the open passenger window of Rubén Arenal's truck, a low croaking sound, and Ernesto Cisneros, make yourself comfortable, here, next to me—Ernesto patting the empty place on the bench of a standard cab—and the Tamaulipas crow, hopping into the cab, a soft-voiced *gar-lik,* looking past the dash out the windshield at the highway, and Ernesto Cisneros, as I get closer to Iguala, a few miles, I'll have a Delicados or Fiesta, or a cigarette out of Rocket's pack of Faros, there isn't a pipe in sight, a little dancing, and then I'll leave my headdress in the F-150, and right before your eyes, my *cuervo tamaulipeco,* I'll change into a macaw-headed man with tail feathers, pound signs my chest, a transformed human, that's what it means, those pound signs, or small circles with dots on my legs or stomach, a bit like a shaman on a Ramos Polychrome, and you'll join me on my journey, *señor Cuervo Tamaulipeco,* a tip of the hat, a sombrero, a broad-brimmed felt hat if it's cold, showing me the way, helping me out, and another *gar-lik* from the Tamaulipas crow, cocking his head, looking at Ernesto as he wiped the perspiration from his forehead with the back of his hand, he couldn't reach for the handkerchief and keep his hands on the wheel, a safe driver, Ernesto, especially in somebody else's truck, then Ernesto hearing the footsteps of the approaching voice, not always a good omen, and Ernesto Cisneros, a little bit of Xipe Toltec, the Flayed Lord, God of the West, of newly planted seed, and sacrificial pain, with the eagle down of sacrifice decorating his robe, shut your eyes and you can see it, sometimes I look at myself with loathing and it's enough to make me break down—because of my guilt for Coyuco's disappearance, parents are as parents think, my *cuervo tamaulipeco*—and the approaching voice, and Ernesto Cisneros, before you say another word, voice, I know you're there, whoever you are, so let's switch on the radio, or I'll play something in my head, a little music to take me away from you, and my pain, plenty of suffering, who needs your dirty tricks, truth or no truth, but a little music, how about "La voz de mi madre," by Los Alegres de Terán, Eugenio Abrego and Tomás Ortíz, who started playing together in General Terán, in Nuevo León—you remember, it's not far from the town of General Bravo—Los Alegres de Terán, Coyuco loves them, Coyuco and Irma, his fiancée, Irma and Coyuco listening to David Záizar, Juan Lopez, and to the guitar of Antonio Bribiesca, the guitar of Augusto "Guty" Alejandro Cárdenas Pinelo, his *canción yucateca,* and to Juanita and María Mendoza, "Corrido de Juan Vásquez," Hermanos Bañuelos, "Marijuana, la Soldadera," Luis Pérez Meza, "Corrido de Juan Carrasco," Trío Los Aguilillas, "Valentín Mancera," Hermanos Yáñez, "Julián del Real," Lupe Martínez and Pedro Rocha, "Rendición de Pancho Villa," Conjunto Tamaulipas, "Amador Maldonado," Hernández and Sifuentes, "Benito Canales"—songs of the Mexican Revolution, I can remember them all—and as often as they could, once a day, usually at night, Coyuco and Irma, playing a recording of "Refugio Solano" by Dueto Sandoval, words that made an impression on them, a song about a rebel, during the *cristero* revolt after 1926, and the name of his mother, my wife, Lupita's name in the song, *bueno,* our Coyuco, *un hijo ejemplar,* always respect for his mother, and I'll recite a verse from "Refugio Solano," *Y el lunes por la mañana, / como a las diez, más temprano: / hubo un combate sangriento / con la gente de Solano. / Sí Lupita, trae tu mano,* "On Monday morning, / a little before ten, / there was a bloody encounter / with Solano's forces. / Yes, Lupita, give me your hand," and near the end, another verse, beautiful and sad, *Le dieron el primer tiro, / se le iba arrancando el alma, / –Arrímate el botellón, / regálame un vaso de agua.– / Sí Lupita, bien du mi alma,* "They shot him the first time / and his soul was leaving him. / 'Bring the jug closer and / give me a glass of water.' / Yes, Lupita, soul of my soul," so Coyuco and Irma, together, all kinds of music, listening to the radio, and recordings, I'll speak in the present when I speak of him, but right now, Los Alegres de Terán, "La voz de mi madre," a little *música norteña,* "My Mother's Voice," a version two minutes and forty-eight seconds long, long enough to wipe the worries from my mind, and no tears, I won't see the road if I'm crying, Ernesto focusing on the highway signs, and Ernesto Cisneros, now there's Mexico 95D, right here, and before you know it, Taxco Cuota/Iguala Cuota, and Guerrero, then it's Mexico 95/Carretera Taxco-Iguala into Iguala.

"Los barandales del puente," "The Railings of the Bridge," a *canción mexicana,* predecessor to *canción ranchera,* playing for Coyuco, nobody else could hear it, not that he could be sure, but Coyuco, his own radio available in his head at all times, day and night, and a voice telling him, just switch it on when you want it, it'll help you live through whatever's going on, and it was Los Texmaniacs, Max Baca Jr. on *bajo sexto,* David Farías, accordion, Óscar García, bass and drums, Lorenzo Martínez, *guitarrón* and drums, Los Texmaniacs, together, playing and singing "Los barandales del puente," and the words bringing a warmth that was a kind of sanctuary to him, *Los barandales del puente, se estremecen cuando paso. / Morena mía, dame una abrazo. / Dame tu mano, morena, para subir al tranvía, / Que está cayendo la nieve fría,* "The bridge railings tremble as I cross. / My dark woman, give me a hug. / Give me your hand, dark woman, to board the streetcar, / for the cold snow is falling," the song accompanying Coyuco and the other students, maybe they heard it maybe they didn't, it was his music, and the two buses with the other students arriving, making the almost twenty miles in no time, everyone pouring out of their respective buses, the second- and first-year students with shaved heads, T-shirts and bandanas covering their faces, not much of a disguise but they had to do something, breaking a window in Coyuco's bus to free them, Coyuco and the other students abandoning their bus, *normalistas* charging the station, commandeering three more buses, Coyuco, José Ángel, and the eight other students having left their bus behind, and not a creature was stirring except the *normalistas,* the students from Ayotzinapa, a *Escuela Normal,* no police, nothing, now they had five buses altogether, it was nine twenty-two, the students telling the drivers to get them out of there as fast as they can, the buses leaving the central bus station, two of them heading toward the highway, three others heading toward the center of Iguala, there still weren't any police anywhere to be seen, five buses taking off, Estrella Roja 3278, leaving from the back of the terminal for Calle Ignacio Manuel

Altamirano with fourteen students, heading for Periférico Sur and the road to Chilpancingo, Estrella de Oro 1531 with fifteen to twenty students onboard, heading for Periférico Sur and the road leaving town, two Costa Line buses, 2012 and 2510, and another Estrella de Oro, number 1568, these buses following Calle Hermenegildo Galeana, heading in the general direction of Periférico Norte, Coyuco sitting in that one, the Estrella de Oro 1568 bus with José Ángel riding in the seat across from him, and more than thirty students altogether, but the three buses weren't going fast enough, the lead driver in the Costa Line 2012 was slowing down, a light foot on the accelerator, the students trying to get him to step on it, and he wouldn't listen, somebody shouting, more than one, several voices saying the same thing at the same time, get a fucking move on! and the Plaza del Zócalo ahead of them, the three buses in a kind of convoy on Calle Hermenegildo Galeana, and at the central plaza— Estrella de Oro 1568 the last of the three buses, Costa Line 2510 and 2012 forming the column in front of the Estrella de Oro 1568 respectively—a municipal police truck cutting them off, blocking the way, bringing the buses to a halt, and the police firing shots in the air, and at the buses, too, the first calls going out to 066, the emergency services, at around nine fifty-three, shots being fired at the *normalistas,* students climbing down from buses, throwing rocks, trying to move the vehicle that blocked their way, army intelligence agents present, and the police firing at them, everything happening faster than their minds could grasp, but the students forcing the vehicle to pull back, enough rocks and the frightened driver, then the three buses starting off again, approaching Juan N. Álvarez and Periférico Norte, the police went on firing, the caravan of buses moving at a crawl, and now about ten police cars from Iguala in front of and behind the buses, and three units from Cocula, the municipal police forces, together, and the ministerial police and federal police, it was almost ten o'clock, then another police truck blocking the road in front of Costa Line 2012, this time the driver getting out of it and taking off, a few students, including Aldo

Gutiérrez Solano, getting out to move the police truck out of the way, pushing the truck with other students, *normalistas* throwing more stones at the police, and in return more machine gun fire ripping through the night air, a bullet striking Aldo Gutiérrez in the head, falling sideways, hitting the ground, *¡cuidado, cuidado!* blood pooling where he fell, Coyuco and José Ángel, with a couple of others, trying to help him, their hands and clothes stained with blood, they were trembling, students running for cover, *¡ya nos mataron a uno culeros!* hiding behind the police truck or ducking behind the first bus in the convoy, Costa Line 2012, a wretched panic, understanding nothing, *¡bájense!* they were hopelessly wiping sweat from their faces, a fraternity of sweat, or was it tears, *¡güey, hay que tomarle foto a lo otro!* filming with their cell phones, it was night, raining, others crawling under buses, *¡bájense! ¿y los demás?* let's get out of here! they're still shooting at us! *¡ya mataron a uno, háblale a la ambulancia!* call an ambulance, you've killed my friend! Coyuco and José Ángel, icy veins, adding their voices to the plaintive cries, voices shouting at the police, shouting at the emptiness inside of them, *¿por qué recoges los casquillos cabrón? ¿sabes lo que hiciste verdad, mierda? ¿por qué nos andan buscando?* why are you picking up the casings, asshole? you know what you did, don't you, shit? why are they after us? fury in the darkness, *¡pinche perro lame huevos!* and words that wouldn't come out burned their tongues, but a sentence written by Ignacio Manuel Altamirano, from his book, *El Zarco*, refusing to be contained, more powerful than fear, pouring from someone's lips onto the street, diluted by spilled blood and falling rain: "By now the moon had appeared on the horizon and was rising majestically in the sky among clusters of clouds," but there wasn't a moon, or if there was they couldn't see it, there wasn't any room for poetry in language, nothing beautiful or fine, just ugliness, with nothing left to believe in, no dreams or future for anyone crouched behind a bus or truck in a rainy mist, under fire from the municipal police, the ministerial police and federal police, too, firing at the inside of the buses, and window-glass shattering, bullets skipping off the road, Coyuco and José Ángel, without El Santo or Blue Demon to help them, Coyuco and José Ángel, and the others, too, carefully backing away from the fallen body of Aldo Gutiérrez— his spirit like a paper kite floating up to the sky—alive but suffering, *¡cuidado, cuidado!* giving up, there was nothing they could do but join him, "they had nowhere to go except Mictlan, the underworld which lay beneath the great steppes of the north, in the cold, twilit country, Mictlantecuhtli and his wife Mictlancihuatl reigned there: the Mexican Pluto's face was covered with a bony mask, and he sat among owls and spiders," the place one goes after death, the next world, or a better place, and a line from John Marston's play *The Malcontent* present for an instant in Coyuco's mind, "Death's a good fellow and keeps open house," and still there was no ambulance, the police doing nothing but shooting at them, and when the ambulance arrived, the police, not letting the emergency vehicle get through to where Aldo Gutiérrez was lying, breathing but not really there, unconscious, by that time a coma, lost, at last the ambulance circling back, making its way close enough to help, paramedics putting Aldo Gutiérrez Solano in the ambulance, a martyr, and prayers on Coyuco's lips, the other students, too, then words from the New Testament mixed with the rain wetting the lips of dry mouths, *Y Dios limpiará toda lágrima de sus ojos, y la muerte no será más, ni existirá ya más lamento ni clamor ni dolor, porque todo lo viejo ha desaparecido,* "And God shall wipe away all tears from their eyes, and there shall be no more death, neither sorrow nor crying, neither shall there be any more pain, for the former things are passed away," first- and second-year students from Raúl Isidro Burgos Normal Rural School, scurrying phantoms trying to get away from the municipal police, the ministerial police, and federal police, too, Coyuco joining José Ángel, maybe Cutberto Ortiz, Leonel Castro, Jorge Luis González, Emiliano Alen, Marcial Pablo, César Manuel, and the others, victims feeling that moment with fear, a fear that went on and on, those seconds, minutes and more, the whole thing lasting roughly fifty-five minutes, from nine forty-five until ten forty, they were surprised at how much time and no time at all had passed with nothing but death snapping at their heels, rabid dogs wearing uniforms, and about seventy students altogether at the crossroads of Juan N. Álvarez and Periférico Norte, the police arresting as many as they could get their hands on, hitting the driver of Estrella de Oro 1568 over the head, pulling students off the bus, the aisle stained with blood, broken glass, or the police dragging students out of hiding, making them lie facedown on the street, hands behind their heads, Coyuco and José Ángel, together, lying on the street, looking at each other with their cheeks pressed against the ground, and a male *mosquero cardenal,* a vermillion flycatcher, *Pyrocephalus rubinus,* or *tlapaltototl* in Nahuatl, a small passerine bird, bright red with dark brown plumage, landing near Coyuco and José Ángel, hopping first in one direction, then another, there was a lot going on around him, confused, not nervous, and a miraculous change occurring through divine or supernatural intervention, a vermillion flycatcher becoming a *cuervo llanero* right before their eyes, a Chihuahuan raven, Coyuco and José Ángel seeing it clearly even though it was night, lying on the street in a light rain that seemed unnatural, a kind of drizzle more like tears than moisture condensed from the atmosphere falling visibly in separate drops, and the raven jumping with two feet at once, a nice move to within reach of Coyuco and José Ángel, if they didn't have their hands behind their heads and the police around them, Coyuco and José Ángel, staring at the bird, blinking their eyes, trying to shake off the transformation they'd seen, witnesses to something rare, once in a lifetime, but under the circumstances, not so unusual, vermillion flycatcher to raven, who could've dreamed it, and the Chihuahuan raven's dark-brown eyes watching them, eyes shifting from one to the other, calling a high-pitched *a-a-rk,* approaching Coyuco, extending its neck as far as it could go, then *pruk-pruk,* a sadness in its voice, carrying a message from Ernesto, Coyuco shutting his eyes, seeing his father and mother on the lids of his closed eyes, seeing Irma, too, Coyuco, no longer afraid, but sorry for them, all of them, everyone, full of the feeling of sorrow and compassion caused by the suffering and misfortunes of Ernesto, Guadalupe, Irma, and all the others, his eyes weren't shut anymore, but looking twice, the raven was still there, no conjuring trick, no sleight of hand, but he couldn't speak the bird's language, only a taste of its mournful voice in his mouth, the raven nodding its head, saying, I know what you don't know yet, but the conversation was interrupted, a policeman seeing the raven, walking over to it, standing above Coyuco and José Ángel, and since all birds speak to each other, the flycatcher returning to itself, a male *mosquero cardenal,* of a large order distinguished by feet that are adapted for perching, including all songbirds, the policeman aware of nothing, reaching out and swinging his stick at a bird, large or small, black or bright red, it didn't make a difference to him, a goon in a uniform, trying to chase it away, the *mosquero cardenal,* a vermillion flycatcher, looking up at him, a menace of bodily harm, such as may restrain a bird's freedom of action, then lifting off the ground, and the policeman pulling Coyuco and José Ángel off the street, throwing them into a truck with the others, a real tragedy, not out of a book, but right there in Iguala de la Independencia, and the vermillion flycatcher, a red dot, circling above the truck, then disappearing in the night sky, its wings moist with rain the color of blood.

Rubén Arenal starting off for his sister's house, going to see Luz Elena, Avelina, Perla and Cirilo, and a freezer full of *paletas,* his way of walking an irregular gait, accompanied always by Little Pascuala, she's strolling through his mind, a picture of her on his eyelids when his eyes were closed, and some music, it wasn't an irregular gait but moving with the rhythm of a song, "Jacinto Treviño," a *corrido,* Los Pingüinos del Norte, Rubén Castillo Juárez, Hilario Gaytán Moreno, Ricardo Escalante, and Rumel Fuentes, but now only Rubén Castillo, the only remaining original member, playing with Raúl Torres on bass and Antonio Pérez Rodríguez, bajo sexto and second voice, he'd seen them in Piedras Negras, in the state of Coahuila, Piedras Negras, more than eight hundred feet above sea level, at the northeastern edge of the state, across Río Bravo del Norte from Eagle Pass, Texas, Rubén Arenal visiting the Catedral de los Mártires de Cristo Rey de Piedras Negras, erected by Fray Raúl Vera López, but now, on his way to Calle Álvarez de Arcilla, heading for Luz Elena's house, a small two-bedroom house not far from the Parque San Filipe, not much of a park, but something green, and the Parish Church of San Felipe Apostle, around a three-minute walk for Avelina, Perla—not Cirilo, he was too young—Rubén Arenal's nieces and a nephew, coming home from school, Avelina, Perla and Cirilo, music in every name, Rubén Arenal looking forward to seeing them on a scorching afternoon, and Rocket, I'm crushed by the heat, but love is a sun that revitalizes with its beams all that exists around us, *La Pascualita*, it's too hot, and the wind, a poet's nightmare, Rubén Arenal in love, and that accounted for everything.

But Rubén Arenal, his stride now half-sluggish and half-deliberate, no more music, indicating that something was wrong, the beams of love not sufficient for stamping out the suppurating wound, a weeping wound on behalf of Ernesto, Guadalupe, and Coyuco, whose homeless ghost was likely drifting about in an unwanted daze, with the other missing teaching students from the Raúl Isidro Burgos Rural Teachers College, known as Ayotzinapa, a college founded in 1926, Rubén Arenal hearing a Mexican jay, *grajo mexicano,* or *chara mexicana,* a large songbird with a blue head, blue-gray mantle, blue wings and tail, a bird of the crow family, calling *quenk, quenk,* coming all the way from Nogales, a passing car with a broken muffler drowning out the bird's call, Rubén Arenal hearing his own scraping footsteps, really dragging his feet, and Rocket, the word, which is memory's strongbox, how much more how much more, something's happened, something that wasn't written, except by God, Rubén Arenal's vision got blurry as if his eyes were full of splinters, seeing everything in a blur, then a few more tears, his anxiety reflected in the windows of a passing bus, reflections in glass, or a window of a taxi gliding in close to the sidewalk, but reflecting his uneasiness, anyway, rubbing the calluses on the palm of his right hand with his right thumb, taking a turn at Domínguez de Mendoza, not so far from Hundido Park, a playing field on the opposite side of the street, hot air burning his lungs as he reached the gate to the entrance of Luz Elena's house.

Avelina and Perla, playing outside with another girl from the neighborhood, Cirilo, on the living room floor, surrounded by building blocks in half-a-dozen colors, Cirilo placing one block on top of the other, making towers and barriers, then knocking them down, Cirilo turning his head, eyes blinking at a familiar face, but that was all he gave his uncle by way of greeting, Rubén Arenal, used to it, touching the boy's thick black hair, ruffling it, Luz Elena shaking a chubby finger at her son, but the boy's back was already turned, Cirilo's eyes fixed on the developing construction site, quick fingers capable of stacking at high speed, a wall of blue with yellow trim, meandering like a Great-Wall-of-China snake on the living room floor, Luz Elena tugging her brother's sleeve, a sleeve rolled up to the elbow, pulling him toward the kitchen, and Luz Elena, with respect to the sun in the sky which is roasting us, and the wind, one of the six pernicious influences—let's take a look at your tongue, is it red or is it wearing a yellow coat? are there thorns on the lung area?—we'd better have a cold drink, *Xihuitl*, my comet, my brother, with respect, of course, to the weather we're having, and Rocket, you're talking Chinese medicine, and I've been waiting all day for a popsicle, I know you've got them in the freezer, I wonder if I'm dreaming, without knowing I am, and Luz Elena, stop talking nonsense, have one if that'll make you happy, what's got into you lately? and Rocket, it's Coyuco, and Ernesto and Lupe, all of them, but Coyuco and the other students, it's the kind of thing I can't shake off, a heartache, a new denial each morning, then a quick glance at the mirror—bang! a truth too much to take, a complete loss of hope exploding in my face, and Luz Elena, with respect to the awful truth, a pitiless situation, and the Cisneros family, of course, little by little, your thoughts are yielding to sensations, and Rocket, you aren't kidding, it's more than Ernesto and Lupe can stand, and me, too, all of us, Rubén Arenal taking a deep breath with the admission, the depth of it, as deep as a bottomless well, and a feeling that pulled him below the surface of the earth, straight into a hole with dirt thrown over him, the emotion this revelation created in him, it wasn't a sequence of resignation, acceptance, and peace, but an irritating, chafing emotion of helpless frustration which made him want to crawl around his sister's house rubbing his back and the side of his body against her furniture to ease the discomfort.

Rubén Arenal taking another deep breath to slow him down, and Rocket, a day's the sum of one thousand four hundred and forty minutes, inhale exhale, Rubén Arenal not moving a muscle of his face, he didn't raise his eyebrows, he was frozen there, a fixed gaze resting on Luz Elena, his sister narrowing her eyes, worried, but not a frown, while her brother was up to his shoulders in sadness, standing in a hole looking up at her, blinking, and Rocket, let's look at things as they really are, I gave Ernesto my truck, he's gone to look for his son, may the most holy Virgin help him, and Luz Elena, to herself, is he going to climb out of his hole, *Xihuitl,* my comet? and Rocket, I bet right now he's driving on Mexico 95D toward Taxco Cuota/Iguala Cuota and Guerrero, or it's Mexico 95/Carretera Taxco-Iguala, heading into Iguala, may Zacatzontli take him safely on his journey, and I pray to Our Lady of Guadalupe that he'll find Coyuco alive, *Creo en Dios, Padre Todopoderoso, Creador del cielo y de la tierra,* and Luz Elena, God bless him, yes, and tears in her eyes, no teardrops, and Luz Elena, with respect to the Ford Lobo, you already told me, the F-150, and I lit a candle, a prayer, at San Felipe Apostle, for Coyuco, Ernesto and Lupe, Rubén Arenal nodding his head yes, then shaking it no, gripping his guts, a sharp pain, a knife slicing his intestines, no *La Pascualita,* or Little Pascuala—a revitalizing sun far away, almost forgotten—and Rocket, what're they

going to do? Ernesto and Lupe, searching for Coyuco the rest of
their lives in that rust bucket of theirs, the Renault 8, and it's not
easy to ask a stranger, are you my son? each of them with their son's
face, but strangers, a face mocking their anxiety, Ernesto and Lupe,
asking questions day and night, excuse me, is that you? until from
so much seeing Coyuco's face in the faces of others, they'll forget
who they are, because, after all, their son's face is a reflection of their
own, Ernesto and Lupe, night and day, what're they doing in Iguala
de la Independencia, another day searching, another night wringing their hands in Iguala, sixty-seven miles from Chilpancingo, and
looking high and low for him in the capital city, too, what do we
lose? we've already lost our son, he could be anywhere, *mi ángel
triste,* and what's that sticking out of the rubbish? is it Coyuco, alive
or dead, and what about Ernesto and Lupe? if they can't find him,
not ever, but turning the earth inside out and dreaming, always
nightmares, turning the earth but it isn't a garden, a plot of land,
just a hole like the one I'm standing in, it's got to make them really sick, and Luz Elena, hold on, *Xihuitl,* and it also means year,
grass and turquoise, *xihuitl* in Nahuatl—our Nahuatl, a language
that sings—get a grip on yourself, with all respect to hardship and
unity, *bendito sea el lazo que une,* blessed be the tie that binds, like
the hymn by John Fawcett, keep going, my big brother, you won't be
of any help to anyone in a state like this, wiping tears from her eyes
with her bare arm, now they were running down her cheeks, supporting herself with the back of a chair, and Rocket, *¡cuidado!* watch
out! or we'll all fall down, Rubén Arenal, a sudden ladder coming
out of nowhere and offering to take him out of the hole, kissing his
sister on the cheek, wiping away her tears, then heading straight for
the freezer.

And Luz Elena, help yourself, Rubén Arenal choosing a Germania-
brand strawberry popsicle, from the town of Santa Isabel, and
another, but no, one at a time, *paletas,* Germania popsicles, based
on milk or water, Luz Elena's freezer full of creamy and fruity flavors, *aguacate, nuez, plátano, limón, chocolate o durazno,* avocado,

pecan, banana, lemon, chocolate or peach, his fingers as busy as the tongue in his mouth, not a handful, but one at a time, Luz Elena smiling, her brother, a paper towel in his hand, a finished popsicle in his belly, wiping his mouth, licking his lips, a strawberry ice pop, tasty fragrant fruit, his left hand opening the freezer, taking a pecan *paleta,* and Rocket, you don't mind? Luz Elena shaking her head, blowing her nose with a handkerchief, and Luz Elena, to herself, no more tears, not for the rest of the day, but it's only late afternoon and who knows what the night's going to bring, slowly slowly don't rush headlong into—and Luz Elena interrupting herself, but you aren't going anywhere, there are children to look after, and dinner to cook, but where's the husband, that's what I'm asking myself, and at about this time every day, Luz Elena watching her older brother eating a creamy nut-flavored *paleta,* then looking up, skyward, and Luz Elena, what next, and which will it be? oh, flavor of flavors, *aman xtechmaca tlen ticuasquej on yejhuan mojmostla ica tipanoto-quej,* yes, I've said it, give us this day our daily bread, and in the Nahuatl of Guerrero, ¡aguas! *chica,* careful, girl! you're going to impress yourself, but a humble look on her face, Luz Elena opening the refrigerator, then turning to her brother, and Luz Elena, a cold glass of water? a soft drink?—with respect to eating ice cream and popsicles, and how thirsty they make us, what'll you have to drink?

Rubén Arenal finishing his ice pop, reaching past her and the open refrigerator door, eyes looking in the freezer, and Luz Elena, excuse me, *Xihuitl,* then shutting the refrigerator door, Rubén Arenal seeing nothing, but his eyes asking, vanilla, coffee, peanut or avocado? batting it around, what'll it be? casually proposing flavors to himself, and more of a thirst now than when he was moving with the rhythm of "Jacinto Treviño," a *corrido,* played by Los Pingüinos del Norte, and Rocket, a song whose history's as rich and diverse as the Mar de Cortés, Luz Elena staring at him, what're you talking about? and Rocket, Jacinto Treviño, a man from Los Indios, on Río Bravo, a community south of San Benito, a few miles upriver from

Brownsville, Jacinto Treviño, an ordinary *ranchero,* he ran into trouble with the *rinches,* the Texas Rangers, in 1911, revenge on an Anglo who'd killed his brother, but the *corrido* by Los Pingüinos del Norte, a different ballad, the ballad of Ignacio Treviño, or a little of each, Ignacio Treviño, a Brownsville policeman, a gunfight with the *rinches,* Ignacio Treviño barricading himself in the White Elephant Saloon, funny name, and in both cases, each with the same kind of trouble and the same result, Jacinto Treviño and Ignacio Treviño, finding refuge on the other side of Río Bravo, living to a ripe old age on the Mexican side, there's more to it, reading Américo Paredes will tell you what you want to know, Luz, Rubén Arenal choosing a coffee-flavored popsicle, a little energy, sugar, and coffee, then sitting in a chair, and Luz Elena, with respect to worry, nervousness, we're jittery, an uncertain future, that's the source, a river that never dries up, I can tell you, we don't want to wake up, we think we're better off that way, in the darkness that surrounds us, but we aren't indecisive shadows, you've got to take a position, a stand, you can take it from me, and you know the story of my husband, El Güero, as dark and untrustworthy as a black mamba in eastern Africa, you know the place, but you've never been there, I know that because I know you, Luz Elena opening the refrigerator again, and Luz Elena, let me pour you a drink, your stomach will freeze with so many popsicles lying in there, a fresh *agua de Jamaica,* a hibiscus flower drink, a little ginger or cinnamon, my recipe, it's not too sweet, what do you say, *Xihuitl,* my comet, it'll lower your blood pressure, and it'll make you pee, an eternal truth and good custom, and Rocket, along with reciting prayers, before you get up, before going to bed, that's an eternal truth and good custom, too, Rubén Arenal crossing himself, almost staining his shirt in the gesture with the last drop of the coffee-flavored *paleta,* Luz Elena pouring him a glass of fresh hibiscus flower juice, setting it down on the table in front of him, and Luz Elena, and with respect, or lack of it, to El Güero—how he got that nickname I'll never know—a poisonous snake, an immoral coward, but I loved him with all my heart, and you know the man, may he wither like a plant without water in the desert, and I pray that God blows his dried-up dusty balls into a foul hole in the earth, a friendly gust of wind, that's all I ask, so you know I know what suffering is, my comet, and I hate him with every little piece of my broken heart—thank you, JP Harris—listen to the clock ticking away the minutes of our lives, I'm thinking of Ernesto, Lupe, and Coyuco, too, Rubén Arenal reaching out for her, taking gentle hold of a brown arm, and Rocket, your needle's stuck playing a broken record, El Güero's long gone, you'll never see him again, not if you're lucky, but for Ernesto, Lupe, and Coyuco, it's another story, as sad as stories can be, their sorrow, because Coyuco's out of it, God forgive me, the edges of the night clinging to his mouth, he's better off dead than in the hands of psychopaths, and that's giving them more credit than they deserve, I'll bet you a five-peso silver 1954 Hidalgo—mint, my year of birth—that's what's happened to him, in Guerrero, a cursed state, drug trafficking and cultivation, gang battles, extortion, illegal logging, land disputes, theories flying like sacks of shit, or it's the police inside the police, *los bélicos,* motherfuckers, they probably turned him over to a drug gang, and they're all connected to Alacrán and his wife, to say nothing of the whole stinking government, *¡claro!* we'll never know the truth, they haven't turned up anything to confirm one thing or another, Rubén Arenal shrugging his shoulders as if to shake off an unwelcome thought, and Luz Elena, nobody'll forgive them, and especially not Tlazolteotl, you know her, the Nahua goddess of vice, the filth goddess, with four aspects that're the four phases of the moon, and in her third aspect, the Power of Purification, sweeping away sins, power over all forms of unclean behavior, she'll never forgive a single one of them, *los bélicos,* the police, gangsters, and she'll wash her hands of the fucking mayor and his filthy wife, so relax, drink your hibiscus flowers, and let me tell you a story, *Xihuitl,* my comet, a word or two from the Legend of the Suns, if you know it, one of two Nahuatl texts preserved in the *Codex Chimalpopoca,* my story may be true, or I'll make it up as I go along, out of whole cloth, inventing everything, or only parts, and a little of the *Anales de Cuauhtitlán*, with respect to everyone and the birth of this world, it's to put your mind at ease for a couple of minutes, a way to unwind, and Rocket, I've got as much time as your story takes until the sun sets or the children eat their supper, then—the sound of Cirilo's building blocks spilling out across the living-room floor, tumbling and rolling, skipping along noisily, towers and walls of a city falling down, a snake sliced into bits and pieces, and the blocks colliding against metal, wood, lying concealed beneath chairs, under the sofa, Luz Elena and Rubén Arenal poking their heads around the corner to see what he was up to, and Cirilo, on hands and knees, reaching for a single blue building block, not a yellow one, disguised in the elongated shadow thrown by a lamp shade in the afternoon sunlight, the hardly deafening sound of Cirilo's small construction falling down, a wall or a tower, blocks spilling out across the living-room floor, interrupted Rubén Arenal's conversation with his sister.

Cirilo's building blocks back where they were meant to be, in his tiny hands, fingers grasping one, then another, different colors symbolizing different parts of the tower, Cirilo stacking them slowly, a face full of concentration, and Rubén Arenal, adjusting himself in the chair at the kitchen table, looking at his sister's face, a face he loved more than his own, Luz Elena taking a chair, drawing it near to her brother, Rubén Arenal swallowing homemade hibiscus juice, and Luz Elena, let's swat away the flies of despair, the worrying thoughts of Coyuco, and Ernesto and Lupe, at least for the moment, my comet, it's too painful right now, and Rocket, do you have a cigarette, a Delicados or Fiesta, and an ashtray, I need a smoke, and Luz Elena, I keep a pack of Faros for you in the drawer of the table, out of time and reality, take a look, Rubén Arenal opening the drawer, removing the pack, lighting one, it could've been a Delicados or Fiesta, it didn't matter, whatever it was, he needed a smoke, taking a long pull off it, and Luz Elena, reciting with her eyes open, "but he could not carry the jaguar, it just stood next to the fire and jumped over it, that's how it became spotted," a couple of sentences I've always liked, and we can thank John Bierhorst—the words of books I've read—and with the sentence of the jaguar, a sentence I've always liked, that's how I'll begin my story, and Rocket, then you've started, right now, so go on, and Luz Elena, but first a temporary amusement that fits with what goes after it, an interlude, where are we? *nochan,* my home, in Nahuatl, we remain behind, like shadows, watching the world change, the surface of the earth's a great saucer, like an enormous coin, positioned in the center of the universe, extending horizontally and vertically, you can see it, of course you can, we can all of us see it, not in the mirror, and don't look out the window, you won't find it, and when the saucer turns, if we aren't careful, then suddenly, zoom! we'll fly off its surface, like Cirilo's building blocks spilling across the living-room floor, Rubén Arenal, another long pull on the cigarette, and Luz Elena, now, my story right now's about the Fifth Sun, its date-sign is 4 Movement, and it's called 4 Movement because on that day it began to move, the five suns are five worlds created out of destruction—we can thank Cottie Burland, Burr Brundage, Manuel Aguilar, Miguel León-Portilla, López de Gómara, Chimalpahin, whose parents were *huehue Chichimeca pipiltin,* ancient Chichimeca nobles, Fray Diego Durán—and so, the Fifth Sun, named 4 Movement, *nahui-ollin,* of the *tonalamatl,* the book of day-signs, the pages of days, a divinatory calendar, the Fifth Sun, and it's our sun, we who live today, but it's a signification, the representation of meaning, because the sun itself fell into the spirit oven and burned up—"out of death and destruction, a new and better world is born"—and there were five of these suns, or ages, not cyclic, but unique and unrepeatable, and they were limited in number, just five, you can count them on the fingers of your hand, there'll be no more, but before our sun, the Fifth Sun, was called the sun, it was called Nanahuatl, *Pobre Leproso,* patron saint of the diseases of the skin, the Pimply One, afflicted with pustules, the most humble of the gods, whose home is over there in Tamoanchan, which means "we go down to our home," the humid lowlands near the Gulf Coast, home to the Huastec—you could fill a stadium with what I don't know—Luz Elena pointing a finger toward the living room, and Luz Elena, which direction's that? well, the spirit oven, the fire at Teotihuacan, burned for four years, and Tonacateuctli, lord of our sustenance, living in Ilhuicatl-Omeyocan, the highest heaven, Tonacateuctli, who set the world in order at creation, dividing sea and land, the being at the center, the still point of the center of a moving ring, Tonacateuctli, describing an ideal existence, where everything is at balance and at rest, and another god, Xiuhteuctli, god of fire, day and heat, lord of volcanoes, the personification of life after death, warmth in cold, light in darkness and food during famine, also named Cuezaltzin and Ixcozauhqui, but let's stick with Xiuhteuctli, so, together, Tonacateuctli and Xiuhteuctli called for Nanahuatl, telling him that his job's to keep the sky and the earth, a kind of guardian, but he didn't have much faith in himself, Nanahuatl, wondering why they'd chosen him when there were better gods to do the job—you see, it's like that for everyone, even the Fifth Sun, 4 Movement, before he was our sun, of course, and nothing really changes does it, insecurity and fear—then Tlalocanteuctli, lord of Tlalocan, god of rain, and Nappateuctli, Four Times Lord, a transfiguration of Tezcatlipoca, patron deity of Chalco, together, Tlalocanteuctli and Nappateuctli, they called for the moon, named 4 Flint, and Nanahuatl, fasting, taking his spines and needles, giving thorns to the moon, Nanahuatl and the moon doing penance, puncturing themselves with thorns to draw sacrificial blood—all part of the undertaking, nothing's easy for anybody—Nanahuatl bathing first, then the moon, each in his turn, Nanahuatl's needles were now plumes, his spines were jade, and four days pass—are you following me, *Xihuitl*?—and when they've gone by, those four days, Nanahuatl, well, the gods feathered him, then chalked him, because as a rule, as you might already know, sacrificial victims were smeared with chalk and crowned with heron feathers—it sounds pretty awful, but that's how things were done—and 4 Flint, the moon, a basin that held in its expanding and contracting interior the waters of the sky,

Coyolxauhqui, Golden Bells, the sister of Tezcatlipoca, or Meztli, often called Tecciztecal, the moon starting to dance for him, singing, too, always a little entertainment, and Nanahuatl, bang! into the fire he goes, a lot of courage, but the moon, a little slow, for all we know a lack of bravery, only fell into the ashes.

Rubén Arenal putting his cigarette out in the ashtray, and Rocket, in the codex, it's the story of the Fifth Sun, I've read it, give me another cigarette, will you? Luz Elena smiling, an untroubled Rubén Arenal in front of her, a brother who might be more relaxed now than he'd been a few minutes ago, as far as she could tell, a sister's love for her brother, and a diverting story, Luz Elena opening the drawer herself, sliding the pack of Faros across the table toward him, and Rubén Arenal, lighting another one, a real coffin nail, a long drag, a pull that filled his lungs, and Luz Elena, and Nanahuatl, out of the fire, grabbing the eagle, carrying it off with him—and this is where my favorite words come in—"but he could not carry the jaguar, it just stood next to the fire and jumped over it, that's how it became spotted"—its spotted coat symbolizing for almost all peoples in the central region of America the night sky glittering with stars and the interior of the earth, and as a god in his own right, the jaguar was Tepeyollotl, Heart of the Mountain, the Jaguar of Night—and the falcon became smoke colored, the wolf was singed, they didn't fall into the fire, so those three couldn't go with Nanahuatl to the sky, but the sun-to-be was able to take the eagle with him, and when Nanahuatl got to the sky, Tonacateuctli and his wife, Tonacacihuatl, together, the two of them, they washed him, bathing him with sacred waters, sitting him in a flamingo chair, a *quechol* chair, Tonacateuctli and Tonacacihuatl, decorating him with a red band, and Nanahuatl stayed for four days in the *quechol* chair without moving, while the gods were asking, why doesn't he move? what's the matter with him? so they sent the blade falcon to ask him why he wasn't moving, and Nanahuatl—it was obvious to him—why do you think I'm just staying in one place, not revolving or traveling the sky, falcon? it's because I'm waiting for them to spill their blood, their precious substance, I'm waiting for their sacrifice, Luz Elena taking a breath, getting up from her chair, going to the refrigerator with an empty glass in her hand, she poured herself a glassful of hibiscus juice, while her brother, following her with his eyes, a calm expression on his face, and Rocket, there are weeks that begin that don't end, not lives, and all things are dictated by nature herself.

And Luz Elena, it'd be great if life didn't make us old, we're heading somewhere, you and I, and what I'm telling you is less of an invention than I thought it'd be, so with respect to the Legend of the Suns, and the words I've got to say, this myth begins and ends with darkness, even though it's solar in character, night encloses the light and is its inevitable shell, since you know the story, you know the Fifth Sun will finally be stolen by Tezcatlipoca, the day 1 Death in the Aztecs' augury table's dedicated to him, Tezcatlipoca, and his home was everywhere, in the land of the dead, on earth, in heaven, he's a trickster god, a sorcerer, a seer, a shapeshifter, whose favorite outward appearance was a jaguar, an animal known to be an evil omen, associated with nighttime and sudden death—it's like the darkness surrounding Coyuco, dead or alive, and it's fallen soundly on the heads of his parents, too—yes, this myth begins and ends with darkness, Luz Elena pulling her chair close to the table, facing her brother, taking a sip from her glass, wetting her whistle, and Luz Elena, the gods got together and held a meeting, it wasn't natural that Nanahuatl, as the sun-to-be, wasn't moving, he didn't budge, and right away, Tlahuizcalpanteuctli, Lord at the Time of Dawn, the personification of Venus, the Morning Star, overcome with anger, that's just the way he was, a quick temper, ready to bite, Tlahuizcalpanteuctli, I'll shoot him, he can't just stand still, not moving, not after choosing him over the others, not with the ritual we've gone through—just like Popeye, that's all I can stands, I can't stands no more—so the Lord at the Time of Dawn, the personification of Venus, acting in his capacity as the god of ice, in the splendor of his rising as a doomed star, Tlahuizcalpanteuctli, really angry, shooting arrows at Nanahuatl, trying to hit him, look out! duck! and Nanahuatl, who wasn't moving a muscle, didn't flinch, motionless as a lead weight in the sky, the Lord of Dawn, Tlahuizcalpanteuctli, missing his target, not a very good shot, I guess, or the other was a lot stronger than he was, because, before you know it, the sun-to-be, Nanahuatl, succeeded in hitting the Lord of Dawn, the personification of Venus, the Morning Star, Nanahuatl's arrows striking him with shafts of flame, and the nine layers, the Place of Duality, which is how the sky is arranged, you can count them on your fingers, the nine layers covered Tlahuizcalpanteuctli's face, and that was it, the Lord of Dawn was the frost, finished, that's how I see it, Tlahuizcalpantcuctli was kaput—with respect to the books I've read, I'll nod my head in recognition, as many times as my neck will allow, there's arthritis up there, or a painful inflammation at the cervical, or a pinched nerve, a little tingling in my fingers, no, not that, I can't take anything as serious as that, but it's playing with Avelina and Perla, at their age, and mine, it isn't easy, not Cirilo, he's a cinch, a snap, so let's hope he grows up like his namesake, a musician in the family—and the gods, without Tlahuizcalpanteuctli, came together again, a few words passing between them, or they didn't use words at all, but a big decision to make, the gods getting together, Titlacahuan, or Tezcatlipoca, known as Smoking Mirror, The Prince of this World, and Huitzilopochtli, Blue Hummingbird of the Left, or of the South, and the women, too, Xochiquetzal, Flower Quetzal, goddess of the flowering and fruitful surface of the earth—she's worshipped on the Day of the Dead by offerings of marigolds—and Yapalliicue, Black-Her-Skirt, and Nochpalliicue, Red-Her-Skirt, or Her Skirt is Prickly Pears, their decision, all together, with or without words, their duty, really, Titlacahuan, Huitzilopochtli, Xochiquetzal, Yapalliicue, Nochpalliicue, they were going to die a sacrificial death—no other choice, that's the way it goes—a sacrificial death in Teotihuacan, a city in a sub-valley of the Valley of Mexico, the only way the sun would go into the sky, the big leap, and at last, at their death, Nanahuatl went into the sky, starting to move, 4 Movement, it was something he'd been waiting for, Nanahuatl, the sacrifices of the others behind him, the birth of the Fifth Sun out of the ashes of the god Nanahuatl, and the sun was in the sky where it was supposed to be, the moon following him, on its way, not too fast, taking his time, hesitating, the moon that wasn't burned in the fire but had fallen into the ashes, and now Papaztac, *el enervado,* a god of drunkenness, one of the Centzontotochtin, or four hundred divine rabbits, Papaztac watching the moon, and when the moon got to the edge of the sky, Papaztac, hitting him in the face with a rabbit—that explains what we see when we look at the face of the moon!—dimming his light, and the moon moving on, slowly slowly, like it wasn't a good day for the moon, trying to ignore what Papaztac had done, breaking his face with a rabbit so he couldn't be a second sun, and when the moon was at the crossroads, he met *tzitzimime,* large round-eyed figures with disheveled hair, skeletal heads and limbs, each a protruding tongue in the form of a sacrificial knife, a snake dangling between their legs, or blood instead of a knife coming out of their mouths, the blood pouring onto the ground in front of their outspread legs, *tzitzimime,* the *coleltin,* star spirits, frightening things, but of which sex? it's not like we can tell, Luz Elena finishing her glass of homemade hibiscus drink, Rubén Arenal shrugging his shoulders, and Rocket, it doesn't really matter, some say male, others female, according to their dress, and Luz Elena, they could be spirits of women who died in childbirth, anyway, they're dangerous as a miserable death, the *tzitzimime,* the *coleltin*—we're almost at the end of my story, invention or reality, who can say—and *tzitzimime,* I don't know how many there were but it wasn't just one, *tzitzimime* calling the moon, waving at him, shouting, come here! come here! terrifying the moon by showing their fleshless faces in a fixed or vacant look, and holding him up, interfering with him, keeping him for a long time, dressing him all in rags, while the sun of 4 Movement, Movement Sun, appeared in the sky, and maize was grown for the first time, fire was domesticated, nightfall was established, *octli* was brewed—did you ever taste it? not as good as my homemade hibiscus drink—4 Movement, the Fifth Sun, and it's our sun, we who live today, and at that time, too, it was their sun, we're standing each day under the same sun as our ancestors, waiting for the end of it, and the earthquakes, at the hand of the god of ill omen, Tezcatlipoca, nestling in the interior of the earth, wielding sacrificial knives, the end of time's within his dark power, the black Tezcatlipoca, and the collapse occurring on a day 4 Movement, according to another codex, *Telleriano-Remensis,* pictures and text—I've got a copy if you want to look at it, a genuine photographic color facsimile, but it weighs a ton—Tezcatlipoca, stealing the sun away, earthquakes swallowing all things, shaking stars down from the sky, plunging us into eternal night, but that's as far as I can go, it's time to get the girls in from playing outside, they'll have to wash themselves, then there's reading to do, school-work, Rubén Arenal, at once, reaching for his sister's arms, laying his open palms on them firmly but gently, nodding and smiling as if he couldn't speak, emotions wrapped within him unfolding and presenting themselves as a curious brightness in his eyes.

Ernesto rolling into Iguala, Rubén Arenal's Ford Lobo bringing him safely into the city, population more than one hundred twenty thousand, Ernesto wondering if that number included Coyuco, alive, or his son, already buried, not in a cemetery, but charred to blackened remains, dumped somewhere with dozens of other bodies, or what was left of them, who knows where, Ernesto switching off the engine after parking the Lobo, between Calle Ignacio Manuel Altamirano and Calle Hermenegildo Galeana, farther away, not so obvious, or on Calle Melchor Ocampo, making sure the doors were locked and nothing was left in the bed of the truck, but Ernesto walking along Ignacio Manuel Altamirano, past Abarrotes Carol, a grocery store, and crossing Las Margaritas, walking slowly toward a car wash, *lavado y engrasado,* the sun stretching itself with a yawn in a lower corner of the sky, Ernesto trying to find the courage to walk to Bandera Nacional No. 83, the bus station, Estrella de Oro, and Ernesto Cisneros, but there isn't a golden star taking me there, no guiding light, not now, anyway, in the land between the waters, Anahuac, and it's dark and the sun's still out, that's my mood, what do you expect, and it's the same for the parents of the others, forty-three victims, plus mine, the world's spinning away from us, heading straight for a reflecting wall, a giant mirror, where it can see its reflection, but it can't stop, heading straight for its end, and that's where we are, all of us, the mirror-wall weeping with blood for tears—wipe your face and your snotty nose, I can't stand looking at you—that's what they'll say, and you want to bet it's their words, the army, the 27th Battalion, the *Policía Federal,* the mayor and his wife, words like that belong to the stupid, so I bet more than I've got and it's my future I'm counting on, *¡cabrones!* it's just like the saying, "Better to die on your feet than live on your knees," they think they've got honor, but they don't have shit, that's the world for you, *¡hijos de la chingada!* it's our blood, *nuestros hermanos,* and they're students, are they dead or alive? and Lupita, all she does is cry and sleep, worse than a bad day, it's the end of our life, and Coyuco's, too, our son, Lupita's and mine, my son and Lupita's, Coyuco dragged away, beaten, it could've been on Boulevard Vicente Guerrero, named after a revolutionary general of the war of independence, a stand-up guy, Vicente Ramón Guerrero Saldaña, born in Tixtla, his father a mestizo, his mother an African slave, Vicente Guerrero, militant and leader of the insurgency, it was the period of resistance, and the second president, in 1829, of our Mexico, and *Mi Patria es primero,* the motto of this state, in his honor, so what happened on Boulevard Vicente Guerrero, like I said, whatever it was it wasn't an honor, and the municipal police, the federal police, the soldiers of the 27th Battalion, drug gangs, fat fingers wearing the same pair of gloves, you can't tell one pair of hands from another, then Ernesto, without realizing where he was going, walking away from Calle Melchor Ocampo, approaching Café Morelos on Reforma, right

next to Florería Lupita, he'd been walking with his head down, now
lifting his eyes, worried and tired with circles under both of them,
lifting his eyes from the sidewalk, the last rays of the sun stretched
out in front of him, and Ernesto Cisneros, rays that're leading me
God knows where, or it was after sunset, a kind of murkiness, a
false, absurd, or distorted representation of whatever light remained in the air of Iguala de la Independencia, around sixty-seven
miles from Chilpancingo, the capital city of the state of Guerrero,
the travesty of light, measured along with a burden weighing a ton,
together, crushing his lungs, dragging his chin to his chest, Ernesto
raising his head with difficulty, up down down up, the weight of the
world, walking into Café Morelos, Reforma 16-D, standing at the
S-shaped bar, ordering a coffee, but something cold to snap him out
of the doldrums, a double espresso from the machine, a Sanremo
Verona, sugar and a little water, no milk, blending the ingredients,
adding ice cubes and cold water, Ernesto reaching for the glass, a
straw sticking up out of it, a really cold glass, his fingertips dancing,
then sitting himself down at a small round red table, a chair with a
red seat, his back to the reddish-brown patterned wall and a television mounted between two framed pictures, a couple of young men
wearing glasses, they looked like brothers, playing chess at a table
beneath the TV that wasn't on, a teenager sitting alone reading a
book, *Caballo de Troya,* two young girls whispering, a living world,
a kind of sanctuary, free from tension and anxiety, but Ernesto, not
part of it, seeing only Coyuco's face, a missing son, taking the straw
between his fingers, drinking his iced coffee, and he was wondering
what his wife was doing right now if she hadn't thrown herself on
the mattress like a rag doll, folded up, lying in the foetal position,
their darkened bedroom, shoulders jerking up and down, sobbing,
crying without making a sound.

The ice cubes clinked at the bottom of the glass as Ernesto shook it
gently, freeing coffee and sugar, no milk, from the unmelted ice and
mixing together what was left of the iced coffee, putting the glass to
his lips, tilting his head back, and Ernesto Cisneros, good to the last

drop, that's what they say, an icy freshness in his brain, cells beginning to send word to other cells, wake up wake up, faster and faster,
Ernesto was ready to go out into the world he no longer related to
except as a sort of detective of the missing and dead, a very sad one,
shuffling his feet, but he didn't have time to waste shuffling anything, not cards, papers or feet, and definitely not shuffling off
responsibility, in this case, Coyuco, his son, Guadalupe's son, their-
boy-now-a-young-man, a student, or a former student, at the Raúl
Isidro Burgos Normal Rural School of Ayotzinapa in Tixtla, and
Ernesto Cisneros, how do I start, but I just want to sleep, I haven't
got what it takes to get me going, what envy to know what you want,
but who am I fooling, I know exactly what I want and why I came
here, Iguala de la Independencia, I'll use your formal name, you,
Iguala, we aren't on familiar terms if what happened to Coyuco really happened here, in this city, I don't care if it isn't your fault,
fucking city, fucking everything, now that's the way to get things
going, anger'll do the trick, *ce, ome, yei, nahui*, counting in Nahuatl,
Ernesto pushing his chair back as he got up from the table, rubbing
his hands together, feeling the cold moisture from the glass of iced
coffee, Ernesto, on his way out the door of Café Morelos, not a
glance at the game of chess, but goodbye to the young man and
woman behind the bar, a nod not a wave, but making the effort to
give them a smile, and Ernesto Cisneros, human after all, I wouldn't
have guessed I had a drop of it left in me, pissed away with my tears,
that's what I thought, and the tears of my wife, Lupita, a crying machine—we're no longer human, or we're too human—and I don't
know how to help her switch it off, I can't afford to cry because
there's just one way I'm going to help and that way, the way to help
her, both of us, whether I like it or not, is to make an investigation
of my own, no matter who or what gets in my way, and the result,
it'll be a real tragedy, because I'm not optimistic, not now, probably
never again, I'm going to try my best, I've got to find Coyuco no
matter what condition he's in, but what am I going to find, a burned
ankle in a blackened shoe, skin and bone black as charcoal, or his
teeth set in the lower jaw bone, *¡Madre de Dios!* and *¡Dios mío!* don't

think about it, wait and see, *por el amor de Dios y todo lo que es Santo,* yes, for the love of God and all that's holy, I'll need a lot of help, all the help I can get, maybe El Santo, Rodolfo Guzmán Huerta, El Enmascarado de Plata, he was born in 1917 in Tulancingo de Bravo in the state of Hidalgo, the most famous of wrestlers in Mexico, the masked Mexican *luchador,* a folk hero, symbol of justice, and my hero, dying in 1984 and buried in Mexico City, Mausoleo María del Ángel, that's where you can find him, but his spirit lives on in all of us, you think I'm crazy but what else is there for any of us who've suffered this tragedy of a mass killing—I'm getting ahead of myself—than to rely on the power of being out of our minds in a world that's already lost its own, and El Santo, from his first movie in 1958, playing El Enmascarado in *Santo contra cerebro del mal,* or later, in another movie, *Santo contra las bestias del terror,* 1972, with Santo and Blue Demon—his real name was Alejandro Muñoz Moreno, like my wife's *apellido paterno*—not wrestling each other, but in a couple of arena matches, nothing out of this world, but the story, it isn't bad, working with Tony, a private detective, helping Tony escape from Sandro, a former professional wrestler who's now a crook, and his thugs—César del Campo's playing Tony, I remember them all like it was yesterday—so El Santo and Blue Demon, together, and an investigation, solving crime, and El Santo and Blue Demon defeating villainy and corruption, I need all the help I can get, a pair of wrestlers at my side, and *Santo vs. la invasión de los marcianos,* wrestling with Wolf Ruvinskis as Argos, leader of the Martians—it doesn't matter who's in it as long as El Santo's in it, or El Santo in *El mundo de los muertos,* again with Blue Demon, an inspiring movie right now, in the world of the dead, and El Santo, a move like the *Pescado,* a slingshot plancha from inside the ring, a flying plancha, or a hold called *A Caballo,* meaning "on horseback," invented by Gory Guerrero, a kind of chinlock, or Blue Demon's own finishing move, *El Pulpo,* the octopus hold, but I'll need more than that, this isn't a game or a movie or a comic book, it's Coyuco's life, our son, and gone gone gone, so thrown together it adds up to an ugly picture, Ernesto crossing the street without looking left or right, almost hit by a 1981 bright orange two-door Dodge Magnum, the sounding horn making him jump like a frightened cat, a real Mexican Mopar, it had a 5.9 liter 360ci V8 engine with a Carter Thermoquad four-barrel carburetor rated in 300 hp, a muscle car with an A833 four-speed manual transmission, but that's all Ernesto put together in his mind, there wasn't a lot of time, he'd hurried to the other side of the street, his heart pumping blood like jet fuel, the Magnum taking off and making the nearest corner, a hard right, and Ernesto Cisneros, my memory's as clear as if the angels had washed it this morning, thanks to an iced coffee and how I inhaled with joy that delicious smell of burned rubber tires and exhaust, my memory rising to the occasion, here it goes, I see his face, Coyuco, the baby's face that changed slowly, becoming another, and I see his mother's face, Guadalupe's, a young woman in a library reading a book whose title I couldn't see no matter how hard I concentrated in the dim light from where I was sitting at the other side of one of many long tables for students, studying students—the books we read, the books we forget—breathing students, half-awake or day-dreaming, pencils and notebooks, and the on-the-ball students with faces determined to solve the mystery before them, scribbling, underlining, scratching their heads through strands of greasy unwashed hair, the waste gasses or air expelled from an engine, turbine, or other machine in the course of its operation, and the stink of a tough elastic polymeric substance made from the latex of a tropical plant, that's what's reminded me, and Lupita, wanting to squeeze her until she burst, flooding my arms, her wetness seeping into my skin, ever since that first time in the library, until now, this moment even, while she's crying, but now it's her tears I want to swallow, along with my own, and our son, Coyuco, a baby's face growing into a man, a young man, but here, look for yourself, I've got a snapshot in my wallet, see? but who am I talking to except to myself, that's it, no one's listening, you can almost hear a pin drop, only pockets of listening, of course there're ears that hear it, the crying, but before you know it, something else will replace it, another nightmare taking it's place, but not now, not while I'm still breathing, walking away from Café Morelos, Reforma 16-D, then almost flattened by a 1981 bright orange two-door Dodge Magnum, a real Mexican Mopar, it had a 5.9 liter 360ci V8 engine, nearly killed before I started, what a pity, a tragedy you could've added to a long list of tragedies, my country's full of them, but I'm still here, Lupita, too, and Irma, Rubén Arenal, Luz Elena, and don't forget Ignacio, a second father to me, his father's first *apellido* the same as the former editor-in-chief of *Política*, so Rubén Arenal, Luz Elena, Ignacio, to name three, and me and Lupita, but the other parents, worried sick, the parents and families of Álvarez Nava, Sánchez García, Gómez Molina, Castro Abarca, Rosas Rosas, Gaspar de la Cruz, known as Pilas, "the pillar," he was calm, intelligent, reliable, and the thirty-eight other families, not including ours, so better make it forty-three souls and our Coyuco, that's the total, a lot of tears, add it up, and more if you figure what it means, because it isn't just the forty-three, and our Coyuco, a voice for the voiceless and a fact, it's every death and disappearance from the beginning of time, more than thousands, stadiums full, not just forty-three, that's only here and now, okay, that's a mouthful, but don't you think it's true? and I can hear my voice echoing, it's a big empty world, a vacuum, like I said, who's listening? but one thing comes after another, and each life counts.

Rubén Arenal, a couple of kisses for Luz Elena, then Avelina, Perla and Cirilo, his nieces and a nephew, and Rocket, eat everything your mother tells you to eat, *mis niños,* and his sister handing him the half-empty pack of Faros, not Delicados or Fiesta, not a white and green and black pack of Aros, but Faros, real coffin nails, and Luz Elena, you might as well take them, I bought a carton, hiding packs all over the house, but you'll never find them, you've got to ask, Rubén Arenal, another kiss for his sister, and Rocket, El Güero'll never know what he's missing, *¡qué idiota!* Luz Elena smiling an accomplice's smile, shaking her head, and Luz Elena, don't mention it, and don't mention his name either, gently closing the front door, Rubén Arenal hearing her turn the latch, and Rocket, a locked door is a closed door, a spring lock after El Güero moved out, remembering his sister's words the week El Güero left, "with respect to privacy, nobody in everybody out, unless I let them in, *¿entiendes, mi Xihuitl?* "understand, my comet?" Rubén Arenal, a swift turn on his heels, leaving her small two-bedroom house behind him, not far from the Parque San Felipe, but not much of a park, and heading home, the sky slipping slowly into darkness, rubbing the calluses on the palm of his right hand, and his fingers itching to make a *hidria* for Luz Elena.

Unlocking the front door, the foyer lit by an electric bulb hanging from the ceiling, a foyer separating his apartment from the street entrance, the door closing behind him, opening the door to his ground-floor apartment, a simple home, and his pottery studio, Rubén Arenal shutting the door, moving across the floor like he was floating, tapping gently with his knuckles on the rough wooden table in the center of the room, a kind of kitchen in the medium-sized studio, looking at the refrigerator, and a few shelves with spices and canned soup, but no time for food, Rubén Arenal heading straight for the part of the studio he called his workshop, an island in the grid-patterned city, no windows here, high capacity fuses, cables, and outlets, switching on the standing lamps, changing his shoes, finding the least worn pair in a pile of mostly worn-out shoes, light illuminating the potter's wheel, Rubén Arenal using a potter's wheel, not always, but most of the time, an old kick wheel, and the standing lamps illuminating a secondhand, front-loading electric kiln, a wedging table, light thrown on fettling knives, fluting tools, wires, paddles, ribs and scrappers, a few things he'd brought from Mata Ortiz, and a hacksaw blade lying on the wooden stool where he'd left it, but it was clean, keeping everything in order, and a heavy-duty trash container on a dolly with heavy-duty casters storing reclaimed clay, Rubén Arenal opening a box containing a fifty-pound bag of stoneware clay, not from Mata Ortiz, a clay gray-tan in color with mid-sized particles, slicing open the bag with a utility knife, caressing the coarse-grained clay, giving it a pinch, tender skin, and a familiar only just moist surface, Rubén Arenal, a sort of daydream, maybe a vision, seeing the form of the pitcher, as if he'd already drawn it without using a pencil, a vision of the *hidria* he was going to make for his sister, something the whole family could use, Avelina and Perla, but not Cirilo, not yet, he wasn't old enough, a pitcher for Luz Elena's fresh *agua de Jamaica,* a little homemade hibiscus flower juice, and ginger or cinnamon, juice poured from the pitcher he'd made for her.

Rubén Arenal, without a sketch or drawing to follow, hunched over the wheel head and his clay, working with the pleasure of concentration only pottery gave him, time passing silently as he worked, but traveling as fast as a train moving freely on rails without a signal to slow it down, faster than a speeding bullet, not only on his feet, a *hidria* taking shape, the wheel moving steadily, controlled by the wisdom of his foot on the flywheel, Rubén Arenal, already feeling a little pain in his knee, nothing new, but he felt it, and the clay he was working into a pitcher, part of the material environment, this world, and coming from the land, the clay agreeing with the spiritual nature of the universe, coinciding with it, so he didn't bother himself with the discomfort of his knee, and he was thinking, not of the *hidria,* but of Ernesto, Guadalupe, and Coyuco, and Rocket, human suffering! how many sad words are still hidden in the belly of man, his thoughts returning to the pitcher, a gift for his sister, he'd pulled the *hidria*'s handle before he started on the pitcher itself, using a lot of water so it didn't break, the handle draped over the edge of the wedging table, hanging there to dry in the air, losing some of its moisture so it'd be easier to work with, the *hidria* at his fingertips, the wheel spinning, the flywheel an extension of his

legs and feet, limbs with roots the strength and weight of the rein-
forced concrete flywheel, and the bell at the street door ringing in
his ears, it took him a minute to know where the sound was coming
from, his foot rising from the flywheel, fingers putting the finishing
touches on the *hidria,* the wheel head slowing down just a little, a
long exhalation, a drawn-out wisp of air, the pitcher not suffering
the consequences, it was finished except for the spout and handle,
Rubén Arenal, stopping the wheel, forming the spout with his index finger, pinching softly with the thumb and second finger of the
other hand, cutting the form from the wheel head using a wire, the
wheel was still turning, lifting the form, setting it gently on a ware
board, and the doorbell ringing again, or a stroke or two from a
clapper against both sides of a bell that finally awakened him from
his waking dream.

At the open street door, Rubén Arenal blinking, his eyes focusing
on the boy, a young man, standing in front of him holding out a
sealed envelope in a very formal way, not a large envelope, about 6
x 9, bigger than a standard letter, the young man waiting for him to
take it so he could get back on his scooter and go home, there wasn't
a receipt to sign, the boy, or young man, with a purple Dorados de
Chihuahua baseball cap on his head, wearing a personalized T-shirt
with Héctor Espino Gonzalez's picture printed on it, and his nickname, El Niño Asesino, written below, and Rocket, more than a few
words to himself, Héctor Espino, one of the best hitters in baseball,
also known as El Rebelde de Chihuahua, born in Chihuahua on
June 6, 1939, Rubén Arenal scratching his head, yes, Calle Cayetano
Justiniani 34, that's it, not far from Escuela Secundaria Guillermo
Prado, six minutes on foot, taking a left on Avenida Independencia
and a right on Eduardo Urueta, try to get your bearings, can you see
it? and the school, even if the school wasn't there then, just to get an
idea where Espino was born, the neighborhood, and Héctor Espino,
his first semi-pro team in 1959, the Dorados of the Chihuahua
state league, a team named after Pancho Villa's bodyguards, Héctor

Espino, the Liga Mexicana del Pacifico declaring that he hit 299
winter ball home runs in twenty-four short seasons, the Mexican
Baseball Hall of Fame setting that total at 310, eleven home runs
unaccounted for, and over the summer, in the Liga Mexicana de
Béisbol, he hit another 453 home runs, for a total of either 752 or
763, and then the three home runs in Jacksonville, don't forget three
more, making the total either 755 or 766, and counting the twenty-
four home runs Espino hit in the Mexican minors, listen, the total's
at 779 or 790, and you don't have that many fingers, *hermano,*
Héctor Espino Gonzalez, "El Superman de la Dale," a right-handed
hitter, a real king, retiring in 1984, Rubén Arenal, shaking off the
numbers, taking the envelope from the boy, his thumb sweeping
across the letters of his name written in ink, a woman's handwriting, and good quality paper, the young man looking at the ground,
reserved or bashful, Rocket reaching out with an open hand and
a reassuring voice, and Rocket, a player to be proud of, El Niño
Asesino, and the young man, maybe seventeen years old, maybe
less, without a word, taking a few steps back, raising his baseball
cap, tipping it, offering a shy smile, a wave, *¡adiós por ahora!* bye for
now! Rubén Arenal, not knowing what the boy meant by it, saying
goodbye for now, watching him get on his spotless wine-red Vento
Phantom 125cc four-speed scooter, disappearing down the street,
not fast not slow, Rubén Arenal, a smile on his face, and remembering the *hidria,* unfinished, a gift for his sister, shutting the street
door behind him, turning the lock of the door of his ground-floor
apartment, a simple home, his pottery studio, and a song playing in
his head, "Perdón mujer," a *ranchera* by Gilberto Parra, performed
by Las Abajeñas, a duet singing the lyrics, two women, Catalina
and Victoria, with Narcisco Martínez, El Huracán del Valle, on accordion, born in 1911 in Reynosa, Tamaulipas, Mexico, and now,
Catalina and Victoria, Las Abajeñas, voices filling him with melancholy, singing, *Qué bonito que quisieras volver, / tu cariño me hace
falta mujer,* "How beautiful that you would return, / I've missed
your loving, woman," and without knowing the contents of the letter, Rubén Arenal, a partnership with the envelope in his hand, a

subliminal bond between man and words, hearing the song "Perdón mujer," a slow sad song, Rubén Arenal making his way to the wedging table, leaving the letter unopened, returning to his work on the pitcher for Luz Elena, taking the handle from where it was hanging, draped over the edge of the wedging table, working it slowly, the clay a little harder but soft enough to move it, a dry surface that didn't leave fingerprints, cutting off the piece he'd use as the handle, scoring the end to help attach it to the pitcher, tapping the scored end with his index finger to widen the surface slightly, applying a slip to fix it, and attaching the top end, letting it sit like that for five minutes to help the clay of the pitcher draw water from the handle so they'd be at the same stage of dryness, hanging the other end of the handle, adding slip, smoothing the joint and the handle where he'd left a few fingerprints, lightly pulling the handle with water, adjusting the handle's curve, cutting the excess clay off, a drop of water at the base of the handle, a little pressure to attach it, Rubén Arenal smoothing the edge of the lower part of the handle fixed to the body of the *hidria,* and Catalina and Victoria singing the last of the lyrics, "There is no other who would love you / like I, you are good and will return to me, / my garden will again bloom, / and this time it will be for you," Rubén Arenal all at once seeing the woman who was a double for Little Pascuala, her alabaster fingers pushing a few strands of hair away from her face, a picture of her at night the last time he saw her, Rubén Arenal bathing in a romantic vision of the woman who looked like *La Pascualita,* leaving the pitcher covered with a soft sheet of plastic for a day or until it's leather hard, Rubén Arenal, deciding on the glaze, looking at a selection of colors, a cautious turn, a cautious look, Rubén Arenal, a dreamer's face, seeing a finished *hidria* the whole family could use, not Cirilo, he wasn't old enough, but Luz Elena, Avelina and Perla.

The open envelope on the kitchen table, a first-rate piece of stationery in his hand, and the handwriting, not scribbling or scrawling but elegant, definite, each word laid out like adobe bricks drying in the sun, using a fountain pen, bottled ink or a cartridge, bold or extravagant gestures of controlled fingers and a slender wrist, not young, no doubt old, a pair of transparent hands, now you see them now you don't, but Rubén Arenal, staying with what he could see, not looking deeper than the fine paper it was written on, there wasn't any need, it was enough just as he saw it, and the feminine hand that'd written the letter, conveying a voice unleashed, weighty and confident, a mighty missive, not long but official, in a private sense, words asking him, but not a request, a statement of fact, the words in the letter saying, if a divine dweller of this divine city of Chihuahua were to rise in the air and fly southeast to a distance of eighty-two or eighty-three miles—one hour and forty-seven minutes by car—as the angel flies, he would see La Presa de la Boquilla, also called Lago Toronto, a dam located in the riverbed of Río Conchos in San Francisco de Conchos, Chihuahua, and La Presa de la Boquilla, a little more than twenty-four miles southwest of Santa Rosalía de Camargo, still flying, now Camargo City, named after Ignacio Camargo, a Mexican insurgent, hero of the independence of Mexico, and La Presa de la Boquilla, a dam that has a hydroelectric power station capable of generating 25 megawatts, with a total capacity of almost three thousand cubic hectometers—Esteban Armendáriz swam 1500 meters of it in eighteen minutes, thirty-two seconds—the area of the reservoir, more than sixty-five square miles, and if it's running at seventy percent capacity, it's generating more than enough electricity to light our eyes and heart, my daughter and myself, in the same way we're lighted by your work, ignited really, I'm not exaggerating, and so we ask to see you, at your studio, on Thursday, tomorrow, in the afternoon, not too late not too early, with the same desire we have to see the sea touching the slope of the sky, there isn't a doubt, it's your pottery we want to buy, no rhyme intended, but refinement and grace, and some tenderness, our señor Arenal, Rubén Arenal, Rocket to your friends, *Xihuitl* to your sister—what I know about you could fill a notebook, not too big not too small—a student of Mata Ortiz, a *ejido* years ago, but it's on the map, not far from the ruins of Casas Grandes, and the city Nuevo Casas Grandes, Rubén Arenal studying near Paquimé, a fourteenth- to fifteenth-century prehistoric settlement, not hitting the books, but hands on, a student of experience, not relying only on text books, a mind as fast as his legs can carry him, returning to Chihuahua, refining your technique, an amalgam of the traditional and the modern, a mixture or blend, not as curious as people might say, a natural development of your artistic brain, making pots with narrow spouts—I've seen them—mugs, bowls, plates, a jar or pitcher for water, cups for tea, mugs for coffee, a vase for flowers, but don't forget your enormous debt to Mata Ortiz, I'm not shaking an index finger, I wouldn't dare, not me not ever, and you already know, a nod and a bow of your head in recognition, a modest view of yourself, a paramount perception, so Thursday, that's tomorrow, Thursday afternoon, not too early not too late, be prepared, I want to see everything, and maybe what I need is more than you've got—*ser claro*, let's be clear, what I've got is what you need—there's no surprise, so collect what you can, lay it out to its full extent, bowls, plates, pots, pitchers, jugs, vases, cups and saucers, even an urn, you never know, Rubén Arenal contemplating the overconfident complementary poetry of the words, admitting that there's no question, a real buyer, and Rocket, it's a sure thing, and none too soon, *así es*, that's right, you can believe your eyes, *mi hermano,* his words joined with optimism and the promise of a sale, financing for Ernesto and Guadalupe, their search for Coyuco, *su hijo,* their son, Rubén Arenal, not needing more in life than he already had, and Rocket, enough is more than enough, Rubén Arenal leaning back in his chair, hands resting on the tabletop, fingers fingering the superior stationery, A1, top-notch, and the ink, a deep blue midnight blue, a hint of green, making him think of Chalchihuitlicue, Lady Precious Green, storm goddess, "the personification of youthful beauty, of whirlpools, and the violence of young growth and love," Rubén Arenal thanking Cottie Burland, just like his sister'd done, a chip off another chip off the old block, Luz Elena, with all the references at her fingertips, and stored away in her head on a Rolodex, don't probe just believe, it's all in there, your filled-to-overflowing mind, a head with plenty of files, Rubén Arenal taking stock of more than the individual words, wide awake and tuned in, their overall tenderness and consideration, shuffling the romantic images like cards but not dealing them, staying with an empty hand except for the letter, there was plenty of time, and Rocket, slow down, *'mano,* it's a buyer not a wife, don't jump when you don't know where you'll land, and who's the other part of *we,* bringing the letter close to his eyes, a squint, and the signature, and Rocket, a curious coincidence? the possible isn't impossible, the letter was signed Pascuala Esparza.

Coyuco was tied up, not a cord but Flex-Cuffs, the plastic stuff the army and police use nowadays, or just plain rough rope binding his wrists but not his ankles—you can walk around but I don't want you guys jerking off or getting yourselves into trouble—pacing the room where he was held with almost thirty others, not much air and what there was of it he couldn't breathe, it was the piss and shit from nerves, students of the Raúl Isidro Burgos Normal Rural School of Ayotzinapa, evacuating what'd turned liquid in their guts, a real scare that emptied the bowels, bladders letting go in a closed room like a big cell, or a garage, José Ángel, a voice of experience on account of his age, a father of two, sitting on a dry spot on the concrete floor, his back against the wall, and José Ángel, take it easy, *'mano,* we don't know what they've got in mind for us yet, but thinking to himself, we'll never get out of here alive, no more wife and kids for me, José Ángel calling him brother after what they'd been through, keeping a steady gaze, Coyuco looking at José Ángel, giving him a if-you-weren't-here-to-give-me-a-little-confidence-I-don't-know-what-I'd-do smile, a forced smile, but a smile just the same, a look of appreciation, really, and José Ángel, a song'll bring you out of it, *compa,* remember on the bus, you were listening, hearing music, I could see it in your eyes, and it's the time for something to get you out of the fear you're in, I do it myself, I'll do it myself, Coyuco hearing a *canción-vals* written by Marco Antonio Velasco, "Jardín de las flores," Flaco Jiménez playing a 3-row button accordion, Max Baca, Jr. on bajo sexto, the words swaying in triple time in Coyuco's heart, *Flor de las flores, flor de una flor, bien de mi vida, dame tu amor,* "Flower of the flowers, flower of a flower, love of my life, give me your love," Coyuco, not knowing what José Ángel was hearing in his head, José Ángel, no longer a steady gaze, not quite a look of relief on his face, eyes glazed by melancholy, or a kind of dreaminess, maybe a tear forming in the corner of an eye, his eyes, they were moist, both of them, Coyuco could see José Ángel's eyes in the glaring light, fluorescent tube lighting above them, eyes saying, what you see is where you are and where you are is nowhere, *mis amigos,* José Ángel, feeling a pair of sympathetic eyes looking down at him, turning his head, looking up at Coyuco, and José Ángel, Las Jilguerillas, Coyuco, that's who I'm listening to in my head, Amparo and Imelda Higuera Juárez singing "Una Palomita," by Felipe Valdés Leal and Ramón Ortega, accompanied by Los Alegres de Terán, can you hear it? a short song, but tears to my eyes, 'mano, a sad waltz:

> *Una palomita que tenía*
> *Su nido en un verde naranjo*
> *Lo dejo solito porque su palomo*
> *La estaba engañando*
> *Yo y esa paloma sentimos iguales*
> *Los mismos pesares*
> *Con lágrimas mias y lágrimas de ella*
> *Llenamos los mares*
> *Hay palomita*
> *Como le vamos hacer*
> *Si a ti te hirió tu palomo*
> *Y a mi me hirió su querer.*

What do you say, a killer, isn't it, a heartbreaker, and Los Alegres de Terán, I know you love them, because I remember everything people tell me, but this song, "Una Palomita," *algo especial,* it's something special, and it's burning a hole through my heart, and Coyuco Cisneros, a wound for the rest of our lives, *mi maestro,* and that's if we live through this, but who can tell? and in the closed room like a big cell, an empty garage, fluorescent tube lighting above them, it was hard to see what the roof was made of, and the impression of a great stain of gold hanging on the horizon, even if they couldn't see beyond the concrete floor and walls, no windows, and for a moment, a breath of fresh air, imagined not real, but it was giving way slowly as storm clouds rose in tin plumes, surrounded by whirling orange-colored veils veiling the stain of gold that might've been the sun if they could see it, but it was night and the students of the Raúl Isidro Burgos Normal Rural School of Ayotzinapa with their piss and shit, a real scare that emptied the bladders and bowels, no matter what song any one of them was hearing in their head, what remained was just a stain, not the sun, and the stench of a filled-to-capacity closed room like a reinforced-concrete hangar, but a lot smaller than a hangar, more like a garage, a stainless steel security door rolled down, sandwich steel panels with foamed-in-place chlorofluorocarbon-free polyurethane core and surrounding seals, U-form bottom seals, keeping out freezing air, humidity and water, and shutting them in good and tight, maybe automatic, maybe not, José Ángel and Coyuco, a silent where-the-fuck-are-we? you can dream up what you want to but here we are and here we'll stay, the music to soothe them evaporating, long gone and nothing left, faded solace, and José Ángel and Coyuco Cisneros, at the same time with a single voice, that was quick! it was a thick solid iron door only wide enough to let one man in at a time, single file, that kept them confined in a cramped room.

Coyuco and his father, Ernesto, on the same wavelength, communicating thoughts, from the living to the almost dead, and so a little wrestling in Coyuco's mind, as the others fell asleep, even José Ángel, a *normalista,* he was tipped forward like a sack of flour, head resting on his raised knees, not snoring but asleep, exhausted, and the other students, too, but Coyuco and El Santo, a team, Coyuco replaying *Santo contra las bestias del terror,* or Santo in *Atacan las brujas,* he liked it for the women, Ofilia the blonde, Elisa the brunette, and for Santo's courage, but most likely seeing *Santo contra cerebro del mal* by Joselito Rodríguez, made in Cuba in 1959, the first appearance of El Santo in movies, not called Santo in *Cerebro del mal,* but El Enmascarado, playing a masked police secret agent, no wrestling just fighting, and Santo looking slim, featuring Joaquín Cordero as Dr. Campos, with Fernando Osés in the role of El Incógnito, a police sergeant, Coyuco remembering the line, "They are citizens of the world—their duty has no frontiers—they hide their identities behind a mask to do good for humanity," then growing sleepy, his wrists burning, *Santo contra cerebro del mal* didn't lift him out of the misery he felt, a nightmare since the bus station in Iguala de la Independencia, Coyuco going back to *Atacan las brujas,* 1964, absurd but fear bringing all kinds of fantasies, ways of escape, El Santo driving a Porsche, Lorena Velázquez playing Elisa, María Eugenia San Martín playing Ofilia, and a great wrestling bout in an arena against a character played by Fernando Osés, with Corona Extra, Bacardi, and Radio 660 *Música Deportes* advertising on the walls, Coyuco finding courage in the dialogue at the end, "I don't understand, Santo," and Santo's reply, "When a cross destroys a witch, her evildoing disappears with her," a grin tinged with disbelief and sorrow on Coyuco's face, his eyes were growing heavy, lids drooping, heavy-lidded leaden eyes coated with ash and wet with tears even as he was falling asleep, facing death, his own ashes falling from the sky into his eyes, and his shoulder touching José Ángel's shoulder, they were sharing a dry spot on the concrete floor, their back against the wall.

A noise waking up the students of the Raúl Isidro Burgos Normal Rural School, more than twenty, almost thirty students, including José Ángel, plus Coyuco, all of them hearing an industrial stainless

steel door rolling up, or it was the weight of a man heaving himself against a solid iron door, the guy behind him saying, *pinche
puto pendejo, hijo de tu rechingada madre,* put your fucking weight
into it! but none of the students hearing the voice, just the creak-
ing hinges, and the heavy door scraping against the concrete floor
like fingernails on a blackboard, a grating sound that finally woke
them up, and the rattling keys, too, four armed men coming into
the room, a suffocating room with a concrete floor and walls, no
windows, a reinforced-concrete garage, or a fortified private hangar,
the four men in uniform, dark blue or black, no hoods, no insignia, no names, One Two Three Four, moving like dark phantoms in
the blurry vision of almost thirty pairs of bloodshot eyes, counting
them one at a time, maybe as many as fifty-four, and four shadows in the ghastly glow of light, fluorescent tube lighting taking the
color out of their skin and clothes, out of everything, even the piss
on the floor, and the students, their skin almost white with fear and
no fresh air, blue veins, and the smell, everybody wide awake now,
their noses and mouths breathing in the odious odors of more than
twenty, almost thirty young men packed into a small space, closer
to thirty, and Coyuco, but who could count, and one of the four
men dragging something heavy across the concrete floor, a dark
green cylinder, and two of the other three, a couple of metal folding
chairs, and a large roll of plastic sheeting, the fourth man dragging
a square metal folding table and a wooden straight back chair made
of poplar, he was bigger and stronger than the other men, setting up
the table and chairs, one of the four armed men in uniform taking
the roll of plastic, laying out a sheet like an enormous heavy-duty
shower curtain covering the floor not far from the iron door, the
only entrance or exit from the room, the students watching them,
but their eyes couldn't focus or didn't want to see what it was because they knew, another sense added to the five others, numb as
they were right now, telling them it wasn't any good whatever it
was and they'd better start praying, and a voiceless voice replying,
as if we ever stopped, *mis amigos,* and right next to José Ángel, but

standing up, not leaning his back against the wall, Doriam or Saúl or Jorge, Coyuco couldn't put a name to the face, not right now, possibly never again, panic erasing his memory, wiping it clean, having temporarily no knowledge or understanding, his stomach aching, and whoever it was that was standing there was vomiting what was left of the contents of his stomach which consisted mostly of acid that was burning tiny holes in the stomach's lining, liquid streaming down the wall looking almost transparent blue, almost colorless in the fluorescent light.

And Coyuco Cisneros, to himself, they haven't got scissors or knives to cut the cuffs, so they'll use an acetylene torch, it's a B-size forty-cubic-foot tank, and it looks like it weighs a lot, Coyuco wanting to rub his eyes with his closed fists but they were tied behind his back, Jorge Manuel, Doriam or Saúl, no longer sick, trying to wipe his chin on his left shoulder, moving like he had a twitch, José Ángel humming a *canción,* thinking of his wife, Blanca, and his two children, América and Gabriela, but interrupting himself from time to time, and José Ángel, it just doesn't get much worse than this, Coyuco and the others not hearing his voice, their eyes fixed on the four armed men in uniform, trying to figure out where they'd seen a uniform like it before, and watching without realizing what they were seeing, No. 1 setting up the acetylene torch next to the square table, the straight back chair made of poplar two feet in front of it with its back to the students, No. 4 putting a notebook and ballpoint pen on the tabletop, No. 1 loosening his belt, unbuttoning the collar of his shirt, making himself comfortable, Nos. 2 and 3 drawing up the metal folding chairs like they were getting ready to watch a few reels of home movies, No. 4 leaning with casual indulgence on the palm of his hand flat against the surface of the metal table, standing next to No. 1, then straightening up, whispering in No. 1's ear, nobody else could hear him, and not a sound in the room, a pin could've dropped, No. 1 nodding his head, No. 4 going for one of them, and the first tortured student of the Raúl

Isidro Burgos Normal Rural School of Ayotzinapa screaming so loud it nearly broke the eardrums of all the others with their eyes shut tight unable to look at what was happening, Antonio or Jonás or Christian or Adán, whoever it was, a howl rising from his guts, fingers shriveling and crisp like burned sausage before what was left of his hands, all ash and bits of bone, bound by melted Flex-Cuffs, parts of his hands, scraps of cooked meat, dropped to the concrete floor, Coyuco and José Ángel, opening their eyes at the same moment, their jaws set with a grimace they didn't know they were making, and Coyuco Cisneros and José Ángel, the two of them saying through clenched teeth, I must be going crazy, *chúntaro* motherfuckers, and tears in their eyes that didn't fall, just burning them, Nos. 2 and 3 getting up from their folding chairs, dragging the unconscious student across the concrete floor to where they'd laid out a plastic drop cloth not far from the narrow door, then two shots fired, a Jericho 941, a couple of 9x19mm rounds, one in the chest, one in the head, leaving the body where it was, the two men wiping the spray and a bit of brain from the legs of their trousers, and Nos. 2 and 3, we'll have to burn these, too, when we're through, wiping off their uniforms, and Coyuco Cisneros, asking himself, what else are they going to burn? and No. 1, the man with the torch in his hand, you better have a change of clothes, *jotos,* and Nos. 2 and 3, the same voice at the same time, who're you calling faggot with that pointed nozzle in your hand, No. 1 doubling up with laughter, then waving at another student, and No. 4, right this way, asshole, a few students retching, gasping for air, vomiting nothing, Nos. 2 and 3 looking at their leader, and No. 1, lighting the torch, mumbling *vete a la madre* to the two men returning to the corner of the room, sitting on their folding chairs, hands folded, not praying, but ready and waiting for the next reel of film that wasn't a movie, No. 4 taking one of the students by the sleeve of his shirt, pulling him across the room by the sleeve, tearing the fabric, and No. 4, repeating, right this way, shoving the student until he was standing in front of No. 1, and the student's knees trembling, finally giving out, the student crumpling to the floor, pissing himself, No. 1, the leader, a voice like tearing a phone book in half, leaving ragged edges, and No. 1, where do you want it, *pajero*, fucking dickhead, holding the torch's flame away from himself as he scratched his nose, and more than one of the students of the Raúl Isidro Burgos Normal Rural School huddled together as close as they could get, the room like a reinforced-concrete garage or a fortified private hangar, as far away from the men in uniform as they could stand, more than twenty, almost thirty students, and Coyuco, saying to themselves, worse than a nightmare! cursing God's name, then looking up, heavenward, for an angel there, any sign of life that wasn't the kind of life they knew on earth, right here, but they couldn't see one, no sign of a miracle regarded as evidence of supernatural power, not anything but the ceiling and those awful lights polluting the air, and at once, a prayer of contrition, and their voices, *Señor mío, Jesucristo, Dios y Hombre Verdadero, Creador, Padre y Redentor mío, por ser vos quien sois, bondad infinita, y por que os amo sobre todas las cosas, me pesa de todo corazón haberos ofendido, también me pesa porque podéis castigarme con las penas del infierno. Ayudado de Vuestra Divina Gracia, propongo firmemente nunca más pecar, confesarme y cumplir la penitencia que me fuere impuesta,* and they all said, *amén,* and the four men in uniform, an automatic response, saying *amén* along with the others, not out of fear, not them, No. 1, adjusting the flame on the torch, while No. 4, unsheathing a military-style knife, a Kershaw or a fixed-blade Gideon Tanto, and No. 4, let's have a slice, like pizza in New York, a grin on his sadistic face, an animal, but an ape was a lot prettier than No. 4, an ape was a real human being if you put him next to No. 4, Coyuco shaking his head no without moving it, and Coyuco Cisneros, silently, they can't do it they can't do it, but knowing they'd do whatever they wanted to do right before their eyes if the students were brave enough to look at them, and José Ángel, the world as he'd known it slipping away, no song could stop what was happening to another student of the Raúl Isidro Burgos Normal Rural School, maybe Marcial, Jonás, José, Doriam or Saúl, nobody could focus on his face, if it wasn't one, it was another, but a long strip of skin sliced off his back, then roasted while stuck to the knife point by the flame of the acetylene torch, the smell making them choke, not the men in uniform, not One Two Three Four, but the others, gagging, the nearly thirty-students-minus-one right now— the corpse leaking blood on a plastic drop cloth near the narrow door—that'd been taken prisoner and held in the reinforced-concrete garage or fortified private hangar.

And Ernesto Cisneros, like I said, I can hear my voice echoing, it's a big empty world, nothing out there, listen, a vacuum, but each life counts, so what the fuck! and you've heard it before, it isn't just Coyuco and the forty-three, it's every death and disappearance from the beginning of time, and so there're dead people everywhere, centuries of them—there aren't enough fingers on our hands, check out your fingers, a pair of hands makes ten at best, you'd need a city of them—and the ghosts of the dead, wandering without a place to rest, no peace of mind or body, you can hear them, it isn't just furniture scraping the floor, a malediction, and more than a jinx, a real curse, a noise that's rasping the fatty sheath off my nerves, and it hurts, my nerves are killing me, they're really painful, it makes me shiver, right to my fingertips, and Lupita, too, arctic, glacial, we're freezing without being cold, shivering because we've got a chronic case of raw nerves, and think of Irma, what'll she say, she'll be a widow before they're married, and Mictlantecuhtli, the Lord of the Land of the Dead, a skeleton with bloody spots, or a plain skull, an obsidian knife through his nose, and his wife, Mictlancihuatl, but it's Mictlantecuhtli, lord of the dead land, sending owls out into the night, calling for those destined to join him, to live in his world, Mictlan, but I didn't hear an owl, Lupita didn't hear a thing, a sound sleeper, not a screech, nothing, no wings, no announcement, maybe Irma heard it, I'll have to ask her, if she can stop the flood of tears for a minute, never easy, like stemming the flow of blood, a hemorrhage of sorrow, the damage their disappearance has caused, listen to it, disappearance, in coded political language, but let's call a spade a spade, being killed, that's what it means, and it's derived from a phrase in classical Greek, so all of them, the forty-three students of the Raúl Isidro Burgos Normal Rural School, and Coyuco, probably dead, and a suffering that extends beyond any measureable distance, why were they taken away from us, a crime on a mountain of crimes, Mictlantecuhtli, the Head-Downward Descender, and Mictlancihuatl, a hideous woman with a bare skull for a head, the god and goddess of death and the underworld, waiting to care for the souls of the dead if only the souls themselves find their way to their restful silent kingdom in the Aztec world, Mictlan—life in Mictlan wasn't unhappy—the underbelly of the Earth, a belly full of souls, stretched wide, the place of the dead beneath the Earth, where the soul was thought to retire quietly in the Land of the Dead, and the souls of missing missing students of the Raúl Isidro Burgos Normal Rural School weren't infants who'd died still nursing, if they were they'd go to El Chichihuacuauhco, meaning "in the wet-nurse tree," and they weren't soldiers who'd fallen in war, nor mothers who'd died in childbirth, going to Tonatiuh-Ilhuicac, the Heaven of the Sun, and their deaths weren't related to water, a journey to Tlalocan, the paradise of the rain god, the place of the nectar of the Earth, if they're dead, better make it forty-three victims, and Coyuco, but why stop there? forty-four, forty-five, forty-six, forty-seven, a hundred, a thousand? and the worst nightmare we could've imagined, if they're no longer living they're in Mictlan, a region of uncertainty and mystery, one of the four stopping places of the soul, but in life, in the Aztec world, all happiness came from hard work and suffering, we know it now, too, and the struggle for growth, followed by a faltering step with the passing of time, we all get old, there's no escape, and at last death, certain, sure and fixed, it was good enough, not bad, and wholly acceptable because it was inevitable—the only possible offering to God in return for life, was life, but now I'm talking about sacrifice, and that's something else—their view in the Aztec world wasn't fatalism, but a true recognition of the nature of human life, so nod your head, because it's true, now as then, then as now, take a look at yourself, and be honest, what do we know about it, the reality of this life is like that of a dream, and in an Aztec poet's words, "Let us consider things as lent to us, oh friends; / only in passing are we here on earth; / tomorrow or the day after, / as Your heart desires, oh, Giver of life, / we shall go, my friends, to His home," death, word-perfect, after which we enter the world of the beyond, the region of the dead, there wasn't a clear picture of hope for a life after death, except after a stay in Mictlan, that's what I've read, the soul might reach a central fire, becoming a part of fire from which new souls are born, according to Cottie Burland, "the heart of everything was fire, and fire to them was the symbol of life," and before all that, to reach Mictlan, the dead were required to undertake a long journey filled with treacherous natural obstacles to be overcome in nine separate phases, first having to cross the Apanohuaia River, or Itzcuintlan, in Nahuatl, "place of dogs," *donde se pasa el río, donde se pasa el vado del río,* through which the river passes, through which the river valley passes, accompanied by a small mute dog, or riding on the back of a little dog, *donde está el río caudaloso y los muertos lo cruzan sobre el lomo de un perro,* where the river is deep and the dead cross it on the back of a dog, but let's not get ahead of ourselves, I don't want to think of Coyuco there, not a wandering soul, either, we've done enough crying and there's always time for more, we don't know if he's dead or alive, Ernesto, almost stumbling on a paving stone, or it was the curb, a heel caught on a crack in the sidewalk, not watching where he was going, walking along Reforma against the traffic in the direction of the distant hills, not heading back to his car, and to catch his breath, leaning against a wooden telephone pole in front of Depósito Flores, or farther on at the corner of Guillermo Prieto and Reforma, looking up at a leafy palm behind a beige-colored wall, Ernesto, worn out by an emotion that'd siphoned off his energy, almost failing, and no more gas, and Ernesto Cisneros, they've vacuumed up my determination, so they're not only criminals they're vampires, too, but he felt a tingling in his skin and the growing presence of something within him, maybe the Prince of this World, Tezcatlipoca, Mirror that Smokes, the trickster spirit, worshipped by warriors and magicians, Ernesto missing only the black obsidian mirror for scrying into the future, but acquiring the strength of Tezcatlipoca, he felt it, Tezcatlipoca, who'd replaced Quetzalcoatl in the later Toltec times, Mirror that Smokes, the shadow side of the human personality in a very clear form, and Ernesto Cisneros, I can almost see him, but seeing isn't what's important now, "I yam what I yam, and that's all what I yam," a quote from Popeye, Ernesto breathing his own words, and Ernesto Cisneros, Tezcatlipoca, Lord of the Surface of the Earth, his symbol's a mirror with flames coming from it, Ernesto's legs holding him upright like pillars of stone, hands grasping the telephone pole for support, and Ernesto Cisneros, the Prince of this World had another title, Titlauacan, "he who is at the shoulder," the god standing beside the shoulder of every human being, whispering thoughts into his mind, suggesting violence and trickery, diverting every action towards his own direction of darkness and cruelty, and it's this voice I'm hearing, Tezcatlipoca's, a terrible deity, leaving a footprint in the night sky that's the group of stars we call the Great Bear, Ernesto straightening his bent shoulders, rising to the situation with a greater strength of body and mind than he'd felt since he'd left Chihuahua for Iguala de la Independencia in Rubén Arenal's Ford F-150 Lobo pickup, and then the words that Titlauacan whispered in his ear, not for everyone to hear, definitely not a child, no one under the age of eighteen, a few sentences more useful to him now than youth itself and the energy that went with it, Titlauacan, or Tezcatlipoca saying, I'll give you the strength to find him, your son, Coyuco, and it won't cost your soul a centavo, a little bloodshed, that's all I ask, because in all my forms, I'm the patron of warriors and of war, Ernesto trembling, unaccustomed to the fiery coursing of blood through arteries and veins weakened by mental or emotional strain, tension resulting from adverse or very demanding circumstances, and Ernesto Cisneros, it's impossible for me to walk anywhere without being inundated with pain and suffering because of death and tragedy, so whatever you are, whoever you are, Tezcatlipoca, Titlauacan, the Prince of this World, Smoking Mirror, I'll take what energy and courage you're giving me, it's an offer I can't refuse, not now after all that's happened, then Ernesto, a flutter, an itch, his right hand letting go of the wooden telephone pole, Ernesto looking down at a figure standing next to him, Ixtlilton, the Little Black One, there for an instant before he disappeared, looking up at Ernesto, becoming part of him, not physically, but incorporating himself as only a god can do into the spirit of a living human being, Ixtlilton, Tezcatlipoca's lieutenant, who visited children in their beds and brought them darkness and peaceful sleep, it was this god, and Tezcatlipoca himself that made the blood in his veins boil, Ernesto, sharing without knowing it, going fifty-fifty with Tezcatlipoca, straight down the middle from head to toe, everything on his left side, including his face showing an expression of surprise if he could see it, sensing his disjointed body, fingers of one hand not matching the fingers of the other, and Ernesto Cisneros, which side is mine, and what does it mean? he was sure that something had happened and he wanted to give himself the once-over, Ernesto hurrying to a window pane, the light was just right, looking at his reflection, seeing half a mask of Tezcatlipoca, an iron pyrite eye in a ring made of shell, half his nasal cavity lined with bright red, thorny oyster shells, alternate bands of turquoise and lignite mosaic built over half his own skull, the left side of his face straight out of the Mixtec Nahuatl codex, the face of Tezcatlipoca, representing one of the two sides of the human mind, the other, Quetzalcoatl, Feathered Serpent, representing conscious intelligence, was nowhere to be seen, and Ernesto Cisneros, one half me, the other half Tezcatlipoca, and that side of my face isn't looking too good right now, Ernesto examining the features of his face, a fixed expression and frightened, because it was the unconscious shadow he was looking at in the window pane, the terrible Tezcatlipoca, wizard god.

Ernesto, asking himself where the other side of the human mind was hiding, knowing it wasn't on his face, not in the reflection he was looking at, but convinced it was in his heart, a good place for Quetzalcoatl's judgment and reasoning, so Ernesto, counting on the half of himself that was still Ernesto Cisneros Fuentes, with a lively vein of the football midfielder, thanks to the happy coincidence provided by his father, invested with Quetzalcoatl's mental ability, Quetzalcoatl, also the Power of Kingship, First of the Lords of Toltecs, the Precious Twin who was thrown together now with the terrible Tezcatlipoca, two mighty forces in cooperation, right side left side, and Ernesto Cisneros, a real pair, you can't beat 'em, and since they've joined me, I'll ride an exceptionally fine and well-kept steed, wearing a *canana,* a wide double band of leather with compartments stuffed with cartridges, the two bandoliers worn by Pancho Villa, right out of the picture from the Bain News Service, George Grantham Bain, and Francisco Villa, commander of *División del Norte,* the *caudillo* of the state of Chihuahua, provisional governor—the meaning isn't lost on me, not you either, I can see it on your faces, *mis amigos,* my right side, my left side, because it's going to be a struggle, and finding Coyuco, I'll need all the help I can get, Ernesto taking on the role with enthusiasm and unselfishness, purposeful perception, calculated cleverness, and insight, a kind of brilliance born of suffering, starting with the responsibility he'd assumed the minute he learned that Coyuco had disappeared—a duty to deal with, and the unique opportunity to act independently and make decisions without authorization—Coyuco and the forty-three other *normalistas,* together, more than a few of them dead, six extrajudicially executed right from the start at four different crime scenes, including a tortured student, another two who were shot at point-blank range, and Ernesto Cisneros, point blank, that's less than 15 cm, almost six inches away, ask Dr. Francisco Etxeberria Gabilondo, a forensic doctor from the University of the Basque Country, ask anyone anywhere, Ernesto, right now, on his own in Iguala, things that were difficult or impossible to understand or explain, looking at his reflection in a shop window, standing there, revitalized, breathing a breath of new life with oxygenated blood, and Tezcatlipoca's desire for revenge, maybe Ixtlilton, Little Black One's brain making sounds, thinking, click click click, but not out loud, Tezcatlipoca and Ixtlilton and a fifty percent solution of Quetzalcoatl's conscious intelligence, whether he saw it on his face or not, Quetzalcoatl, god of the winds and the breath of life, personification of wisdom, symbol of the origin of everything precious, Ernesto—*in qualli yiollo, in tlapaccaihioviani, in iollotetl,* "his good heart, humane and stout"—confident he'd get to the bottom of it, find his son, he couldn't miss, Guadalupe's Coyuco, Irma's Coyuco, his Coyuco, and Ernesto Cisneros, so if it's Tezcatlipoca and his lieutenant making my heart race, pushing blood through narrow roads under my skin, I can promise myself, and anyone listening, that my goal's the opposite of theirs, especially Tezcatlipoca's—feigning miracles, "gathering disciples and wicked people to molest those honest men and to banish them from the land," Fray Diego Durán wrote it, I read it, and what I want is the opposite, not punishing honest men, because now I've got the right blend, a real complement, together with Quetzalcoatl, the plumed serpent, a god who demanded no sacrifice but fruit and flowers, and in the *Codex Vindobonensis,* a history of Quetzalcoatl, and the creation of the world, Quetzalcoatl as a god and later a divine king, human, and the possessor of greater wisdom than other men, representing a set of ideas and symbols revealing the profound and intricate philosophic world of the peoples living on the Central Plateau, and in the very first myth, Quetzalcoatl, the spirit of the waters flowing along the winding bends of rivers, Ernesto knowing his own history, making an urgent request of the spirit of Quetzalcoatl to dominate and turn the terrible Tezcatlipoca, and Ernesto Cisneros, we've got to work together, make him listen, and his lieutenant, too, Ixtlilton, Little Black One, Ernesto looking away from the plate glass window and moving down the street, a twin-powered Ernesto, wanting to help himself, and honest men, women, and children, sorrowful and grief-stricken, wanting to help Guadalupe, Irma, abandoned dogs and cats, starving turtles in their terrariums, birds left to their last grain, unwatered plants with shriveling leaves, all because their owners, disappeared or dead, couldn't attend to them, too many miserable living things to count, it was impossible to live with a untroubled heart, their wretched roots—human, plant, animal— buried deep in the earth's flesh, he wasn't dreaming, it was a fact, and Ernesto Cisneros, you're awake now, but what profound in-duced sleep's kept you ignorant for so long?

Ernesto watching the passersby, head to the left head to the right straight ahead, no one seemed to notice his transformation, it was Ernesto's unchanged face, Ernesto Cisneros, husband of Guadalupe, father of Coyuco, that passersby could see when they looked at him, nobody running away, not a shout or pointed finger singling him out, he was just another man in not too much of a hurry, mak-ing his way in the fading warm sunlight of late afternoon, a few last rays and shadows stretched out on Iguala's east-west streets like long lying dogs in summer, and Ernesto Cisneros, these events don't have to be, there's a glaring question of right or wrong, so bright it blinds anyone who asks it, burning our eyes catching in our throats breaking the backs tearing out the hearts, sounds familiar, doesn't it, Ernesto walking against the traffic down Calle Guillermo Prieto, arriving at the corner of Eutimio Pinzón and Guillermo Prieto, taking a left, again against the traffic, and Ernesto Cisneros, I hope it's not a sign, and continuing until he reached Netzahualcóyotl, a right turn, Ernesto wondering where he was going, and Ernesto Cisneros, I'm not ready for Central Estrella Roja, not yet, but head-ing in the general direction of the bus station just the same, Ernesto walking at a leisurely pace all the way to Manuel Ávila Camacho, a left, and a right on Calle Juan R. Escudero to the Hotel Obregón, not far from Periférico Sur, and Ernesto Cisneros, I'll take a room for the night, maybe two, but the bright blue and white, an orange spiral staircase to the first floor, a modern design that's enough to make my eyes water, not tears of joy, at least it isn't run-down, Ignacio had given him the name of a different hotel in Iguala, El Andariego, Carretera Iguala Lots 29-30 in the industrial section, just beyond Calle Periférico Norte, in another part of town, not anywhere near Central de Autobuses, Estrella Roja, and Ernesto Cisneros, so it's here that I'll stay, even if it's killing my eyes, I'm too tired to go back the other way, Ernesto paying in advance for two nights, climbing the orange-painted stairs, washing his face in the sink in his room, then leaving the hotel for Central Estrella Roja, a six-minute walk, Avenue General Álvaro Obregón to Nabor Ojeda, named after Nabor Ojeda Caballero, *agrarista,* soldier, revolutionary and politician, Ernesto taking a right turn, and a block later a left on Hermenegildo Galeana to Calle de Salazar and straight to the bus station, stopping at Taquería Nayra or Taquería Martha, plenty of choices for a bite to eat and something to drink, a watermelon-flavored Jarritos, Ernesto standing with the bottle in his hand, a straw sticking out of the mouth of it, staring at the front of the Central Estrella Roja, a long sip through the straw and a big swallow of Jarritos cooling his throat, a taco in his belly, the sunset in the sky, and Ernesto Cisneros, time to get back to the car, Rubén Arenal's Ford pickup, because the night's got eyes, I'll have to get my things out from under the seat, in the shadows, how far is it to Calle Ignacio Manuel Altamirano and Calle Hermenegildo Galeana from here? or Calle Melchor Ocampo? I never remember where I park, and Lupita's the opposite, a real compass in her head, North South East West, a finger pointing over there, that's Guadalupe, my Lupita, and our Coyuco's the same, now don't start thinking about it or tears'll get in the way, remember Big Joe Turner, Joseph Vernon Turner Jr., Kansas City, "Turn off the waterworks, baby, they don't move me no more, / When I leave this time, I ain't comin' back no more," I've got the blues myself, and it's the same for the others, parents of forty-three victims, or as many victims you can count on all the fingers of all the hands, and what I keep asking myself, what I don't understand, is why their leaders, the student leaders, keep putting them in danger, risk their lives, from the perspective of revolutionary ideology, the forty-three students and Coyuco are victims offered up by their leaders in a utilitarian sacrifice, and there's a long history of it, look up the words of Kain Guek Eav, Comrade Duch, a monster in his own right, warden of S-21 prison under the Khmer Rouge, denying the cruelty of his actions and those of his subordinates, and the Nazis' categorical imperative, big words coming from my agonizing heart, *¡Dios mío!* what crimes! … the world's whirling away from us, heading straight for *teotalli iitic,* under the holy plain, another term for Hell, but resurrecting forces are at work in Tamoanchan, "place of our origin," the paradise of Omeyocan, the thirteenth sky, presided over by Ometeotl, Lord of Duality, in Omeyocan, dwelling of the supreme beginning, life emanating from here with its two faces, its two opposing forces, and where our bones are ground by Quetzalcoatl, with the help of Cihuacoatl, with a headdress of eagle feathers in the *Florentine Codex,* or the Woman Serpent, together, using the remains of human beings from previous ages, and putting the ground bones in a precious clay pan, or a jade bowl—the bones were broken on their way from the underworld, humans of the Fifth Sun, our sun, we're many different sizes, some people are tall, others short— Quetzalcoatl, giving us life with his own blood by piercing his penis—*¡ay!*—in self-sacrifice, "upon them Quetzalcoatl bled his member," *Leyenda de los Soles,* a new population appearing thanks to what he'd done, creating the first human beings of the Fifth Sun, *in macehualtin,* "the deserved ones by the penitence," and later, the common people, according to the *Florentine Codex,* like you and me, like most of us, *mis amigos,* Ernesto leaving the bottle of soda on the countertop, Taquería Nayra or Taquería Martha, heading for the Ford Lobo, a right on Hermenegildo Galeana, two blocks, another right at the corner, leaning to catch his breath against the rounded iron bars painted yellow and red on the sidewalk opposite the serving window and counter of Pollo Feliz, the façade painted brick red, a glance at the sunset sky, and Ernesto Cisneros, death and life are no more than two sides of the same reality, you know it and I know it, and the potters of Tlatilco, in the Valley of Mexico, know it, too, making figurines with double faces, one half alive, the other skull-like, they're duality masks, I don't need more proof than that, so I'll buy it ten times over, Ometeotl, "our mother, our father," as a symbol of his intangible quality, as the heart of wisdom and of the only truth on earth, and Quetzalcoatl put a face on him, identifying him as Ometecuhtli-Omecihuatl, Lord and Lady of Duality, who live above the highest of the heavens in Omeyocan, but it's time to come back down to earth, maybe life's just a bunch of made-up facts, Ernesto, gathering his thoughts, his taste buds tickled by the smells coming from a take-out chicken stand on Calle Joaquín Baranda, taking two dozen steps past Pollo Feliz, *No Hay Otro Mejor—EXPRESS Sólo para llevar*—heading straight to where he'd parked Rubén "Rocket" Arenal's pickup.

Under the seat of the F-150, a parcel he'd put together before leaving Chihuahua, clothes wrapped in yesterday's newspaper, making an anonymous thing out of it, tied with string he'd found wound in a ball in a drawer in the kitchen when Guadalupe was taking a bath, a parcel concealing a dark-blue uniform, resembling the uniforms of the *Policía Municipal,* or the *Policía Nacional,* whatever he could get away with, including the belt but without a gun, insignia and Mexican flag sewn on late at night, Ernesto working until daybreak, hiding the short-sleeved shirt where his wife wouldn't find it, not with his clean clothes, not there where she'd see it when she put away the laundry, hiding it in a trunk with old books, nobody looked at his old books, Ernesto accepting that the shirt might smell of the mustiness of aged paper, decaying paper, rosin, acetic acid, furfural and lignin, chemically related to the molecule vanillin, a hint of vanilla, not so bad, but mostly a stale, moldy or damp smell, a reader's dream, and it was all he had, Ernesto locking the Ford pickup, turning back in the direction of Hermenegildo Galeana, not retracing his steps, unreadable footprints, walking roughly six blocks to Antonio de León, a right, one block to Álvaro Obregón, returning to his room at Hotel Obregón, the parcel tucked under his arm and Rubén Arenal's pack of Faros in his shirt pocket, Ernesto undressing, unlacing his boots, and a pair of socks that stood up by themselves, taking a shower, washing his thoughts off his skin, agonizing anxiety anxious agonizing, and fear for Coyuco, Ernesto washing himself, trying to eradicate the indecent, to loosen the particles of contaminated foul fear that came out of his pores along with the sorrow in his heart, two or more for the price of one, Ernesto having no answers to any questions, not his own, not Guadalupe's, not Irma's, not Ignacio's, not Rubén Arenal's or Luz Elena's, and for sure, not the other parents of the disappeared, Ernesto, using a hand towel, scrubbed and scoured the reddening skin on his chest, arms, and legs, dead cells raining down with the water in the hot shower, and Ernesto Cisneros, I'll add those cells to the heap of the already dead and disappeared, a pile as high as a low mountain range, Ernesto shaking his head of wet hair, gray strands falling in front of his eyes, but there're enough dead out there without me throwing in my used-up worn-out overworked skin cells, Ernesto rubbing his eyes, gargling mouthfuls of water and spitting them out, a rinsing of death and decay without an antiseptic, watching the tarnished blemished water circling the drain, Ernesto stepping out of the shower stall, drying himself off, not feeling clean but awake, and a rumbling in his stomach, a deep resonant sound, a real hunger because a taco and a bottle of Jarritos wouldn't fill a cat, Ernesto staring at the bed and the parcel, the towel over his shoulders, wishing he had a pair of clean underwear and socks, not thinking of everything, unwrapping the uniform and laying it out on the bedcover, just a thin blanket, pressing and caressing the uniform with the palms of his hands, and Ernesto Cisneros, from here on in it's my disguise, and tonight, before I go to sleep, under the mattress you go, a poor man's pressing, that's what you need and that's what you'll get, and Ernesto Cisneros and Rubén Arenal, at the same time in different places, without words but with thoughts coupling like two railroad cars, each surrendering their heart to something, which meant pursuing something, going after it, each in their own way, because the word "heart" in Nahuatl, *yollotl,* was derived from *ollin,* movement.

Rubén Arenal putting the envelope with the letter between the pages of a book, the deep blue midnight blue ink on superior stationery, making him think of Lady Precious Green, Chalchihuitlicue, "the personification of youthful beauty, of whirlpools, and the violence of young growth and love," the storm goddess, and the overall tenderness and consideration of the words, a tumultuous tempest tickling him, enticing pictures filling his head, images sprouting up from the letter's words, twenty-four frames a second, a real series of moving pictures, Rubén Arenal, sitting on the edge of his chair at his desk, hands resting on the cover of the book, Juan Rulfo's *Obra Completa,* fingers drumming gently at first on the paper cover, a skeleton wearing a wide flower-embellished hat looking back at him, maybe a woman, a bluish ink drawing, almost purple, on a washed-out worn-out pink background, published by the Ayacucho Library, an editorial branch of the Venezuelan government, managed by the Fundación Biblioteca Ayacucho, Rubén Arenal, impatience getting the better of him, a nervous drumming on the flower-embellished hat, the cover of Juan Rulfo's book, and Rocket, *¡tranquilo, hermano!* it's a buyer not a wife, but the signature, Pascuala Esparza, and her daughter, *La Pascualita,* or her look-alike, dressed in black, walking next to her mother, a precarious prediction, Rubén Arenal seeing them now like he'd seen them last night, in the burning heat, and Rocket, I don't like my own trick of stumbling like a donkey after whatever comes to my mind, coming when the idea comes to me from wherever it comes, it's passing through where the sun doesn't shine, not too intelligent, not too bright, but where's the source, the birthplace, the origin, encouraging parlous providence, timely preparation for future eventualities full of danger or uncertainty,

and those words, ladies and gentlemen, in deep blue midnight
blue ink, so take care be responsible watch your step slow down,
Rubén Arenal, overwhelmed by anxiousness, oxygen held back in
his lungs, in culminating convulsion, breaking out in a sweat, and
Rocket, breathe, breathe, you fool you clown, knock it off, my thing
is to have my lungs working in tip-top condition, of the very best
class or quality, now and forever, tip-top and not a line guide on
a fishing rod, *no seas tan bobo, hermano,* don't be such a fool, like
the song from 1965 by Luz Esther Benítez, a *Boricua*, a native of
Bayamón, a municipality of Puerto Rico, Luz Esther Benítez, better
known as Lucecita Benítez, ask Roberto Tirado, dedicating his first
release in 1988 on Lando records to Lucecita Benítez, Rubén Arenal
rising from his chair, walking to the kitchen, heading straight for the
refrigerator, and Rocket, first things first, reciting part of the letter's
contents, without moving his lips, hearing Pascuala Esparza's voice
through the words she'd written in a standard-size letter, sealed in
a hand-delivered envelope, 6 x 9, my daughter and myself, we're
lighted by your work, and so we ask to see you, at your studio, on
Thursday, tomorrow, in the afternoon, not too late not too early, it's
your pottery we want to buy, Rubén Arenal, using different words,
or the same words in a different order, and Rocket, but it's the thrust,
the meaning, the drift that counts, the substantial substance of a
message of striking proportions, a sale to pay the rent, and a woman
I've been wanting to meet, Rubén Arenal, his hand on the refrigerator door, a photograph stuck there by a magnet, Luz Elena, Avelina,
Perla and Cirilo smiling back at him, and a pitcher of pulque waiting
for him behind the door, fermented agave nectar extracted from the
maguey and mixed with *xnaxtli* seed, or the *ocpactli* root, aiding the
fermentation, Mayáhuel, "Goddess with the four hundred nipples,"
the personification of the maguey plant, the goddess who invented
pulque, and Patécatl, "God of medicine," Lord of the root of pulque, and god of healing and fertility, pulque, seen by the ancients as
the result of the union between female and male archetypes, Rubén
Arenal opening the refrigerator door, and in front of him, a nearly

empty refrigerator, but the pitcher of pulque, a path to sleep and dreams, connecting the divine and earthly realms, and Rocket, impatience will lose you the jackpot, because *La Pascualita,* or Little Pascuala, with her veined hands and wide-set sparkling glass eyes, the woman that's a dead ringer, *una doble de la Pascualita,* will wait for me, brother, if I wait patiently for her, breathe breathe, Rubén Arenal pouring himself a tall glass of pulque, raising the glass to his lips, swallowing a mouthful of chilled pulque, not getting drunk but taking enough to dream, sitting on a chair at the rough wooden table in the center of the kitchen area, Rubén Arenal raising his shirt, looking down at a tattoo of a maguey on his stomach, rubbing his belly, taking another mouthful of pulque, warmth pouring into him like a tender fire, charitable and caring, remembering the Nahuatl story, "The Horticultural Boy," "Xochicualtequitca Piltontli," a folk tale, Rocket, putting a few sentences of the story into his own words, "earlier the healer had seen that on his stomach the boy had a maguey painted in blood, and she said to his mother, look, madam, this maguey that's painted on his belly means that he'll have to be raised on pulque, and while he's growing, feed him what I've told you; when he reaches the age of seven, then we'll change his nourishment, in the meantime let's heal him, and she began to heal him, she sucked the blood on his belly, she perfumed him with burnt St John's wort, palm, incense, many other medicinal herbs, she rubbed rooster blood on his stomach, erasing the maguey painted on the boy; she burnt incense later so he wouldn't cry again, after she healed him he didn't cry again, he was always calm, once they'd given him the pulque they didn't have to give it to him again, he'd fall asleep and they'd give him more the next day," Rubén Arenal taking a drink from his glass, licking his lips, dry after recounting part of the story, "The Horticultural Boy," taking another slug of pulque, feeling a little sleepy himself, and Rocket, I wasn't like him as a child, but *I've* been drinking the stuff all my life, so thank you thank you Don Pablo González Casanova, born in Mérida, Yucatán, on 29 June 1889, tireless researcher, teacher, editor and director of the Sunday supplement of *El Universal,* member of the Mexican Academy of Language, but without a seat since no seat became vacant, so no acceptance speech—*toma, por mala suerte,* that's too bad—thank you Padre González Casanova for a million things, and for collecting and translating those stories from Nahuatl to Spanish, Rubén Arenal finishing his glass of chilled pulque, the pulque in his veins making him sleepy, all at once his eyelids weighed a ton, and Rocket, it's time to read and go to sleep, I've got less than a day before they come here to see my things, Rubén Arenal putting the empty glass in the sink without rinsing it, leaving the kitchen to get his copy of Juan Rulfo's *Obra Completa,* the bluish ink drawing, almost purple, of a skeleton wearing a wide flower-embellished hat looking back at him from the cover, and he thought he saw it give him a wink, a nod, and then Rubén Arenal, undressed, no pajamas, and straight to bed to read a few pages before falling asleep.

"Una noche serena y oscura," played and sung by Cuco Sánchez and Dueto América, Cuco Sánchez, José del Refugio Sánchez Saldaña, born in 1921 in Altamira, a port city on the Gulf of Mexico, in the state of Tamaulipas, and Dueto América, Carolina and David González from Aguascalientes in the state of Aguascalientes, and "Una noche serena y oscura," "One Dark and Serene Night," a melancholy song of love and betrayal:

> *Una noche serena y oscura*
> *cuando en silencio juramos los dos*
> *cuando en silencio me diste tu mano*
> *y de testigo pusimos a Dios*
>
> *Las estrellas, el sol y la luna*
> *son testigos que fuiste mi amada*
> *hoy que vuelvo te encuentro casada*
> *ay que suerte infeliz me tocó*

Soy casada y amarte no puedo
por que así lo dispuso la ley
quiero serle constante a mi esposo
y en silencio por tí lloraré

Cuando estés en los brazos de otro hombre
y te creas la más consentida
espero en Dios que te maten dormida
por infame y traidora a mi amor.

One night, serene and dark
when in silence we both promised,
when in silence you gave me your hand,
and for a witness we appointed God.

The stars, the sun and the moon
were witnesses that you were my beloved.
Today I return and find you are married,
Oh, what sad luck I have.

"I am married and cannot love you,
because the law has made it so.
I want to be true to my husband,
and I will cry for you in silence."

When you are in the arms of another man,
and you believe you're the most pampered one,
I hope to God they'll kill you while you're sleeping,
for being ungrateful and a traitor to my love.

Rubén Arenal listening to the song, shrugging off the love, concentrating on betrayal, already afraid of what might happen if he fell in love, a premature paranoia setting in, and a little wounded unwarranted jealousy even before he'd met her face to face, the daughter of

Pascuala Esparza, getting up from the wooden table in the kitchen area with a second cup of coffee in his hand, walking to where he'd laid out as many pieces of pottery as he could without making it look like a garage sale, his best work, free from flaws or mistakes, displaying his modest skill, know-how, artistry, imagination in earthenware and stoneware, with the heart of Mata Ortiz, a small land-grant village with adobe dwellings, a village four and a half hours south and west of El Paso pumping its blood into each piece, Rubén Arenal refining his technique, an amalgam of the traditional and the modern, and an enormous debt to Mata Ortiz, and now, a stab of love stuck into him sharp like a cactus thorn, waiting, pacing, and Rocket, I wonder if I'll hear the bell or the knocking at the door, leaving the pottery studio for the entrance to his ground-floor apartment, a simple home, checking to see if the bell worked, a buzzer, and Rocket, asking a passerby, a fifteen-year-old kid, maybe younger, standing there with a gym bag slung over his shoulder, *¿ese, me gustaría que hicieras algo por mí?* can you to do something for me? and the boy, a puzzled look, *¿estás en serio o me estás tomando los pelos?* are you serious or are you kidding me? the boy, his gym bag in his hand, faltering steps, not dragging his feet, but slowing down, stopping out of curiosity, and Rocket, can you do me a favor, *manito?* this is a test, sounds like American TV in the sixties, but you're too young, so what I'm asking is, will you start out by ringing the buzzer, or it's a bell, it doesn't matter, and then knock on the door, at first not so loud, this door, right here—Rubén Arenal laying the palm of his hand on the face of his door—I'll go back inside, right now, that's the test, and if I don't come to the door, if I don't open it, it's because I didn't hear you, and so you start banging on it, louder, you can lay into it, I won't object, nobody will, and keep it coming until I open the door, got it? good, and I'll give you a hundred pesos, okay? just to know if I can hear when somebody's there at the door while I'm inside, it's no joke, not from where I'm standing, which is right here waiting for somebody to show up, I'm itching, and I don't want to miss them, they're more than a somebody, not one but two, a woman and her mother, what do you say? and the boy, *chido, güey,* okay, Rubén Arenal, without another word, shutting the door behind him, standing in the foyer separating the street entrance from his apartment door, deciding he'd better go inside, closing the apartment door behind him, staring at the kitchen area of his studio, clicking his tongue, rubbing the calluses on the palm of his right hand, a kind of tic, a habitual spasmodic contraction of the muscles, not in his face, but in his hand, that's how it was, and right away, the doorbell, or it was the buzzer, but Rubén Arenal, waiting a little longer, if he didn't hear it it'd be better to know what the pounding on the door sounded like, so he was frozen to the spot in his kitchen, listening and waiting, waiting and listening, a knock on the door, a thump, followed by another, no echo, just a faraway sound passing through two doors, then a heavier weight against the outer door, the street entrance, a blow with a person's fist or blunt instrument, a hammering sound, dull not sharp, a whack wallop and the fifteen-year-old boy was beating the daylights out of the door, the wood insensible to the attack, Rubén Arenal hurrying to get to it, wanting to stop the violence that made him more nervous than he already was, his skull vibrated painfully, the pounding like hammer blows shaking loose his skull casing, opening up a hole for all his anticipation to bore into the center of his brain.

Rubén Arenal digging into his trouser pocket for a hundred-peso note, unfolding it, and Nezahualcoyotl's crumpled courtly face looking back at him as he smoothed the bill, rubbing it against the leg of his trousers, Nezahualcoyotl, Coyote-Hambriento, "Hungry Coyote," or fasting coyote, Rey de Texcoco, King of Texcoco, poet, scholar, architect, Rubén Arenal hesitating before handing over the one hundred pesos, standing up to the stony stare on Nezahualcoyotl's face, a pair of eyes on cotton-fiber money, not polymer, and Nezahualcoyotl's hard unyielding unbending inflexible inspection of Rubén Arenal's unbuttoned unwound features, a voice, Nezahualcoyotl's voice saying, do I know you? I think I do, and I always will, I sleep on this paper that pays the rent, buys food, cigarettes, and I'm wearing the face of a poet who's first emphasis is a keen awareness of time and change, *cahuitl*, "that which leaves us," Rubén Arenal acknowledging what he heard, nodding his head at Nezahualcoyotl, then looking at the boy, who was shuffling his feet, not knowing what to do except to listen, and Rocket, opening his mouth, speaking to the boy, you've done your duty, and more than your job, *manito*, a royal responsibility, an infinitesimal undertaking, but of immeasurable importance to me, so here's the regal face of Nezahualcoyotl, 1402-1472, that's I Rabbit–6 Flint, a true master of the word, and if you're speaking to him, he's called *tlamatini*, "he who knows something," "he who meditates and tells about the enigmas of man on earth, the beyond, and the gods," an authority on things both human and divine—Miguel León Portilla—Rubén Arenal extending his hand to the boy with one hundred pesos in it, and Rocket, you can take it at face value, here it is, handing the banknote to the fifteen-year-old, with the face of an eleven-year-old, but tall for his age, a bashful boy except when it came to pounding on a door, his gym bag at his feet on a patch of asphalt, or it was concrete, the boy smiling at him, folding the money and putting it in his shirt pocket, with nothing to say, and Rocket, but you've got to listen to what I'm going to say, and these aren't my words, "I comprehend the secret, the hidden: / O my lords! / Thus we are, we are mortal, / humans through and through, / we all will have to go away, / we all will have to die on earth … / Like a painting we will be erased. / Like a flower, / we will dry up here on earth. / Like plumed vestments of the precious bird, / that precious bird with the agile neck, / we will come to an end," and so it continues, *manito*, take the poem with you, it's of more value than one hundred pesos—and what Nezahualcoyotl's doing on a sheet of money I'll never know— maybe a reminder of our past, and a real hero, a man to look up to, the assassination of Nezahualcoyotl's father by warriors from Azcapotzalco, "in the place of the anthills," in the northwestern part of Mexico City, the beginning of a long series of misfortunes and dangerous harassments, Nezahualcoyotl's mental agility, perceptiveness and bravery brought him victory over his enemies, and we can learn from him, *manito*, I've got a friend whose son's gone missing with forty-three other *normalistas*, a friend like a brother to me, and he's in Iguala, searching for him, a hopeless journey, a little of Nezahualcoyotl's shrewdness and guts is exactly what we need right now, take my word for it, the boy looking at his shoes, picking up his bulging gym bag, holding it like it didn't weigh anything, a nervous grin, then raising his head, swept by confidence, and the boy, according to *Historia de los Mexicanos por sus Pinturas,* a post-conquest codex, señor Arenal, probably drafted by Fray Andrés de Olmos in the 1530s, "they had a god whom they called Tonacatecuhtli, whose wife was Tonacacihuatl … who were self-created, and their dwelling place was always the thirteenth heaven, the beginning of which was never known," Tonacateuctli and his wife, Tonacacihuatl, the female half of "the primeval parents of both gods and man," Tonacateuctli, Lord of Our Sustenance, and don't forget the miracle of procreation, in the *Codex Vaticanus A* there're scenes of copulating couples, I know how much you like alliteration, señor Arenal—don't ask me how I know your name, you wouldn't believe me if I told you—and in this world of money, poverty, abundance, ignorance, suffering and death we forget the sources of our lives, our history, I don't have to lecture you, of course, but it's worth remembering, and so with the blessings of Tonacateuctli and Tonacacihuatl—none other than Ometecuhtli, "Lord of the Duality," and Omecihuatl, "Lady of the Duality," living in Omeyocan, "Double Heaven," Ometecuhtli-Omecihuatl, also known as Ometeotl, the god of duality, both male and female at once—with their blessings, I wish you the best of luck with Pascuala Esparza and her daughter, *La Pascualita,* maybe love, maybe children—your sister's got them, but you don't—hey! what's that frown on your face? you haven't seen a ghost, señor Arenal, just touching the money you held in your hand, laying my palm and using my fist against your door, I can see more than you can imagine, the future, not all the details, but what I see I see, so don't underestimate me, I might look fifteen years old, but you know and I know that I haven't got an age, only the years your mind wants to give me, what you think I am I'll be, my spirit expands with the steadily increasing knowledge of our country's past, not just facts, but invisible energy, regular, even, and continuous in development, frequency, and intensity, that's the way it is, señor Arenal, like the title of Elvis Presley's fortieth album, you know it, don't you? *That's The Way It Is,* produced by Felton Jarvis, eight studio tracks recorded in Nashville, four live tracks from the International Hotel in Las Vegas, a hotel built by Kirk Kerkorian on sixty-four and a half acres on the east side of Paradise Road between Desert Inn Road and Sahara Avenue, plenty of Armenian immigrants *en el Norte,* pogroms and genocides, like our homegrown murders right here in Mexico, and everyone everywhere wanting to get away from violence, so Kirk Kerkorian, Armenian, born in the US, and a lot of Armenian families in Southern Nevada—what I don't know could fill a shot glass, señor Arenal—so like I was saying, the nonphysical part of myself that's the seat of emotions and character, my true self, capable of surviving physical death or separation, a highly refined substance or fluid thought to govern vital phenomena flowing within me, an idea no longer in everyday use but something I believe in, and stoutheartedness, resolution, moxie, call it what you like, it's all there, add it up, mix it together, what it amounts to is my soul—it's a big word, I know, you don't have to say anything— growing with a steadily increasing knowledge of once major-league Mexico's past, regular, even, and continuous in development, frequency, and intensity, I'm repeating myself for your benefit, pay attention but don't count the words, they're ingredients to cook by, like music, it's what fortifies me, the boy, slinging the strap of the gym bag over his shoulder, stepping back, Rubén Arenal with a hundred-peso note back in his hand, and the boy, it costs you nothing to believe me, there's the proof, Rubén Arenal steadying himself by leaning his shoulder against the façade of the building, taking a deep breath, he contemplated the one hundred pesos in the palm of his hand, and Rocket, then you know what'll happen to me? and the boy, to know our past is to place ourselves firmly in the present, señor Arenal, the future is a secret.

The boy, starting to walk away, leaving Rubén Arenal leaning against the façade, a bewildered expression on his face, but taking pity on him, far from indifference, a feeling of sorrow and compassion caused by the confusion of others, it wasn't the first time the boy had seen it happen, Rubén Arenal wasn't unique, they'd all reacted in more or less the same way, a touch of the shoulder in passing, buying a newspaper, *El Diario de Chihuahua, El Monitor, El Diario de Juárez,* or *La Prensa* from Mexico city, and taking the paper from the hands of a newsagent, or a firm grip, shaking hands with someone at the post office, that's all it took, a moment of physical contact, and out it came like a rush of wind, seeing more than anyone could imagine, the future, not all the details, but enough of it, and the boy making an impression, whoever was listening to him, baffled by his illuminating insight, judgment, facts and details, the boy, taking pity on him, stopped in his tracks, turned around, and the boy, my last bit of advice—I'm off to exercise my body and mind with an empty gym bag, can't you tell there's nothing in it?—is don't trust what's right in front of you, not every time, without fail, because things aren't always what they seem, obvious and overused but even so it's true, you'll know what I mean when you've got a decision to make, a choice—I know the world and the world knows me—and you'll figure it out yourself, with the help of a warning, a road sign, alarm bells, a colored light or a semaphore, or a straw in the wind will let you know, it might be your intuition, because your brain gets clearer, sharper, then you can do things, think, carry out plans, and in the words of Antonio Machado, *Caminante, son tus huellas / el camino, y nada más ; / caminante, no hay camino, / se hace camino al andar,* "Wanderer, your footsteps are / the path, and nothing else; / wanderer, there is no path, / the path is made by walking," and

Rocket, okay okay, it could be my head's not screwed on right, it isn't the sun, it's not that hot, there's not enough heat cutting through the hat I'm not wearing to make my head so piping hot, I guess I'm really hearing what you've got to say, so you've left your mark, a lasting or significant effect, and the boy, ¡adiós! so long, maybe we'll see each other again, I know the future, you don't, but I'm not saying anything more, and a wave goodbye, the boy walking down the street, his spirit trailing after him, or it was the other way round.

Rubén Arenal wasn't sure of anything, wiping the sweat from his forehead with a handkerchief, always a handkerchief whether he thought of it or not, an automatic better-put-this-in-my-pocket before he knew he'd done it, now folding the hundred-peso note back into his trouser pocket, today, a man of small bags sewn into clothing, and a latchkey in his hand, but elongated shadows drawing his attention, the latchkey didn't make it to the lock, looking down at his feet, shadows stretching across the tops of his shoes, moving in a constant direction on a horizontal surface, shadows whose shapes weren't clouds but two people, shadows so long they must've come from giants, Rubén Arenal wanting the shadows to belong to Pascuala Esparza and La Pascualita, not wanting to look up or turn his head, but he couldn't help it, swinging his head around, moving fast as a whiplash, at first a blur due to his unfocused vision, then eyes popping out of his head, and Rocket, the boy's just confirmed it, and what do I see? there they are, evidence, endorsement, the seal of approval, and definitely based on facts, he was rubbing the calluses on the palm of his right hand with his right thumb, the common flexor sheath, or ulnar bursa, and Rocket, shut your eyes, they'll go away even if you don't want them to, and at the same time, a kick, an exhilaration, a rush, controlled by chance rather than design, recognizing the contradiction, or there was a harmony, and Rocket, in the afternoon, not too late not too early, that's what she wrote, so it's a plan or blueprint, not chance, Rubén Arenal seeing the words, "with the same desire we have to see the sea touching the slope of the sky, there isn't a doubt, it's your pottery we want to buy," printed in red letters on the yellowish air in front of his eyes, and Rocket, it's luck, and thanks to that kid I'm out here instead of in there, the earth's really spinning, or it's my head, but hang on, it's just a little dizziness, don't collapse, they aren't insects, not *zancudos,* they won't bite, Rubén Arenal with his heart in his mouth because it meant so much, not just a sale, but love, and Rocket, answering himself, yes, love, his eyes squinting against the sun, his eyes on the figures drawing near, ignoring for the moment the silhouette of Pascuala Esparza, his eyes trying to distinguish the features of the other face hidden behind a veil hanging down from a wide-brimmed hat shading her head against the heat of the sun, Little Pascuala, or a dead ringer for *La Pascualita,* her look-alike, her twin, a carbon copy and the mirror image.

Rubén Arenal jangling his keys in his hand, trying to wake himself from a dream, and Rocket, am I standing here? or in front of the plate glass window of La Popular, Calle Victoria 801 and Avenida Ocampo, Zona Central, he was both here and there, seeing a woman's tall, slender figure in a bridal gown, her veined hands, wide-set sparkling glass eyes, eerie smile, real hair and blushing skin tones, *esa mujer celestial,* that heavenly woman, and later, after his visit, treating himself to breakfast at Mi Café, nourishment after gazing at *La Pascualita,* a couple of scrambled eggs and fresh juice, maybe *jugo verde,* vegetable juice, because watching her drained him of his strength, and the café was nearby, nothing more, and Rocket, coming to his senses, that was there, but now I'm here, and a strong gust of wind was slicing at his skin, his feet planted firmly in front of his ground-floor apartment, a simple home, and his pottery studio, and Rocket, it's time for the wind, that's Chihuahua, you can count on it here like you can count on the thirsty earth of arid plains split with cracks and dry arroyos in northwestern Mexico and the inland northern areas, just like Juan Rulfo's story, "Nos han dado la tierra," "They Gave Us The Land," and the hustling current of air encouraging the two women, bringing them closer to him, propelled by wind, he could smell their perfume, and his own desire, Pascuala Esparza and her daughter, *La Pascualita,* not walking on earth but gliding, defying gravity, mother and daughter, arm in arm, Little Pascuala dressed in black, and her mother, also dressed in black, a *rebozo* draped over her shoulders, her mother's shoulders not *La Pascualita's*, a shawl from Pátzcuaro in Michoacán, black and deep-blue with knotted fringe, Rubén Arenal recognizing it from last night, or it was the night before last, Little Pascuala, a few remarks to her mother, not really hearing what she said, just the sound of her voice, the heat, the wind, the night, mother and daughter taking a stroll, getting some fresh air, the last time he'd seen them, and right now the sultry afternoon air, fiery and feverish, a few small bubbles filled with serum appearing on his skin, or a rash, he was so excited, and in no doubt, on the outside, appearing composed collected self-assured, looking first at Pascuala Esparza, then straight at a pair of veiled eyes, *La Pascualita,* and Rocket, *bienvenidos, señoras,* thank you for coming, and an idiosyncrasy, almost bashful, cupping his hand, palm up, beckoning them with four fingers pinched together, and a little bow and a shy smile, unlocking the street entrance, holding the door open for them, a queen and her princess, and Rocket, you're welcome you're welcome, hearing the street door shut behind him like it was miles away.

Ignacio Pardiñas fastening the ties of a trash bag, propping it against the back door, watching it slide in slow motion onto its side, but nothing spilling out, and it was late afternoon, the sun was setting, Ignacio looking out the little window set in the upper part of the back door, the last few rays of sunlight like arms stretched across the cement in the alley behind the house, asking himself if he should call El Andariego, a hotel in the industrial section of Iguala, on Carretera Iguala, lots 29-30, just beyond Calle Periférico Norte, and Ignacio Pardiñas, Ernesto might be taking a siesta, but Ignacio, shaking his head no, and Ignacio Pardiñas, continuing, it's too early, he's out on the streets, not wasting any time, parked and walking and not even checked in someplace where he could sleep, I can see it when I close my eyes, if I had a custom-built mirror I'd show you, Ignacio with a scarlet iridescence in his eyes, imperfections that were always there, particles representing some kind of electro-magnetic radiation, or it was just the way the light struck them, and for Ernesto it was like a caress, a son's plea to his father for affec-tion, and then granted, not a grunt or slap on the back, that's how it was, that's how it always was and always would be until one or the other, Ignacio or Ernesto, substitute father or son, or both, ceased to exist, no longer living on this earth, but Ignacio heading out the front door, thinking that it was his substitute grandson, a young man by the name of Coyuco, a student at the Escuela Normal Rural Raúl Isidro Burgos, Carretera Nacional Chilpancingo-Chilapa, Ayotzinapa, Tixtla de Guerrero, who had left this earth, land as they knew it, fertile—wheat, cotton, maize, sorghum, peanut, soy, alfalfa, green chile, oats, corn, beans, potato, watermelon, melon, thirty va-rieties of apple—and also made of wood, stone and steel, Coyuco, never to be seen again, abducted with other students, disappeared, maybe dead before his own father and mother, the worst kind of tragedy for a parent, and Ignacio Pardiñas, a line from the Bible, *Acuérdate que mi vida es un soplo, / Y que mis ojos no volverán a ver el bien,* "Remember that my life is a breath; / my eye will never again see good," Ignacio, narrowing his eyes, locking his door, and the iron gate that protected it, leaving his house on Barrancas del Cobre, turning right, walking slightly uphill toward a cement stair-case, something like nine steps up, a railing on the left-hand side, nothing on the right, moving through the darker stage of twilight toward Calle 38A, using a hardwood walking stick, hand painted with the design of an eagle and snake, not many trees on his street, carefully crossing Calle 38A, continuing on Barrancas del Cobre, and Ignacio Pardiñas, that's the hill, and now a slight climb ahead of me, continuing with the words of Job, *Los ojos de los que me ven, no me verán más; / Fijarás en mí tus ojos, y dejaré de ser,* "The eye of him who sees me will behold me no more; / while your eyes are on me, I shall be gone," but take it literally, *mis amigos,* as I say it, not only in the Bible's context, Job, 7:7-8, but in mine, Ignacio, used to hearing his own voice, out loud or in his head, moving on with the help of his walking stick, a gift from his father, an inheritance from father to son, but Ignacio, without children or a wife, it was supposed to be Coyuco's stick, not now, but one day in life, a future Coyuco might never see, an old walking stick, like an artifact, an object made by a human being, and at the same time, more than object made by hand, a pair of skilled hands, an eagle and a serpent painted in colors of the living earth, an item of cultural or histori-cal interest, an object with magical powers, bringing visions and good luck, Ignacio and a long life, and the people in it he'd loved, and some that he'd cherished, and now an insistent suffering that brought to mind that of Job, asserting itself like nothing else but suf-fering could, as if it were a test or proof, Coyuco lying on an untidy collection of dead, a mound of student teachers, a burning pile of men in a furnace, or soaked in gasoline before striking the match, there weren't limits to what his imagination came up with for him to see on the closed lids of his weeping eyes, a lot of people expelled from this world, it wasn't pleasant, nothing to look at, and it made his stomach sick, a man of his age who'd seen a lot, and Ignacio Pardiñas, you couldn't say everything, but a lot of ugly things had passed before his eyes, not just in his imagination, so it must've been something, and Ignacio Pardiñas, fuck and fuck! those pictures on the closed lids of my eyes, Ignacio thinking all that when he stopped in front of a house so close to his own house that he could've thrown a baseball—if he still had a good arm, a high arcing ball—from his cement porch on Barrancas del Cobre straight up across Calle 38A and it would've hit one of the two pillars before him painted purple like the house itself standing quietly here with its white iron-barred windows, Ignacio's knees were weak, it wasn't a long walk, he had his hardwood walking stick, a cane painted with a serpent and an eagle, to keep him on his feet, and he wanted to take a breather from what was on his mind, exchange a few words, sit down in a chair with his legs extended, ankles crossed, and not be the one that always gave everybody else good advice, it was his turn, after all, to listen to a handful of comforting words from friends he'd known since he was a kid, and Ignacio Pardiñas, depending on what you call a kid, we grew up awful fast, and so he started toward the white door of the single-story house in front of him that was like an extension of the house standing to the left, sharing a wall with it, and to the right, a car covered by a tarp parked in the narrow space behind a locked iron gate painted white, the purple façade of the house wasn't painted by a professional housepainter, the owner had done it himself, his wife mixing the paint until she'd got the color she was after, her choice, nobody else's, pouring slowly into a five-gallon paint bucket, no bubbles, the initial pour no more than three gallons, using a bucket screen over the lip of the five-gallon bucket, a paint roller brush, an arm moving in an up-and-down W-pattern, Ignacio keeping them company, drinking from a bottle of beer at the time, while his friend and neighbor did his best to make his wife happy with the color she'd mixed.

Mariano Alcalá Reyes and Rosalía Calderón Alcalá opening the door together, sharing arms and hands, Ignacio couldn't tell who'd turned the knob of the door, which one of the two had drawn the door back toward them, pulling it gently out of the grasp of its frame, swinging the front door open on its hinges to let the non-light of twilight scratch at their feet wearing well-kept polished shoes, and Mariano Alcalá, a retired shoemaker, come in come in señor Pardiñas, *nuestro* Pardiñas, our house is always open to you, it's small as a shoebox—hehe!—you know it, and you know it well, but my Rosalía, a magician for a welcoming home, a marvel at the management of household affairs, right this way, Rosalía and Mariano, each indicating with an outstretched hand the small combination living room and dining room, it was a two-room house, and there was a sofa, Ignacio making his way on tired legs and a cane to the inviting cushions, burying himself in them, they were plump and deep, and the fabric worn, Mariano rubbing his hands together, and Mariano Alcalá it isn't cold outside, but Rosalía's going to make us a champurrado, *masa de maíz,* not *masa harina* or corn flour, dark chocolate, milk and panela—vanilla or cinnamon? she'll make it like you want it, señor Pardiñas, and a few words from Edgar Allan Poe, *Desde el tiempo de mi niñez, no he sido / como otros eran, no he visto / como otros veían, no pude sacar / mis pasiones desde una común primavera,* "From childhood's hour I have not been / As others were—I have not seen / As others saw—I could not bring / My passions from a common spring," what do you say to that? I didn't just fix and polish shoes and boots all these years, and Ignacio Pardiñas, you don't have to tell me that, why do you think I'm here? you're the one I'm talking to, don't sing the same song, *comp,* and hearing these words, Mariano, not amazed or struck dumb, a smile on his lips, his face expressing happiness and satisfaction with a further proof of friendship, one more after so many years and a lot of proofs, actions and words, Mariano, Rosalía, and Ignacio, in the comfort of Mariano's small home, a couple of rooms, but a garden at the back, Rosalía now stirring the champurrado in the kitchen, using a *molinillo,* a wooden whisk, rolling it between her hands, then moving it back and forth in the mixture until it was full of air and frothy, the rhythm and the spin, Ignacio and Mariano hearing her make the champurrado, Ignacio discharging releasing leaking a few words about Ernesto, Guadalupe, Coyuco, the missing son, Mariano having heard it before, knowing what Ernesto and Guadalupe were going through, a quick and delicate appreciation of others' feelings, imagining the pain and suffering, maybe knowing it firsthand, and Mariano Alcalá, don't let it get you down, not when people need you, and besides, nobody understands it, we live in fear of the lights going out, you get what I mean? from one minute to the next, snap! and somebody's hit the switch, it's not just because we're a lot older now than we were twenty years ago, even five minutes ago, don't look at your watch, take my word for it, Ignacio leaning forward, using his cane to balance himself, putting some of his weight on it, and Ignacio Pardiñas, what I've heard, there were six extrajudicially executed right from the start in four different crime scenes, including a tortured student, and another two who were shot at point-blank range, point blank, that's less than fifteen centimeters, almost six inches away—ask Dr. Francisco Etxeberria Gabilondo, a forensic doctor from the University of the Basque Country—and on the same night in different parts of Iguala, and outside, too, at other locations, the list: at the crossroads of Juan N. Álvarez and Periférico Norte, from around nine forty-five to ten forty, that's where they collared Coyuco, taken into custody, and I'll bet all I've got, my life savings, but I haven't got much, and a bus driver, "ya estando en la patrulla observé que los policías tenían amarrados y tirados en el piso a unos estudiantes y los estaban contando del uno al cuartro, siendo aproximadamente un total de veinte etudiantes," "once I was already in the patrol car, I saw that the police had some students tied up and thrown on the floor and they were counting them by fours, with a total of maybe twenty students," that's what a woman told me, the driver's sister, or word of mouth, unofficial, and the exit to Chilpancingo from Iguala, right in front of the Palace of Justice, lasting almost an hour, beginning about nine forty, at the same time as the attack at the intersection of Juan N. Álvarez and Periférico Norte, I know it because I've heard people talk, witnesses, you see it and tell somebody else and they tell you, that's how it goes, and the exit from Iguala to Chilpancingo, just before the Palace of Justice, between ten and eleven, but no shooting, not then—it makes me sick, the police, the army, they were going crazy, they're out of their minds, and I don't know who was telling them to do what they were doing, but that fucking Alacrán, and his wife, that bitch! the first lady and the Queen of Iguala, you can figure they had a hand in it, and there was a kid with his T-shirt pulled up to his chest, heavy bruising, no ears, no eyes, and the skin of his face removed from his skull, did you see the picture? and an attack on a bus with the *Los Avispones* soccer team, a couple of other vehicles into the bargain, at the Santa Teresa crossroads, fifteen kilometers, almost ten miles from Iguala on the way to Chilpancingo, it might've been eleven thirty, not late but too late, police and the army, the whole bunch of them, raving mad cops, berserk, unhinged, not all there, and at eleven forty, a second attack in the same place, on the road into Iguala and Periférico, another taxi and a truck, and the municipal police, from Iguala and Cocula, maybe the state police, maybe not, but a selection, a fine blend of motherfuckers, stopping a bus—ministerial police were there, too—*normalistas* taking off for Colonia Pajaritos or 24 de Febrero, hiding in a house, and on a hill, and later in the night, at twelve thirty on the 27th, at the intersection of Juan N. Álvarez and Periférico Norte, a press conference, shooting and chaos and death, and finally, at Camino del Andariego, in the industrial area, probably between one and two in the morning on the 27th, a *normalista* tortured and executed, a little information goes a long way, Mariano listening without blinking his eyes, he'd heard some of it before, read it, a telephone call, or there were people talking about what'd happened, nothing anyone could believe even listening to the words coming out of the mouth of someone they trusted, and Mariano Alcalá, *Mis días son como sombra que se va, / Y me he secado como la hierba,* "My days are like an evening shadow; / I wither away like grass," that's Psalm 102:11, señor Pardiñas, our Ignacio, El Fuerte, *mi Fuerte,* and Ignacio Pardiñas, *mi amigo,* I know it, and Psalm 102:12, *Mas tú, Jehová, permanecerás para siempre, / Y tu memoria de generación en generación,* "But you, O Lord, are enthroned forever, / you are remembered throughout all generations," and there aren't prayers enough for the suffering I feel, not for myself because I'm not in the middle of this story, but for Ernesto, Lupe, and then there's Coyuco, if he's still in one piece, Ignacio sinking back into the worn cushions, letting his body collapse, Rosalía coming into the room, three hot bowls of champurrado, *masa de maíz,* not *masa harina* or corn flour, balanced on a tray, setting the tray on the low table, and Rosalía Calderón, you're weeping over what you can do nothing about, señor Pardiñas, our Pardiñas, take a bowl, drink, it's warm but it'll cool you down, quench your thirst, fill your stomach like it's the first time, because we're being crushed, eaten by the jaguar-serpent-bird, with its human head, we need to keep our strength up to live with the jaguar-serpent-bird, the frontal war serpent, common among the Maya, traveling here all the way from Piedras Negras in Coahuila, three hundred thirty-seven miles, a thirty-six-minute flight, if it's really a kind of bird, and Mariano Alcalá, Rosalía's right, we've got to keep up our strength, did you know that in some places, when the ice melts after thousands of years, the bones of the dead appear, the dead who once lived from the Pliocene epoch, five million years ago, and into the Holocene, we're wading through a river littered with bones, a sea of them, señor Pardiñas, and one day they're going to be our bones and the bones of our children, and we don't have to wait more than a thousand years, *mi amigo,* it's happening now, ice or no ice, check the garbage dumps and the furnaces, Ignacio bringing the thick liquid made with hominy flour to his lips, taking a drink of champurrado, but his throat tightening, a reaction to Mariano's words, the truth in them, a reality he believed from the moment he'd learned of Coyuco's disappearance, an anxiety making it difficult to breathe, not just any bones, but those of a human being, a young man studying to be a teacher, a *normalista,* but it was a magic mixture prepared by Rosalía's hands that passed his lips—she hadn't added any unusual ingredients that didn't belong in the champurrado, with vanilla, not cinnamon—magic and magic, irresistible champurrado, Rosalía didn't know it, Mariano didn't know it, Ignacio didn't know it, swallowing it now without a clue of its potency, the *atol de elote* sliding down his throat, and bang! gone the winter of other countries located farther north, a wintry sentiment suddenly cleared of cold and fallen leaves and snow, a passable path of summer warmth and brightness, his feelings, his disgust, his disappointment soaring away from him, evaporating in the heat of the sun that Rosalía's champurrado released in the east of a black stinking place he'd carried within him since breakfast, a reawakened faith and enthusiasm for mankind, amid all the horror, a little corner of brotherly love making life bearable again—a hot lunch didn't rid him of the terror that felt like nightmare-filled dreams—but Coyuco and forty-three others, burned brittle like bacon or their bloated bodies buried in a trash heap, and Mariano Alcalá, I can read your mind, a question rising, what'd they do to deserve it? is it the god of stone and coldness, castigation, Itztlacoliuhqui-Ixquimilli, with his face and curving forehead of banded stone, in Nahuatl, the expression for punishment, *tetl-cuahuitl,* meaning "wood and stone," a little justice is blind for all of us, so where are they? they couldn't be dead, leaving their bones for future archaeologists, forensic detectives, to dig up after the ice melted, and Ignacio Pardiñas, his own voice echoing in his head, they're dead, I'm sure of it, sure as fate, and no two ways about it—a total of more than one hundred eighty victims, that many human rights violations, young men, and minors, too—then Ignacio stood up, pushing off with the muscles in his legs, lower belly and back, his legs supporting him, he didn't need his cane, a hand-painted wooden stick, and his ears tingled with the sensation of ants radiating heat, running up and down, down and up, from his earlobes to the top of his pinnae, insects marching deep within the rigid cartilage of the external part of his ear, a complex social colony with one or more breeding queens, wingless except for fertile adults, or it was a colony of pollinating, stinging winged insects rushing down his face, traveling to his legs, hips and feet, bees inspiring a dance straight out of Karl von Frisch's dance language of bees, the round dance, with swift, tripping steps, Ignacio running in a circle of such small diameter that for the most part only a single chair or vase lay within it, then running about in the room, suddenly reversing direction, then turning again to his original course, between two reversals, one or two complete circles, Ignacio capturing the two pair of eyes and individual spirits of Mariano and Rosalía, seeing an example of what they'd read about in a book, that in the case of bees, there wasn't any dancing on an empty or sparsely occupied comb, the dancer in her circling, coming at once into contact with other bees, but here the dancer was a man, their señor Pardiñas, and so, in the combination living room and dining room, Mariano and Rosalía, in an appropriate mood, having finished their bowls of champurrado, *atol de elote,* with vanilla, not cinnamon, following Ignacio, tripping excitedly after him, Mariano and Rosalía receiving information, holding their arms instead of antennae against his abdomen, Ignacio drawing along with him a train of two followers imitating his circlings and changes of direction, Ignacio growing weary, completing his dance, slowing down, stopping all together, Mariano and Rosalía letting go, turning away, returning to their chairs, Ignacio dropping gently to the cushions of the sofa, knowing that the round dance was a sign that there was something to be gone for and brought back, not to the hive but to their moral or emotional nature, their sense of identity, and Mariano Alcalá, bright as a button, I get it, señor Pardiñas, *Pues a sus ángeles mandará cerca de ti, / Que te guarden en todos tus caminos. / En las manos te llevarán, / Para que tu pie no tropiece en piedra,* "For he will command his angels concerning you to guard you in all your ways. / On their hands they will bear you up, / lest you strike your foot against a stone"—a psalm I've always liked, *Salmo 91:11-12*—and add the ingredient of Itztlacoliuhqui-Ixquimilli, the god of stone and coldness, castigation, our punishment, *tetl-cuahuitl,* so what we've got to get and bring back to us is help from God, maybe we've sinned, maybe we haven't, *mi amigo,* señor Pardiñas, but with our faith we must seek Him out, that's what you're trying to say, that's what your dance was telling us, yet it's difficult, almost impossible, a job that's hard to figure on doing with any kind of enthusiasm—how fucking angry are we at what they've done to those young men!—so what I taste in my mouth isn't the sweetness of the presence of God but the taste for revenge because we're suffering, all of us, and the *normalistas,* they're suffering or already dead, so having led us in the round dance of the language of bees—Ignacio interrupting him, rubbing

his eyes in a discouraged gesture, and Ignacio Pardiñas, I can't forgive a crime like that and search for God at the same time, I'm lost
and I don't know what to do, *mis amigos,* yes, my friends, that's what
you are and always have been, my brother and sister, too, whether
you call me señor Pardiñas or Ignacio, today isn't the day it was
when I woke up, I don't know what came over me, it must've been
something I drank, and Rosalía Calderón, you can't blame me because I didn't add an ingredient that wasn't supposed to be
there—cross my heart—but what we're feeling, the thing that's tearing up our guts, the corpses, the smell of death, the outrage at blood
that stings us like maguey thorns—I read it somewhere—it's our
world, here, *Treinta y un Estados Libres y Soberanos y el Distrito
Federal,* every state's got its troubles, take a look around, Rosalía
looking at her husband, Rosalía looking at Ignacio, and Rosalía
Calderón, *mi marido, y nuestro amigo, nuestro hermano,* smiling, an
awkward movement of her lips, but with a sadness in her eyes,
Ignacio saw it, his vision sharp, his body numbed with age, not dull
but less functional, and Mariano Alcalá, if God intended us to escape the pain we run up against every day, then He'd lift us out of
the way, but there's a lesson in it, I just can't abide the condition of
being a pupil, not with the crazy municipal police, ministerial police, federal police and army when they're doing business with
criminals, and Ignacio Pardiñas, "To govern by fear … surely God
can leave that to Stalin or Hitler, I believe in the virtue of courage, I
don't believe in the virtue of cowardice"—I read that in a book by
Graham Greene, and Rosalía Calderón, *pero en el Salmo 34:19,
Muchas son las aflicciones del justo, / Pero de todas ellas le librará
Jehová,* "Many are the afflictions of the righteous, / but the Lord
delivers him out of them all," and Ignacio Pardiñas, in Elena
Poniatowska's book, *Massacre in Mexico,* a government repression
in October 1968, *noche triste de Tlatelolco,* she spent three years
tape-recording interviews, "a collage of voices bearing historical
witness," and one of them, an eye witness, right there in the middle
of it, Diana Salmerón de Contreras, "Now that I managed to get

Julio and we were together again, I could raise my head and look around, the very first thing I noticed was all the people lying on the ground; the entire Plaza was covered with the bodies of the living and the dead, all lying side by side, the second thing I noticed was that my kid brother had been riddled with bullets," and Mariano Alcalá, I read it, too, *La noche de Tlatelolco,* and the mother of a family, Matilde Rodríguez, saying, "I'd seen things like that on the *Gunsmoke* series on television, but I never dreamed I'd see them happening in real life," she'd been standing behind one of the pillars supporting the Chihuahua building, her daughter'd pushed her there, then she was dragged to safety into a store, a flower shop or gift shop, but before she got there she was wounded by machine-gun fire, hit in the leg by a fragment of a dum-dum bullet, in the Plaza de las Tres Culturas in Tlatelolco, it happened then, it's happened now in Iguala de la Independencia, and in other places, too, our many times momentous Mexico, regrets and tears, and Rosalía Calderón, my husband's a poet, but don't worry, he's harmless, no threat to anyone, and the three of them, by a sudden effort, snapping out of the gloom, Mariano, Rosalía, and Ignacio laughing, and the three pairs of eyes saying, when you've got to laugh instead of cry, it's a message sent directly to us from emotional Ernesto without him knowing it, "Cry! Cry! Cry!" sung by Johnny Cash, like the waterworks of Big Joe Turner, "You're gonna cry, cry, cry and you'll cry alone / When everyone's forgotten and you're left on your own / You're gonna cry, cry, cry," a song playing in Mariano and Rosalía's combination living room and dining room, Ignacio rising from the sofa, putting his weight on his hand-painted wooden stick, a serpent and an eagle to keep him upright, and Ignacio Pardiñas, hey! enough already! and that goes for all of us, "The road of good things is filled with light, the road of bad things is dark," Juan Rulfo put those words into Macario's mouth, Macario, a simpleminded boy, a halfwit, the town idiot, Macario saying, "that's what the priest says," and, *mis amigos,* my sister, my brother, it's that straightforward, uncomplicated, entry-level and 101—you can believe it because it's true, and Mariano Alcalá and Rosalía Calderón, with the same voice at the same time, we believe it! and Ignacio Pardiñas, I don't know more about my belief in God than I did when I came here, but my faith hasn't left me, *muchísimas gracias* for the champurrado, the dancing and a song, Mariano and Rosalía accompanying him to the front door, watching him walk carefully to the street, Ignacio turning around, and a friendly wave goodbye from Barrancas del Cobre, Mariano and Rosalía gesturing, nodding their heads at the same time, with the same motion, sharing a single head, separated from the rest of the body by a neck, going fifty-fifty on the thing that contained the brain, mouth, and sense organs, viewed as the location of intellect, imagination, and memory, a couple living together for as long as they'd been living together knew that two heads weren't better than one, Mariano and Rosalía keeping an eye on their friend on the downhill grade, Ignacio heading home with the help of his cane, a hardwood walking stick, Ignacio walking toward the intersection of Barrancas del Cobre and Calle 38A and the nine cement steps and a handrail on Barrancas del Cobre, seeing a sea blue-green house on the right as he descended the nine stairs, Ignacio, even-tempered, alert, but a thread of regret pulling him down, what he couldn't do because of his age, and his helplessness in the face of authority, the police, the army, the world itself, the sun longtime gone, Ignacio opening the front door to his house, his fan turning, whispering, not whirring but oscillating, a room with no lights on, silence washing over him, no sound, no voices, inner and outer wordlessness, switching on a lamp to light his way, half a dozen paces and he was standing in the kitchen, turning on an overhead light, Ignacio smelling the garbage that'd started to stink, and the question of pursuing God with a taste in his mouth for revenge, possible or impossible? Ignacio knowing no more now than he'd known before, and with that letdown, no sense of humor about anything, Ignacio hearing crickets, and Ignacio Pardiñas, they might be real, they might not, but I hear them, crying for the souls suffering in purgatory, where's the place for God in all this, I've done one right thing, encouraging Ernesto, buoying him up, Ignacio switching off the overhead light, parting the worn-out curtain over the window in the back door, the air in the kitchen stale, heavy with the remaining heat of the day, the glow of the moon making an effort to break through the curtain of clouds, Ignacio looking for God in the alley behind the house, letting his fingers play with the edge of fabric, then a glance at the bag of garbage that'd slid down but hadn't spilled, if Ignacio could see himself in a mirror, the scarlet iridescence still in his eyes, imperfections that were always there, particles representing some kind of electromagnetic radiation, he was alive and not everybody could say the same thing, and Ignacio Pardiñas, not forty-three *normalistas,* and Coyuco, that's for sure, it might be a drop in the bucket, but it's a drop that weighs a lot, bluish-gray, soft, ductile metal, the chemical element of atomic number 82, sending out waves, *hablemos claro,* let's be clear, our world isn't the same as it was, a hefty rock thrown into the middle of our unlucky lives, and ripples of pain, like we need more of them, fucking ripples, what the fuck!—this garbage bag reeks, out it goes, Ignacio bending over, taking hold of the bag, moving it away from the door in order to open it, at once a gust wind blowing into the kitchen, brushing against his face, drying his tears, and Ignacio Pardiñas, Proverbs 3:1-4, *Hijo mío, no te olvides de mi ley, / Y tu corazón guarde mis mandamientos; / Porque largura de días y años de vida / Y paz te aumentarán. / Nunca se aparten de ti la misericordia y la verdad; / Átalas a tu cuello, / Escríbelas en la tabla de tu corazón; / Y hallarás gracia y buena opinión / Ante los ojo de Dios y de los hombres,* "My son, do not forget my teaching, / but let your heart keep my commandments, / for length of days and years of life / and peace they will add for you. / Let not steadfast love and faithfulness forsake you; / bind them round your neck; / write them on the tablet of your heart. / So you will find favor and good success / in the sight of God and man," Ignacio putting the bag in a trash container, and Ignacio Pardiñas, so let's take a good look at it all, life here on earth, and in the sky—where'd I leave my stick? but he didn't turn around to look for his hand-painted cane that was leaning against the kitchen countertop, faith in the knowledge it was where he'd left it, Ignacio's eyes drawn elsewhere, narrowing them to focus as he tilted his head back, the turning sky making him dizzy, and Ignacio Pardiñas, balance balance, *mi amigo,* then he looked at the curtain of clouds, his head rolling with them, traveling traveling, listing farther backwards, and Ignacio Pardiñas, it may rain, a heavy black cloud passing over his head, his face open to the gaze of the moon, and Ignacio Pardiñas, and it may not.

The pottery lay spread out on a hand-woven Saltillo rug from the state of Coahuila, or from Teotitlán del Valle, a small village, Teotitlan, in Nahuatl, "place next to God," in the state of Oaxaca, he couldn't remember, but a hand-woven rug, 69 x 49 inches, roughly 5 ½ x 3 ¾ feet, an orange rug, blue and brown stripes, a little staining and fraying, laid on the floor of Rubén Arenal's studio, he'd cleared away enough space for Pascuala Esparza and Little Pascuala to get a closer look at his pottery, moving around without bumping into anything, not the lights on tripods, a potter's wheel, a front-loading electric kiln, a wedging table, a heavy-duty trash container on a dolly, boxes containing fifty-pound bags of stoneware clay, not the rough wooden table with chairs in the kitchen area, or a low table near to his bed on the far side of his studio, a table with five painted plaster mariachi figurines, dressed in elegant black suits trimmed with white, musical figurines, Pascuala Esparza, crouching in front of the rug, examining a vase for flowers, pots with narrow spouts, a bowl for fruit, mugs for *posol,* mugs for coffee, cups for tea, a *hidria,* a jar or pitcher for water, and Rocket, *primero la pinto con aceite por dos razones, el aceite hace la olla impermeable y la olla brilla más,* first I paint it with oil for two reasons, the oil makes the pot more impermeable, and the pot will shine more, Pascuala Esparza turning a black ashtray in her hands, a long and slender object, curved sides like a high-sided canoe with extreme rocker, the upward sweep of the keel toward bow and stern, and Rocket, leaning close to her, *siempre estoy pensando en los diseños, cuando estoy caminando, estoy pensando en las formas y los diseños,* I'm always thinking of the designs, when I'm walking, I'm thinking about forms and designs, I studied at Mata Ortiz, you mentioned it in your letter, *señora,* but many things have changed since then, *pero muchas cosas han cambiado desde entonces,* looking up at *La Pascualita,* she was standing with her arms folded across her chest, the hat with the veil on her head, but the veil itself drawn back, away from her face, revealing shiny brown eyes almost black reflecting light from spotlights on tripods surrounding the Saltillo rug on the floor, Rubén Arenal turning to face Little Pascuala, not able to keep his eyes off her, a few shadows across her face, shadows light as clouds, a black-and-white photograph in living color, and Rocket, *me gusta trabajar por la tarde y la noche, son los tiempos más tranquilos,* I like working in the evening and in the night, they're the most peaceful times, *La Pascualita,* an understated smile, not obvious, but he saw the corners of her mouth rising, and Rocket, *cuando vivía en Mata Ortiz usé tres colores de pintura: negra del manganeso que saco de las montañas, rojo del polvo de piedra y barro, y blanco del barro blanco, y usé cabello de niños para la brocha,* when I lived in Mata Ortiz, I used three colors for painting, black from powder of magnesium that I got from the mountains, red from powder of stone and clay, and white from white clay, and I used hair from children for the brush, and *La Pascualita* touching neither fine nor course strands of her straight black hair, medium, moving a thumb and index finger downward with hair like cotton thread pinched gently between them, fingers like fine-grained, translucent form of gypsum, maybe a veined hand, he couldn't say because she tucked it away in a shadow falling across the left side of her body, Rubén Arenal crazy about her eyes, her hair, Pascuala Esparza, standing up straight, she held one of his mugs in the palm of her hand, a mug for *posol,* balancing it there, and Pascuala Esparza, a faraway voice, moist on the lips, seductive, you're work is beautiful, you're inhabited by the miracle of being alive, what I mean is how beautiful is beauty, and for some time I've wanted to sink my teeth into something, what I mean is is it magnetism or mojo? attractive for what it has of proven prophecy, typical and topical, we're enthusiastic with the signs of enthusiasm that've got their origin in our stupendous grand unequalled interpretation of your work, embellished by your presence, you're a maestro, virtuoso, authority and champion, a crackerjack potter, worthy of praise, how can I say it in a way that what I say says what your work means to us, we want to buy as many pieces as you're willing to sell, what I mean is that we want all of it, believe me, and we're together, Pascuala Esparza looking at her daughter, and Pascuala Esparza, don't we, *niña*, my child? Rubén Arenal swimming in a tremulous and deep dream, and Rocket, to himself, they're as real as I am standing here in front of them, but their words—no, I haven't heard *La Pascualita*'s voice— not timid people, courageous, vivid, and bold, as the definition goes, so confident as to suggest a lack of shame or modesty, *La Pascualita*, giving the nod, agreeing with her mother, not submitting to her, but with desire in her black eyes, beautifully quiet before the silent acclamations and unusual admiration of a real fan, an acolyte, Rubén Arenal, enticed and drawn, a follower of two temptresses, Pascuala Esparza with her shawl over her shoulders, long straight black hair without a streak of gray, a few wrinkles, lines, crow's feet, extra skin under the chin, but mother and daughter spitting images of each other, each of a different generation, *La Pascualita* the sole heiress to the distinctive looks of her mother, a revised edition, and Rocket, mumbling, *primero la torta y luego el chorizo,* first the torta and then the chorizo, talking about work, trying to keep his mind off the explosions in his head, but forced to give an explanation, and Rocket, I'm talking about the clay, the torta's a flat piece, lifting it while it's inside a plaster mold, forming a pot, the chorizo, a kind of band, a strip of clay for the lip, that's what they're called, at least in Mata Ortiz, Pascuala Esparza, putting the mug back on the Saltillo rug, looking up at Rubén Arenal, and

Pascuala Esparza, a benign lunatic, that's your psychic category, señor Arenal, with explicit emphasis on the benign, but I guess all
artists—don't you think, *niña,* my child? Pascuala Esparza looking
at her daughter, Little Pascuala, then turning to Rubén Arenal, and
Pascuala Esparza, *tan seco como el desierto,* as dry as the desert, can
you offer us something to drink? from here, where I'm standing,
something as refreshing as a swim in Río Bravo? if you get my drift,
we're fish fished out of the river, a major tributary, Río Conchos,
enters at Ojinaga, Chihuahua, below El Paso, in our state, "The Big
State," maybe we're a couple of Chihuahua catfish, they're big! or
west Mexican redhorses, blue suckers, or Mexican stonerollers, it
doesn't really matter, there're something like 166 species of fishes in
Río Bravo when both freshwater and brackish water species are
considered, that's according to Benke and Cushing in 2005, and the
lower Río Bravo contains nearly twice as many species as Río
Conchos, three times as many as the upper Río Bravo—a few indispensable facts—so our fishy lips are dry, and talking about thirst,
there's a line by Robert Benchley, *un gabacho brillante,* "why don't
you get out of that wet coat and into a dry martini?" a funny guy, we
can see through the *jarillas* that've grown up really thick, wind or
no wind, it's that time of year, but it isn't alcohol we want, is it, *niña,*
my child? it's your pottery and something fresh to drink, and Little
Pascuala, shaking her head no, then nodding her head yes, and
Pascuala Esparza, she's quiet, isn't she, silent as a man being shaved,
in the words of the thirteenth century Italian poet Niccolò degli
Albizzi, and Rocket, yes, "Prolonged Sonnet: When the Troops
Were Returning from Milan," I know it, and later Rossetti, so I'll
check the fridge, *señora, señorita,* and bring you a selection, or what
I've got, and there's a special treat, my sister made it for me, *tepache,*
fermented but not much alcohol, the Rarámuri people, in our
Estado Grande, and it's made from peel and rind of pineapples
sweetened with brown sugar, the Rarámuri, long-distance runners,
and if you ask one of them what their souls do when they drink? the
answer is, "they go over there," because, as I see it, drunkenness is

what comes from the departure of their souls during drinking, and Pascuala Esparza, I'll try your sister's drink, but my daughter, a Chaparritas grape, or a Jarritos tamarindo or hibiscus flower, if you've got one, señor Arenal, Rubén Arenal with a bashful bow, looking away from the glorious gaze of Little Pascuala's black eyes, leaving the mother and daughter for the safety of the kitchen area and a refrigerator with cold drinks, clean glasses, no cups, pouring a glass of Luz Elena's *tepache,* opening a bottle of Jarritos tamarindo, and placing everything on an old tin serving tray on the countertop, the tray a gift from his mother, a snow-peaked mountain, trees, a house, cactus, and a burro with a saddle carved into the unscratched worn surface with soft lines and shading, a bottle of Topo Chico mineral water for himself, Cerro del Topo Chico in Nuevo León, or a Peñafiel from Tehuacán, "place of the Gods," in the state of Puebla, and Rocket, out loud without realizing it, *por la fe y la esperanza,* by faith and hope, Rubén Arenal not believing what Pascuala Esparza'd told him, hearing the words in his head, not for the last time, not for the first, "we want to buy as many pieces as you're willing to sell, what I mean is that we want all of it," and Rocket, to himself, maybe the drinks will wash down the purchase of as many things as they can carry, setting the tin tray on the rough wooden table in the kitchen area of his studio, a sturdy table serving as work bench, not his desk, leaving the drinks as a ceremonial presentation, a still life, Rubén Arenal walking back to where they were standing, mother and daughter, not far away, it wasn't a big studio, but it wasn't small either, mother and daughter languidly looking at him, and Rocket, right this way, another bashful bow, a gesture toward the kitchen area, and Pascuala Esparza, let's drink to it, your work, señor Arenal, but there's nowhere for you to sit, not enough chairs, and after we've made a toast, we've got to sit down, the massive Sierra Madre, giving birth to life not only for her residents, but for untold thousands of other Mexicans, boundless measureless unpublished, in the foothills and plains below, and you can count us among them, and you're included, and Rocket, you can count me in, Rubén Arenal dragging another chair from his desk, pouring Little Pascuala's glass of Jarritos tamarindo, handing them around, right and left, with only two guests who were of consequence, not counting himself, they were standing, glasses raised, *La Pascualita*'s eyes looking at nothing in particular, but glowing anyway, they didn't need a drop of light to ignite them, and Pascuala Esparza, it's not a question, and not a foolish little number that fills the repertory of time, clocks nodding and waving their little arms, not some sugary nonsense to sweeten the cheap taste of connoisseurs of lower forms of skill, craft, technique that I sing your praises, señor Arenal, Pascuala Esparza drinking from her glass of *tepache,* the thyroid cartilage of her larynx moving with two swallows, *La Pascualita* concealing a burp coming from the descending, then rising bubbles of carbonation of a Jarritos tamarindo, covering her mouth with a delicate hand, pale as an angel of the grave, but a twinkle in her eyes, an embarrassed smile at the corners of her mouth, and Little Pascuala, almost in a whisper, excuse me, and Pascuala Esparza, she's a balanced woman, in charge of every one of her acts, acts over which she exercises enviable control and maneuvering invigorated by evening mass at the cathedral, seven fifteen at the Catedral de Chihuahua, or at six, Templo de San Francisco de Asís, *delimitado de manera aproximada por la Calle Niños Héroes al norte, la Avenida 20 de Noviembre al sur, la calle 27ª al este y la Avenida Ocampo al oeste,* bounded roughly by Niños Héroes to the north, Avenue 20 November to the south, 27th Street to the east and Avenue Ocampo to the west—but what am I telling you, you live here—or Capilla de Santa Rita de Casia in Colonia Santa Rita, at seven in the evening, you know it, don't you, señor Arenal? it's one of our favorites, Pascuala Esparza, a beautiful swaying of hands, without spilling, and the cheeks of her face, no injections no surgery, a little cream foundation, one shade lighter than her skin tone, a base two shades darker below the cheekbones, a little blush on the apples, and liquid highlighter at the top of the cheekbones, or a matte bronzer, brushed into the hollows of her cheeks, swiped to the very top of her ear and into the hairline, avoiding the apple, bronzer to the outer corner of her forehead and along the jaw line, and cream highlighter at the very top of the cheekbones and edge of the eye, as youthful as her daughter, and Pascuala Esparza, what I mean is let's tie up the deal, you don't want a check and I don't remember the last time I wrote one, well, just listen to me, it's cash in pesos, not dollars, not yuan, señor Arenal, and I'll bet what I've got that you'd rather have cash than a piece of paper with scribbling on it, what I mean is we'll be thankful to you, and here's a little on account, and don't ask on account of what, that's too silly, but you can say what you want, you're our maestro, expert, genius, wizard and pro, but I'm repeating myself, not exactly, but with lightning lucidity, and here's a few crisp notes, I didn't print them, don't worry, did I, *niña,* my child? and *La Pascualita,* a sharp shake of the head indicating no, her black hair beneath the hat and veil flying briefly in front of her face, and a seductive glance at Rubén Arenal, and Rocket, thank you, a modest voice, a hint of self-confidence, folding the bills into his shirt pocket without counting them, reaching out to shake Pascuala Esparza's hand, turning toward her daughter, looking straight at *La Pascualita,* and she returned his gaze, head-on, Rubén Arenal swearing to himself that he'd seen her wink.

And Pascuala Esparza, coming soon on this face, and my daughter's, too, isn't that right, *niña,* my child? a happy and triumphant beam, a grin from ear to ear, and that makes four of them, ears I mean, count 'em, señor Arenal, we've each got two, nicely formed nicely sculpted, ears to pierce ears to clean ears to listen with, but I'm talking about satisfaction, the gratification of possession, and in this case, it's really something special, not a luxury car, not a yacht, but crockery, ceramics, earthenware, stoneware, pottery made from your skillful hands, payment in full on delivery, name a price, it's yours, you'll get exactly what you ask for, señor Arenal, "then good luck, and remember the sky's the limit," words straight from the *Syracuse Herald,* September 1911, the first time the words were put in print, the *Syracuse Herald*, a broadsheet covering Syracuse, Onondaga, New York, 1904–1939, but you'll come to our place, not tonight, but tomorrow at twilight, between daylight and darkness, or after the sun's set, night, with its electric light, bring everything with you that you can carry, getting away once and for all from that hot wind that cuts through clothes, you've felt it, we've all felt it, that's Chihuahua, in *El Estado Grande,* when you get to our place, you might hear the struggle of the river, even if there isn't a river, you'll hear it, and you'll remember it forever like the echo of a distant hello, wondering if you're hallucinating, but you aren't, trust me, it's there, we all hear the river, a path to follow, running ahead, behind, or beside us to show us the way, upstream or down, a squiggly blue line on a map, thick or thin, it doesn't matter, it's a river, señor Arenal, maybe walking sideways, moving like a crab, and you've got to follow it because it'll lead you to us, you'll head straight to our front door, with all the beauty you can carry on your back, or on a small donkey used as a pack animal, a car, a truck, or a cart, it doesn't matter, a vehicle is any means of transport as far as we're concerned, you're our maestro, bright spark, enchanter, brainiac—nothing like the Mexican horror movie, *El barón del terror,* 1961—and we'll be expecting you, *No ya el desasosiego / pero sí el deseo / la esperanza / de encontrarte a la vuelta de la esquina,* "No longer the restlessness / but the desire / the hope / to encounter you turning the corner," that's part of a poem by Claribel Alegría, isn't that right, *niña,* my child? *La Pascualita* knitting her eyebrows in a frown of concentration, and Little Pascuala, almost a whisper, it's time to go, *ahora es el momento para ir,* and her pale hand reaching out to Rubén Arenal, his hand grasping hers, a poised Little Pascuala, a graceful and elegant bearing, and *La Pascualita,* a few words, *Y si me duermo y sueño que estoy muerta / y en realidad he muerto / y no lo sé,* "And if I fall asleep and dream that I am dead / and in fact have died / and don't know it," I know her poems, too, *amá,* Claribel Alegría, and Rocket saying to himself, that's the first real sentence I've heard her say, his skin with the hairs erect, and a trembling in his muscles, charged particles, dynamically as a current, passing through him with the sound of her voice, Pascuala Esparza and *La Pascualita* putting their drinks down on the table, and Pascuala Esparza, you'll walk us to the door, readily accompany us to the wonders-will-never-cease world inspiring delight and a measure of the heebie-jeebies to anybody who's got a head on their shoulders, señor Arenal, what I mean is when this staggering phenomenal extraordinary world isn't scaring the hell out of us, making our hair curl—you've noticed our hair's as straight as a stretch of two-lane blacktop—a world that's a crocodile's mouth, wide open, not a yawn, but waiting for a snack, this world, our world, the living or the dead, it's true, in my blissful euphoria I'd forgotten about it—outwardly it looks like ecstasy or rapture, but upon closer examination, take a good look, it isn't exaggerated and out of proportion, Rubén Arenal leading them to the door of his studio, opening it, letting them get in front of him, then opening the outer door, the three of them standing on the sidewalk, *La Pascualita* pulling the veil down in front of her eyes, Pascuala Esparza gripping an edge of her black and deep-blue shawl with knotted fringe, the wind had blown the yellowish air away, but there was plenty of sunlight to light their way, a glowing globe of reddish-yellow light like a ripe orange throwing three shadows, a sphere about to fall off the edge of the earth, and Pascuala Esparza, so until the next time, goodbye, ¡adiós! señor Arenal, words that strike right between the eyes, and a friendly wave, the two women turning their backs on him, Rubén Arenal, forlorn, a wretched blue knot in his stomach the shape of *La Pascualita*'s fist, watching them walk away, but Pascuala Esparza's daughter, Little Pascuala, turning her head to look back at him, a momentous moment, a young woman's gaze fixed in time, hanging in the air between them, Rubén Arenal and *La Pascualita*, while her mother, looking straight ahead, moved like she was floating on the surface of the sidewalk even though her feet were touching the ground, *La Pascualita*'s feet faltering, she was half turned around, the upper half, not tangling her legs, but not looking where she was going either, Rubén Arenal clearly saw her dark brown, almost black eyes behind the patterned veil, the picture of her face just before she turned away, rounded the corner and disappeared was printed on the retinas lining the back of his eyes as he unlocked the street entrance, locked the door behind him, stood for a moment to adjust to the darkness, he hadn't switched on the electric bulb hanging from the ceiling, then unlocked the door to his ground-floor apartment, a simple home, and his pottery studio.

Two women, then three

Luz Elena inviting Guadalupe to her house, inviting Ernesto's wife, Coyuco's mother, Guadalupe, meaning "valley of the wolf," always punctual, arriving on time, on the dot, a weekend day, Saturday, or Sunday, Luz Elena waiting for her, and Luz Elena, to herself, there she is, not too soon and not too late, Luz Elena unlocking the gate, a warm smile under the circumstances, not ear to ear, but dimples forming in the cheeks, Guadalupe kissing her, then a hug, Luz Elena holding the gate open, letting her walk past the gate, locking it, Luz Elena following right behind her, Guadalupe taking long strides to the entrance of the house, buoyed up uplifted spurred on by the show of Luz Elena's love, and a feeling in common of worry, nervousness, and unease for Coyuco, they all feared the worst, not wanting to say it, one big unhappy family, Guadalupe, Ernesto, Irma, Luz Elena, Rubén Arenal, Ignacio, Mariano, Rosalía, each hour a prayer, Psalm 31:9, "Be gracious to me, O Lord, for I am in distress; my eye is wasted from grief; my soul and my body also," Guadalupe waiting for Luz Elena to open the front door, then following her into the house, one trailing after the other, and Guadalupe Muñoz, where are the kids? knowing they were there somewhere, at least Cirilo, he was too young to go out alone, and Luz Elena, with respect to where people are, Lupe, what we know is that we don't know where your son is!—I've been smelling smoke coming all the way from the Cocula garbage dump in a city in another state ever since Coyuco disappeared, with respect to Iguala in Guerrero, if you'll forgive me, 'mana—but Cirilo, he's in the living room, and the other two are playing in their room, or they're outside, I can't keep track of them, they're always up to something outdoors, it's good for the health and brings color to their cheeks, keeps them in the pink, they look so nice, a pair of sisters in tip-top shape, and their brother, too, have you looked closely at the color of their skin? Guadalupe shaking her head no, and Guadalupe Muñoz, not lately, m'hija, the two women standing in the kitchen in front of the refrigerator, and Luz Elena, park yourself there on a comfortable chair, indicating one of the kitchen chairs at the kitchen table, and Luz Elena, a suggested scheme or plan of action, with respect for tired legs and an emotional state of mind, we've got to start somewhere so why not sitting on a chair, Luz Elena asking Guadalupe to join her for a fresh agua de Jamaica, a little hibiscus flower drink, with a little ginger or cinnamon, her recipe, not too sweet, pouring a couple of glasses of agua de Jamaica, offering Guadalupe a tall glass filled to the lip, not frothing to the brim, it was homemade hibiscus flower juice in a glass nothing like the empty jam jars she used as glasses for Avelina, Perla, Cirilo to drink from, washing out what was left after they'd finished the guava jam, and Luz Elena, with respect to age and who's got more or less than one or the other, the jam jars are more for Cirilo, the other two are too old for anything but a grown-up's drinking glass, Cirilo still runs his little fingers over the diamond-shaped ribbed glass on the outside of the jar, saying mine mine mine, and how many times he's said it I don't know, like the scene in Los Olvidados, Marta, Pedro's mother, played by Estela Inda, bringing her son a large piece of raw meat, there's lightning, thunder, Marta advancing towards him, holding out the piece of meat to her son, played by Alfonso Mejía, and Pedro, reaching out to take it, the wind blowing harder and harder, but a hand emerging from under the bed, Jaibo's hand, it's Roberto Cobo as Jaibo, and Jaibo grabbing hold of the meat, taking it away from Pedro, and Pedro shouting, give me the meat, it's mine! that's what I think of when I talk about

Cirilo and his jam jars, and Guadalupe Muñoz, possession is nine
points of the law, a logical rule of force, thank you *m'hija,* taking
the glass from Luz Elena's hand, and Luz Elena, *agua de Jamaica,*
it'll lower your blood pressure, which I'll wager the hundred pesos
I've got in my pocket is skyrocketing with all the worry and sadness you're suffering, with respect to the awful truth, an inhuman
turn of events, that's what I told my brother, municipal police, the
ministerial police and federal police, even the army, madmen are a
curse—men can be a pain in the neck—and that's what they are if
they've done what I figure they did to forty-three student teachers,
and Coyuco, the smoke I've been smelling with my nose in the air,
a suspension of particles of only God knows what coming all the
way from Cocula, maybe we *are* all travelers passing between different times, we're here, then we aren't, and it goes so fast you don't
see it happening, unless you keep your eyes peeled, count the days,
months and years, but what they've done to Coyuco, we don't know
but we can guess, no excuse, a crime, it's perverted, twisted, and
a fucked-up situation for everyone in formerly foremost Mexico,
which makes me think of El Güero, *'mana,* as dark and untrustworthy as a black mamba in eastern Africa, a venomous serpent,
a dishonest weakling, a fucked-up guy, I can't forgive him for not
wanting to support his own kids, *Y mientras se confunde / la tierra
con el cielo, / unos sueñan con Dios / y otros con el dinero, / pero eso
mi amor, / es lo que se ve en la calle,* "At some point on the horizon /
sky can be confused with earth / some people dream of God / while
others dream of wealth / but of course my love this is what you
see out on the street," that's Carlos Varela, and Jackson Browne—so
frontwards or backwards, however you swing, El Güero's a con-
temptible coward, but don't tell me, I know, there's no comparison,
reducing your suffering to an observation so lacking in originality
as to be obvious and boring, *perdóname, no era mi intención hacerte
daño,* forgive me, it wasn't my intention to hurt you, for you and
Ernesto, it's another story, as sad as stories can be, but I can't get him
out of my head, El Güero, my needle's stuck, not even a shaman can
set me free, and talking about a person regarded as having access

to the world of good and evil spirits, and influence, too, there's Rocket's pottery, shamanic spiritual journeys on earthenware vessels painted with various colors, geometric motifs, human, animal, or plant designs, and looking a lot like the pottery of the Medio period of the Casas Grandes culture—but in his own way, and with his skilled pair of hands—a culture from right here in northern Mexico, including southern New Mexico and Arizona, and west Texas, the various Medio polychrome types, you can break them down into two basic painting styles, Babicora and Ramos, but the finest polychromes from Casas Grandes are Ramos Polychromes, I know about it just like Ernesto knows about it, because Rocket's my brother, and a brother confides in his sister, 'mana, but as far as El Güero's concerned, I've tried everything, you know as well as I do I'm stuck like a cockle burr to a sheep's coat, El Güero's long gone, and I'll never see him again, okay, I'm a little misty-eyed, close to tears, or just plain angry, and it could be the song I'm hearing right now, a duet by Carmen and Laura Hernández, born in Kingsville, Texas, listen, it's just two minutes, forty-three seconds, "Qué cobarde," "What A Coward," accompanied by Paulino Bernal and Conjunto Bernal, a *ranchera*, and a woman's disillusioned love:

> *Qué cobarde,*
> *me enseñaste a querer,*
> *y luego, y luego me dejaste.*
> *Pero, qué cobarde,*
> *cuando más enamorada*
> *me encontraba sin piedad me abandonaste.*
>
> *Qué cobarde,*
> *marchitaste la ilusión*
> *de todos mis quereres.*
> *Ya que no hay amor, verdad,*
> *yo maldigo con razón*
> *el ingrato corazón*
> *de los infieles.*

What a coward,
you taught me how to love,
and then, and then you left me.
What a coward!
When I was most in love,
you abandoned me without pity.

What a coward,
you withered the illusion
of all my love.
Now there is no love, no truth,
so I damn, with good reason,
the ungrateful heart
of the unfaithful.

Guadalupe hearing the song, somebody playing a record, the radio, or nothing at all, a timely tune coming out of the blue, Carmen and Laura's voices breaking anyone's heart, and in this song, a *ranchera* by Nico Jiménez, hope ground to dust, but an easy danceable beat, and Guadalupe Muñoz, you're right, *m'hija*—you know that I call you my daughter because I've got enough affection in me to give plenty to you, and I'm older than you—you're stuck there like a curious seal, in the words of Michael Drayton, 1563–1631, but enough with the similes, they're splintering my spirit, what I'm thinking about is why I haven't heard from Ernesto, not in twenty-four hours, good news bad news, there's a difference that can kill, he was swept along by the wind, lost in low dense layers of clouds blocking out the stars, I'll never know what's going on if I don't have his words to listen to, a reassuring voice, and a few facts, and Luz Elena, or worse, with respect to danger, and the police—municipal, ministerial, or federal—it doesn't matter which one, or all three, if he's sticking his nose into what they've done with forty-three *normalistas,* and Coyuco—knuckles rapping at the window interrupted her, a hand reaching through the bars, it must've been a slender hand, a child, but it was Irma, named after Irma Serrano, La Tigresa, Luz Elena pulling aside the curtain, face to face with a smiling face, a little pain painted into it, too, Irma running her hands through her hair with a gesture of studied indifference perfected in the intimacy of her bathroom mirror, she wasn't old enough to get rid of the habit, younger than Coyuco, Luz Elena waving at her to head for the front door, turning to Guadalupe, and Luz Elena, I must've left the gate open, it's Irma, and Guadalupe Muñoz, you invited her, *m'hija?* or is it a kind of spontaneous apparition? Luz Elena giggling from the joke, covering her mouth with her hand, she had most of her teeth, and a dental bridge, nothing to be ashamed of, but that's how she was, and Luz Elena, I invited her, Lupe, and I'll just let her in, relax and finish your drink, Irma standing impatiently at the kitchen window looking in, Luz Elena turning to see her still standing there, and Luz Elena, no voice, mouthing the words, well, go around to the front, *'mana*, what're you waiting for?

Guadalupe, Irma, and Luz Elena sitting at the kitchen table, each with a glass of fresh *agua de Jamaica* within reach, and Irma Payno, I've got to have a smoke, Luz Elena getting up, bringing an ashtray to the table, Irma lighting a cigar, an Aromas de San Andrés or a Capa Flor by Puros Santa Clara, or a Te-Amo Clásico, from the Turrent family, in the San Andrés Valley in the southeast of the state of Veracruz, Irma, a volunteer for a few words, pinched by instruction, and Irma Payno, the volcanoes give the soil in the valley of San Andrés Tuxtla plenty of potassium, and the *maduro* tobacco's sweet and spicy, Irma and a fleeting look of contentment on her face as she leaned back in her chair, exhaling a pearl-gray cloud rising toward the kitchen ceiling, and Guadalupe Muñoz, you're sweet and spicy yourself, *niña mía,* and I get a kick out of the smell of your cigar, it makes me want to have a smoke myself, and a few tears, too, because I'm sure Coyuco loves the smell of it, our Coyuco, my Coyuco, Guadalupe waving her hand like a fan to gather a noseful of tobacco smoke, and Irma Payno, even if he's good and dead? her own tears falling on the wrapper of her cigar, and Guadalupe Muñoz, no, don't believe it, you'll see, as soon as Ernesto's brought him home and you feel the warmth of him right next to you, the wind that blows a little before dawn on the day before you'll see him will carry away your worst fears, and Irma Payno, speaking of wind, my mouth gets dry just listening to you, it's the place that loses its moisture when my heart's dried up for good, she took another pull on the cigar, a cloud of smoke hiding her eyes, red from the tears she'd cried for days, and Irma Payno, and take a look at my skin, like fish scales, my whole body's parched withered longing for a drink, and not just hibiscus juice, Irma resting the cigar in the ashtray, rubbing her hands together, and Luz Elena, with respect for the thirty-one states of our Mexico, *La Patria es primero*—I've heard Ernesto say it—a healing treat from the southeast and west of the Yucatán Peninsula, there's nothing like a little aloe from the Estado Libre y Soberano of Campeche to help your hands, and a little almond oil, it's a long time I haven't seen such a sad look as the look I see on your face right now, dry skin or no dry skin, and Guadalupe Muñoz, I saw that same look when I washed my face this morning, raised my head from the sink, and looked at myself in the mirror, Irma wiping the tears from her cheeks with a handkerchief Luz Elena gave her, lightly brushing away the teardrops on the cigar wrapper with an index finger, Irma raising the cigar, a 5x40 Capa Flor, raising it to her lips, a dry smoker except for her tears, she sat staring at the ceiling, taking a drag now and then—spicy Nicaraguan tobacco blended with sweet San Andrés leaves bound in San Andrés Marrón leaf rolled in a cinnamon-brown Colorado wrapper grown in Ecuador—her shoulders shaking with quiet convulsive sobs, Luz Elena reaching out to take her hand, a comforting contact, skin on skin, Guadalupe did the same thing, reaching for Irma's free hand, while the Capa Flor, clenched between her teeth, stood straight out of her mouth like a thermometer.

Luz Elena, letting go of her hand, standing up, and Luz Elena, with respect for a special kind of thirst, you need something stronger to drink, and Guadalupe Muñoz, I could use a drink myself, even if it's just after two, because our ancestors originated in semi-arid northern Mexico, not so far from where we are, why don't we each have a *pulque muy fermentado,* in Nahuatl, *yztac octli,* a little white pulque, that's what we want, *m'hija,* fermented from maguey sap, *aguamiel,* although I hate that you've got to kill the plant for it, it takes twelve years for the maguey, *metl* in Nahuatl, to mature enough to make the sap for pulque, and Fray Bernardino de Sahagún, *auh in icoac ocōtoiauh octilj nimā ic muchi tlacatl quiya in vctlj, nimā ic peva in tetlavātiloya,* "and when they had poured the *octli* then everyone drank it; then they began to serve the people *octli,*" that's what Sahagún wrote in *Primeros Memoriales,* a Nahuatl-language manuscript, with many thanks to Francisco del Paso y Troncoso, Mexican historian and archivist, and Luz Elena, I was telling my brother the story of the sun of 4 Movement, the day sign of the Fifth Sun, Movement Sun, before he was our sun, of course, I told him that nothing really changes, insecurity and fear because of our sun, "in its time there will be earthquakes, famine," but when the Fifth Sun appeared in the sky, maize was grown for the first time, fire was domesticated, nightfall was established, and *octli* was brewed, 4 Movement, the Fifth Sun, it's our sun, we who live today, and at that time, too, it was their sun—we're standing each day under the same sun as our ancestors—well, let's see what I've got in the cupboard, the refrigerator, or our imagination, white pulque, and we'll drink to Coyuco, our ancestors, the present and the past, Luz Elena searching the kitchen, finding three glasses of the frothy drink standing on the countertop where she hadn't left them, *un truco de magia,* a magic trick, not a lot of pulque but enough to feel the effects, as if the glasses had been waiting for her to find them, and Luz Elena, I don't know if I prepared them, I don't remember, and I didn't put them here, that's for sure, but maybe a time-space event's come our way, right out of a book of science fiction, a movie, or something for TV, let's drink up, here's your glass, Irma, and yours, Lupe, we'll raise them to our lips in the name of Coyuco, and forty-three others, we're all in it together, and leave frothy moustaches for our tongues to clean, Guadalupe, Irma, and Luz Elena downing the contents of their glasses, setting them on the table in front of them, watching the glasses disappear, dematerialize, becoming spiritual rather than physical, and Guadalupe Muñoz, solidarity's our thing, between women it's as common as sunrise, Irma cocking her head slightly to one side, eyes shining like pools lit up by the moon, hearing a duet by Ninfi and Nori Cantú, born in Falfurrias, south Texas, and Irma Payno, do you know Hermanas Cantú? listen, it's a song just two minutes fifty-one seconds long, "Mil puñaladas," "A Thousand Stabs," accompanied by Los Alegres De Terán, a *ranchera* of romantic misery, a song that causes overwhelming distress:

> *Estoy perdido sin esperanzas,*
> *sin esperanzas de tu querer,*
> *lo que te adoro, con toda el alma.*
> *Y tu me hieres con tu desdén.*
>
> *Mejor me dieras mil puñaladas*
> *mil puñaladas en el corazón.*
> *Pero no quiero ya tu desprecio*
> *que así me matas sin compasión.*
>
> *Si me marchara, lejos muy lejos*
> *a donde nunca me oigas hablar,*
> *siempre me llevo mis sufrimientos*
> *que tal vez nunca pueda olvidar.*
>
> *Mejor me dieras mil puñaladas*
> *mil puñaladas en el corazón.*
> *Pero no quiero ya tu desprecio*
> *que así me matas sin compasión.*

Si me marchara, lejos muy lejos
a donde nunca me oigas hablar,
siempre me llevo mis sufrimientos
que tal vez nunca pueda olvidar.

Mejor me dieras mil puñaladas
mil puñaladas en el corazón.
Pero no quiero ya tu desprecio
que así me matas sin compasión.

I'm lost without hope
without hope of your love,
I who adore you with my entire soul.
And you hurt me with your disdain.

It's better that you give me a thousand stabs,
a thousand stabs in the heart.
But I don't want your contempt anymore
because you're killing me without compassion.

If I were to go far away, very far away
to where you'd never hear me speak,
I'll forever take my suffering
that I'll never be able to forget.

It's better that you give me a thousand stabs,
a thousand stabs in the heart.
But I don't want your contempt anymore
because you're killing me without compassion

And Guadalupe Muñoz and Luz Elena, two voices at the same time, I hear it, and Guadalupe Muñoz, continuing on her own, you can stretch it out and it's a song about our pain, too, not just romantic misery, your pain, mine, Ernesto's, and our Coyuco's, all of us, take these words, "If I were to go far, very far away, / to where you would never hear me speak, / I will always carry my sufferings with me, / that I may never be able to forget," no, what I feel isn't romantic love, not for Coyuco, he's my son, Ernesto's too—Irma, you can sing the romantic version of it, it's as sad as teardrops, and Luz Elena, speaking tenderly, earnestly pious, *claramente, es más que puede soportar,* clearly, it's more than you can bear, Guadalupe Muñoz repeating the words, and Guadalupe Muñoz, clearly, it's more than *we* can stand—you, me and the rest of the world, and Irma Payno, so what're we going to do about it? we can't leave it up to Ernesto alone, and Luz Elena, with respect for the weight of a word, nine words in total, and the value of a single life, forty-three altogether, and Coyuco's, Irma's right, and Guadalupe Muñoz, of course she's right, *m'hija,* we can organize a march, a protest, and go all the way to Mexico City, it's not far, and Luz Elena, let's start with where we are, *'mana,* and move on from there, we'll make banners, *Alcalde de Iguala ¿puedes dormir por la muerte de nuestros hijos?* Mayor of Iguala, can you sleep even with the death of our children?—fucking José Luis Alacrán and his dragon wife—and Irma Payno, *¡ayúdanos a localizarlos!* help us find them! posters with the their faces, names, and placards, *¡vivo se los llevaron! ¡vivos los queremos!* they took them alive, we want them alive! *Ayotzinapa ¡ni perdón, ni olvido!* Ayotzinapa–no forgiving, no forgetting! *¡tu familia te espera!* your family is waiting for you! and Guadalupe Muñoz, we give birth to them, raise them, nursing them from our breasts, but we can't bury them when they're dead, when they've disappeared, lost lost lost, that's what those villains did to us, everything's going from bad to worse, our Mexico, you said it, *m'hija, La Patria es primero,* listen, what's that sound? the first howl, sharp and piercing, their voices, tortured children, murdered, burned to a crisp, left for bird food, or buried in a mass grave, their cries rising out of it, tearing the membrane of my middle ear, and what remains is their shadows—not my own, if that's what I see when I look down at the earth—their shadows, and ours soaked through with fear and hatred, shaped "into a resistance that hinders all movement," our souls together, the living and the dead, hovering in the air, crippling our thoughts, our arms and legs, numbing our skin, and Irma Payno, it's the "deglossing of a daydream," reality, and a slap in the face, and Guadalupe Muñoz, a knife heated red hot in a flame, blade flat against my wrist just to wake me up, that's reality, and wide awake, tattooed by exposure to heat or flame, all we can do is stay huddled together straining to take a deep breath—not any longer, I've had enough, it's time to do something, hours have passed, days, we've been watching the water falling from a sky ruined by sadness, mourning, so now's the time, their bodies are drying in the sun far from home, and Irma Payno, okay, Lupe, okay, *tienes razón,* you're right, there's no truth like yours, so where'd I put my cigar? Irma reaching for the box of matches and her cigar, no trembling hands, but steadiness, not faltering or wavering, not shaking or moving more than gently biting down on the end of the cigar and striking a match, and Luz Elena, the sooner we get started doing something, organizing mobilizing, the sooner we'll climb out of the hole we're in, more like a grave, where they've put us knowing full well that we're dying right along with our children, a day or two, a week or a month ahead of us, who got there first doesn't matter, but we're dying in any case, there's evidence, proof, documentation, and we don't need it, we've got just cause, a legally sufficient reason, somebody else living somewhere else with other things on their mind might want more than that, but we've got all the proof we need, and Guadalupe Muñoz, right now a breath of fresh air is what's required, a little oxygen to fill our lungs, not literally, but a look at your children, *m'hija,* innocent offspring, they're the future, even if we're afraid of what the future will bring, Guadalupe looking at Luz Elena, raising her eyebrows, a question without words, and Luz Elena, with respect to a refreshing change, coming out of a clinch at the referee's command, the girls are out playing somewhere, but Cirilo, a cinch, a snap, like I said, he's in the living room, quiet as the tranquil sky, in the words of Henry Wadsworth Longfellow—poet and educator from *el Norte,* in

Portland Maine, it was part of Massachusetts at the time—but that's
Cirilo today, an exception, he's got nothing to complain about,
maybe a lost building block, a misspelled word out of wooden alphabet blocks, otherwise, *darse buena vida,* or as the *gabachos* say,
the boy's living the life of Riley, and the three women, Guadalupe,
Luz Elena, and Irma, moving like birds, extending their arms, feet
barely touching the ground, exaggerated steps light as feathers taking them to the entrance to the living room and a moment to
observe irreproachable innocence, Cirilo, on the living room floor,
surrounded by wooden alphabet blocks, each letter a color, a red *A,*
a blue *S,* a green *L,* a yellow *J,* a green *V,* a red *Y,* and two of the three
women wondering if at his age Cirilo could really spell, and Luz
Elena, reading their thoughts, with respect to intelligence and family resemblance, just because he looks a lot like El Güero—how he
got that nickname I'll never know—it doesn't mean he's as stupid as
his father, and as my brother said, El Güero will never know what
he's missing, *¡qué idiota!* a son like Cirilo is a gift from God, may He
hear my thanks, Luz Elena pinching the cross hanging from a thin
chain around her neck with a couple of chubby fingers, Guadalupe
and Irma, shaking their heads no at the same time, no words but a
motion conveying plenty, united against El Güero, confederates for
life, and unanimous in their fondness for Avelina, Perla, and Cirilo,
and Guadalupe Muñoz, look at him, *un verdadero ángel viviente,* a
real living angel, Cirilo's mesmerized, the alphabet spread out in
front of him, tiny hands forming words with wooden blocks, breeding thoughts, performing specified logical operations at a level
above that which is normal or average, a first-rate gifted boy, while
the life we're leading is no life at all, yes, he's innocent, and in the
clear, and he's got to stay that way for as long as he can, stay a child,
Cirilo, that's all, and nothing more, you'll know soon enough—*disculpa, por favor,* excuse me, but these are words I've got to say—the
minute life's got you by the balls, and Cirilo, hearing a familiar voice,
warm-hearted Guadalupe, not the words, and what did he know
about balls at his age, Cirilo, not mesmerized at all, but concentrating,

turned his head, eyes blinking at the faces peering at him, each with a smile on their lips, dropping a letter-block to the floor, a yellow J, playing with a curl in his thick black hair, a boy who flirts, and Irma Payno, no likeness to El Güero, *un hombre muy bruto y mal criado,* a rough and bad man, Luz Elena, Guadalupe, and Irma gliding farther into the living room, Luz Elena sitting down on an armchair, Irma sitting sideways on the arm of the same chair, turned away from the windows, toward Cirilo, Guadalupe standing over him, Cirilo looking up at her, and then his attention drawn back to the alphabet blocks, Guadalupe on her hands and knees, getting comfortable, sitting right next to Cirilo, thinking to herself, this is a boy like my boy when he was younger than he is now, another tear, and visions of a moment that couldn't be put into words, because it was all noise, fear, bullets, bus windows shattered into slivers and shards, and Luz Elena and Irma Payno, saying in the same voice at the same time without a word out loud, it doesn't do any good to miss people, but why not dream a bit? and Guadalupe Muñoz, answering without speaking, *¿me estás vacilando?* are you kidding me? and then out loud, what's left to dream about, a burial next to what's supposed to be Pancho Villa's tomb in the municipal cemetery of Hidalgo del Parral, *m'hijas?* a hundred forty miles southeast of us, heading out of Chihuahua on Mexico 16, using twenty-three miles of the Cuauhtémoc highway, then taking Mexico 24, crossing Río Parral before San José, taking Vía Corta, that's what it's called, turning off heading west, joining Avenida Tecnológico and on to Panteón Dolores, two arched stone entrances, or exits, depending on whether you're coming or going, a salmon-colored wall, but we don't even have Coyuco's body, so don't hold your breath, we aren't going anywhere right now, and Luz Elena, with respect to a map in our hands and which way to turn—and we all know that the only way's toward God—you don't have to give us directions, 'mana, we've been there before, whether Villa's buried in Hidalgo del Parral or Mexico City, it's a journey we've made, all of us, *¿adónde vas? ¿qué haces?* where are you going? what are you doing? a visit to the grave of our José Doroteo Arango Arámbula, but right now, right here, we're beginning a journey of protest, and there are banners, posters, and placards to make, and Irma Payno, you're right, what're we thinking about if we aren't thinking about the loved ones we've lost, maybe the loved ones we're going to lose—and now it's my turn to say, *disculpa, por favor,* excuse me—in this fucked up world, our world, the one in which we live, that looks nothing like the world I dreamed of when I didn't know any better, Irma folding her hands in her lap, and then a song coming out of nowhere, playing for Irma, "Pero hay qué triste," "But Oh How Sad It Is," a tender song with unhappy words played on 12-string guitar and sung by Lydia Mendoza, and recorded in San Antonio, Texas, in 1934:

> *Pero hay qué triste*
> *es amar sin esperanza.*
> *De mi pecho–mi corazón latiendo,*
> *de mis ojos–una lágrima vertiendo,*
> *y desde entonces, no hay*
> *consuelo ni esperanza para mí.*
>
> *Pero hay qué triste*
> *es amar sin esperanza.*
> *De mi pecho–mi corazón latiendo,*
> *de mis ojos–una lágrima vertiendo,*
> *y desde entonces, no hay*
> *consuelo ni esperanza para mí.*
>
> *¿Pues si no me quieres,*
> *pues para qué me miras?*
> *¡O, qué misterio encierra tu mirada!*
> *De mis ojos–una lágrima vertiendo,*
> *y desde entonces, no hay*
> *consuelo ni esperanza para mí.*

But oh, how sad
it is to love without hope.
From my chest my heart is beating,
from my eyes a tear is falling,
and ever since then there is
no consolation or hope for me.

Well, if you don't love me,
well, why do you look at me?
Oh, what mystery your gaze contains!
From my eyes a tear is falling,
and ever since then there is
no consolation or hope for me.

The three women, together, a moment of silence for the purpose of listening, clearly sensibly logically, the three women, an appropriate, relevant resolve, no drama but a general feeling of discomfort, illness, or uneasiness from the words, and Irma Payno, smoking is permitted, a spot of pulque, and judgment, so the one who wants to know something new, don't listen to this song, it's what's become of us, all of us, an old story that isn't so old, and the other parents, wives, girlfriends, brothers and sisters, it's driven like a nail into our hearts, where the nail is known to act as habitual intruder, an imprecise—who knows where it's going to hit—and finally precise something, involving pain, disappearance, the missing and dead with their eyes a gift to the swarm of flies, a swarm of flies that are stitched to them like a shroud, our Coyuco, yours and mine, forty-three other students, and a come-as-you-are funeral, none of the *normalistas* were invited, which brings me to our curiosity as to the fate of Coyuco, and Ernesto's search in Rubén's F-150, where are they? what're they doing? and why don't they come home, together? "but oh, how sad it is to live without hope," and Guadalupe Muñoz, take a look at Cirilo, what he's spelling with his wooden blocks—not something to miss! Luz Elena getting up from the armchair, Irma standing with her head bent trying to see past Cirilo sitting on the floor, Guadalupe, leaning forward, putting her hand on the boy's shoulder, while Luz Elena and Irma walked closer to where they were sitting, Luz Elena and Irma standing now above Cirilo and Guadalupe, the three adults looking down at the word he'd formed with his alphabet blocks, a multi-colored word as linear as a strip of wood typically marked at regular intervals, to draw straight lines or measure distances, *fantasma,* ghost.

E rnesto, after a good night's sleep, looking at himself in the mirror of his room at the Hotel Obregón on Avenue General Álvaro Obregón, at the corner of Calle Juan R. Escudero, not far from Periférico Sur, admiring the dark-blue uniform, resembling the uniforms of the *Policía Municipal,* neatly pressed after spending the night under the mattress, a poor man's pressing, a uniform including the belt but without a gun, flag and insignia that he'd sewn on at home late at night, working until daybreak, hiding the short-sleeved shirt where his wife wouldn't find it—a pair of blue trousers just a pair of blue trousers, nothing to hide—a shirt now adorning his sunken chest, he wore a sleeveless T-shirt against his skin, but no clean underwear or socks, he couldn't think of everything, and he wasn't the most imposing figure for a member of the *Policía Municipal* without a cap, but it'd have to do, Ernesto sniffing the air, turning his head and raising his arm to smell the fabric of the shirt, the mustiness of aged paper, decaying paper, rosin, acetic acid, furfural and lignin, not so bad, but mostly the stale, moldy smell of where he'd kept the shirt at home, and despite the uniform, still no answers to any questions, not his own, not Guadalupe's, not Irma's, not Ignacio's, not Rubén Arenal's or Luz Elena's, not the other parents of the disappeared, and he wouldn't get any answers to whatever questions he had, much less anybody else's questions, until he got himself outside and walking on the streets in the city of Iguala, Ernesto combing gray strands of hair away from his forehead and eyes, using his fingers because he didn't have a comb, he gave himself a thorough examination in the mirror, not squinting but taking advantage of the sunlight streaming in through the window to make the final touches, adjusting the collar, straightening the shoulders, brushing the trousers with the palm of his hand, slapping them clean of dust and lint, the sting of the slap stimulating the flow of blood under the skin, wiping his black leather boots clean with a towel, until he decided he looked as fit for the role as he could be.

Ernesto talking to himself, with no voice but his own, and Ernesto Cisneros, head up, eyes straight ahead, shoulders back, while it seems like everything's within my reach, and I see it plain as day, it feels like my mind's slipping, I've got a cramp in my brain, and the only solution, just like getting rid of a kink, a real stiffness in the back or neck, is to shake off the persistent gloom, leave the hotel—a modern design that's enough to make my eyes water and my throat dry—and try out this uniform, put an authoritative expression on my face, not a frown, just confidence, and a measure of the law and the right it gives me as a cop, let's call it a trial run before I go into that single-story white building, the *Policía Municipal,* with a door painted black, climbing ocher-colored steps, more orange than yellow, four of them, I've seen it, and I know where I've got to go to get there, an unimpressive imposition, I'll find out what they can tell me about the disappearance of forty-three student teachers, *normalistas,* and our Coyuco, Lupita's and mine, and Irma's too, because he belongs to all of us, even our friends, and his friends, we've got a right to know what happened to all of them, uncertainty's erasing the contours of things, Coyuco, gone like a cow washed away in a rising river, the heavy water hitting her flanks, I bet she bellowed for help, and only God knows how *he* bellowed, right out of Juan Rulfo's story, "Es que somos muy pobres," "We're Very Poor," a poor cow, but if she's borne more than one calf, she's left at least one life behind her—not us, Coyuco's an only child—while ours is a miserable life

we're living if we aren't already dead, a lost world in the time of dinosaurs, devoured carcasses, plants crushed, trees knocked down,
and an imitation of a dinosaur's heavy stride with big legs, substantial legs, monster legs, stridently slicing through the primeval forest,
because that's where we are, we've gone back more than centuries,
tens of thousands of years, or in the case of dinosaurs two hundred
million years ago, living like we've haven't got any laws—don't look
them up in a book, you won't find them, and if you do, they aren't
for us—and it's nothing but eat somebody else before you get eaten
by something that's got the face of the ministerial police, the *Policía
Federal,* the municipal police, the 27th Battalion, the Guerreros
Unidos, and Iguala's fucking mayor and his wife, the first lady and
the Queen of Iguala, add it up and we've lost, it's an insurmountable
wall, and the struggle to get beyond it quickly becomes an inability
to act, a wounded world walking with a limp, Ernesto, a protesting
snort breaking out of his throat wrapped up in weeping, and Ernesto
Cisneros, we all get emotional in a crisis, it's a time of intense difficulty, trouble, and danger, and it might as well be on paper, a
document containing a populational census that assures us of a
critical scarcity of brains that work of brains that reason of brains
being brains that do what they're supposed to do, and the same document, maybe I'm imagining it, but whether it's true or not it might
as well exist because it predicts the ruthless premeditation—plotted
schemed organized—that's behind the beginning of the end, right
now, today, not even waiting for a maybe later, and it makes my
head swim, my blood run cold, I can't swallow it, I won't swallow it,
and if they sweeten it for me with syrup I won't swallow it because I
can't put up with defeatism, and a few words from another time,
originating in the same place, a poem by Cuauhtencoztli, *Yo,
Cuauhtencoztli—exclama—aquí estoy sufriendo ... / ¿Tienen verdad,
raíz, los hombres? / ¿Mañana tendrá todavía raíz y verdad nuestro
canto? / ¿Qué está por ventura en pie? / ¿ Qué es lo que viene a salir
bien? / Aquí vivimos, aquí estamos, / pero somos indigentes, / ¡Oh
amigos nuestros!* "I, Cuauhtencoztli, suffer. / What is truly real? /

Will my song still be real tomorrow? / Do men truly exist? / What will survive? / We live here, we stay here, / but we are destitute, oh my friends!" an approximate translation, but you get the idea, so what's the choice, it's a short list, don't look for more, and I haven't thrown away a page, nothing on offer appeals to me, keep ourselves happy with winks and pats on the back and a buy this buy that you can't live without it, or keep your head down, don't look anybody in the eye, and if that doesn't work and it gets to be too much you can always run away, but it cuts no ice with me, and you, *mis amigos,* brothers and sisters, mothers and fathers, what kind of life is that? I wonder if behind my back they've organized a state of well-run well-regulated disorganization, turn around, you'll see something different, but I won't put a peso on it, behind my back or yours, it's all the same, it's a valueless vacuum sold right off the grill, fresh out of the oven, and we've got to put up a fight, let me flip through a book, a point of reference you can sink your teeth into, but it isn't anything on a map, just a little quote from a book I haven't got in my hands, "Aztec religion, on the mystico-militaristic level, sought to preserve the life of the Sun, threatened by a fifth and final cataclysm, through ceremonial warfare and human sacrifice ... At the same time, however, many of the wise men, living in the shadow of the great symbol of Nahuatl wisdom, Quetzalcoatl, attempted to discover the meaning of life on an intellectual plane. These almost diametrically opposed attitudes toward life and the universe existed side by side—a situation similar to that of Nazi Germany in our time, where a mystico-militaristic world view and a genuinely humanistic philosophy and literature coexisted," according to Miguel León-Portilla, and I see his point, it's not a leap or a jump to make the connection, humanism and barbarism, hand in hand, shoulder to shoulder, it's human nature, but that doesn't make it right, you see what I'm talking about, a fucking nod is as good as a wink to a blind horse, and not just then but now, the human species is perhaps two million years old—prehistorians keep pushing our birth date further back—the incidence of clearly recognizable artifacts dates back only fifty to a hundred thousand years, more fingers than we can count, and in that modest span, we've come from stone axes and spears to intercontinental missiles with nuclear warheads, but maybe my brain's turned to mush, like I've taken more than a handful of *ololiuhqui,* the seed of the *Rivea corymbosa,* a species of morning glory, or swallowed a drink with *sinicuichi* of the Mexican highlands, *Heimia salicifolia,* you know it, don't you? a perennial shrub with small narrow leaves and yellow flowers, leaving the crushed wilted leaves in water in the sun, brewing and fermenting them, and when the mixture's just right, downing a glass or two, look out stomach here it comes, generating the divine within, an entheogen, and down to earth, no abstruse, cryptic or transcendental messages, down on earth, right here, let's be honest, my voice's echoing, it's a big empty world, nothing out there—a good idea's worth repeating—and *ach ayac nelli in tiquitohua nican,* "it may be that no one speaks the truth on earth," what do I know except what I've seen, and what I've seen doesn't look good, more like hell than anything else, so what I'll make of it is the quality of the revenge I'll get if I don't find Coyuco alive, and all the good will in the world won't save me from trying to get it, brains or no brains, sense, judgment, wisdom, my mind's made up, my enemy's apathy and fear in the face of bullying, cruelty, and repression, when push comes to shove—the other side of the ten-peso coin—that's a good one we'll see who's going to do the pushing now, it's something to believe in, with a cry squeezed out by the hangman's spasm, I raise my cleaver, no holds barred, yes, something can be done, carried out, pulled off and wrapped up to make it right, even if it's inflicting hurt or harm on someone for an injury or wrong suffered at their hands—look it up, that's what it says, it's the world as it is and there's nothing out there but suffering, why try to change things when they've been working for hundreds thousands millions of years, who's the dinosaur now, the meat-eating ball-biting animal, I raise my hand, call on me call on me, but the result has yet to be seen, give me the spyglass, and the quartermaster, the navigator's enlisted assistant,

reaches for a wooden box containing the small, hand-held tele-
scope, offering it to me with the solemnity of a long-established
ceremony, I'm the navigator, not the ship's captain, that's how I'll
know the result, using an optical instrument designed to make distant objects appear nearer, lenses, or curved mirrors and lenses,
rays of light collected and focused, shutting one eye, concentrating
with the other, dealing with one particular thing above all others, a
forecast or a verification, "the proof of the pudding is the eating," it
might be Miguel de Cervantes, and "if you seek truth you will not
seek victory by dishonorable means, and if you find truth you will
become invincible," Epictetus, a Stoic philosopher born a slave,
read, read, and never stop, "it's a long trip, we are the only riders,"
that's William Burroughs, and my mind's turning to mush, I haven't
got anywhere in this business but dressed in this uniform and hanging on to a rough idea of what I'm going to do once I get myself out
of Hotel Obregón, on Avenue General Álvaro Obregón, and into
the light of day, not in the splendor of the moon in the distance, not
now, I couldn't take it, too many ghosts floating above the tall grass
lit by moonlight, and not a figment of my imagination, our previously prized and even now material—important essential
relevant—Mexico's supplied plenty of them, ghosts crashing into
me, drivers without eyes, *fantasmas peatonales*, pedestrian ghosts
with no sense of direction, a direct hit, one after the other, you've
walked in the countryside, the towns and cities at night, I swear it's
true, it can happen to anyone, keep your eyes open, let your skin feel
the contact of the dead we can't see, they'll caress your cheeks with
phantom fingers, beyond our eyes the picture is vague, a useless
clarity, not faulty but to no effect, what we can't see, provoking, dis-
orienting, so let's go outside, face the world, maybe the daylight will
protect us, no further need to explain excuse produce any arguments or facts in support of the decision, it'll soon be neurologically
impossible to oppose or even to question, on that account, therefore
and thus, splashed with blood from head to foot, I'll jet sprint zoom
away into the streets of Iguala de la Independencia singing, *La*

verdad es que cuesta trabajo aclimatarse al hambre, "The truth is
that it's hard work to get used to hunger," or *Cola de relámpago, re-
molino de muertos,* "Tail of lightning, maelstrom of the dead," take
your pick, one line's as good as the other, accompanied or not by
music, it's all the same to me, what do you think, a Mexican-style
instrumental version of "Noche de ronda" by Agustín Lara—he of
the very long name, Ángel Agustín María Carlos Fausto Mariano
Alfonso del Sagrado Corazón de Jesús Lara y Aguirre del Pino, born
in Tlacotalpán, Veracruz—no, it's too sad, a song dedicated to María
Félix, because things don't always work out the way we hope they
will, here I go again, but take a look around you, then and now, now
and then, a highball glass of *torito veracruzano,* cane alcohol flavored with fruit, *guanábana,* removing the seeds first, or with *jobo,*
nache, coffee, coconut, peanuts, walnuts, or chiles, a little cinnamon
sprinkled on top, mixed with crushed ice, or none at all, and that'll
bring the daylight down on top of us, Agustín Lara drank them at
Cantina Blanca Nieves, or Tobi's, not far from the wide Río
Papaloapan, but let's get back to going out into the street, Avenue
General Álvaro Obregón, you've got to start somewhere, and that's
where I'm going to put down my foot, both of them, Ernesto turning the doorknob, the door shutting behind him, headed down the
corridor to the stairs and out the door of Hotel Obregón into
daylight.

Ernesto, one boot in front of the other, laced-up tied-up leather
boots he'd carried with him from Chihuahua, and Ernesto Cisneros,
count your blessings, I've got one left, Lupita, and I used to have
two, my Coyuco, Lupita's and mine, but I don't want to get ahead
of myself, I've said it before and I'll probably say it again, there's
still hope and maybe he's alive, the dry wind cutting slices out of
his skin, the sun more terrible than he remembered it being as it
tried to flatten him against the walls of buildings, or demoralize
him with its intensity, its brightness, but the question of whether or
not the searing sunlight was taking the wind out of his sails floated

for a second, then became a part of the zone of the forgotten when Ernesto, raising his eyes from the path, the direction his feet in their boots were taking him, saw a boy and girl, around fifteen years old, schoolmates, or a teenager holding hands with his girlfriend, the girl dropping an ice cream wrapper, a Holanda-brand Mordisko *clásico* ice cream sandwich, Ernesto, out loud, and with an authority that surprised him as the words came out of his mouth, pointing at the wrapper, words not shouted but at a commanding volume, and Ernesto Cisneros, pick it up, don't be a lazy slob or you'll get yourself into trouble, then watching as the boy stepped back, let go of her hand, and the girl, bending at the waist, her skirt rising to the back of her thighs, reaching for the brown, red and white wrapper fluttering like a leaf on the street, and Ernesto Cisneros, telling himself, beginner's luck, I'm using the voice of the official organization that's responsible for protecting people and property, making people obey the law, then Ernesto swinging around, saluting the couple without breaking his stride, twin teenage souls amidst a multitude of strangers on a street in Iguala de la Independencia, a gust of wind swirling at the girl's ankles, climbing her legs, raising her skirt, Ernesto, still walking, caught a glimpse of what she was wearing beneath it, then turned around to face the direction he was going in without knowing exactly where he was going, and before he knew he'd got there, another street corner, an intersection, not counting the blocks he'd walked, trying to orient himself, it was around Avenida Adolfo Ruíz Cortines, named after the Mexican president who granted women the right to vote, Ernesto looking at the streets ahead of him, figuring on straight ahead to Calle 5 de Mayo, where he wanted to turn right, but a distracting thought got in the way, that with a short prayer and a shorter benediction, he'd turn out all the lights in the Iguala police station, between Calle Prolongación Celestino Negrete and Izancanac, and in total darkness hit every cop he could find with a chair, drawing blood, breaking bones, bestowing unconsciousness and death on everybody who crossed his path, a perfect revenge because they'd never see his face and

wouldn't know what'd hit them but their own furniture, punishment punishment was the name of the song, and Ernesto Cisneros,
to himself, a lawnmower's trimmed my brain, I don't even know
where I'm going, then taking a long stride without confidence, but
a firmness of purpose on automatic pilot, starting out for Calle 5 de
Mayo, he collided with a policeman at the corner of Río Velero, a
block from Calle Río Papagayo, and Ernesto Cisneros, excuse me,
officer, I wasn't looking where I was going, or I was looking, but
not at you, my mind's full of pictures and thoughts that'd interfere
with anyone's thinking, Ernesto regaining his senses, seeing who he
was speaking to, and Ernesto Cisneros, adding, officer of the law or
not, I'm not paying attention to what's going on around me, and the
policeman, mistaking Ernesto for a superior, a higher-up, you don't
have to apologize to me, sir, you've got important things to do, a lot
on your mind, it's written on your face, and I'm on my way home,
lunch with the kids, I've got five and they've all got to eat, it's a little
early, but that's the way it is, at least for the young ones, as for the
two older kids, they do what they want, you know how teenagers
are, it's the same everywhere—do you have kids? excuse me, never
mind—so I'll join them, and my wife, too, family's the most important thing, *fundamental y el gran secreto,* the big secret to a long
life, and that's why I work like a brick, sir, in the words of John Lyly,
an English poet, playwright, the works—I read a lot when I've got
the time—so we all have at least one meal together, no matter what
time of day it is, today it's lunch, except when work keeps me away,
but you know how it is better than I do, sir, it's our duty our mission
our role in this life, Ernesto resting a firm hand on the policeman's
shoulder, and Ernesto Cisneros, you're right, *colega,* it's our responsibility, but if you don't mind, a moment's delay, a diversion, a little
sidetrack from routine, I need the advice of a *compañero,* a fellow
soldier *del orden público,* a little favor, *por favor,* how about going
with me to get some beer at Modelorama, it's just over there on
Ruíz Cortines, I can see it from here—Ernesto pointing down the
street—and if you walk this way, I mean if you take this route home,

you'll already know it, Modelorama, I've got a hard time deciding what to buy and how much I can carry, it's a special occasion, I won't bore you, my meticulous attention to detail, but since we're going the same way, I thought that you'd give me a hand, and an ice-cold beer is in it for you because you're you're taking a break for lunch, I'm a generous man and a good leader of men, and a couple of six-packs for me, a celebration always calls for beer, and what we've got going, my colleagues and I, officer, *mi colega,* it's an important event, almost historically significant, momentous, so what do you say? on a day like this, a cold beer, if you've got a minute to spare, the policeman, wanting to please his superior, lifting his cap from his head, wiping the perspiration from his forehead with the back of his hand, and the policeman, it'd be an honor, sir, to accompany you to Modelorama, and to give you a helping hand, even if it looks to me like you're in very good shape for a man your age, if you don't mind my saying so, sir, and in fact, because of the feeling I have right now, courtesy and admiration and a little affection, I'd follow you to the end of the world, as long as I get to my house in time for lunch, Ernesto, a salute, an informal wave of the hand, and they were walking down Ruíz Cortines toward Río Papagayo in the mildly buzzing silence of noon.

Ernesto, resisting the desire to put his arm over the policeman's shoulder, not out of any affection, but to be sure he didn't get away, veer off in another direction, or decide his family lunch was more important than helping a higher-ranking member of the municipal police, instead Ernesto kept an eye on him, trying not to be obvious but interested in the man's comportment, a bearing befitting a young officer of the *Policía Municipal,* Ernesto and the policeman entering Modelorama, and Ernesto Cisneros, nothing too strong, we're on duty tonight, the policeman nodding his head, and the policeman, if you want to keep your head clear after a couple of beers, this is a good choice, only 4% alcohol, Ernesto taking the man's advice, deciding on two six-packs of Victoria, and a Negra

Modelo for the policeman, Ernesto paying, carrying the two six-packs, the policeman by his side, an open bottle in his hand, and together, rounding the corner and walking down Río Papagayo, and Ernesto Cisneros, you'll walk me to my door, my wife'll be glad to meet you, and my colleagues, you might recognize a few faces, *compañero,* it isn't a barbeque but there'll be something to eat—I know you've got to get home for lunch—just shake a few hands, it'll do you good, your career, too, you never know, and without breaking his stride or speech, Ernesto looking at the pistol in the policeman's holster, wracking his brains, remembering the pictures of handguns he'd seen in a catalogue, Ernesto patting his empty holster, making a show of it, and Ernesto Cisneros, you always wear your pistol? I check mine in, I'm off duty, rules are rules, but from where I stand, it's a Glock, a Jericho 941, a Heckler & Koch USP, or a classic Parkerized .45 ACP M1911, but I won't put a peso on it seeing that I can't make a solid survey while we're walking, the policeman slowing down, hearing the words but not believing them, a superior officer with a pair of really sharp eyes, but Ernesto urging him on, a hand at the elbow of the arm holding the beer, the policeman taking another swallow from the bottle, wiping his chin with the back of his hand, then smiling in admiration and high regard at the estimable Ernesto, and the policeman, it's a Glock, sir, and you're right, you've got your guns straight, what I'm carrying is thanks to a friend I've got in the *Policía Federal,* not a classic .45, they don't carry them, he gave me a good price, sold it at a discount, a real friend, Ernesto nodding, but looking straight ahead at a tree standing alone in the middle of the sidewalk, concentrating focusing keeping his mind on its leafy branches reaching over part of number 10 Río Papagayo, a single-story washed-out yellowish-beige house, and extending more than halfway across the deserted street like an open umbrella, and Ernesto Cisneros, self-defense's an indispensable part of our line of work, *colega,* and when they got to the shade beneath the tree, the policeman turned to look at him, a wide grin on his face, Ernesto, holding the two six-packs cradled low in his left arm as ballast, swung around with all his weight and hit him with a strong right, right on the nose, coldcocking the man whose legs were giving way beneath him, eyes open but seeing nothing, his body wobbling, Ernesto catching the Negra Modelo in midair with his free hand before the bottle hit the ground, and ignoring the fact that the policeman slobbered all over the mouth of the bottle, Ernesto took a swig, nearly finishing the dark-style lager, then setting his two six-packs on the ground in order to drag the policeman into a sitting position, leaning him against the yellowish-beige wall of the house, looking up and down the street, finding nobody and nothing watching him, a sigh, Ernesto shaking his head, surprised at himself, or at the strength he could muster in his fist, and a well-aimed sock on the nose, with the help of the two six-packs to improve his stability, Ernesto, without a sound, not speaking but thinking, and Ernesto Cisneros, with pain and pleasure limits defined, and the juxtaposition formulae set up, it's fairly easy to predict what people will think in a thousand years or as long as the formulae remain in operation, Ernesto giggling to himself, undisciplined thoughts accompanying savage actions, and Ernesto Cisneros, adding, *El hombre invisible,* where are you now? I was just doing a little target practice, a private joke, not mine, out of *Lady From Shanghai,* and now to work, he fumbled with the policeman's belt, drew the Glock out of the holster, the policeman's unconscious body tipping sideways, Ernesto straightening it with his boot, then lifting the sweat-stained cap off the policeman's head, examining the inner band of the cap, gripping it between his thumb and forefinger, rubbing off the man's perspiration, wiping his fingers on the front of the policeman's shirt, he put the cap on his own head, slipped the Glock into his holster, fixed the strap, tapping the butt of the pistol with the heel of his hand, caressing it with the tips of four fingers, and he took the time to look down at the policeman whose eyes were closed, a smile on his face, and a little saliva or beer at the corners of his mouth.

Ernesto standing there, and Ernesto Cisneros, this has gone too far, but it hasn't gone far enough, maybe I'll kill him, unsnapping the strap that kept the pistol in place, weighing the Glock in his hand, and Ernesto Cisneros, no, he's got a family so I won't kill him, one thought in another thought out, drive-in arguments, so he put the Glock back in the holster, snapped the strap in place, turned around and started walking back in the direction of Modelorama, leaving the two six-packs and a nearly empty brown bottle of Negra Modelo next to the senseless body of the policeman, asleep without dreams, one two three four five six steps away, he turned back, stopping in front of the policeman still sitting upright against the wall, and Ernesto Cisneros, a few words from the poet Tecayehuatzin, Lord of Huexotzinco, offering an interpretation of the nature of poetics, and speaking of another poet, Ayocuan of Tecamachalco, a prince:

> *Como esmeraldas y plumas finas,*
> *llueven tus palabras.*
> *Así habla también Ayocuan*
> *Cuetzpaltzin,*
> *que ciertamente conoce al Dador de la Vida.*
> *Así vino a hacerlo también*
> *aquel famoso señor*
> *que con ajorcas de quetzal y con perfumes*
> *deleitaba a nuestro Dios.*

> Like emeralds and fine plumes,
> your words rain.
> Thus also Ayocuan Cuetzpaltzin speaks,
> who surely knows the Giver of Life.
> Thus he also came to do it,
> that famous lord,
> who with quetzal bracelets and perfumes,
> delighted the only God.

Ernesto, ignoring that "flowers and songs" might be a language for speaking with the Giver of Life, the only memory of humanity that will remain on earth, perhaps enduring in the beyond, "the dream of a word," the holiness of life, Ernesto started kicking the policeman, swinging his leg connected to a well-oiled pivot in his hip, repeatedly striking the knocked-out policeman with the toe of his boot, hearing ribs break, internal organs trying to avoid the blows, look out look out, and Ernesto Cisneros, what's right and what isn't? there isn't any poetry in what I'm doing, or maybe there is, and each kick is a line in a stanza, but the question he asked himself, like the question of whether or not the searing sunlight was taking the wind out of his sails, floated for a second, then quickly became a part of the zone of the forgotten.

It was the first gathering of members of the *Policía Municipal* that impressed him as big enough to serve the purpose, constituting more than two and less than five men, a group of three men, a couple of cigarettes, not off duty but taking a break, a squad car parked a few feet away in an illegal spot, not illegal for them, but for any other citizen of Iguala, a gathering big enough for Ernesto to consider as interesting since he'd started walking from Modelorama the entire length of Avenida Adolfo Ruíz Cortines to Juan Aldama, then Diagonal Juan Aldama, past Privada Bandera Nacional to Avenida Bandera Nacional and the Estrella de Oro station, it could've been the station at Calle de Salazar and Calle Hermenegildo Galeana, or the Estrella Blanca station, it didn't matter, any connection to the buses of Iguala and the missing students and Coyuco was good enough for him, it was the police he was looking for, Ernesto couldn't resist the beauty of such a gathering assembled and ready for harvest in front of him, and behind the bus station itself, a small but efficient group, suiting his purpose like a pile of shit suits a fly, but he wasn't a flying insect of a large order characterized by a single pair of transparent wings and sucking, often piercing mouthparts, a vector of disease, even death, and right before his eyes, the image of

a slow debilitating crippling paralyzing disease befalling the policemen of Iguala, not a select few but handfuls, by the dozen, hundreds,
it'd be a plague of disease-carrying flies if he had a say in it, an almost but not quite fitting convenient tailor-made execution, except
for the fact that he wasn't a fly but the carrier of a naturally unnatural death by shooting, and Ernesto Cisneros, but a disabling disease,
not a bad way to go, worth the wait, a long-drawn-out suffering, not
for me, but for the rest of them, the municipal police, the federal
police, the ministerial police—maybe I should branch out, throw
on a whole different kind of uniform? the army, the 27th Battalion,
after all, it's variety that counts, keeps the mind fresh, the clothes
pressed, the hair combed, tidy neat well-groomed—an invasion, an
epidemic, only if I could watch observe take notes, I'd publish a
medical memoire of satisfaction and distribute myself to anyone
interested in the product of untreated unprocessed raw natural and
crude justice in the form of reprisal, handwritten notes! a copy for
you, you, and you, I'm all those flies, you can't count them on a hundred hands, a large order of insects comprising the two-winged or
true flies, their hind wings reduced to form balancing organs, including many biting forms, such as mosquitoes and tsetse flies, holy
vectors of disease, and that's me, Ernesto Cisneros Fuentes! named
after the football midfielder, if you divide and multiply me, a convergence of man and fly, intersected infected living things, and it's
these three guys, here and now, members of the municipal police, a
relaxed smoke before the execution, they're going to get bitten by a
savage insect, and they don't even know it, and it's best that way, a
surprise, a revelation, and because it isn't the station at Salazar and
Hermenegildo Galeana, or the Estrella Blanca station, they aren't
paying attention to what's going on around them, where's the hot
spot, hazardous, perilous, high-risk, don't touch it, you'll burn
yourself, don't look, turn your head away or your eyes'll melt in
their sockets, they won't know what hit them, as long as they don't
survive, a forensic scientist communicating with the dead could tell
them, it'll put the federal police, the ministerial police, the 27th

Battalion on their toes, and the Mayor of Mayors, and his cold-blooded reptile wife, a lot of toes in laced-up boots, except the Reptile, she'll be wearing heels, the authorities, government, administration, establishment, police, losing a few of their own, more than a few if I've got anything to say, it's a start that'll put them in the picture, if they're listening, that they ought to strip off the corruption double-dealing murder greed and solve the mystery of the missing *normalistas*, Ernesto approaching the three policemen, not close enough to fire, pulling the brim of his cap down, the cap was a size too big for him, a detail working to his advantage in the striking daylight, a cap protecting his head, the brim creating a little shade for his eyes, concealing them and the upper part of his face, while his anger and despair wrapped around his body like a living thing, a snake squeezing him, taking his breath away, or he was holding his breath, keeping it in his lungs, anticipating, and the tightness he made for himself in his chest forced him forward, motivating him, the two policemen facing him were smoking, leaning against a wall, the third had his back to him, sitting on the hood of the patrol car, and Ernesto Cisneros, to himself, ten to one he's eating, head down with his chin on his chest, maybe a snack, *cuerno de azucar*, with refined sugar spilling on the front of his uniform, a bag of *rosquitas con miel,* or simple *rosquitas souflee* with sugar, Ernesto's mouth watering at the thought of sugary fried *rosquitas,* flavored with vanilla, Ernesto, without taking a breath or exhaling, nothing keeping him from breathing, really, he was making himself ready for use, a convergence of man and disease-carrying fly, drawing the pistol, lightweight in his hand, extending his arm, readying himself without knowing what he was doing, he'd never fired a gun before, not trembling, or he was trembling but couldn't see it, standing a couple of feet from the policemen, arm outstretched like he was pointing at them, but it was a Glock and not a finger, the two policemen astonished, each with a cigarette pinched between thumb and second finger, staring at him, and the third policeman swung around, pivoting his upper body, shirtfront covered in refined sugar

and holding what was left of a doughnut in his hand, a grin on his
face, granulated sugar caught in his moustache, and perfect white
teeth, Ernesto pulled the trigger without centering his finger on it,
and nothing, no sound, no kick, the external integrated trigger
safety, a trigger with a spring-loaded lever in its lower half, preventing him from firing, or the magazine was empty, or there wasn't a
magazine, one of the policemen threw his cigarette away, took a
couple of steps toward him, nothing pressing in his movement,
reaching for the pistol in Ernesto's hand, not taking it away from
him but covering the top of it with the flat of his hand, lowering the
pistol for Ernesto, whose arm followed the downward pressure the
officer put on it, Ernesto's eyes searching for fear in their faces, but
there wasn't anything like it, twinkling bright eyes, opened wide,
and an abrupt snort coming from one of them, the sudden forcing
of breath through his nose, Ernesto wasn't sure if he was expressing
indignation, derision, or incredulity, and the officer with the sugary
doughnut in his hand, still chewing, popped the rest of it in his
mouth, then swallowed, clearing his throat before speaking, and
policeman No. 1, what do you think you're playing at, *cabrón*? and
now that the Glock was pointing at the ground, Ernesto's arm at his
side, the policeman who'd lowered his arm for him, taking another
step toward Ernesto, putting his hand on Ernesto's shoulder, and
policeman No. 2, take it easy with the kidding, mister, nice weapon,
where'd you get it? we aren't issued anything like it, a .38 Special,
that's our brand, *colega,* but I've heard there are 9mms circulating,
replacing these worn out .38s, have you heard anything about it? is
the word spreading? are we getting new weapons finally positively
once and for all and at last? Ernesto, effortlessly putting the pistol in
the holster, no embarrassment on his face, and Ernesto Cisneros, to
himself, I won't show them anything owing nothing to my intelligence or practice but to the fact that I don't know what I'm doing
and I don't want them to know it, and Ernesto Cisneros, I got it
from a friend in the *Policía Federal,* maybe you know him, or you've
heard of him, his nickname's El Lápiz, tall, skinny, and all muscle,

Inspector Jefe Calderón Hinojosa, two stars, carrying a Heckler &
Koch, *un hombre imponente,* an imposing man, the three policemen
listening intently to the description of a man they didn't know, and
the officer with granulated sugar in his moustache, policeman No.
1, let's drink to it, I've got a bottle behind the seat of my Toyota, the
four of them moving together down the street toward a second vehicle, a pickup, Ernesto hadn't noticed it, he'd been concentrating
on the promise of killing three members of the *Policía Municipal,* a
triple play for a start, not the same as a defensive play when three
runners are put out, impeccable timing, in accordance with the
highest standards of artistry, and accurate throws, like flinging
knives at a human target spinning round on a wheel, Ernesto on the
offensive, a powerful throwing arm, his vision sharp, accepted now
by the three policemen who were fooled by a fine homemade uniform, Ernesto sewing like a seamstress after fifty years on the job,
they were tricked, by his worthy bearing, too, an actor's skill even if
he'd never performed for anyone but himself in front of the bathroom mirror, clowning around when he had the spirit to play the
fool, long before what'd happened to Coyuco, and now, Ernesto
feeling a gust of hyena laughter building up in his lungs waiting to
come out, his body, led by an anguished brain, out of control after
the emotional wound he'd suffered, a long-drawn-out illness of his
own, impairing his brain's usefulness and normal function, and before he could swallow it the laughter broke out, a crazy laughter
bursting from his throat, the lungs had pushed with all their might
and there was no stopping the laughter, and the four of them standing next to the Toyota, the passenger door open, the officer with
granulated sugar in his moustache didn't have any sugar there now,
he'd wiped his mouth with the smooth skin of his arm after taking a
swig of tequila, a hand as big as a baseball mitt wrapped around the
bottle, and policeman No. 1, not the best quality, but on our pay,
10,000 a month, pesos not dollars, what do you expect, eh? shoving
one of the two others, officer No. 2, making him stumble backward
while he was reaching for the bottle the other was holding out to

him, officer No. 2 catching the neck of the bottle with his fingers, getting his balance along with a firm grip on the bottle, taking a swallow, wiping his chin, then swallowing another mouthful of tequila, chiming in with a wise crack, and policeman No. 2, not including the 7,000 pesos a month you'd get working with a gang, Los Pelones, Los Rojos, Los Metros, or Los Tequileros in Tierra Caliente, for example, and I'm not talking about the song by Los Tigres del Norte or Los Alegres de Terán, and then there's CJNG, Los Caballeros Templarios and Guerreros Unidos, the cartels, and the big time, more money than you'd see in dream, and policeman No. 1, or it's death and a funeral, if you're lucky, 'mano, or no funeral at all 'cause they'd never find the body, and policeman No. 2, I swear I haven't touched a centavo ¡claro! no matter who's pushing what in my hands because if I did, and I don't know anybody who hasn't been tempted, I'd turn into a flesh-and-blood paradox, and then I break out in a rash, exanthema, urticaria, that's just the way I am in a world of give-me-this-I'll-give-you-that—officer No. 3, who hadn't said a word, interrupting him, and policeman No. 3, you're one of the few, seeing as I've met plenty with their hands open, then closed tight on a nice handful of cash every month, but 'mano, give me that bottle, I'm thirsty, and knock off the yackety-yak about Los Caballeros Templarios, Guerreros Unidos, shakedowns, palm-greasing graft, it's a way of life, we've had plenty of trouble here, and it's just the beginning, officer No. 2 still holding the bottle, and policeman No. 2, let me think, he shut his eyes in order to see the list that unfolded before him, officer No. 2 feeling his colleagues' impatience, officer No. 3 trying to pry the bottle from his fingers, without luck, and policeman No. 2, hang on, just give me a minute, then opening his eyes, a wide smile and another set of perfect teeth, and policeman No. 2, yes, that's right, now I've got it, Guerreros Unidos, first it was El Tilde, after the business with La Barredora, then El Sapo Guapo, and his brother, El Chino, but definitely Gonzalo Martín Souza Neves, Benjamín Mondragón in Morelos, and now El Chaky, I think it's El Chaky who's the boss, Ernesto saying nothing, just listening, officer No. 1, the policeman who didn't have sugar in his moustache, extending his arm, his fingers wiggling, beckoning the bottle, ignoring officer No. 3's turn at the tequila, and policeman No. 1, the sugar-free policeman, hand it over, 'mano, your reciting another litany always makes me thirsty, a real fountain of facts, that's what you are, come on come on, give it to me, but the bottle passed to the third policeman, so he reached into his shirt pocket for a pack of cigarettes, lighting one, taking a long haul on it, and policeman No. 1, El Chaky, whoever the fuck that is, and even if I do know who he is I don't want to know, if you know what I mean, and policeman No. 2, you know and I know it's Arturo Hernández, known as El Chaky when he was a lieutenant in the late-but-not-great Amado Carrillo Fuentes' cartel in Chihuahua, Amado Carrillo, El Señor de los Cielos, Lord of the Skies, on account of his jets, dying fresh off the operating table after trying on a new face, but since we're talking about Guerreros Unidos, let's talk about Arturo Hernández, a real family man, El Chaky, devoted to family and home, a man who's got a wife and one or more children, you can count them on one hand, at least as far as I know, because I can tell you a story, two stories, and it isn't the tequila talking, it was in the papers, maybe you read it, maybe you didn't, or it came your way by word of mouth, El Chaky's son, Emmanuel Hernández Tarín, known as El Pepino, "The Cucumber," driving drunk in his gray Nissan Pathfinder, plate number 194WDA—I've got a memory like a steel trap and a passion for lists, that's me—and El Pepino, finding his way into the offices of the *Policía Ministerial*, walking right in, on purpose? who knows, but blasted trashed stinko and completely impaired, getting himself killed in January 2009, not ancient history but not so long ago, right here in the Free and Sovereign State of Guerrero, and then El Chaky's other son, Christian Arturo Hernández Tarín, El Chris, head of La Barredora, the *Policía Federal* caught him 2011, and he's in jail stir the big house the penitentiary—they drop like flies or end up in prison, you need a scorecard to keep track of them—El Chris doing time in La Palma, or

Almoloya, in the municipality of Almoloya de Juárez, around fifteen miles from Toluca, officer No. 1 dropping his cigarette, crushing it with his boot, then police officer No. 3 passed the bottle to Ernesto, who lifted it to his lips, swallowing three mouthfuls, no need to wipe his chin with his sleeve, and at last, a few words from Ernesto, and Ernesto Cisneros, *mi colegas,* in the pertinent words of a Nahua poet, relative to the matter at hand:

> Oh you friends!
> You, eagles and jaguars.
> In truth here it is like a game of *patolli!*
> How can we gain something in it?
> Oh friends … !
> We all must play *patolli:*
> we must go to the place of mystery.
> In truth before his face,
> I am only in vain,
> destitute before the Giver of Life.

And Ernesto Cisneros, continuing, that's from the *Cantares Mexicanos,* a special thanks to Miguel León-Portilla, you can find a reproduction of the manuscript in our National Library, so throw your bright-colored dice, and your beans, or maize, it's up to you, *colegas,* pray to your gods with the hope of winning the game, and if I have anything to say about it you won't, *perdone,* but that's the way it is, my position on the subject is well-known, locally if nowhere else, can we take a walk, go somewhere where there's nobody to interrupt us, you'll see what I mean, I've got more to say, what do you think, is it okay with you, all three, of course, that's what I meant, right this way, *yo indicaré el camino, y ustedes siguen con las vacas,* I'll blaze the trail, you follow with the cattle, just like in a Western, you can leave your vehicles where they're parked, you're the police, after all, and so am I, Ernesto leading them away from the Estrella de Oro station, toward the statue, *La Patria Trigarante,* reminding him of the flag of the Three Guarantees of Mexico, walking along Heroico Colgio Militar, past the Unidad Habitacional Militar, a military housing unit, and Ernesto Cisneros, you can pick which entrance you want, *colegas,* the red on the left or the green on the right, and the three men following Ernesto, approaching the double arches painted red, white and green, police officer No. 2 using the bottle to point at the red entrance, the four of them taking the left entrance, heading in the direction of an empty soccer field near Unidad Deportiva de Iguala for the players of the Liga Municipal de Futbol Amateur AC, but there wasn't a match going on right now, officer No. 1 ambling next to Ernesto, a confidence, a whisper, and policeman No. 1, you're a little old for being a cop, aren't you, *tata?* excuse me, *'mano,* but you remind me of my father, and Ernesto Cisneros, what do you think of him, your father? is it love or hate, a fistful of indifference? and policeman No. 1, I loved him all right, but he's dead, and when he was alive he was a living son-of-a-bitch, and Ernesto Cisneros, who really knows what a man's tastes or intuitions are based on, then turning his head, throwing words over his shoulder at the other two, that's what I say, boys, aspirations, dreams, hopes, what d'you suppose your mothers and fathers bathed you in besides water, hot when they could get it, cold when there was no choice? instilling what sort of principles, ethics, moral codes, standards? Ernesto turned to look at officer No. 1, adding, have you got any idea? obviously not, it's written on your ugly face—blank with a broken nose, I'm talking about your son-of-a-bitch father, what do you figure he taught you? officers No. 2 and 3 passing the nearly empty bottle back and forth between them, giggling like children, Ernesto catching a couple of sentences coming from officers No. 2 and 3, and policeman No. 2, *¿desde cuándo se viste él como un joto?* since when does he dress like a faggot? and policeman No. 3, *desde que él tiene dinero,* since he's got money, and policeman No. 2, *así, él no está maldiciendo su mala suerte,* so, he isn't cursing his bad luck, and policeman No. 3, *¡sobres!* you said it, and they went on like that, officers No. 2 and 3, exchanging observations that meant nothing to Ernesto, jokes that were more empty and meaningless than offering a house to a nomad, and when the last drop was drained from the bottle, police officer No. 2 tossed it in the air as they were walking next to a fenced-in grassy playing field, not green but dusty brown, and in the far distance a mountain range watching over them, Ernesto hearing but not seeing the bottle shatter, turning around when he got to the leaning trunk of a tree, Ernesto face-to-face with officer No. 1, and policeman No. 1, they finished the bottle, which is, deep down, so familiar, and Ernesto Cisneros, in other words, they're drunk again, and policeman No. 1, to the other two officers, what the fuck! and officers No. 2 and 3, a big laugh from their guts filled with tequila, staring at the glass on the sidewalk glittering in the sunlight, not a single car or truck passed the four men gathered on the sidewalk, there wasn't a pedestrian in sight, Ernesto, looking away from the two drunken policemen, staring at his hands, wondering what to do with them, and Ernesto Cisneros, where on earth will I put them now? his hands fidgeting without a word from his brain, hands impatient to do something, Ernesto knowing what his hands were thinking, knowing what they wanted to get their hands on, recognizing their needs even though the needs were outside the laws of nature, against his own nature, too, but they were his hands, he couldn't refuse them, and he knew himself, his personality, disposition, temperament, makeup, a modified altered revised version of the old familiar Ernesto, transformed the moment Coyuco disappeared, and anger was only part of it, and Ernesto Cisneros, silently, a sadness as deep as the Sigsbee Deep, or the Mexico Basin, a triangular basin, the deepest part of the Gulf of Mexico, 12,000, even 14,000 feet, so deep it's fathomless, that's a lot of sadness, more than a man can handle, and three hundred miles long, our Barranca del Cobre under the sea, so when the spark that's lighted in situations like this has been lighted, not fireworks, not having a good time like someone on a merry-go-round, no trio of trumpeting trumpets, but an explosion outburst flare-up of anger, drowning in the deep of the Mexico

Basin, floating facedown on a salty sea, or cursing the hope that's been lost, *nuestra intranquilidad, nuestra dependencia, ha ido en aumento, también la crudeza de nuestros insomnios,* our restlessness and dependency have only increased, as well as the severity of our insomnia, we're all in the same boat, nobody's closing an eye at night to sleep, we're afraid of what we'll dream or what we'll see in our dreams, and during the day we're wide awake waiting for the least bit of news, we're locked out and don't have the key, that's me, that's Lupita, and it's the parents, wives, girlfriends, brothers and sisters of all the others, forty-three, plus our Coyuco, *los desaparecidos,* hundreds, or thousands—the missing, no end to them, and policeman No. 1, so where to, *tata?* where are you taking us? destination unknown, not into error or morally questionable behavior, I hope, but my fingers are crossed, you just can't see them, here, take a look, and he waved a fat-fingered hand in front of Ernesto, and Ernesto Cisneros, a broad smile on his face, we're going straight to the center of the earth, officer No. 1, not really paying attention, looking with narrowed eyes for the entrance to the playing field, no sunglasses, just a hand like a visor on his forehead, and policeman No. 1, let's climb the fence, I don't feel like walking, and I've got to take a piss, Ernesto offering him a leg up, and policeman No. 1, *tata,* you're stronger than you look, then Ernesto helping the other two officers up and over, the fence wasn't high but a bit wobbly, Ernesto making it over by himself, dropping gently to the dried-out grass on the other side, officer No. 1 scanning the landscape for a place to take a leak, Ernesto looking down at the shadow of a tree cast by the sun between the wire-mesh fence they'd just climbed and the white wooden fence staking out the field, turning his eyes to a goalpost without a net, the four men stepping over the white wooden fence, advancing toward the middle of the field, officer No. 1, eyes moving left to right right to left, searching for a tree a shady corner a clump of shrubs somewhere to take it out and let the stream flow freely to relieve his bladder, Ernesto leading the way, the others behind him, not a real Francisco Vázquez de Coronado, but with his own ideas in mind, Ernesto hearing mumbling voices, indistinct words coming from officers No. 2 and No. 3, the two-fisted tone of officer No. 2's voice, and then the words themselves, and policeman No. 2 speaking to officer No. 3, *este pinche cabrón me pone los nervios de punta,* this fucking shithead gets on my nerves, and policeman No. 3, *¡a poco!* no shit! I can see it on your face, *cabrón,* the four men now standing in the center of the soccer field, forming a kind of circle, positioned not too close not too far away, officer No. 1 still looking for a place to piss, while officer No. 2, drawing attention to himself, a drunken selfish self, moist on the lips, tequila forced out of his mouth by a torrent of saliva, sickeningly seductive, moving slowly but surely toward Ernesto, edging his way closer, officer No. 1 taking a step back, Ernesto focused on the distorted deformed expression on officer No. 2's face, skin turning a shade of purple, a face growing larger as he approached Ernesto, a balloon with bulging eyes and a wide-open mouth with shiny saliva-covered teeth, Ernesto hearing nothing at first because there was nothing coming out of the other's mouth, just lips shaping silent words, then officer No. 3 trying to hold back officer No. 2 by gripping his shoulder, twisting his body in the effort, making a Quasimodo out of him, as the other fought to pull himself free, and policeman No. 3, in the words of Edward Bulwer-Lytton, he's as strong as the voice of Fate, then officer No. 2, with nothing holding him back, standing as close to Ernesto as he could get, an unwanted Siamese twin, a furious bag of hot air fueled by alcohol, not a dry brain cell left to suppress any parts considered obscene, personally unacceptable, or a threat to security, officer No. 3 covering his ears as the words started to come out of officer No. 2, officer No. 1 holding his breath, ignoring the membranous sac in which his urine was colleted, ready to overflow, Ernesto listening without understanding at first what he was hearing, hateful words pouring from officer No. 2's mouth, his extended arms waving like the sails of a windmill, shouting at Ernesto, covering Ernesto's face with a spray of saliva and tequila, aggressive was the chest officer No. 2 shoved forward, imaginary masses getting out of their cars, the masses shaking their fists, the masses declaring a fight, the masses calling for blood, but there wasn't a crowd, only four of them, and one was out of his mind, and policeman No. 2, his voice now a whisper, this is a country of plain and simple observers, officer No. 2 sticking his arm out with his hand raised like he was one of The Supremes, stopping Ernesto before he could say a word, and policeman No. 2, I'll anticipate what's going to come out of your mouth, *tata,* you're going to tell me we've got great poets in these parts, and it's true, I'm one of them, no one can deny it, and now, out of the blue, straight into your elephant ears, you'll hear a shout, an enthusiastic exclamation of intelligence coming from yours truly, *estúpido,* maybe you haven't got any brains horse sense know-how, *cabrón,* but I can help you out, you're gonna get a break, I can do that for you, you faggot son-of-a-bitch, cop or no cop, *tata,* you aren't one of us, that's for sure, ever since the 26th September, here in Iguala, you can't trust anyone, who was there, who wasn't, who's gonna say something, or who's gonna keep their trap shut, *hijo de puta,* son of a bitch, are you gonna make apologies, turn yourself in, *pinche huele-pedos,* you fucking fart-smeller, you blank piece of paper, a nobody, you get what I'm saying? Ernesto not saying a word, and policeman No. 2, *¿naciste lento, o pasó recién?* were you born this slow, or did it just happen recently? *arbeit macht frei!* upside-down B or not, work sets you free, you prick, that's where you belong, you'd better keep your mouth shut, whatever you know, if you know anything at all, which I doubt, so if there's something on your mind, a little guilt, something to confess, *bendígame Padre, porque he pecado,* bless me Father, for I have sinned, like some kinda *marica?* a sissy, then swallow it, not a word, or do I have to shut your mouth for you, and all those weeping parents, wipe away your tears, *hijo de la chingada,* son of a bitch—*¡vete al coño podrido de tu puta madre!* go to the rotten cunt of your whore mother—officer No. 2 turning to the other officers, indicating Ernesto with a jerk of his head, and policeman No. 2, *se busca por tonto,* wanted for stupidity, then turning back to Ernesto, so close that Ernesto felt his stinking

breath on his face, and policeman No. 2, not to mention the eman-
cipated and intellectual women who work in circuses, *¿qué chinga'os
buscas, pinche pedazo de mierda? hijo de la chingada,* you fucking
piece of shit, what're you looking at, you fucking dick? Ernesto
spreading his arms like wings, reaching around the other's waist,
drawing officer No. 2 closer, belly to belly, squeezing him, holding
him in an embrace, Ernesto unholstering officer No. 2's .38 Special,
pressing the muzzle against the other's guts, firing a round, then
another, turning on his heel, firing a shot between the eyes of officer
No. 1, then firing a couple of bullets into officer No. 3's chest and
neck, killing all three of them on an empty field used for outdoor
team games, a soccer field near Unidad Deportiva de Iguala for the
players of the Liga Municipal de Futbol Amateur AC, Ernesto, wiping the grip, trigger, barrel of the .38—any part he might've
touched—with the tail of his shirt, dropped the gun in the dry grass
next to officer No. 1's dead body, trousers stained with piss, relief at
last, Ernesto looked up at the welcoming sky, with no hope now for
getting to that single-story white building, the *Policía Municipal,* its
door painted black, no hope of climbing the ocher-colored steps,
more orange than yellow, and Ernesto Cisneros, out loud to himself,
now what've you done.

I f you turn around now, a cautious turn, a cautious look, you'll see
them changing her clothes, *mi amigo,* but you've got to have X-ray
eyes like Ray Milland in the International Picture by Roger Corman,
because twice a week *La Pascualita's* outfits are changed behind
curtains put up in the shop window, always using the more classic
bridal styles that the store's owner, Mario González, and his staff
consider more appropriate and dignified, so the curtains are up in
the shop window to preserve the dummy's modesty, women are like
that despite what men want to see and what they might show them,
the ones they're interested in, of course, and that isn't just anybody,
mi amigo, that's right, only if they're interested, and that's called

seduction, a big word for a lasting effect, I'm talking about erections, *mi amigo,* yours and mine, well, yours because of my age, now where was I? telling a tale, a fable myth parable or allegory, take your pick, and Little Pascuala's still spawning supernatural spectral tales, maybe it was last year, I can't tell you exactly, my memory's not what it used to be, but let's say within the last couple of years, or more recently, it's the story that counts, a woman was having a violent argument with her boyfriend right here in front of La Popular, macho macho macho, that's what we are and that's how we're going to be, *mi opinión,* my generation, too, because whether or not you can see it I'm more than seventy years old, *mi amigo,* maybe you're different but it's in my blood, stale as it is, not a tasty drop for a vampire to drink, which makes me think of Julio Cortázar, then straight to Curzio Malaparte—something I've read is something I remember—"everyone knows how egoistic the dead are, there's no one but them in the world," and you might as well put *La Pascualita* in the same boat, rowing, here we are and we're still talking about her, that's something special, so when the woman who's having a fight with her boyfriend turned her back on him, what else was she supposed to do, insults, and who knows what, the boyfriend, a slow burn, you follow me, don't you? a scene out of the movies, the woman walking away, taking her time, and music playing, but it wasn't Les Baxter, he didn't write the music like he did for Roger Corman in *X: The Man with the X-Ray Eyes,* that's asking too much, if we could only hear a soundtrack without those goddamn things stuck in our ears, no wires dangling tickling getting in the way, just a living soundtrack playing when we want it to, not for everyone to hear, a personalized private accompaniment to life, and a loving multitude twirling to the beat of a music that nobody else hears and others don't even know is playing, citizens inhabitants aficionados swaying back and forth in enormous waves that can only be seen from a distance, appreciated from far away, a bird's-eye view with a wink and a smile, if you follow me, but I'm dreaming out loud, let's get back to the woman, a topical topic, since it happened right here,

not more than a few feet from where we're standing, in front of La
Popular, a popular port of call, *mi amigo*—you're my friend even if
I don't know you—but the woman didn't get far, barely stretching
her legs, you'll see what I mean in a minute, plain as day, the boyfriend, more than irritated, you could say he was hot under the
collar even if he wasn't wearing a shirt, okay, a T-shirt, but seeing
red, pissed off, and reaching into the waistband of his trousers, pulling a pistol from beneath his jacket—dressed to the nines, and
wanting to create a striking impression—the boyfriend, no hesita-
tion, shot his girlfriend in the back, nobody remembering if it was
a revolver or an automatic, it all happened so fast, that's what the eye
witnesses had to say, and there were plenty of them, La Popular's a
popular place that people make a special trip to visit, and maybe the
street was busy, maybe not, but a few pedestrians, enough to make
a difference, and when she fell, striking her head on the pavement,
or the sidewalk itself if she hadn't reached the crosswalk, a second
pool of blood forming quickly, spilling out without mercy, one for
the wound in her back, one for the blow to her head, it didn't look
good and every passerby near enough or who'd heard the shot fired
from across the street, people gathered around her as she twisted
her body around in order to look up at Little Pascuala in the window of La Popular, they hadn't drawn the curtains, she was dressed
in her finest as she was dressed in her finest every day, the wounded
woman throwing a pleading look at *La Pascualita*, a lifelike figure
behind glass, and out of the woman's mouth, a weak but distinct cry
of hope and no shadow of a doubt, you can call it faith, *mi amigo,*
and the woman shouted with all her strength, save me, Pascualita,
save me! and she survived—the final phrase or sentence of my tale
fable myth parable or allegory, take your pick, providing no humor
but a crucial element—the enchanted enchantress, Little Pascuala,
I'm not the only one to think of it as something otherworldly spiritual mystic, straightaway the locals remembering what they'd seen
and heard a long time ago, they were my age, probably older, I can't
always be sure of the date of my birth, I might be older than I think

I am, you know how it is, *mi amigo,* "the passing years are like a mist sweeping up from the sea of time so that my memories acquire new aspects," from *A Writer's Notebook* by W. Somerset Maugham, the passersby at the time of the shooting, a collective memory of the moment *La Pascualita* made her first appearance in the shop window, March 25th, 1930, dressed in a spring-season gown, who could forget it, nobody who'd been there or stopped by for a visit, giving the window display the once-over before going to the cantina for a beer or to the casino, the passersby now eyewitnesses to a sort of miracle nodding their heads at the communal recollection of Pascuala Esparza's daughter, she didn't have a name, or if she did we didn't seem to remember it, what's the difference, *La Pascualita's* good enough, and she looks a lot like her mother, that's what everyone said, and Pascuala Esparza, getting abusive phone calls from angry citizens accusing her of embalming her daughter, the phone ringing off the hook, that's the saying, isn't it, Pascuala Esparza, a formal denial through a public notary—I heard it myself, or I read it in *El Correo de Parral,* or *Voz del Norte,* I don't remember, I've got a habitually forgetful disposition, it's a lapse of memory, abstraction, I can't explain it, but in the words of George Payne Rainsford James, "memory's like moonlight, the reflection of brighter rays from an object no longer seen"—Pascuala Esparza issued a statement denying rumors the mannequin was the preserved body of her daughter, that's the way it went, but it was too late, nobody believed her, you can't blame them, take a good look at her hands! but for Pascuala Esparza, the questions were answered and there was nothing more to say or do, in the words of a Nahua poet, "the fleeting pomps of the world are like the green willow trees, which, aspiring to permanence, are consumed by a fire, fall before the axe, are upturned by the wind, or are scarred and saddened by age," but our curiosity, *mi amigo,* yours and mine, makes speculation a responsibility, a shop worker, her name's Burciaga, told me that every time she goes near Pascualita her hands break out in a sweat, because *La Pascualita's* hands are very realistic, and she's got varicose veins on her legs, so she believes Pascualita's a real person—maybe Burciaga's affected by the same condition, swelling and tortuous lengthening of veins—I guess that's why we're here, you and I, maybe a couple of others, but not as often as *we* are, it's a weekly requirement for keeping our heads above water, a glance or a stare at *La Pascualita,* that's what it takes, if you don't mind that I speak for you, *mi amigo,* essential to our well-being, comfort, and I've got to say it, our health, am I right? but what really matters for a man aggressively proud of his masculinity, erection or no erection, and I'm only speaking for myself, you're a lot younger than I am, *mi amigo,* is that she looks good for all the years that she's been here, and then a long silence, Rubén Arenal saying nothing, the old man savoring the impact of his tale, looking at him with a hint of pride as the bearer of this news, a kind of dispatch without the paper, a correspondent's report sent in from a faraway place that was the old man's memory, as if what he had to say was something new for Rubén Arenal's ears, most of the locals had heard it a hundred times, the stories were for out-of-towners, but the old man had an audience, speaking at last to a fellow member of the club, an association dedicated to a particular interest, and Rocket, thanks for reminding me, saying the words with a smile, bowing gracefully and taking a few steps back, turning on his heel and heading for his ground-floor apartment, a simple home, and his pottery studio, where he'd put together everything he thought Pascuala Esparza wanted to buy, as much as he could put in a truck, packed carefully, wrapped carefully, carefully handled, and at last Rubén Arenal nearing the street entrance that led to the foyer and his front door, remembering Pascuala Esparza's words, "with all the beauty you can carry on your back, or on a small donkey used as a pack animal, maybe a car, truck, or cart, it doesn't matter," Ernesto somewhere in Iguala with his Ford pickup, so Rubén Arenal borrowing a two-wheel drive manual transmission Suzuki Carry Truck with right-hand steering from a neighbor who'd brought it down from Texas and hauled fruit and vegetables with it and it didn't have anything bigger than a

660cc engine to carry the load or do the work for him, not a Hyundai H100, it would've been a lot easier to find than the Suzuki, but for Rubén Arenal the Japanese minitruck was exactly what he wanted for the job.

The bed of the truck was almost overloaded with his pottery, bundled up and protected by rags and crumpled newspapers, a couple of hand-woven Saltillo rugs from the state of Coahuila, or from Teotitlán del Valle, tied with string, and wedged between larger pieces of pottery, Rubén Arenal wanting to present his work in the best light and on fine hand-woven materials in a pattern of colors and a traditional style, justifying their decision to buy so many of his works, everything covered by a waterproof tarp, Rubén Arenal behind the wheel, and on the seat next to him, on the left because it was right-handed steering from Japan, a bottle of homemade pulque, full to the brim and brimming full but with a top sealed by wax, a traveling companion from Luz Elena, who was not only a virtuoso of voluptuous hibiscus flower juice, the sun had fallen past the horizon, there was a faint dying glow of reddish-orange light that slipped away the minute he pulled the minitruck out of town, heading for where they told him to go, not following directions, but an instinct for the route he'd have to take, an instinct introduced by the prior presence of Pascuala Esparza and her daughter, Little Pascuala, and Rocket, not so little, a young woman as beautiful as an *oropéndola,* in the words of John Keats, and me, too, that's a golden oriole, listen to it sing, I'm listening now, but if I wait long enough, what do I hear? maybe Our Lady, Our Great Mother, Cihuacoatl, the Serpent Woman, mythical mother of the human race, bringing nothing but misery toil death, the lower part of her face a crude bare jawbone, her mouth stretched wide, hungry for victims, Cihuacoatl, that's the woman, with long and stringy hair, two knives forming a kind of diadem on her forehead, clothed and painted in chalky white, hearing her voice now, and asking myself, why why why, why now? when *La Pascualita*'s waiting for me, and

I'm waiting for her, and a special kind of love, no cunning maneuvers, no cat and mouse, fine and refined, a love that's protected in its shell and hasn't been broken yet, nothing spilled, no yoke or white, a pure oval object, a jewel of incalculable worth laid by a Sierra Madre swift, a bird living in the *barrancas,* or steep-sided valleys, mountain slopes, waterfalls, and then there's the money I'll earn that's a reward for the pottery I make, an amalgam of the traditional and the modern, my debt to Mata Ortiz, a *ejido,* not far from the ruins of Casas Grandes, and the city Nuevo Casas Grandes, near Paquimé, but what I'm thinking while I'm driving is what happened to Coyuco and the others, nobody knows where they are or whether they're alive or dead, and it's a real-life factual nonfictional delivery direct from the hands of Cihuacoatl, the most feared and effective of all the goddesses, yes, the legendary rain's started coming down for real, a downpour soaking us through to our souls, going that deep because of the municipal police from Iguala and three units from Cocula, the ministerial police and federal police, the army, the 27th Battalion, working side by side, hand in hand, our night-walking evil spirits, shouting and screaming, not changed into a serpent, or a beautiful young woman, that'd be too shrewd, a sign of mastery talent genius artistry, not likely even in a dream, their methods are more direct, a modern clumsy version of what Cihuacoatl's capable of, they've got power and the right to give orders make decisions enforce obedience, with official permission, and a lot of bullets, Rubén Arenal, sick to his stomach, shuddering with his hands gripping the steering wheel, tight and tighter, chalky white knuckles, feeling as if Cihuacoatl was riding in the passenger seat beside him, popped right out of the bottle of homemade pulque, wearing the face of an ugly municipal policeman from Iguala, and Rocket, shake it off, *'mano,* you've got a place to go and two people to see, even if you don't really know where you're going, the streets taking him more or less south out of Chihuahua, or it was the Suzuki with a mind of its own, on Calle Apicultura past the Díaz building supply store in the Colonia Zootecnia, driving toward the mental hospital off Calle Apicultura, the night falling heavily on the winding and twisting and slithering moonlit road without streetlights, the Suzuki moving on the back of a snake through a landscape of mesquite, silver-leaved guayule shrubs, and ocotillo with its red flowers, and Rocket, I might as well be a resident at *Salud Mental,* and not know it, Rubén Arenal driving toward Mápula, a location in the middle of nowhere, on a plain between the mountain ranges of Santo Domingo and Yerbabuena, cattle territory in the 1880s, it's possible the road he was traveling on didn't exist, as far as he knew there was nothing out there, the old train station, where Don Abraham González, serving Francisco Madero as Secretary of the Interior, arrested by General Antonio Rábago on the orders of Huerta, was murdered with his hands and feet tied to the rails, run over by an engine, *La Decena Trágica,* and the Hacienda of Mápula, two and a half miles from the station to the west, and nothing where he was right now, the Suzuki's engine and cargo keeping him at less than forty miles an hour, the bumpy road didn't make things any easier, he'd borrowed the vehicle after all, and Rocket, caution caution, and respect for a favor, a generous neighbor is a true friend, but Rubén Arenal, distracted by what he could see and what wasn't there before his night-soaked eyes, the headlights' beam bouncing on the potholed road ahead of him, rough rutted, nonexistent, nothing like Mápula, and then snowflakes fluttering down on the windshield of the Suzuki like dried leaves in autumn, Rubén Arenal catching a glimpse of a house surrounded by a low stone wall, set back from the road on the rise of a hill, its roof turning white with snow, he'd seen a photo once of a house just like it in the mountains outside Reno, Nevada, in the high desert at the foot of the Sierra Nevada, and his intuition speaking without a voice, this is it, you can slow down, there's a welcoming driveway ahead of you if you keep your eyes peeled for it, Rubén Arenal turning into the drive, climbing the narrowing access road, hesitating at the private driveway, he stared at a house he'd never seen before, a whole house, not run down or weather beaten, and a corrugated roof covering a place to park a car, a stack of cut wood, more than a cord, at least two, and a tall single street lamp that wasn't on the street but just behind the low wall with what looked like a faintly glowing bulb in the globe throwing almost no light on the house, but it was a gas lamp with a finial, rain shield, a gas lamp spreading a tiny bit of warmth like only a flame could do on a day like this, warm and bright when he left the city, and daylight, too, but here it was like a place out of time, almost night, snowfall, and with the window open, not cold but fresh mountain air, Rubén Arenal inhaling deeply, smelling the smells and hearing the sound of a generous river he couldn't see, a pre-winter unfrozen strong and fast-moving stream of water catching snowflakes like feathers from a night sky, it was out there some-where even if he couldn't see it, Rubén Arenal pulling into the drive and parking under the corrugated roof, turning off the windshield wipers he'd turned on in the sudden snowfall, hearing Pascuala Esparza's words, "you might hear the struggle of the river, even if there isn't a river, maybe wondering if you're hallucinating, but you aren't, trust me, it's there, a path to follow, running ahead, behind, or beside us to show us the way, upstream or down, a squiggly blue line on a map, thick or thin, it doesn't matter, it's a river, and you've got to follow it because it'll lead you to us," Rubén Arenal switched off the Suzuki's engine, stood outside the minitruck, looking up at the sky, his face tickled by snowflakes melting on his skin.

There wasn't anyone answering the door after he'd knocked on it, no doorbell or buzzer to call to the unreachable depths of a house that was a lot bigger than it looked from the side of the road, Rubén Arenal rubbing his hands together, even if he wasn't cold, in an-ticipation of seeing Little Pascuala again more than the hope for a sale, and the river's gurgling sounds, rushing water, bubbling as it struck rocks that got in its way, a river heading rapidly down from the mountain top, turning this way and that, the sounds calling him away from the wooden porch, descending the stairs, dragging his feet in order to feel them on the surface of the earth, not because he was tired or anxious, a simple need to feel he was part of what the house was standing on, what everyone on earth was standing on, this surface or that, enemy or friend, it didn't matter, where else were human beings supposed to go, Rubén Arenal walking around the house, following the voice of the river he couldn't see, no lights showing at the back of the house either, but he knew without knowing it that it was where he was supposed to meet Pascuala Esparza and her daughter, grateful he'd thought to cover his carefully wrapped pottery with a tarp against a high desert climate that included snow, where the snow came from he didn't know, it gave the surrounding landscape a comforting quality he felt in his own blood, a kind of drugged pleasure, not woozy or numbed but fully conscious of movements and thoughts, gliding along the thin layer of slowly increasing snowfall, and Rocket, a motivating song, just a verse, *He llegado aquí, / soy Yoyontzin. / Sólo flores deseo, / ha venido a estar deshojando flores / sobre la tierra. / Allá corto / la flor preciosa, / corto la flor de la amistad: / junto contigo, con tu persona; / ¡oh príncipe! / Yo Nezahualcoyotl, el señor Yoyontzin,* "I'm coming, I, Yoyontzin, craving flowers, hatching flowers here on earth, hatching cacao flowers, hatching comrade flowers. / And they're your flesh, / O prince, / O Lord Nezahualcoyotl, O Yoyontzin," and Rocket, in a lower voice, the flowers are warriors, that's the symbol, and in the rest of the song, a dance, a poem—I've got more pages in my head, it's full full full—Nezahualcoyotl arrives from the other world bringing his flowers-warriors to the dance floor-battlefield, according to John Bierhorst, in the first stanza of song II in *Romances de los Señores de la Nueva España,* and the words of the Aztec *cancionero* giving him courage, the night was dark, the snow was falling, it wasn't cold, and there was no one in sight, and Rocket, the same Nezahualcoyotl on the hundred-peso note, King of Texcoco, poet, scholar, architect, he's called *tlamatini,* "he who knows something," "he who meditates and tells about the enigmas of man on earth, the beyond, and the gods," a voice to listen to, a voice to follow, so I, the maker of pottery, student of Mata Ortiz, a *ejido* not far from the ruins of Casas Grandes, a song of my own is what's missing, I'll have to write one sing one play one one day, but I'm here now to see *La Pascualita*, she'll be a sumptuous stimulant to my song, and then there's the business of selling my pottery, a gift from Xochiquetzal, patroness of craftsmen, protector of painters and artisans, with golden earplugs and a golden ornament in her nose hanging over her mouth, her head crowned with a garland of red leather woven like a braid, round green feather ornaments looking like horns emerging from its side, a divinity wearing a blue tunic decorated with woven flowers made of feathers with plaques of gold all over them, in the words of Fray Diego Durán, and creating the objects I make with my a wedging table fettling knives fluting tools wires paddles ribs and scrappers, a potter's wheel, an electric kiln, or using the coil method, scraping pots with a hacksaw blade to shape them, an inverted flowerpot sagger covered in cottonwood bark, my debt to Mata Ortiz, a gift from Xochiquetzal, it adds up to an honor and my duty, and I'll follow this path that's a river, real or imagined, drawn on earth where it's snowing, until I achieve both targets, Little Pascuala and a memorable transaction on a red-letter day, "for each of the directions of the universe, there's a particular tree; and in the center, another," Ángel María Garibay Kintana, priest, linguist, historian and scholar of the culture of the Nahua peoples of the central Mexican highlands, I don't always know what it means but it means a lot to me just hearing myself say it, not just the words, it's the range scope depth, since what I'm thinking about now makes me blue, and worse, a jab from a needle of heartbroken melancholy, the disappearance of the student teachers, it's ruined everything because I can't go on smiling or talking bullshit when I know a thing like that's happened, leaving me nothing to hold on to, *Entonces el rey respondió y dijo: Dad a aquella el hijo vivo, y no lo matéis; ella es su madre,* "Then the king answered and said, 'Give the living child to the first woman, and by no means put him to death; she is his mother,'" *1 Reyes 3:27,* that's the way it was in the Bible, and that's the way it should be, justice, the one up above will call for an accounting of all that we've done in our lives when he comes down, or we go up, but now it's time for *La Pascualita* and her mother, and selling them more than a fewof what I spend all my time and energy making—how generous they are!—and the unswerving arrow Rubén Arenal, standing at last on the bank next to a flowing river coursing where there was nothing like it on any map, not snow-covered or icy, not resembling an ocean of dry sand with hardscrabble desert plants, a river in the state of Chihuahua, an area of more than ninety-five thousand square miles, where there wasn't a river, and Rocket, now you see it now you don't, Rubén Arenal sniffing the air like Ernesto always did, breathing in its freezing freshness, hearing it seeing it, and if he reached down to dip his hand in it, cold cold cold, he knew he'd remember this river forever.

Rubén Arenal spotting a pair of shadows out there in the snowy landscape, Pascuala Esparza and her daughter, each standing beneath a wide umbrella deflecting snowflakes from their faces but gathering the water vapor frozen into ice crystals and falling in light white flakes on the surface of the circular canopies of black skin stretched above their heads, watching the river's current as it flowed from its faraway source in the mountains, two women, slender and elegant shapes in the whitening terrain beside a half-frozen river bubbling as it rolled hurriedly past them, like spun silk, uninhibited, powerful, and taking small bites out of the river's icy edge, Rubén Arenal lifting one foot after the other from the earth moist from freshly fallen snow, still it wasn't cold, the flakes fell in bunches like flowers thrown out of the sky, a pair of celestial hands up there he couldn't see, but forming a visor out of the palms of his hands, peering at the grayish-black above him, locating nothing that could give him an indication of what kind of sky it was, who was up there, which season it was, not even the time of day, as if where he'd arrived wasn't listed in any time zone except the time zone belonging to Pascuala Esparza and her daughter, only they'd know how to read a clock and set it right in the house where they lived, and as for a compass, finding North South East West, Rubén Arenal didn't bother thinking about it, things appeared the way they were, it wasn't worth coming to any conclusion but the one he'd reached in Chihuahua, and Rocket, to himself, I'm here to see *La Pascualita,* and to sell as many pieces of pottery as I can to mother and daughter, Rubén Arenal cupping his hands on either side of his mouth to help his words carry in a shout to where Pascuala Esparza and her daughter stood gazing at the river, calling out to them, and Rocket, here I am! trying to make his voice heard over the hastening river which, from where they were standing, must've been more like a sustained rumble than a full-on roar of a speeding current, the river wasn't very wide, but enough sound to keep their attention along with the silvery reflection of moonlight on the water's surface, the two women turning their heads, protected from the elements by two umbrellas, *La Pascualita* raising a slight hand, not waving, it looked like she was beckoning with four of her fingers, Pascuala Esparza turning away from his direction, leaving it to her daughter, a gift not resignation, Rubén Arenal continuing toward them as the snowfall rose undeniably on the ground, the soles of his boots slipping, losing his balance, one leg extended far in front of him, but standing upright, an acrobat, pulling a muscle in his thigh, the groin, using one of his hands on the near leg to bring himself into a normal standing position, and Rocket, shouting, it's okay, an artful chance thanks to the snow, meant to show you that I've got more than a single creative skill, "Bend and stretch, reach for the stars / There goes Jupiter, here comes Mars," a little something from *el Norte,* a television show, 1953, originally from Baltimore, franchised and syndicated, not the city but *Romper Room,* Rubén Arenal getting close enough to see the smile on *La Pascualita*'s face, no veil no wide-brimmed hat, but her mother, Pascuala Esparza, standing with her back to him, not unfriendly but preoccupied beneath an umbrella's shadow, his boots crunching in the frozen snow, with or without a cold wind, it was winter, night was near, Rubén Arenal face to face with *La Pascualita,* feeling the edge of Pascuala Esparza's umbrella tickling his neck, and Rocket, I hope when I turn she doesn't poke out my eye, but it's nice to have her close by when I'm standing in front of her daughter, nearest and dearest, a family, Rubén Arenal, searching for words to say to Little Pascuala, ruminated over nothing like the nature of existence but more on the order of how he'd get himself into bed with *La Pascualita* and what her mother would say about it if she had the right to say anything at all, because Little Pascuala wasn't a child, he wasn't a child, and the world wasn't ever going to be like it used to be, he wanted the sale, financing for Ernesto and Guadalupe in their search for Coyuco, as much as he wanted to spend his life with *La Pascualita*, Rubén Arenal rushing ahead of himself, but a dose of timidity, and an attractive clumsiness, awkward in his movements when he was nervous, Pascuala Esparza at last turning around from her contemplation of the coursing river with its ragged icy edges, the twirl of the umbrella sending a shiver down his spine as it brushed against the back of his neck, now the three of them were in a little circle, and Pascuala Esparza, looking at her daughter, we've seen what we have to see, haven't we, *niña,* my child? and it isn't cold, the snowflakes are like tissues, soft and smooth, but our señor Arenal, our maestro, not a novice, he's got exalted examples of his work to sell us, and it's time time time for the sublime, pottery of such excellence, grandeur, or beauty as to inspire great admiration or awe, *La Pascualita* taking Rubén Arenal by the elbow, drawing him under the canopy of her umbrella, encouraging him forward on the slippery snow while tucking her hand into the crook of the left arm he'd bent just for her, Pascuala Esparza following closely behind, conscious of the danger of the tips of her umbrella's folding metal frame, no stabbing no gouging, revered Rubén Arenal entered the back of the house through a door almost blocked by a heap of snow blown by a sudden gust of wind that preceded them.

The swerve that gets you out of the hole, a dog sniffing your shoes, Pascuala Esparza putting her damp folded umbrella in the umbrella stand alongside *La Pascualita*'s umbrella shaken free of moisture before stepping over the heap of snow, not through it, and over the threshold into the house, and Pascuala Esparza, like I was saying, it's the swerve that gets you out of the hole or around the dog sniffing your shoes, we just missed stepping straight in running straight into that pile of snow gathered all of a sudden at our door, ruining our shoes, my shoes and yours, our delicate shoes that might've cost us six months earnings if we had a job, but we don't, money isn't anything for us, in this time and out of it, isn't that so, *niña*, my child? and Little Pascuala, and don't forget our estimable guest—the two women looking down at Rubén Arenal's boots, damp where the soles met the uppers, a little water-stained but in good shape, wiping them dry on the indoor floor mat, a product by WeatherTech, or a simple rug—and Pascuala Esparza, a daughter whose lips move, a daughter whose voice's heard above the din, I'll hand over transfer relay my right of speech to my daughter, there wasn't a loud, unpleasant, and prolonged noise when they entered, the house was quiet, peaceful, a little humid, but there was the weather to account for that, and Rocket, to himself, a bit too chilly if you ask me, but the chill's only here or there, in one corner or another, in front of a door that's shut, not everywhere, hotspots that're cold, grinning at his little joke, Little Pascuala and her mother, off with their identical long dark red cotton coats, hung up to dry but not near a fire, there wasn't a chimney where the three of them were standing, maybe in the next room, but Rubén Arenal didn't see one, peering down a passageway through an open door into a room for general and informal everyday use, and Little Pascuala, your smile is welcome, refreshing agreeable promising, my praiseworthy person, Rubén Arenal noticing right away she'd substituted the word *our* with the word *my*, and Rocket, you can call me Rocket, my closest friends do, when they don't call me Rubén, señor Arenal's more formal, but Rubén's a name I like, always liked, a gift from my father and mother, "behold, a son," the name given the oldest son of Jacob and Leah, that's the Old Testament, but here, under this roof and in these circumstances, call me Rocket, because all roads are long and improbable, and I suspect even our dreams won't be revealing, that's how it is, here and now, *ahora y aquí,* and Pascuala Esparza, wisdom can hardly be termed a virtue, for it's made up of intellectual qualities one man has and another not, Rubén Arenal looking at them as though for the first time, Little Pascuala and her mother, each elegantly dressed in traditional clothes, *La Pascualita* wearing a *chincuete,* from the Nahuatl, *tzincueitl,* a pleated knee-length skirt of satin and lace worn by Mazahua women in the state of Mexico, the Mazahua, *tetjo ñaa jñatjo,* "those who speak their own language," "the owners of deer," and beneath the *chincuete,* an underskirt with an embroidered edge showing, a *quechquemitl,* meaning "tip of the neck" in Nahuatl, a kind of shawl, and a woven sash worn around her waist, the center of energy, an energy relating to Mother Earth, a sash decorated with plenty of birds, Rubén Arenal not seeing the solitary bird with a thorn in its leg, a sign of spiritual pain, not seeing anything but her beauty, his eyes examining Pascuala Esparza's long skirt with ribbons, a long blouse embroidered at the bottom and around the neck, a belt strapped on the back, a dark blue rebozo with narrow pale stripes and orange knotted fringes, *rapacejos,* and a reddish apron, traditional dress not from the state of Mexico, but Michoacán, Rubén Arenal and a coincidence, both women wore clothes from places where the Mazahua people live, San Felipe del Progresso and San José del Rincón in the state of Mexico, near Toluca, and in parts of Michoacán, even Querétaro, and Guadalajara in Jalisco, according to migration, economics, and the passage of time, Rubén Arenal, a quick investigation of their faces, a peek, the once-over without staring, their features weren't easy for him to identify, faces describing the history of much-loved Mexico, and Rocket, I'm straight out of a *casta* painting, too, an illustration of a stratified social system trying to impose an objectionable odious order based on ethnic inequality in the Spanish possessions, *los españoles,* the Spanish colonial state and the Church, *etiquetas,* the flaws of time, stains of loss, inaccurate or restrictive, *morisco con española, chino con india, mestizo con español, castizo con española, español con mulata, español con negra, indio con mestiza,*

in all our faces—what does it matter now? it might to some, but
not others, not me not now—but Little Pascuala and her mother,
milk-white skin almost colorless, deathly pale, and *una enfermedad del fantasma, una enfermedad de fantasmas,* a ghost disease,
a disease of ghosts, but they look healthy enough, *La Pascualita,* a
beauty without a veil, they're part of me, I'm part of them, a tie, a
link, Rubén Arenal averting his gaze, he'd seen all he had to see, and
what he saw he appreciated very much, the beginning of friendship,
too, Rubén Arenal following the two women down the passageway
into the living room, standing at one of the windows, looking out
at the snow falling on the earth, and a vague outline that was the
river's edge, winding bending, and Rocket, to himself, "it's not a
question of poverty, a man's word is enough, we are all poor, when
a man gives his word to another at a great distance … the one who
gave his word must keep it," Mohammed Mrabet wrote it in a letter, and I believe in these words, that's what I'm doing, keeping my
word knowing they'll keep theirs, turning to Pascuala Esparza and
her daughter, and Rocket, I've got everything in the minitruck,
pottery protected like precious stones under the corrugated roof,
and Pascuala Esparza, you'd better go out the front door, it's closer
to your vehicle in these times of inclement weather, our luminous
luminary, and a real-life royal Rubén Arenal, what I mean is that
we respect you so much, like a persistent rain, the slow surprise
of respect swollen with pride, your work, and who you are, what I
mean is it goes without saying, but I've said it, out it comes from between my lips, a fountain, we know everything about you, don't we,
niña, my child? Rubén Arenal blushing, her heartfelt words touching him, there wasn't any derision in her voice, no charade, it's how
they treated him, and Rocket, without moving his lips, I'm better
placed here than anywhere in the world, at least for today, and like
the Arabic proverb, "The world is like a cucumber—today it's in
your hand, tomorrow up your arse," and *La Pascualita,* a song to
accompany you on your journey to and from the minitruck, "Viviré
para ti," "I'll Live For You," by Agustín Lara, sung by Antonio Badú,
born in Real del Monte, Hidalgo:

Viviré para ti,
nada más para ti,
para ti viviré
mientras pueda vivir.

Viviré para ti solamente
nada más para ti, ¡para ti!
¡Y seré para ti únicamente
aunque tú nunca seas para mí!

Yo quisiera esconder mis angustias,
en tu boca color carmesí,
y secando tus lágrimas mustias,
viviré nada más para ti.

I will live for you,
nothing more for you,
for you I will live
as long as I can live.

I will live for you alone,
nothing more for you, for you!
And I will be for you alone
although you'll never be for me!

I'd like to hide my anguish,
in your crimson mouth,
and dry your sad tears,
living only for you.

Rubén Arenal bowing as Little Pascuala accompanied him to the door, the music taking him out of it into the snowy night, a night that wasn't cold, but no explanation, there was snowfall that fell in the high mountains, but Pascuala Esparza and her daughter didn't live in the high mountains, but the foothills, that was the way to describe where he was right now, even if the setting, the house itself, looked like a picture of a house he'd seen in the mountains outside Reno, Nevada, Rubén Arenal standing beneath the corrugated roof protecting him from a heavy snowfall, the overloaded bed of the truck covered by a waterproof tarp, he started by rolling back the tarp, reaching for pottery bundled and protected by rags and crumpled newspapers, carrying them to the open front door, Pascuala Esparza and her daughter weren't anywhere in sight, but he smelled meat cooking on a grill or baking in an oven.

The second time he went out the front door, moving back and forth between the house and the Suzuki, the Suzuki and the house, he returned with only the hand-woven Saltillo rugs from the state of Coahuila, or from Teotitlán del Valle, each tied with string, untying them now, spreading them out on the living room floor, wanting to present his work in the best light and on fine hand-woven materials in a pattern of colors and a traditional style, but he'd forgotten the bottle of homemade pulque on the passenger seat of the Suzuki, still no sign of *La Pascualita* or her mother, the odor of grilled onions joined the smell of cooking meat, it might've been a real breakfast in the afternoon, *machaca con huevos,* grilled dried spiced beef, eggs, tomatoes, chopped onion, salsa, or they were preparing a kind of Jalisco *birria,* a spicy lamb stew, or *picadillo,* salted pot roast beef with onion and garlic, shredding the meat, sautéing diced onion and chopped green tomatillos, adding the meat, and later a sauce of *guajillo* chiles, or a simple *carne asada,* marinated flank steak, sliced and grilled, burritos with wheat-flour tortillas, refried beans, red rice, *salsa verde,* a little smoke in the air, whatever it was it smelled delicious, Rubén Arenal, his mouth watering, hoping no saliva fell on an ashtray, a pitcher, a bowl for fruit, a mug for coffee, a mug for *posol,* as he carefully unpacked them all and set them out on the hand-woven rugs he'd brought with him, not knowing before now that he was hungry, laying the objects out to show them to their best advantage, the smells from the kitchen pouring over him, moving three tall Japanese paper *kaku-andon* lamps toward the Saltillo hand-woven rugs so the soft beams of atmospheric light fell diagonally across all the pieces of pottery, a caressing hand, and Rocket, I listen to them in the kitchen like I listen to the rain, but now the snow's falling silent as the slain, the *normalistas*, I can't hear them breathing, all the disappeared, I'd like to free them, at least their souls, but I can't find them anywhere, not even in my clothes, but if I reach into pockets that aren't sewn shut—Rubén Arenal interrupting himself, there was nothing like a *normalista* in his pockets, bulging with keys, chewing gum, loose change, folding money, but no student teachers, he knew it before he looked but he didn't think it wasn't worth a try, and Rocket, because after all who knows and what've I got to lose, I'll look anywhere—there's always the chance, but even a human being burned to a crisp wouldn't fit into a man's trouser pocket, and another trip to the Suzuki, followed by another until he'd emptied it and brought everything inside and laid each piece out for Pascuala Esparza and her daughter to look at.

Little Pascuala carrying a platter of hot food into the dining room, Rubén Arenal standing as she came in, watching her go straight to the table, putting the platter with marinated flank steak, sliced and grilled, a stack of wheat-flour tortillas, a bowl of refried beans, another of red rice, no cheese, a bowl of *salsa verde,* a bowl of *salsa roja* made with *chile morita,* smoked jalapeño, and Pascuala Esparza right behind her, plates and serving spoons and napkins, and a table laid out, Little Pascuala returning with glasses and bottles of beer, Noche Buena, and Pascuala Esparza, I've got a case of it I saved from Christmas, and the snow, a delicate balance between its present age, the beer, and a lost one, where we are now, neither here nor there, but somewhere special, isn't that right, *niña,* my child? but I promised to leave the talking to my daughter, what I mean is I'll have less to say when my mouth's full, what I mean is it smells good doesn't it, and it tastes better, we've prepared our best for you, our authority, champion, virtuoso potter, so sit down and dig in as the unrefined uneducated *gabachos* say, *La Pascualita* pouring him a glass of beer, the dreamy odor of the grilled marinated flank steak, from another world, a better world, was floating in the air like he'd seen it float in the air in a cartoon, the weather outside, out of time, another world, too, Rubén Arenal taking a bite of his burrito, a lot of salsa verde, and a swallow of beer tasting like Christmas day, and Rocket, aren't you going to eat, I can't eat on my own, it isn't polite, and you've made all this food, which is so good my mouth's watering while I'm chewing it, Pascuala Esparza and her daughter shaking their heads no at the same time in the same rhythm, mechanical dolls that weren't machine-driven but full of life, emotion, and a scent he couldn't identify, a floating fragrance drawing him to daughter and mother, an aroma impossible to escape in a house surrounded by a low stone wall, set back from the road on the rise of a hill, its roof white with snow, just like the house he'd seen in a photo taken in the mountains outside Reno, in the high desert at the foot of the Sierra Nevada, and the more he ate and drank, another burrito with plenty of salsa, adding spoonfuls of *salsa roja* made with *chile morita*, a blaze in his belly and fire in his heart, a second beer, then a third, his head feeling like the beer he was drinking was laced with a very strong pulque, something hallucinogenic, Rubén Arenal wiping perspiration from his face with a handkerchief, Pascuala Esparza and her daughter, the very pleasant and pleasing Little Pascuala, mother and daughter not touching a forkful of beans, meat, rice, no wheat-flour tortillas, but through unfocused eyes it seemed they were drinking from tall glasses, icy cold, tequila mixed with Jarritos-brand *toronja*? clinking ice and sweating glasses, Rubén Arenal observing them, not staring outright, a subtle raising of the eyes now and then while putting the brakes on his stomach-driven single-minded tunnel vision of bountiful beef burritos and Noche Buena, and a reciprocal street-crossing eye to eye with *La Pascualita,* and Rocket, to himself, I see you and you see me, she doesn't miss a beat of my pulse, she can probably hear it, a beat that carries, and she isn't sitting in another room, not far away, but right here right there, within arm's reach and fingers' grasp, Little Pascuala tuned in, effortlessly adjusting to the frequency of the required signal, *nos telepateamos,* our telepathy, signals signals signals, something like a gesture, action, or sound used to convey information or instructions—I can't quite read them now, but there's time ahead of us—by prearrangement between the parties concerned, that's me, and *La Pascualita,* you can throw Pascuala Esparza into it, too, since nothing would've happened without her, no letter, no meeting at my pottery studio, and then there's the fifteen-year-old kid—"maybe I look fifteen years old, but you know and I know that I haven't got an age, only the years your mind wants to give me"—and Nezahualcoyotl's face on a crumpled hundred-peso note, Rubén Arenal and more of the kid's words, "to know our past is to place ourselves firmly in the present, señor Arenal, the future is a secret," and Rocket, a boy with wisdom range insight, you couldn't tell as much by looking at him, and for the moment Rubén Arenal was forgetting or not needing to rub the calluses on the palm of his right hand, returning to the present and the genuine conjugation between himself and *La Pascualita,* apparently unavoidable, and Rocket, but no possession's worth much when there's nothing to spend, so I'll spend what I've got which is who I am, Rubén Arenal and a mouthful of refried beans, red rice, *salsa roja* and grilled flank steak in a wheat-flour tortilla, but his skin, inside and out, was parched and cracked since Coyuco and the other *normalistas* disappeared, forty-three and Coyuco, whose fault was it? the student leaders, the politicians, the military and police, he could hear his own silent shrieks given to grieving stones, and Rocket, a variation on Ecclesiastes 10:9-11, my mind's alert, Rubén Arenal convinced of everyone's misfortune, high and low, and frightened as well, split down the middle, suffering and pleasure, he was in love with Little Pascuala, but his ripped-out soul, as it came out of his mouth, claw marks leaving bloody scratches in his throat, always thinking of Coyuco and the others, and Rocket, no one's safe these days, if it weren't for God, we'd all be dead, I pray to Nuestra Señora de los Dolores because she's Our Lady of Sorrows, and always a handful of prayers to Nuestra Señora de Guadalupe,

Mother of all Mexico, how are the parents brothers sisters wives girl-friends going to live when they've got to live without them, because if you ask me they're dead and gone, *La Pascualita* reading his mind, reaching across the table, taking his hand in hers, Pascuala Esparza turning her head away, ladylike behavior, respectful and considerate of others, Rubén Arenal catching a glint of light and unspoken signs in Little Pascuala's eyes, and a little music to go along with the moment, "Contestación a mujer paseada," "Answer To An Easy Woman," by Manuel C. Valdez, sung by Juanita and María Mendoza, return of the old duet, Hermanas Mendoza, a powerful testimony of female independence and agency, a personal response to a two-faced false and slanderous statement made in a song by her former lover:

> *Si fueras hombre formal*
> *no andarías divulgando.*
> *Si me quieres como dices*
> *¿Para qué lo estás contando?*
>
> *Si he sido mujer paseada*
> *es porque a mí me ha gustado.*
> *Pero del hombre que es hombre*
> *nunca jamás me he burlado.*
>
> *Si yo te llegué a querer*
> *fue porque nunca pensaba*
> *que anduvieras difamando*
> *a la mujer que te amaba.*
>
> *A los hombres como tú*
> *pronto les doy su cortada,*
> *porque yo tengo palabra*
> *aunque sea mujer paseada.*

Grito:
¿Y tú, qué dijistes ya?
¡Pero no se pudo, chiquitito!

Si fueras hombre formal
no andarías divulgando.
Si me quieres como dices
¿Para qué lo estás contando?

Si he sido mujer paseada
es porque a mí me ha gustado.
Pero del hombre que es hombre
nunca jamás me he burlado.

Si yo te llegué a querer
fue porque nunca pensaba
que anduvieras difamando
a la mujer que te amaba.

A los hombres como tú
pronto les doy su cortada,
porque yo tengo palabra
aunque sea mujer paseada.

If you were an upright man,
you wouldn't go around making it all
public.
If you love me like you say you do,
why do you go around telling stories?

If I've been an "easy woman,"
it's because I've enjoyed it.
But of the man who's a real man
I've never ever tried to make a fool.

If I ever came to love you,
it was because I never thought
that you would go ruining the reputation
of the woman who loved you.

Men like you,
I cut them off quick,
because I keep my word,
even though I may be an "easy woman."

Shout:
And you, what do you say now?
But you just couldn't do it, could you,
"little boy"?

If you were an upright man,
you wouldn't go around making it all
public.
If you love me like you say you do,
why do you go around telling stories?

If I've been an "easy woman,"
it's because I've enjoyed it.
But of the man who's a real man
I've never ever tried to make a fool.

If I ever came to love you,
it was because I never thought
that you would go ruining the reputation
of the woman who loved you.

Men like you,
I cut them off quick,
because I keep my word,
even though I may be an "easy woman."

That's what Rubén Arenal heard, Little Pascuala, too, a shared instant of melodious music, a complementary coloring to the touching of hands, away from the dusty plains and distant seas and the snow falling outside like it was winter when he knew it wasn't winter in Mexico but only here and here alone in the neighborhood of Pascuala Esparza and her daughter's house, resembling a house he'd seen in a photograph taken in the high desert at the foot of the Sierra Nevada, Rubén Arenal having arrived there on a rough rutted road, nonexistent, with snowflakes fluttering down on the windshield of the Suzuki, not knowing what to expect and certainly not expecting what was happening right now before his eyes, something preventing him from giving his full attention to the sensation of her fingers touching his skin, it wasn't the music, he was catching more than light right now, Rubén Arenal looking at Pascuala Esparza, a change of clothes without changing clothes, Pascuala Esparza wearing a white blouse with embroidery around the neck and on the sleeves, Rubén Arenal wiping his face with a handkerchief that didn't succeed in removing his doubts, she wasn't wearing what she'd been wearing a minute earlier, and Rocket, to himself, how the world turns and the people with it going around and around interchangeable and never the same dissimilar twins new and unfamiliar, and there's got to be something in the Noche Buena, Rubén Arenal dropping his napkin on the floor, looking up under the table at Pascuala Esparza's long dark blue skirt with stripes of embroidered flowers in vivid colors at the waist and near the bottom, a traditional skirt from Tabasco, sure that what he was seeing on her now wasn't what she'd been wearing then, Rubén Arenal straightening up with a worried look on his face, not trying to hide it, and Rocket, what's the point in dissimulated truth when honesty's my goal, I don't care what they think of what they see that's written on my face, but perilous perilous, as certain as a tail will follow a comet, she wasn't wearing that when she came into the room, but not a word from *La Pascualita* nor her mother, he was rubbing his eyes, shutting and opening them as quickly as he could, but the sweeping lids swept nothing away, he saw what he saw when his eyes were open wide, then Pascuala Esparza nudging her daughter, her lips were moving, but there wasn't a sound, Rubén Arenal swearing he heard the words, "destiny is nothing but a trickster demon," but not wanting to give the words any importance, Rubén Arenal under their spell if there was one, a silent incantation from the very start, not a hex but an enchantment, or it was the weight of the second burrito and three bottles of Noche Buena turning against him, turning his head, but love was love, and he was here where they were living, and Rocket, to himself, a sale's what's called for if the fruits are put to good use, but now, look here, *La Pascualita*, it's her turn if it's turns they're taking, Little Pascuala wearing a dress typical of Chiapas, handmade in the town of Chiapa de Corzo, Rubén Arenal, a fount of knowledge, forcing himself to stay in his chair, dropping his napkin again to get a good look, Little Pascuala in a handmade wide black skirt with a full decoration of stripes with colorful flowers embroidered in silk, flowers symbolizing the region's diversity, representing the jungle, mother and daughter, their clothes changing from one moment to the next, this region or that, without lifting a finger, he was struck by a figurative hammer with a large wooden head, startled out of his chair, and standing up so fast his chair tipped over, Pascuala Esparza offering him a smile, raising her glass, tequila and grapefruit soda, the ice cubes clinking, Rubén Arenal staring at the overturned chair, his eyes returning to Pascuala Esparza's smile, then looking at *La Pascualita*, love with lyrical eyes, but now Pascuala Esparza, a long-sleeved high-collar simple white shirt, and Rocket, now you see it now you see it, a shirt without embroidery around the neck and on the sleeves, Rubén Arenal setting his chair upright, a moment of embarrassment, shaking his head and catching his breath, then bending at the waist, a foolish act, an indiscretion, no furtive glances sneaking out of the corner of the eye, like it or not he had to do it, another peek under the table, Little Pascuala's mother dressed in an ankle-length skirt with horizontal stripes decorating the bottom, an example of turn-of-the-century Chihuahua, and Rocket, if this keeps happening I'm going to throw up, not from the spinning in my head but from the switching of their clothes at such high speed, remarkable transformations for a pair of stationary statuettes sitting in chairs, Pascuala Esparza gracefully wiping her lips with a lace napkin, and then it was *La Pascualita*'s turn, Little Pascuala wearing a dress with a huipil blouse, black thread embroidery around a square collar, Rubén Arenal, before sitting down again, peering beneath the surface of the table at the ankle-length dress in the Campeche style that she was wearing, and Rocket, okay enough is enough, I won't look again, pressing his napkin against his mouth, a filter against the noxious fumes that must've been affecting his head, but the napkin didn't change anything, a last glance at Little Pascuala's delicate crossed ankles, no stockings or shoes, a seductive siren from Mexico, not Greece, alluring and fascinating, dangerous in some way, and *La Pascualita,* it's comfortable without shoes in a house that's your own, each time we go our own way, we carry a piece of the other, mother and daughter, our feet without shoes are more sensitive to each step, forward or backward, between identical beings, I'm speaking for both of us, and Rocket, not a word from Pascuala Esparza, less talkative than the last time he'd seen her at the pottery studio, leaving the words to her daughter, now wearing a white wide waving skirt with embroidery and lace, a white blouse, a black apron with embroidered flowers, a shawl, and three flowers on the left side of her head, meaning that she's single, typical of the state of Veracruz, Rubén Arenal regaining his place at the table, reaching for another serving of meat, beans, rice, *salsa verde,* not *salsa roja* made with *chile morita,* and a tortilla, pouring himself another beer that stayed ice cold without an ice cube or ice bucket, and Rocket, a rigorous reminder, a mental note, what can be obtained in this life without payment? everything must be paid for, or redeemed, even the shortest happiness.

Little Pascuala leading him away from the table to the living room, his belly full of burritos and his lips still wet from the head of a Noche Buena that'd left a mustache he didn't wipe from beneath his nose, Pascuala Esparza nowhere in sight, the hand-woven Saltillo rugs, from the state of Coahuila, or Teotitlán del Valle, laid out before them on the living room floor, a presentation in the best light and on fine hand-woven materials, Little Pascuala turning to face him, using the back of her index finger to wipe the foam from his upper lip, licking it from her own fingertip, then making an elegant and discreet long curving movement with her hand to indicate the range of pottery he brought for them, a set of different objects of the same general virtuosic type, and *La Pascualita,* the value of people and things truly depends on their setting, your pottery's magically magnificent, delightful in such a way as to seem removed from everyday life, and here we are, you and I, in another world, and not only thanks to the works you've brought to our modest home, Rubén Arenal appreciating himself, Little Pascuala raising him from artisan to artist, putting them on a more equal social footing, his head swelling without changing shape, just on the inside, but a greatly gratified and gracious Rubén Arenal standing still, a smile on his face, divine grace, like he'd been praying to a new Virgin in the church who could work miracles, and then *La Pascualita,* taking him by the hand, a wide welcoming hallway ahead of them, he hadn't noticed it before, but he'd been looking less and feeling more since they'd arrived in the living room, on the right-hand side halfway down the passage a door, and the door opened without anyone touching it, swinging on silent hinges, Rubén Arenal stumbling, his own left foot catching on the sill or threshold where there was nothing in his path on which to trip, momentarily losing his balance, trying to get in his own way, a subliminal screw-up, but letting Little Pascuala lead him into the room, and Rocket, look after me, *Virgencita,* look after both of us, and the *normalistas,* too, past and present, he hadn't lost touch with the all-around inner feeling or voice acting as guide to the rightness of his behavior, a blanket of principles values morals joining him as he wrapped his arms around Little Pascuala, Rubén Arenal looking at his surroundings, it wasn't a bedroom, there wasn't any furniture but a mattress on the floor and several paper lamps in a Japanese style, *andon*, popular in the Edo period, elaborate *ariake-andon*, or bedside lamps, or *bonbori*, with its hexagonal profile, standing on a pole in two corners on one side of the room, like in the Room of Storks in the Nishi Hongan-ji, Western Temple of the Original Vow in Kyoto, northwest of Kyoto Station, his lips numb, not cold, but tingling when they came in contact with *La Pascualita's* lips, his head was heavy, his nose and mouth breathing in silvery smoke from censers swinging invisibly nearby, the tattoo of a maguey wide awake on his stomach, and Rocket, Our Lady of the Sacred Heart, pray for us, pray for us, Little Pascuala's arms wrapped around him, her hands clasped behind his neck, drawing his face toward hers, and *La Pascualita*, whispering, *Nuestra Señora del Sagrado Corazón*, you're right to pray, señor Arenal, Our Lady of the Sacred Heart is ageless, just like my mother and I, we're eternal, we never grow old, in the words of Wordsworth, we're "continuous as the stars that shine," a handy little phrase for the sky at night, above us now, but you're of this earth, the present, today and this night, our virtuoso, enchanter, authority, and genius, Little Pascuala wearing nothing, not a veil, not dressed in an example of the Campeche style or a dress typical of Chiapas, *La Pascualita* and the skin she wore when she was born, a thin layer of tissue forming the natural outer covering of her body, yesterday and today and forever, Rubén Arenal's talented hands not getting enough of the feel of her skin, collecting evidence of what was impossible to measure, an hour passed, or it was four, Rubén Arenal lying on top of her now, straightening up and looking down at her neck shoulders hips, his back arched like a curved piece of wood whose ends were joined by a taut string, Little Pascuala stretched out facedown beneath him, arms extended above her head, reaching reaching, her buttocks temptingly twitching, enticing him, and Rocket, I've been under the influence of a powerful attraction for who knows how long, *La Pascualita* rocking her hips, moving them from right to left left to right like she was waging her tail, but nothing like it protruded from the opening at the end of the alimentary canal, Rubén Arenal's pulsating penis waiting patiently, Little Pascuala slowly sliding backward on her belly, edging toward him, not a jaguar that's putting the fear of God into him, and contact, a shiver shared between them, contact again, penetration as he settled himself between her buttocks, her opulent opening opening for him, giving way easily, a yawn on a small scale, a consensual quivering, *La Pascualita* and Rubén Arenal feeling a pair of eyes fixed on them, pinned on the two entwined bodies bound intricately together, not uncommon but always nice to look at, each protecting the other, serpents and their eggs, Rubén Arenal and *La Pascualita* twisted together under a watchful gaze, eyes they couldn't see but felt, not burning a hole in them but warming up the place more than the heat was already turned up, a lot of sweat, damp skin and no friction, Rubén Arenal sliding into her deeper and deeper, insinuating himself, on her invitation, disappearing between the half-moons, and Rocket, you can't resist them, not only thanks to the subtle light from two *ariake-andon*, or the *bonbori*, standing on a pole in two corners on one side of the room, throwing shadows on the two round fleshy parts before my eyes that form the lower rear area of Little Pascuala's body, Rubén Arenal traveling through her intestines, waving at the womb, past her hips to her stomach, a glance at the liver, moving into her chest, a good evening nod along the corridor of her throat, trachea and esophagus, and far out into the heart of places where no one goes, until he thought if she turned around to look at him he'd see his penis piloting out of her mouth.

The screen-fold *Codex Borgia*'s one of the most beautiful and elegant pre-Columbian painted manuscripts, with its detailed depiction of highland Mesoamerican gods and the ritual and the practice of seeking knowledge of the future or the unknown by supernatural means associated with them, an ancient manuscript probably painted somewhere in central or southern Puebla, the area around Tepeaca and Cuauhtinchan, or the Tehuacán Valley, in our

southeastern Mexico, just decades before the arrival of the Spanish—
and you can add the nearby areas of Mixteca Alta in Oaxaca, too,
who can say? it's what the experts think—and in the manuscript, it's
the long supernatural journey that interests me most, we're travelers
who pass between different times, beginning with the five enclosures that serve to make supernatural statements, the story starting
on Plate 29—in that book maybe not in others—the first of several
enclosures formed by the body of a goddess of death, because that's
where I am, rising out of the dark foamy substance emerging from
the large blue vessel on the large black disk, take a closer look, I'm
one of the animate creatures characterized as winds, you can tell by
the features of Quetzalcoatl, there, right there, on my face, can you
see it? and in addition to the many winds, there're two skeletal figures, one a god of death, the other a depiction of Tlazolteotl as the
earth below the blue vessel, in my case three skeletons because I left
three dead bodies behind me, and the fact is, there's nothing as ti-
tanic as the shameful disgraceful dishonorable unforgivable
behavior of a man who throws away what he believes in, just like
that—I'd snap my fingers but you wouldn't hear it—and now I've
got to live with it, I'm exactly like the enemy, those motherfuckers,
but I'm not wearing the same clothes, not now, I had to change back
into my own, get rid of the uniform that was a real job of stitching,
needle and thread, and I ditched the hat, holster and Glock, too, but
when I killed them, that's when I was dressed like they were dressed,
one killer looks just like another, it wasn't so long ago, but you don't
need me to remind you—what's well known is that everything isn't
known to everyone—I was one of them as far as they could tell, the
three officers of the municipal police, and right now, as I'm dressed
today, same day different clothes, no uniform, I burned it, and
dumped the rest, but I've got to live with it because that's what happened, three dead men because I lost my temper, a kind of hell,
that's where I'm going if I'm not already there, I can feel it, maybe
that's why I'm sweating, everybody says it's hot down there, a hell
with plenty of room for me, here's the lamp, there's the armchair,

nicely furnished, no books, my only luxury a photograph by Agustín Casasola, I can't decide which one, there're so many great pictures, but probably a prisoner, a young man with his hat in his hand—I'm not flattering myself, not at my age—arrested by a couple of policemen, a man on the beat in uniform, and an officer holding a revolver, surrounded by a bevy of bystanders in the background, a photograph from around 1930, fitting appropriate suitable, isn't it? my place in hell, not stepping out of my experience, I'll never get far away from what I've done, here's my wrist, you can take my pulse, you'll see I'm almost there, a resident of the beyond, the region of the dead, but walking on two legs, upright and miserable, not in good shape and it's only been a couple of hours, maybe more, since I killed them, but what can I do, it's done, Ernesto looking at himself in the mirror of the bathroom in Hotel Obregón, not far from Periférico Sur, the bright blue and white façade, an orange spiral staircase to the first floor, a modern design that made his eyes water, not tears of joy, and Ernesto Cisneros, but the tears falling right now, that's because I killed three men, *suerte y mortaja del cielo bajan,* life and death come down from Heaven, but I gave death a helping hand, Ernesto, no longer looking at himself in the mirror, head bowed, looking at his boots, Ernesto raising his head, revealing an almost diabolical expression, without blinking, but seeing nothing, or he didn't see himself when he faced the mirror, only a bright blur the color of horror, which he couldn't describe even if he wanted to, a radiant color generating hellish heat, not nice to look at, and he wanted nothing more than to turn back the clock, not only to a time before Coyuco disappeared, and the other *normalistas,* too, but to a minute, an instant before he spread his arms like wings, reached around officer No. 2's waist, drawing him closer, belly to belly, holding him there in a kind of embrace, but no affection, only hatred, unholstering officer No. 2's .38 Special, and firing a round, then another, into his guts, turning on his heel, firing a shot between the eyes of policeman No. 1, then firing a couple of bullets into officer No. 3's chest and neck, and Ernesto Cisneros, okay, turning it back more than a minute, seeing as I might've thought more about what I wanted to do here in Iguala to find my son, and the uniform, even if I made it myself, time and skillful hands, the uniform had an influence on my body, and lesson number one: if you look like a member of the *Policía Municipal,* you're going to act like one, but don't forget, if you don't use your head you aren't using thought or rational judgment, I came here to find out what happened to Coyuco, and now without thinking, I've given the nightmare of the century to myself, my wife, Lupita, and anyone like me who's started off to do something they think is right driven by a force that sounds a lot like there's no choice anyway don't waste time you've got something to do and if you don't do it you'll lose what's left of your mind so get going step on it get cracking get a move on it's your duty obligation and a moral imperative, yes, that's a nightmare you can't shake off like water, entrusted as we are with the timely task of burrowing a tunnel into the painful mournful miserable sad, no matter what's at the end of it, we'll know no rest and won't know any until we've righted the wrong that's been done, remember, "a man sent on a pious mission shall meet with no evil," we've got our hopes and dreams, the parents, aunts, uncles, wives, girlfriends, brothers and sisters of the *normalistas* who've vanished, gone up in smoke, swallowed by the mouth of Mictlan, a reverse journey into a mother's womb, traveling there with the help of the Techichi, a small, mute red dog of the Toltec people, reaching Chicunauhmictlan, the ninth hell, where the lords of night rule over the affairs of men, and the souls of the dead stay for eternity, but the student teachers were thrown there, not led, no volunteers, murdered—stand back, watch out! I shouldn't let my thoughts come out in words—yes, we've got our hopes and dreams, *Adiós O Madre,* maybe I've lost my faith in the Virgin, maybe I haven't, but does the *Virgen del Sagrado Corazón* love a murderer, it isn't like I've just ruined a recipe for *chiles en nogada,* created in 1821 by nuns in Puebla, I feel things growing out of my twice-damaged heart, but they aren't natural things, I don't know what they are, they'll do tests in a lab, my hollow muscular organ pumping blood through the circulatory system by rhythmic contraction and dilation, two atria and two ventricles, a tiny ash tree, two jacarandas, and a pepper tree growing there right now, I can feel the pull on the outside of my heart, and the Mother Mountains of the West are the Sierra Madre Occidental of Mexico, you can read it in a book, their mountain tops gather in the clouds, their slopes send water rushing over cliffs and down deep and wide canyons, and to the east the water finds it's way to the fertile farms of Hidalgo del Parral and Ciudad Chihuahua before continuing an ocean-bound voyage by way of Río Bravo, and in the Sierra Tarahumara, the land of the Rarámuri, a small part of that great mountain wall of northwestern Mexico, I've been there many times, this or that side of the Continental Divide, it doesn't matter where I stand, I know them like I know my right hand and my left, *Ah, pero yo era más viejo entonces, / soy más joven ahora,* "Ah, but I was so much older then / I'm younger than that now," look at them, one at a time, inspect them closely, these hands, I'll hold them in the light, take a good look at them, smooth skin, a few age spots, and this one, the right hand, the same hand that gripped the Glock, and an index finger that squeezed the trigger of a .38 Special, I saw a lot of pines in El Cañón del Cobre, evergreen coniferous trees that have clusters of long needle-shaped leaves, it's the needles that're piercing my heart, not an ash tree, a couple of jacarandas, or a pepper tree, and there's that little matter of the jaguar, it's put the fear of God into me, a terrible thing, slender and silent, thin enough to creep through the veins in my arms and legs, tickling my subclavian vein, a continuation of the axillary vein, or on the other side, an itch in my cephalic vein, communicating with the basilic vein via the median cubital vein, and I don't mean talking, a jaguar stalking God knows what but heading for my brain, give me a minute while I use my right hand to rub the muscles of my upper arm, the cephalic vein's visible through the skin, it's as close as I can get to the jaguar that's in there, scratch scratch scratch, I've got to watch out, there's more than fear of a large, heavily built cat that's got a yellowish-brown coat with black spots, the cannulation of a vein as close to the radial nerve as the cephalic vein can lead to nerve damage, that's dangerous, maybe it's better he's already in there and not out here trying get in, but I'd still like to know what he's doing with the sharp claws he's got, inside or out, there's going to be trouble, hey! can you hear me? I'm asking you a question, not you, I wouldn't shout at you, I'm talking to the jaguar under my skin, and he's maintaining radio silence, *mi diablito*—not a dolly, hand truck, or electrical wiring to steal power from your neighbors—my little devil, even if the jaguar isn't a child, he's got to be pretty small, and if he's in the subclavian vein, a paired large vein, the jaguar's less than normal or usual size, because the diameter of that vein's approximately the size of our smallest finger, and the cephalic vein's diameter is a lot smaller, it doesn't matter, I'm crazy, what does it matter? fiery souls are more open to rage, they aren't born equal, they're like the four elements of nature—fire, water, air, and earth, and you're going to ask me, what's all that? and I say, it's Seneca, and Cortázar, and what I'm feeling now, such very depressed feelings, what the ancestors of a Javanese might've called *nelangsa*—feeling completely alone, still living among others but no longer the same, the heat of the sun's borne by all, but the heat in our heart's borne alone, so the only way to get relief is communion with the hearts of those of a similar fate, similar values, similar ties, with the same burdens, and you can count forty-three families, that's the total, not including ours, that's how I look at it, plenty of tears, and more if you figure what it means, because it isn't just the forty-three, it's every death and disappearance from the beginning of time, nobody's got enough fingers to count up the names we know and the names we don't, you've heard it before, excuse the excusable repetition, but there's no harm in saying it again, there's no distinction between the others, not for Lupita and not for me, but there's our Coyuco, Lupita's and mine, our son, and every time I say his name, I figure he might be alive and stay that way a little longer, long enough for me to find him, my illusion my dream, but there are other dreams, straight out of the exile of Nezahualcoyotl, in the origins of the Tepaneca War, "The Coyohua was fetched, and he came before Tezozomoctli, and when he had arrived in his presence, he said to him, 'Come here, Coyohua,' then he said, 'listen Coyohua, here is why you have been called, who is this truly bad one that I have dreamed about? an eagle is standing on top of me, a jaguar is standing on top of me, a wolf is standing on top of me, a rattlesnake is lying on top of me, my dream terrifies me,'" and that's how life is, at least today, for Lupita and for me, the thing is, we can't fall asleep, we dream horrors, our special nightmares, and now, and now … but Ernesto couldn't finish his sentence because there weren't any words left for him to say, he ran his fingertips over his face as if he were searching for cobwebs.

Closer to the Periférico Sur than Hotel Obregón, a supermarket, *frutas en Iguala de la Independencia, alimentos congelados en Iguala de la Independencia, verduras en Iguala de la Independencia, carnes en Iguala de la Independencia, limpiador en Iguala de la Independencia,* fruit, frozen food, vegetables, meats, cleaning products in Iguala de la Independencia, and Bodega Aurrerá, Ignacio M. Altamirano 89C, not far from the Walmart de México, Ernesto walking down the aisles, looking for nothing and seeing everything, drawn by the magnetic force of a display of masks, and Ernesto Cisneros, faces faces faces, and none of them mine, profoundly popular really respected honestly celebrated wrestlers' masks, El Santo, El Demonio Azul, El Murciélago, Aníbal, El Solitario, Mil Máscaras, Dr. Wagner, Ángel Blanco, all the faces looking back at him, positive in attitude and full of energy and new ideas, a genuinely dynamic display of masks, Ernesto standing like a statue in a town plaza, with no possibility of doubt, full of energy, and a new idea unfolding like the first appearance of light in the sky before sunrise, and Ernesto Cisneros, *un regalo de Dios,* that's the coupling that's missing in my plans, like a fitting on the end of a railroad car for connecting it to another, because I'm not completely here, continuously possessed by something alien, what have I done what have I done, a permanent idiot, I yam what I yam and that's all what I yam, oh Popeye! Ernesto reaching out to touch the masks, undecided, his fingers itching to take them all, as many as he could buy with the pesos in his pocket, but it was the mask of Mil Máscaras, Aarón Rodríguez, "The Man of a Thousand Masks," born in San Luis Potosí, 1942, it was his mask, with the letter *M* in center position on the forehead, not Mil Máscaras' leopard *máscara* that went with the matching costume, Ernesto and a classic mask chosen from a wide range, the sweeping selection of false faces worn as a disguise, or to amuse or terrify other people, but Ernesto, not a result of Valente Pérez's contest, holding a replica of Mil Máscaras' wrestling debut mask from 1965 in Guadalajara, no *Plancha Suicida*, no Mexican Surfboard, known as the Romero Special, or *La Tapatía*, invented by Rito Romero, a.k.a. Rayo Mexicano, no *Quebradora con Giro*, just watchful Ernesto, holding the mask, heading for the cashier, and after he'd paid for it, a search for a mirror, and Ernesto Cisneros, to himself, right this way, señor Cabrón, I pray to San Judas Tadeo, the Saint of Lost Causes, and instead of a flame above my head, I'll wear this mask and the face of Mil Máscaras with an *M* decorating my forehead, it's the only way I can live with myself, Ernesto loosening the laces, slipping the mask over his head, pulling it down in order to peer through the cutouts for the eyes, and Ernesto Cisneros, now take a look at yourself, trained by Diablo Velazco, not you, señor Cabrón, but the face you're wearing, the face you're looking at, Ernesto, inspecting his own profile, seeing a young man in the mirror, a teenager, coming up beside him, admiring the face of the third member of the holy trinity of *enmascarado* greats, without the body to match, not at his age, and Ernesto Cisneros, ay, *jovencito*, will you give me a hand with these laces? the young man, almost an adult and tall for his age, pulling the laces and tying them with all the strength in his fingers, helping Ernesto secure the mask of Mil Máscaras, which was the pride of all and in particular Aarón Rodríguez, a mask tight and laced in place, so

Ernesto wouldn't have to look at a murderer in the mirror, a traitor to all he'd believed in, a disappointment to Guadalupe, his wife, Coyuco, his son, whether living or dead, because the dead could see what the living only imagined, a disappointment to his friend, Rubén Arenal, and to Ignacio, like a second father to him, but Ernesto, a hero to the unforgiving members of the families of the disappeared, or only a handful, or just one, or none at all, because not everyone wanted revenge, but they definitely wanted justice, and the return of their children, and Ernesto Cisneros, I, too, am a witness, I'll give testimony, about what if not myself? Ernesto turning away from the mirror, looking at the young man, and Ernesto Cisneros, what do you think, *jovencito*, how do I look? a hero in my time, a legend in yours, Ernesto feeling better on the inside thanks to how he looked on the outside, in the mirror, and in the noble eyes of the young man, catching a radiant reflection of himself in the expression on the boy's face, appearing at last as the kind of man he'd always wanted to become, and the young man, señor, my name's Aarón, intentionally named after the wrestler whose mask you're wearing, and Ernesto Cisneros, Aarón, *m'hijo*, two good things have struck me at once in a life that's been going from bad to worse, finding this mask to wear as my own face, and you, Aarón, who's fixed it with laces on my head, Aarón took two steps back, maintaining a respectful distance, a warm and friendly smile on his face, Ernesto reaching out, taking him by the arm, leading the boy out to the street, Ignacio M. Altamirano, taking a left, Ernesto not letting go of Aarón's arm, but the young man gently pulling his arm until it was free, snaking out of Ernesto's grasp but continuing to walk beside him until Ernesto, unavoidably attracted by the deep lavender color painted on the walls of a deserted location not far from Bodega Aurrerá, the two of them passing under a rectangular sign prohibiting littering without ducking their heads, Ernesto leaning against the far lavender wall with a painted red line drawing a circle with a large black letter *E* in the middle, and a red line slicing diagonally through it, Aarón standing facing him, looking at a diminished version of Mil Máscaras, and Ernesto Cisneros, do you smoke? and Aarón, I'm not an angel or a saint, señor, reaching into his baggy trousers, removing a crumpled pack of cigarettes, Ernesto watching him closely, eyes on the pack in the boy's hand, not Delicados or Fiesta brand, or a cigarette out of Rocket's pack of Faros, he'd left it on the shelf beneath the mirror in the bathroom of Hotel Obregón, but a gold, red and white pack of Capri, Aarón offering one to Ernesto, and Ernesto Cisneros, I don't really smoke, it's just a habit, but I don't usually kill people either, so I'll take one, his voice a hesitant bell ringing in a busy street, Aarón putting both cigarettes in his mouth, lighting them like he'd seen an actor do in a movie, turning the cigarette and passing it filter first to Ernesto's trembling fingers, Ernesto taking a long haul on it, filling his lungs, smoke flowing out of his mask-covered nose and mouth, blinking his eyes that were the weary eyes of Mil Máscaras, a bluish-gray cloud lingering between them like there wasn't a current of air, all stillness, and a voiceless world making a lot of noise, conversation bargaining chattering discussing terms, and with the nicotine, Ernesto slowing down, the rhythm of his heart stimulated and peaceful at the same time, Aarón watching him, the mask against a lavender background with only part of a red circle visible on the wall, no noticeable letter *E*, Mil Mascaras was in the way, and Ernesto Cisneros, I jumped into a hell I made for myself by losing control of my emotions, the fuse was lit when my son disappeared, and where I've landed is a spiritual realm of suffering I know I'll never climb out of, not even with the world's longest ladder, *m'hijo*, I'm stuck where I am, there's no before, only after, and the space separating then and now can be no longer because the Devil's settled down right smack in between them, blocking my view—he's casting a helluva shadow—and that's the truth, as far as I'm willing to tell it, not to you, not everything, not now, but it's worse than you can imagine for a man like me who's lived without a vicious bone in his body, I might as well hang myself now with a hemp cord, but I'm bleating like a sheep, you've got your own troubles, everybody does, and Aarón, flicking ash off his Capri, my troubles are the troubles of everyone I meet, señor, and you can take my word for it, in these times we're all sitting on the *comal* burning the seat of our pants, but from what I can tell, you're nicely roasted, burnt to a crisp on the inside, and it's only a matter of time before you crumble into a heap of ashes, consumed, so let's take a minute to see what you believe in, señor, if you believe in anything at all, Ernesto inhaling another lungful of smoke, looking at the burning tip of his cigarette, waving it like a tiny flare in front of his mask, and Ernesto Cisneros, what I want to believe in and what I'm feeling now are two different things, no, not just two, but more, let's not make things more complicated, I used to believe in everything a man who's been raised on the words of the Bible is supposed to believe in, and breast-fed on words spoken by the priest in church, but now those words are written on sheets of paper marked with symbols and signs I can't read, it burns my tongue to say it, and that's from somebody who's been reading longer than you've been alive—old enough to be your father, *m'hijo,* older, in fact—but I still have a memory for things I've heard more than once, and what comes to mind are a few words my father used to tell me whenever I slipped into a state of miserable melancholy—why not call him my father, because that's what he is, yes, *m'hijo,* Ignacio Pardiñas, my father of the living because my parents are no longer here on earth— a fiesta of words I have faith in today, right now, and right out of the Bible and Ignacio's mouth, words from Ezekiel 36:26: *Os daré corazón nuevo, / y pondré espíritu nuevo dentro de vosotros; / y quitaré de vuestra carne el corazón de piedra, / y os daré un corazón de carne,* "And I will give you a new heart, / and a new spirit I will put within you. / And I will remove the heart of stone from your flesh and give you a heart of flesh," it fits me like a toreador's suit of lights, and I want to believe them, but those words are shifting altering shining unsteadily before my eyes, symbols and signs signs and symbols, guttering flames, and Aarón, what you're saying, it's very good, tell me your name, señor, and Ernesto Cisneros, Ernesto Cisneros Fuentes, named after the football midfielder, a happy coincidence, my true father's first *apellido, qué en paz descanse,* may he rest in peace, and Aarón, what the words say after that, that's the beginning of my worry for you, señor Cisneros, in Ezekiel 36:27, *Y pondré dentro de vosotros mi Espíritu, / y haré que andéis en mis estatutos, / y guardéis mis preceptos, / y los pongáis por obra,* "And I will put my Spirit within you, / and cause you to walk in my statutes and be careful to obey my rules," and there's more, it's at the heart of your suffering, let's skip a few verses, straight to Ezekiel 36:31, *Y os acordaréis de vuestros malos caminos, / y de vuestras obras que no fueron buenas; / y os avergonzaréis de vosotros mismos por vuestras iniquidades y por vuestras abominaciones,* "Then you will remember your evil ways, / and your deeds that were not good, / and you will loathe yourselves for your iniquities and your abominations," not so good for you, not at all, señor Cisneros, with a conscience like yours, but your cigarette is out, so's mine, let's have another.

And Ernesto Cisneros, to himself, let him talk, it's a great moment, the return of a great wrestler, I can see it, but Mil Máscaras in my body, that's a laugh, Aarón lighting a couple of cigarettes like he'd done before, offering the second to Ernesto, each taking a long drag, and Aarón, the real Mil Máscaras is seventy-four years old, Aarón Rodríguez Arellano, a legendary pankratiast, I know you know that, but you don't know his address, and Ernesto Cisneros, I didn't ask for his address, and I suppose if I was wearing Blue Demon's face your name would be Alejandro, or you'd be calling yourself Roberto if I had on El Solitario's golden mask—I don't know who you are or what you're up to, *m'hijo,* but something tells me to trust you, and I do, so I'll ask the question that's been jabbing me in the ribs, is it shameful for a killer to wear the mask of a hero? I can't walk around with my own face, I'm ashamed to look at myself in the mirror, then Aarón, taking a wallet-sized pocket mirror from his trousers, held it to the pair of eyes staring at him through the mask, and Aarón, take a good look at yourself, the *M* doesn't stand for murderer, it stands for *mil* of Mil Máscaras, nothing more nothing less, a thousand layers of faces to protect you, and they're representing the faces of the families of the disappeared, not the disappeared themselves, *usted está en el lado de los que sufren,* you're on the side of those who suffer, señor, whatever you've done, and I know what it is, don't be anxious brood or lose sleep, señor, do you really think you'll do it again? a repeat offender? what's the likelihood, what're the chances, do you have any statistics to lay out in front of us right here right now? and Ernesto Cisneros, that's not what I'm asking, it's the mask of a hero and it hides my guilt, the young man paying attention but with something to say, and Aarón, according to the Bureau of Justice Statistics, isolating M1 and M2 from the larger category of homicides, in one decade, from 2000 to 2010, national statistics in the US showed a 1.6 percent recidivism rate for murder, you can believe it or not, not that it's of any real use, but you know that statistics—and Ernesto Cisneros, interrupting him, statistics, what a science! and Aarón, statistics are democracy in its scientific state—essences isolated by means of individuals! and Ernesto Cisneros, statistics my ass! you aren't making me feel any better no matter what the recidivism rate is or isn't according to your sources, *m'hijo,* whether it's here in once-great Mexico or *en el Norte,* all I know is that I'll have a lifetime of crying ahead of me, it's what I've done, not whether or not I'll do it again, and Aarón, what we know, and it's according to an expert, is that inflicting pain on the wrongdoer doesn't restore the thing that was lost, and that's a quote, señor Cisneros, don't get me wrong, I understand you, and maybe under the same circumstances I'd have done what you did, what separates you from them, killers who reoffend, is the strength of your religious beliefs, an important factor along with your feelings of guilt, not shame, and Ernesto Cisneros, now you're beginning to get on my nerves, cut out the psychological crap, *por amor de Dios,* I just asked you a simple question, mask of Mil Máscaras, or no mask, *Señoras y Señores, Damas y Caballeros,* may I have your attention, please, I'd like an answer to my question, what's the decision? no wrestling pun intended, and Aarón, you don't have to shout, and Ernesto Cisneros, it's the best I can do to get a little volume through this mask, *m'hijo*, and cut through the wind you're sending my way, meaningless rhetoric, not that you're insincere, but don't be a gasbag, remember who you're talking to, a likeness of Mil Máscaras, in the flesh, not physically, but like you said, look at my face, and by the way, while you're at it, in case you suffer from a weak memory, *m'hijo*, give me an answer, is it a loss of respect or honor for Aarón Rodríguez that I'm wearing the mask of Mil Máscaras? Aarón breaking into a smile, taking a pull on his Capri, a gust of wind catching the bluish-gray smoke and throwing it against the lavender wall behind Ernesto, who took advantage of the breeze to suck in as much air as he could, opening and closing his mouth like a fish, filling his lungs, not with Aarón's smoke but the oxygen that followed it, and Aarón, I answered your question but you aren't listening, you're wearing a thousand layers of faces to protect you, representing the faces of the families of the disappeared, anonymous and familiar faces, changing faces, there's no shame in that, señor, anyway, I don't think he lives here in Iguala, I don't know where he lives, and I believe he'd be honored, under the circumstances, as long as from now on, no matter what, high or low, you follow the unwritten laws of faith and set an example through ethical, righteous, worthy-of-the-mask behavior, Ernesto turning to face the lavender wall, his shoulders unevenly rising and falling, his knees nearly giving way, he was crying discreetly, Aarón swore he heard sobbing before the wind carried the sounds away, and Ernesto Cisneros, with a muffled voice directed at the painted red line forming a circle with a large black letter *E* in the middle, *m'hijo*, the mask feels tight, can you loosen the laces? and Aarón, taking a step closer to him, examining the back of his head, there are no laces, not anymore, and there's no sign except my furrowed fingers that there ever were laces, in fact, there's no mask, no four pieces of fabric sewn together, no cotton, nylon, leather or vinyls, no tongue of fabric under laces to keep it tight, no nothing, señor Cisneros, Ernesto turning around, wiping tears from his eyes, and Aarón, no mask but an additional layer that isn't the usual thin layer of tissue forming the natural outer covering of your face, and there's still *antifaz*, or trim, around the openings for your eyes, nose and mouth, a wrestler's mask that's no longer a mask, but the living Mil Máscaras, with the *M* on your forehead, Aarón taking the mirror from his pocket again, Ernesto seeing himself, watching as the skin of his face started to change color, from a metallic-blue and white to all white with narrow blood-red *antifaz* and a blood-red *M* on the forehead, skin resembling pro-grade Lycra, colors that were almost but not quite transparent, Ernesto breaking into a smile, stretching the elastic polyurethane fiber of his skin, and Ernesto Cisneros, a blessing in disguise, laughing at his joke, a different appearance in order to conceal his identity, no longer having to live with the face of a murderer no matter how he tried to justify what'd happened, with or without Aarón's help, Ernesto knowing his face would keep on changing, he was Mil Máscaras, after all, not the wrestler, not with his build, Aarón dropping his Capri, rubbing it out with the heel of his laced left boot, the wallet-sized pocket mirror returning to his trouser pocket, Ernesto, a final drag to finish the cigarette pinched between steady fingers, extending his arm, his fingers letting go of the butt, Aarón's right heel crushing it, and Ernesto Cisneros, as long as your father's first *apellido* isn't Rodríguez, and Aarón, don't worry, it's not, and it couldn't be, since my name, first and *apellidos,* changes according to who I'm talking to, and what's in a name? as the saying goes, I might as well call you a golem, yes, the Golem of Iguala, or the Monster of Fate, your doppelgänger, like Pernath's in Meyrink's book, and Ernesto Cisneros, that's a name I know and understand, *m'hijo,* an artificial man of clay made by Kabbalistic magic, created to serve its creator, and Aarón, *The Golem*'s before all else an exploration of identity, a "painful quest for that eternal stone that in some mysterious fashion lurks in the dim recesses of ... memory in the guise of a lump of fat," Ernesto whistling through his teeth behind the lips of his non-mask, and Ernesto Cisneros, from what I've read and with the help of a hint of light in a dimming memory, Gustav Meyrink was a founder member of the

Theosophical Order of the Blue Star, and became a disciple of Bo Yin Ra, a German charlatan—Aarón interrupting him, and Aarón, the idea of a golem originated in mediaeval Jewish commentaries on the *Sefer Yetzirah,* Book of Creation, the central text of the Kabbalah, but in the eighteenth century it became a legend identified with Rabbi Loew, and Ernesto Cisneros, Rabbi Loew, Rabbi Leib, or Rabbi Liva, depending on who you're reading, Chayim Bloch, Isaac Singer, or Yudl Rosenberg, who wrote pulp in the early twentieth century, and there's Meyrink, who doesn't even mention the rabbi by name, and Aarón, and Yitzkhok Peretz wrote a story called "The Golem," and Egon Kisch, a journalist, with his investigation, "On the Track of the Golem," writing, "Standing by his grave, I know why God so willed it, that the Man-automaton, working ever for the welfare of strangers and unconditionally subject to an extraneous will, should be buried here," and Ernesto Cisneros, I'm not dead yet, Coyuco is, that's my son, but today I'm flesh and blood, and according to my reflection in your pocket mirror, it's only my face that's changed, and Aarón, in your case, a transformation, yes, but in your transformation is a reference to the Maharal of Prague, *Moreinu ha-Rav Loew,* our Rabbi Loew, Talmudic scholar, mystic, and philosopher, you can't deny it! and Ernesto Cisneros, it's not our story, not here not now, I can't change what I've done but I can do things to make up for it, and Aarón, you could call it a miracle and exactly what you need, and Ernesto Cisneros, without moving his lips, since Coyuco disappeared I've longed for an answer, one that didn't come from a human mouth, but from the realm of the supernatural, through some nonhuman being as an intermediary, maybe today it's some supernatural being roaming in the daylight like him, and maybe this being, invisible but somehow part of my experience with this mask has whispered the answer to me, I've got to listen to everything I hear, and to everyone I meet, Ernesto leaning against the wall, slowly descending to a crouching position before Aarón, who followed him down to stay on eye level with his companion, Ernesto's wrists crossed with his forearms resting on his knees, and Ernesto Cisneros, let's stick to the mystical, that's where I'm headed, or I'd better say, that's where I am, transcending human understanding, and definitely concerned with the soul or the spirit, not with material things—it's my shot at salvation—I've done enough damage with a .38 Special, bang bang bang, there's nothing more material than that, *m'hijo*, take your pick, the Glock I took off a cop I knocked unconscious, or the .38 Special I used, one weapon's the same as another, death's what I've brought to the world, when I came here to Iguala de la Independencia just to find my son.

Aarón reached out toward Ernesto's face, Ernesto turning his head first this way, then that, left and right right and left, wanting to avoid any human contact, Aarón's finger touching the letter *M* on his forehead, and Aarón, the *M* that stands for *mil* on your brow is your *Emeth*, or Truth, in Hebrew, and in your case, no one can remove the first letter of it, the aleph, to spell *Meth*, or death, but don't get me wrong, señor Cisneros, you can't stop bullets and you aren't going to live forever, with or without your dream question, which you've asked without knowing yourself that you've asked it, and this, your face, is your answer, and Ernesto Cisneros, but *m'hijo*, I never asked you who you are, and Aarón, it's because of that, which I'll call your faith, señor, that I can guide you, another proof in the answer to your question, because in order to perform the tasks you'll carry out to put right what you've done, you must have faith in your transformation, "And the Lord God formed man of the dust of the ground, and breathed into his nostrils the breath of life; and man became a living soul," you've read Yudl Rosenberg, you said so yourself, and Ernesto Cisneros, a smile on his face, there isn't a book about what I don't know that I haven't read, then again there's a lot I don't know and plenty yet to read, Aarón, patting him on the shoulder, helping him stand because the muscles in Ernesto's legs were cramped, he wasn't a young man and didn't exercise, and Aarón, there's nothing mysterious about it at all, it's only magic and sorcery—*kishuf,* a kind of magic—that frighten men, but the rays from the sun of the spiritual world are mild and warming, okay, just in case, let me check, there's probably a scrap of paper, a *shem*, with a magic formula behind your teeth, attracting free stellar energy from the cosmos, like the seal the rabbi forgot in the golem's mouth, then Ernesto, a false long drawn-out yawn, and Aarón peering past the *antifaz* around his lips and into his mouth, a broad grin on both of their faces, and Aarón, remember, whatever you do, there's no amulet to make you invisible when you go to a dangerous place to help others from misfortune and don't want to be seen, but you can always make use of disguises, Ernesto and Aarón walking slowly away from the lavender wall and the red circle with the letter *E* in the center and a red line slicing through it, Aarón, his arm over Ernesto's shoulder, whispering in Ernesto's ear, and Aarón, just beware of the priest Thaddeus or anyone like him, Ernesto nodding his head, in the picture clued in and fully informed by the writings of Yudl Rosenberg and the others, Ernesto and Aarón, together, a steady pace as they left the location not far from Bodega Aurrerá, walking beneath something like a cloak of contentment, arm in arm like old friends, Ernesto was no longer afraid, the oppression in his spirit had been lifted, the message got through, and only if he heard the lonely cry of a bird did he stop and look—Aarón standing by his side—perhaps because the bird was calling after the daylight moon or crying out its longing for a lover who'd never arrive.

Ignacio, hearing all the news that circulated in Chihuahua and other cities in Mexico long before anyone else knew about what was happening there, including Iguala de la Independencia, whether it concerned people he knew or those he'd only met briefly, knowing not by mysticism and magic, because no one could swear to Ignacio's adherence to any belief other than being a good Catholic, but a kind of second sight or sixth sense, an awareness or feeling accompanied by words and pictures that somehow made their way to him, enlightening him to more than just current events, filling his days with the ups and downs, a succession of both good and bad experiences in the lives of human beings he'd encountered in his more than seventy-five years on earth, and so it was that a handful of images and a few words written beneath them featuring Ernesto in Iguala played before his eyes like pictures in a silent movie, Ernesto's face had changed, Ignacio couldn't put a finger on what the difference was, not from the flickering pictures he saw that were passing in front of him so quickly, no close-ups, taken from middle distance, seeing Ernesto speaking with a young man wearing baggy trousers, a couple of cigarettes, and then a zoom straight into Ernesto's face, and the details presented themselves at last, Ignacio wasn't shocked but paid close attention to what he saw, immediately recognizing a version of Mil Máscaras' many masks, Ignacio a wrestling fan himself, going to more than a hundred matches in almost eighty years, Ernesto's skin impregnated with a substance that looked like pro-grade Lycra, elastic polyurethane skin that was all white with narrow blood-red *antifaz* and a blood-red letter *M* on Ernesto's forehead, Ignacio removed his pajamas, showered, and got dressed to go out, taking his hardwood walking stick, hand painted with the design of an eagle and snake, locking his door, and the iron gate that protected it, leaving his house on Barrancas del Cobre, turning right, walking slightly uphill toward a cement staircase, more or less nine steps up, a railing on the left-hand side, nothing on the right, moving through the brighter stage of daylight toward Calle 38A, carefully crossing Calle 38A, continuing on Barrancas del Cobre to see Mariano and Rosalía, and Ignacio Pardiñas, in the words of Charles Reade, novelist and dramatist, "Good advice is like a tight glove; it fits the circumstances, and it does not fit other circumstances," Ignacio heading straight for the white door of the single-story house, almost an extension of the house standing next to it to the left, and the retired shoemaker answering the door, a welcoming smile, and Mariano Alcalá, come in come in señor Pardiñas, our house is always open to you, it's small as a shoebox—hehe!—you've heard me say it more than once, more than a thousand times, and after all the years we've known each other, but I'll say it until my dying day—hehe!—you know it, but thanks to Rosalía, a magician for a welcoming home that folds its arms around you, a real embrace, she's a marvel at the management of household affairs, Mariano closing the door, turning toward the kitchen, and Mariano Alcalá, Rosalía! *jazmín mío,* my flower, our señor Pardiñas is here to see us, then taking his friend by the arm, Mariano indicating with an outstretched hand the small living room and dining room, his fingers and thumb pointing to Ignacio's favorite sofa, the only sofa in the house, Ignacio making his way on tired legs, lightly tapping the floor with his cane, burying himself in the inviting cushions, plump and deep, and the fabric worn, Rosalía drying her hands on a kitchen towel, no apron, and Rosalía Calderón, your turn, *mi Jícama Gigante,* Mariano taking the dishtowel from her, and Mariano Alcalá, back in a minute, a wink and a nod in Ignacio's direction, then disappearing in the kitchen, Ignacio turning the hand-painted cane with his fingers, then rolling it between the palms of his hands like he was starting a fire by friction with a spindle, and Rosalía Calderón, we've got to forgive him with all our heart and soul, then he'll be free of his sin—I'm talking about Ernesto, and Ignacio Pardiñas, you know why I came here and what I'm thinking? and Rosalía Calderón, we haven't been friends for this long without our knowing exactly what's going on in your head, señor Pardiñas, and your hardwood walking stick, a cane painted with a serpent and an eagle, a symbol of *nuestro México,* well, it's a country of ghosts, you've heard Rocket say it, and so have I, let's all call him Rocket, because Ernesto does, otherwise it's Rubén Arenal, so formal so correct and so far away, and Ignacio Pardiñas, well, that's settled, and leaning forward, putting his weight on his stick, shouting in the direction of the kitchen, can you hear this, Mari? Mariano returning from the kitchen, no towel, his hands were dry, and Mariano Alcalá, you haven't called me that since we were kids, when I called you El Fuerte, *mi Fuerte,* always stronger and sturdier, *el fuerte viento,* a strong wind, Rosalía clapping her hands, and Rosalía

Calderón, that's what I want to hear, solidarity, and the energy of youth, a breath of air for our old bones that've grown and shrunk together, at the same time, in a sort of trinity, if you'll excuse the comparison, we've known each other that long, so Mari it is, an off-spring of Mariano—*en los primeros tiempos del cristianismo se asoció con el culto a la Virgen María, un nombre de pila llevado por varios primeros santos,* in the early days of Christianity it was asso-ciated with the cult of the Virgin Mary, a first name taken by several holy Saints—we'll try our best to help Ernesto in our own way, un-conventional as it might be, to return home, here, to our Chihuahua, *Valentía, Lealtad, Hospitalidad,* Courage, Loyalty, Hospitality, *en nuestro Estado Grande,* and Mariano Alcalá, a few words from Borges, but first, when I think of what's happened to Ernesto in Iguala and how he looks today—your vision's passed to us through the symbols of a serpent and an eagle painted on your walking stick, yes, that's our Mexico, sending a wire, direct, and now for Borges, words having a bearing on Ernesto's dream of finding his son, "Oh, incompetence! Never can my dreams engender the wild beast I long for. The tiger indeed appears, but stuffed or flimsy, or with impure variations of shape, or of an implausible size, or all too fleeting, or with a touch of the dog or the bird," and Ignacio Pardiñas, a wise choice, the words of Borges fit like a glove, because what Ernesto's found in his search for Coyuco isn't exactly what he thought he was looking for, instead he's stumbled on a part of himself he never imagined he'd meet face to face, and it could be our fate, too, if we step over the line that's drawn before us we'll discover what we're capable of, and then, like Ernesto, we'll need more than a mirror to see what it's done, *Isaías 35:8, Y habrá allí calzada y camino, y será llamado Camino de Santidad; / no pasará inmundo por él, sino que él mismo estará con ellos; / el que anduviere en este camino, por torpe que sea, no se extraviará,* "And a highway shall be there, and it shall be called the Way of Holiness; / the unclean shall not pass over it. / It shall belong to those who walk on the way; / if they are fools, they shall not wander in it," Isaiah 35:8 and Rosalía Calderón, let's pray that Ernesto's on the right path now that he's wearing the masks of Mil Máscaras, burned into his skin with the brand of a special kind of redemption, and Mariano Alcalá, to the roof, as usual? Ignacio and Rosalía nodding their heads, and Rosalía Calderón, but first a drink to put us in the mood, a glass of *el pipiltzintzintli,* meaning *niñitos,* and not just a dose of *Salvia divinorum,* because *pipiltzintzintli,* by its name, is related to Piltzintecuhtli, Señor Niño, 7 Flower, the Young Prince, a god of the rising sun, healing, hallucinatory plants and visions and the word *piltzintli,* meaning "offspring, child," and they're identified with Xochipilli, the Prince of Flowers, the deity of sacred plants, a solar god and the god of maize, and his twin sister or female counterpart Xochiquetzal, Lady Precious Flower—what am I saying? I know you already know it, I'll be right back, I've got the dried leaves soaking in water in the kitchen, not for me, I'll abstain, somebody's got to look after you, Mariano sitting next to Ignacio on the sofa, and Mariano Alcalá, "the dramas of the modern world proceed from a profound disequilibrium of the psyche, individual as well as collective, brought about largely by a progressive sterilization of the imagination," not my words, El Fuerte, *mi Fuerte,* but Mircea Eliade, and Ignacio Pardiñas, I've read it, and here's more, "To have imagination is to be able to see the world in its totality, for the power and the mission of the Images is to *show* all that remains refractory to the concept: hence the disfavor and failure of the man 'without imagination'; he is cut off from the deeper reality of life and from his own soul," I trust the visions I'm presented with—you get them, too, and Rosalía—thanks to my walking stick, that's why we're united in going to the roof to perform our rituals, the voice of *pipiltzintzintli* will be guiding me, Rosalía returning with three glasses on a tray, two with the infusion, and the third glass, a whisked amber-colored liquid, a beer made from corn, and Rosalía Calderón, yes, it's for me, a homemade tesgüino, or *batári,* the most sacred, according to the Tarahumara, or Rarámuri, depending which side of the street you're on, another recipe from Luz Elena, so you know it's delicious, Rosalía sitting down with them, each taking their time but not too much, there were places to go, things to do, then the empty glasses of tea were returned to the tray, Rosalía bringing the tray back to the kitchen, Mariano leaving the room to assemble the things they needed for the ritual, a dry gourd painted red with red flowers containing dried *jiculi,* from the Tarahumara, *peyotl* or peyote, in case the *pipi-ltzintzintli* wasn't strong enough, two candles, one each for Ignacio and Mariano, a box of wooden matchsticks, incense, a hand-engraved pocket knife with a bone handle, and on the blade, *soy amigo de los hombres,* I am a friend of man, to protect them against those who call them *yn teyxcuepanime yn diablosme yn intlayacahuan yn yztlacati yn titiçi,* "enchanters, devils and their leaders, those who lie, the doctors," a bag filled with handfuls of earth, ash and potsherds from an archaeological site, the ruins of Casas Grandes, or Paquimé, sealed in plastic, airtight packed tight and bigger than a baseball, a couple of saints in plaster, and a mini-ziplock bag holding the powder of a ground bird skeleton mixed with eggshell fragments kept in a drawer in their bedroom closet, Mariano returning to the small combination living room and dining room, opening the bag of powder in front of them, using a couple of spoonfuls to clean his hands, offering the same to the others, eggshell fragments and powder ignited in mid-air by it's own properties, disappearing before it hit the floor, Rosalía gathering flowers from a vase in the kitchen, the three friends climbing a ladder at the back of the house, accompanied by the first stanza of the song "Plegaria," "Prayer," a waltz sung by Lydia Mendoza with María Mendoza on mandolin, a recording made in San Antonio in 1936, playing somewhere in the sky above them, Ignacio the last up the ladder, handing his walking stick to Rosalía in order to get a better grip on Mariano's hand pulling him up onto the flat roof, and the repeating lyrics of the first stanza, a relaxing *vals* caressing their faces: *Traigo estas flores de mi jardín / a tu santuario con devoción / vengo buscando consuelo a mis males, / en el amparo de tu protección,* "I bring these flowers from my garden / to your sanctuary with devotion, / I come seeking solace from my cares / in the shelter of your protection," Mariano putting the dry gourd with dried *jiculi* where the roof abutted the corrugated iron extension, Rosalía placing the saints and a handful of flowers at the edge of the roof, Mariano spreading a thin layer of earth, ash and potsherds gathered at the ruins of Paquimé on the surface of the roof, a bird's-eye view showing the sweeping gestures Mariano's hand made when spreading the earth, ash and potsherds with an arcing movement of his outstretched arm, a human windmill with one vane turning, Mariano and Rosalía helping Ignacio to lie down comfortably on the flat roof with its layer of earth, ash and potsherds, his walking stick within reach, the potsherds not disturbing anyone because Mariano and Ignacio were wearing clothes, no fabric would be torn, no skin scraped by sharp edges, Mariano and Rosalía placing the first of the two candles to the left of Ignacio's head, lighting the candle, and setting the other candle where it'd be nearest Mariano's head once he lay down, Rosalía lighting five cones of gray copal resin incense from trees of the Burseraceae family, neither hardened resin nor sap, borrowing from their ancestors, five to represent their three bodies and the bodies of Ernesto and Coyuco, putting two of the cones next to the two candles, not close enough for the smoke to sting their eyes, Mariano lying down, Rosalía lighting Mariano's candle with a wooden match, then walking carefully across the corrugated iron roof, sitting on the low red brick wall with a satellite dish attached to it, her hands resting on her knees, she tilted back her head, looking up at the streetlight and all the wires extending out from it, phone lines or electricity, the air was still, not a bird flew over their heads, and the three of them kept their eyes open wide searching the noonday sky for clouds, which might present an omen depending on the shape they took, but there weren't any clouds, the sun had burned them out of the sky early that morning, leaving nothing but glare and blue staring down at them, incense smoke rising straight up, nothing else stirred, their clothes didn't move because there wasn't even a breeze or breath of air, Mariano, Rosalía, and

Ignacio set to start and concentrating, a tight-knit trio trying to get in touch with what was above them, not just the sky itself, because it wasn't a matter of high or low, up or down, the important thing was what the blue expanse of the sky represented, arms embracing the earth, "Mexico is a solar country, but it is also a black country, a dark country," and the hope that their voices, when brought together as one, would be heard from one end of the world to the other, and Mariano Alcalá, whispering, I'm ready, and Rosalía Calderón, with a small but single-minded voice, so am I, and Ignacio Pardiñas, unfaltering and a bit too loud, count me in! and Mariano Alcalá and Rosalía Calderón, together, shh! we've got to keep our voices low, our Pardiñas, señor Pardiñas—there's always room for an honorific—words have windows to all levels of understanding, Ignacio exhaling a sigh, and Ignacio Pardiñas, you don't have to tell me, *mis amigos,* how many times have we done this in how many years? and when the time's right—you can count it out in seconds, not minutes—our voices will be filled with a strange force, I've chosen words today that'll carry all the way to Iguala and back again, returning in their own sweet time, of course, it's not up to us, and with Ernesto in tow no matter what he looks like or how he's changed, appearance and temperament, temperament and appearance, and Rosalía Calderón, forgive our impatience, you're our *paini,* señor Pardiñas, our messenger, accompanied today by Mariano, a branch of Mars, second only to Jupiter in the Roman pantheon, as guardian and friend, because you can't be too sure, and as for me, I'll watch over you both, keeping you from getting up, breaking the spell, and taking care that there isn't any noise because that'll drive you crazy, and Ignacio Pardiñas, enough, *mi familia,* I feel it, *el pipiltzintzintli* is speaking now, telling me to begin with a poem by Octavio Paz, a timely choice, who resigned as Ambassador to India to protest against the government's bloodstained suppression of the student demonstrations in Plaza de las Tres Culturas in Tlatelolco, and I'm asking now which poem, and *el pipiltzintzintli* tells me to recite "El pájaro," "The Bird":

En el silencio transparente
el día reposaba:
la transparencia del espacio
era la transparencia del silencio.
La inmóvil luz del cielo sosegaba
el crecimiento de las yerbas.
Los bichos de la tierra, entre las piedras,
bajo la luz idéntica, eran piedras.
El tiempo en el minuto se saciaba.
En la quietud absorta
se consumaba el mediodía.

Y un pájaro cantó, delgada flecha.
Pecho de plata herido vibró el cielo,
se movieron las hojas,
las yerbas despertaron ...
Y sentí que la muerte era una flecha
que no se sabe quién dispara
y en un abrir los ojos nos morimos.

In the transparent silence
day rested:
the transparency of space
was the transparency of silence.
The unmoving light of the sky soothed
the growing of the grasses.
The bugs of the earth, among the stones,
under the unchanging light, were stones.
Time was sated in the minute.
Noon consumed itself
in the self-absorbed stillness.

And a bird sang, slender arrow.
A wounded breast of silver, the sky quivered,

the leaves shook,
the grass woke up ...
And I felt that death was an arrow
that doesn't know who shot it,
and when our eyes open we die.

And Ignacio Pardiñas, *muchas gracias a* Eliot Weinberger for the translation, and his voice didn't have to whisper because it was no longer his voice, and the voice, it's *el pipiltzintzintli* speaking, yes it's me, none other, no whispering necessary, let's get on with it, just no extraneous noise, that'll drive you and your friend, lieutenant, *y compañero de viaje,* a fellow voyager, señor Mariano Alcalá, out of your minds—what'd you say? yes I know you've got señora Rosalía Calderón to look after both of you, I'm not blind or deaf, but I'm not watching or listening either because I'm in charge, what I've got to say speaks through you, may your two friends be witnesses! and the delicious smell of copal, my nostrils are savoring it by candlelight even if it isn't night but a full round blue sky without a cloud, no shapes no omens, we're working on our own, between the two of you, and señor Mariano Alcalá's wife as lookout, shall we try to get your Ernesto back into señor Rubén Arenal's F-150? he's overdue here in Chihuahua, and I don't mean in the process of being carried in the womb between conception and birth, and "not having been born, though beyond full gestation," you follow me, don't you?—the entheogen of prophecy, interpreter of visions, and healer, was silent for a moment while the three friends nodded their heads under a canopy of clear blue sky—and Ignacio Pardiñas, with the voice of *pipiltzintzintli,* I can swear that Ernesto's changed as much as he's going to change, inside and out, the face he saw in the mirror reflected the faces of the disappeared and dead, he knows, and he's one of them, carrying the word, *Emeth,* or Truth, and a symbol of his salvation, and there'll be hell to pay if he stays in Iguala, it's dangerous for him there, so it's Chihuahua and the sooner the better, here everything's waiting for him, with open arms, expectations of a spiritual nature, and when he gets back in town, there isn't just the sacrament of reconciliation, but a duty required of a person as part of this sacrament to indicate repentance, show us show us your mission responsibility role function, and he'll have tasks to perform behind the thousand masks of Mil Máscaras, because freedom doesn't come for free, and if you're wondering if I'm strong enough as a drug, or if you've got any doubts, take my word for it, you've got the dose right, and you won't be needing any *jiculi,* or peyote, I'm plenty strong, this is *el pipiltzintzintli* speaking, testing testing one two three, gently flows the water of the river to the sea, what was I saying? ah, yes, you can't do what Ernesto's done and live with it without sooner or later having to make good put right mend what's been torn in the fabric, so it's good works for him, nothing more nothing less, and in your nonordinary state of consciousness for spiritual purposes we will now recite, not in Nahuatl this time, "En plena primavera," "In Full Spring," from the *Cantares Mexicanos,* and *gracias a* Ángel María Garibay Kintana and Fermín Herrera:

> *Brotaron, brotaron flores:*
> *abiertas se yerguen delante del sol.*
> *Ya te responde el ave del dios:*
> *tú en su busca vienes:*
> *"Cuantos son tus cantos,*
> *tanta es tu riqueza:*
> *tú a todos deleitas,*
> *cual trepidante flor."*
> *Por todas partes grito,*
> *yo el cantor.*
>
> *Bellas olientes flores*
> *se está esparciendo*
> *en el patio florido, entre las mariposas.*
> *Vienen todas ellas de la región del misterio,*
> *en donde está erguida la Flor.*

223

Flores son que a los hombres hacen perder el juicio,
flores que al corazón totalmente trastornan.
Vienen a entretejerse, vienen a derramarse
en tejido de flores, de narcóticas flores.

The flowers blossomed, they blossomed:
they bloom and stand erect before the sun.
The bird of god answers you:
you come in search of it:
"Your songs are many,
your wealth is great,
you delight everyone
like a trembling flower."
Through every region I shout it,
I, the singer.

Beautiful aromatic flowers
are being scattered
in this flowery courtyard, among the butterflies.
They come, all of them, from the region of mystery,
where the Flower stands erect.
Flowers that make people lose their senses,
flowers that derange the heart entirely.
They come to be intertwined, to be scattered
in a weave of flowers, of narcotic flowers.

My friends, you've given me great pleasure, your voices clear as crystal in the clear as crystal sky of noon, a lovely poem, heartfelt voices for a chemical substance of plant origin like myself, *el pipiltzintzintli,* and for my benefit, it's a celebration of me just between us, and we know and we've heard in the words telling the history of things that in this case, this song, a poem, anything like it, well, the magic will disappear if we throw more light on the words, and now we'll send a message to bring your Ernesto back to

Chihuahua, a message in more than one language, maybe he hasn't reached the truck, maybe it's not where he thought he'd parked it, but don't worry, I promise you he'll find it soon, it's within my power, do you see him with the keys to the Ford Lobo in his hand? it isn't me asking, or it is, because this is *el pipiltzintzintli* speaking, but speaking through you, señor Ignacio Pardiñas—if you had a mirror you'd see your lips moving, and Mariano Alcalá, his friend and witness, keep cool keep calm all's well, El Fuerte, *¡mi Fuerte!* but there wasn't time to say more than that because—and *el pipiltzintzintli,* yes, I've got more to say, so señor Ignacio Pardiñas, you're speaking to yourself, listen carefully, the words will come out of your mouth and your mouth alone, and to the understated accompaniment of a *ranchera,* "Cuidado con la lengua," "Watch Your Tongue," by Paulino Bernal, accordion and vocals, *que bueno hermano, Dios le bendiga y siga firme en el camino de nuestro Dios,* good brother, God bless you and continue steadfast on the path of our God, and a suitable selection of a song: *Cuidado con la lengua / Con lo que tú dices / Porque lo que tú dices / Eso lo serás. / Cuidado con la lengua / Con lo que tú dices / Porque lo que tú dices / Eso lo tendrás,* and the chorus: *Soy prosperado / Tengo éxito / Vivo en salud / Porque ando en la luz,* "Watch your tongue / And what you say / Because what you say / Is what you will become. / Watch your tongue / And what you say / Because what you say / Is what you will have. / I am prosperous / I am successful / I have health / Because I walk in the light," perfect, absolutely just right and fitting, don't you agree? I could almost hear it again, but let's move on, there's Ernesto's face wearing the face of another, skin resembling pro-grade Lycra, all white with narrow blood-red *antifaz* and a blood-red *M* on his forehead, not quite transparent colors, dressed as he was dressed when he borrowed señor Rubén Arenal's F-150, I can't call him Rocket, it wouldn't be right, because this is *el pipiltzintzintli* speaking, with respect, as señora Luz Elena says, my mind's arm reaches over the world's details like a benevolent cloud, and this is it, the moment you've all been waiting for, the words to bring your Ernesto back to Chihuahua, in Spanish and English, we'll skip the Nahuatl again, "En el interior del cielo," "In the Interior of Heaven," a poem by Nezahualcoyotl:

> Solo allá en el interior del cielo
> tú inventas tu palabra,
> ¡Dador de la Vida!
> ¿Qué determinarás?
> ¿Tendrás fastidio aquí?
> ¿Ocultarás tu gloria y tu fama en la tierra?
> ¿Qué determinarás?
> Nadie puede ser amigo
> del Dador de la Vida.
> Amigos, águilas, tigres,
> ¿a dónde en verdad iremos?
> Mal hacemos las cosas, oh amigos.
> Por ello no así te aflijas,
> eso nos enferma, nos causa la muerte.
> Esforzaos, todos tendremos que ir
> a la región del misterio.

There, alone, in the interior of heaven
You invent Your word,
Giver of life!
What will you decide?
Will you be angry here?
Will you conceal Your fame
and Your glory on the earth?
What will You decide?
No one can be a friend to
the Giver of Life.
Friends, eagles, tigers,
where will we really go?
We do things badly, oh friends.

But do not distress yourselves so,
that makes us sick, it causes death.
We must be strong,
we will all have to go
to the region of mystery.

Bien hecho, well done, *mis amigos,* a big thank you *y ¡chingón!* that's
what I was hoping for, *me gusta como lo hiciste,* I like the way you
handled it, there's nothing like unity cooperation consensus solidarity—I'm being more familiar, but why not! after all we've been
through together—and now my world's a better place, the great star
appeared, the sky grew brighter from end to end, and this from the
Maya myth, "I am the sweeper of the path, I sweep his path. I sweep
Our Lord's path for him, so that when Our Lord passes by he finds
it already swept," and out of your mouth, señor Ignacio Pardiñas,
with my voice, *el pipiltzintzintli's,* come my last words to Ernesto:
go in peace and don't rest in peace until all is peace, and with these
words they called Ernesto home, Ignacio licking his dry lips without knowing he was doing it, Rosalía wiping her dry mouth with a
handkerchief, Mariano blinking his dry eyes open and shut, two of
the three friends under the influence, and *el pipiltzintzintli,* this is
el pipiltzintzintli speaking, a parting word, *mis amigos,* do you hear
me, señor Ignacio Pardiñas and señor Mariano Alcalá?—always
respect, no matter what drug's speaking—two brothers of my family, users of our ancient herb and hallucinogen, prohibited by the
Spanish during the Inquisition of New Spain, and over there, señora
Rosalía Calderón, watcher and keeper of my brothers, myself, and
so she is my sister, too, I leave you now, wishing you all a glorious
afternoon in the clear light of day above your heads, the sun burning down upon you and the rest of Chihuahua, *Valentía, Lealtad,
Hospitalidad,* in *nuestro Estado Grande,* as señora Rosalía Calderón
put it so nicely, Mariano, Rosalía, and Ignacio baking in the heat,
perspiration covering their faces, each taking a deep breath as they
felt in one way or another the *pipiltzintzintli* moving on into the

world of man to visit friends, users of entheogens, and to look at what man was doing to the world.

Rubén Arenal woke up without a blanket or a sheet covering him, not cold but shivering, drenched in sweat from the efforts of making love, he'd been asleep, not moving, out cold, now rubbing his sleepy eyes, looking at the room that wasn't a bedroom, no furniture but the mattress he was lying on, and several paper lamps in a Japanese style, *andon,* and detailed *ariake-andon,* or bedside lamps, a couple of *bonbori,* with their hexagonal profile, standing on a pole in two corners on one side of the room, not for the Bonbori Matsuri, a festival in early August each year when bonbori lanterns are lit in the sacred precincts of the Tsurugaoka Hachimangu Shrine in central Kamakura city, these lamps were just part of the decoration, Pascuala Esparza and her daughter's decoration, Rubén Arenal's lips tingling like the first time they'd come in contact with *La Pascualita*'s lips, his head felt light, his nose and mouth breathing air he could see because of the low temperature in a room in the house surrounded by a low stone wall set back from the road on the rise of a hill in the fresh mountain air, its roof white with snow, straight out of a photo of a house in the mountains outside Reno, Nevada, Rubén Arenal pulling the covers around himself, hearing the sound of a generous river he couldn't see, a wintery unfrozen strong and fast-moving stream of water still catching snowflakes like feathers, out there somewhere even if he couldn't see it, a flowing river where there was nothing like it on any map, not snow-covered but icy-cold, absorbing each snowflake as it fell, out there where the Suzuki he'd borrowed was parked under a corrugated roof protecting a stack of cut wood, more than a single cord, Rubén Arenal sitting up wrapped in sheets and a blanket, alone in the room, misty-eyed, not from tears, but a blurry setting, not contemporary, of a faraway Japan in the present day, more than a day older than when he arrived, and not an hour younger, the

Tepitotonteotl, a small household guardian, one of the messenger gods, responsible for maintaining contact between human beings and the gods, Tepitotonteotl telling him nothing, Rubén Arenal waking up in an old-fashioned place and an uncertain time that looked a lot like eighteenth-century Japan, and Rocket, am I here or am I there, when here *is* there? what was left of his memory wasn't much of a memory at all, flickering images, bad quality, but the sensations were still fresh, the smell of Little Pascuala on his skin, the odor of burning oil from the lanterns in his nose, Rubén Arenal asking himself how much time had passed, it was daylight, but which day and how long had he been sleeping, questions he couldn't answer, Yoaltecuhtli, the Lord of the Night, giving nothing away, and there was no sound in the house, just wind pushing fallen snow against the outside walls, tickling the window frames, forcing cool air into the room that mixed with his breath, Rubén Arenal getting out of bed, still wrapped in the blanket, bending over to pick up his clothes, putting them on one by one until he was decent, folding the blanket at the end of the bed, walking in his stocking feet to the living room, seeing the hand-woven Saltillo rugs from the state of Coahuila, or from Teotitlán del Valle, and the three Japanese paper *kaku-andon* whose soft beams of atmospheric light had fallen diagonally across all the pieces of his pottery, presenting his work in the best light and on fine hand-woven materials in a pattern of colors and a traditional style, but there wasn't a single piece of his work on the rugs, the lamps without electric current stood where he'd placed them, unlit, the soft light of day coming in through the windows, and in the dining room not a plate, glass, crumb or dirty napkin, and Rocket, the kitchen's clean as a rose after rain, in the words of James Whitcomb Riley, Rubén Arenal leaving the kitchen, passing through the dining room, one of his ears hearing birdsong, following the vocalizations with his head cocked sideways, the music in his ear guiding him, walking through the living room, then down the wide corridor leading off the living room, Rubén Arenal lured in the direction of the room where he'd spent the night with

La Pascualita but walking past it, catching a glimpse of the mattress and Japanese lamps, Rubén Arenal standing at the far end of the hallway, finding a door he hadn't seen before, Pascuala Esparza's bedroom, knocking at the door, no answer, hearing birds singing on the other side of it, turning the knob, pushing the door open slowly gently without making a sound, and a roomful of birds, three canyon towhees, a couple of hermit thrushes, and more than two but not many rare painted redstarts, eight birds in all, a canopy bed with the ornamental cloth torn and yellowed with age, bedcovers ripped frayed moth-eaten, off-white walls stained with mold, fragile-looking bedposts and bed frame, no rug no curtains no furniture except for a large wardrobe, and the birds flying here and there, fluttering their wings, or walking across the floor, several painted redstarts from the family of wood warblers, the most beautiful of all warblers, black above, large white patches on their wings, red lower breast and belly, white outer tail feathers, flitting through the air, then perched on the frame holding the tattered canopy, and the canyon towhees, large long-legged earthy-brown sparrows with long tails, chunky bodies, short rounded wings, warm rusty undertail coverts, buffy throats and a hint of a reddish crown, scurrying along the floor, two hermit thrushes, motionless, standing upright, slender straight bills slightly raised, round heads and fairly long warm reddish tails, rich brown on the head and back, pale underparts with spots on the throat, smudged spots on the breast, Rubén Arenal taking a closer look, seeing their thin pale eye-rings, hermit thrushes hopping and scraping in the torn bedcovers strewn from bed to floor, now cocking their tails, bobbing them slowly, flicking their wings, Rubén Arenal standing just inside the room, listening to the hermit thrushes' melancholy song, a sustained whistle, ending with softer echo-like tones, *oh, holy holy, ah, purity purity eeh, sweetly sweetly,* pausing between each phrase, and the painted redstarts' two-syllable phrases followed by one or more single-syllable chirps, and loud low-pitched "cheeyu" calls coming out of their mouths, the canyon towhees' typical six to eight repeated, evenly spaced, double syllables, sounding like *chili-chili-chili-chili, chur chee-chee-chee eh,* introduced by a call note, Rubén Arenal sighing, no other sign of life, no Pascuala Esparza no Little Pascuala, and the birds ignoring him, landing on the top of the wardrobe, or standing on the edge of the far-gone mattress facing the window, but there was nothing more of life in the room, Rubén Arenal, hearing the birdsong, thinking of Ernesto, imagining he could hear the lonely cry of his friend, not behind the wheel of the Ford Lobo, but standing somewhere in Iguala, not alone but without hope, carrying a colossal quantity of longing to find his son, Rubén Arenal sinking to his knees, two tears falling down his cheeks, one for each eye, then the ducts drying up, and eight birds in flight, landing on him, a spiraling pattern of flickering light and feathers, settling on his shoulders head arms outstretched hands, birds and man man and birds, a moment of peace for Rubén Arenal, no worrying no thinking, just warm-blooded egg-laying vertebrates and a human being, no words but plenty of talk, and what the birds had to say, repeated and with variations, their voices thrown together, hermit thrushes, *oh, holy holy, ah, purity purity eeh, sweetly sweetly,* painted redstarts, two-syllable phrases, then one or more single-syllable chirps and the loud low-pitched "cheeyu," and canyon towhees, *chili-chili-chili,* introduced by a call note, hidden languages with hidden secrets for an outsider, but Rubén Arenal wasn't an outsider, he knew the coded language, understood every word, and the birds singing, Ernesto's got something to say to you, Rubén Arenal, still as a statue covered in birds, waiting, three redstarts, two thrushes, three towhees, whispering in his ear, their birdsong but Ernesto's words: "I'm still alive for you, you're still alive for me," Rubén Arenal, standing up from the kneeling position, the tear ducts dried up because there was nothing to cry about, what he hadn't known he knew now, Ernesto was coming home, returning to Chihuahua, and Rocket, rebirth's the miracle of life if you aren't the terminal victim of the police, the army, the government, or your own stupid behavior, *ciertamente, oh Jehová,* the thrushes, redstarts, and towhees turning in the air above his head, it was the end of the message, transmitted by birds with unique voices, and the birds circling above him, rising towards the nonexistent ceiling, a piece of sky winking down at him through the tear in a roof in disrepair, birds fading in the cool fresh invigorating light of the room, less color less definition but he could still see them, and before they completely disappeared, two hermit thrushes, three painted redstarts, three canyon towhees, voices in unison, we're playing on your team, and you know it.

Rubén Arenal, leaving the room in his stocking feet, taking a last look around him, and Rocket, if this is Pascuala Esparza's bedroom, and why shouldn't it be, then in what century? and how is it possible? sliding his feet forward on the polished floor like an amateur ice skater, the floor the only part of the house still in good shape, since he'd woken up alone on the mattress where he'd made love with Little Pascuala the night before, Rubén Arenal had seen only a ruin of a house, nothing like what it was when he arrived by way of Calle Apicultura past the Díaz building supply store in the Colonia Zootecnia, driving toward the mental hospital off Calle Apicultura, on the winding and twisting road, a landscape of mesquite, silver-leaved guayule shrubs, and ocotillo, heading toward Mápula, a location in the middle of nowhere, on a plain between the mountain ranges of Santo Domingo and la Yerbabuena, and then the potholed road, rough rutted, nonexistent, nothing like Mápula, with snow-flakes fluttering down on the Suzuki's windshield, Rubén Arenal gliding down the hallway into the living room, finding a chair but not his boots, settling himself there to smoke a cigarette, taking one out of a pack of Faros sitting on the table where he'd left it, and Rocket, a few lines from a flower song, "The Flower Tree," by Nezahualcoyotl, *Tiazque yehua xon ahuiacan. Niquittoa o ni Nezahualcoyotl. Huia! Cuix oc nelli nemohua oa in tlalticpac? Yhui. Ohuaye,* "We will pass away. I, Nezahualcoyotl, say, enjoy! Do we really live on earth? *Ohuaya, ohuaya,*" words from the *Cantares Mexicanos,* Rubén Arenal, putting a cigarette between his lips, a sigh of satisfaction, and

Rocket, repeating the words, I, Nezahualcoyotl, say, enjoy! lighting
the cigarette, the match light flaring in his face swallowed up by his
depthless black eyes, taking deep drags of smoke, exhaling, watching the smoke swirl up and out and break against a silent wall of air,
and Rocket, answering himself, I'm enjoying it, and how! and give
this room the once-over, you don't have to squint, nothing's left of
what I brought here, just the rugs, but there's the furniture belonging to Pascuala Esparza and her daughter, a tumbledown table with
a broken leg, cobwebbed chairs, and three torn paper *kaku-andon*
standing where I put them, no electricity, yes, and everything's in
apple-pie order, decay and dilapidation, no sign of life, but where'd
they go, Pascuala Esparza and *La Pascualita,* and what happened
to my mugs for *posol,* bowls, plates, a *hidria,* cups for tea, mugs for
coffee, a vase for flowers, a couple of ashtrays, and an urn? blowing smoke out his nose, picking loose tobacco out of his mouth,
pushing untidy long hair away from his eyes following from bottom
to top the contours of an uncared-for cabinet with lots of drawers
and shelves, catching sight of an oversized kraft envelope on a shelf,
Rubén Arenal crossing the room, weighing the bulging envelope
in his hands, seeing his name written on it in blue ink, opening the
envelope, spilling the contents out on the horizontal top part of the
table, finding plenty of pesos, paper and coins, 50-pesos banknotes
from El Banco de Londres y México, 1889-1913 issue, on one side
a portrait of Benito Juárez on the left, a gaucho with longhorn cows
on the right, and on the reverse, a golden eagle devouring a snake,
50-pesos banknotes from El Banco Oriental de México, 1900-1914
issue, a portrait of Esteban de Antuñano on the right, Euterpe, the
Muse of music, on the left, 100-pesos banknotes from El Banco de
Durango, a steamship on the left, seated Justice on the right, and on
the reverse 100 printed three times, and like shuffled cards, 5-pesos
banknotes from El Banco de Nuevo León, a vignette of a jaguar on
the left and a portrait of General Ignacio Zaragoza on the right,
the reverse, Indians with a shield, Mexican revolutionary 2-pesos
banknotes, Gobierno Provisional de México, 1916 issue, with a

Christopher Columbus statue on the left, the Aztec Empire Royal Throne Hall in the center, a Toltec stone head on the lower right, and on the reverse, in the center, the Aztec Sun Stone with a young woman in the middle, more than a few 5-pesos banknotes, El Banco de Guerrero, 1906-1914 issue, on one side a Mexican girl holding a basket of pineapples in the center, and on the reverse, a view of the port of Acapulco, a couple of 25-centavos banknotes from El Banco de Santa Eulalia, Chihuahua, series B, 1875 issue, a steam locomotive in the center, a handful of coins at the bottom of the envelope, silver Mexican 8-reales coins, San Luis Potosí mint from 1837, Rubén Arenal, no clue as to the value of the money he found, a costly collection, or what he'd do with it, Rubén Arenal cupping his hand and sweeping the paper money and coins back into the envelope, a hissing sound coming out of his mouth, rubbing the calluses on the palm of his right hand, a habit that never completely disappeared, a tongue that respected nothing but it's own meaning, and Rocket, it's time to leave this house that's straight out of a photo I've seen but can't remember where or when I saw it, like everything around here, in these hills or foothills or right-below-what-looks-like-mountains, snow and a river with a thin covering of ice, unless it's melted, there's a little sun now, and heat comes with it, melt melt my little snowflakes, my little lacy layers of ice.

Rubén Arenal switching on the ignition of the Suzuki, letting the engine turn over a couple of times until it decided to start, it'd been a cold night for cold times, seeing the bottle of homemade pulque he'd left behind on the passenger seat, breaking open the wax-sealed top, swallowing a couple of mouthfuls to warm him up, and now the Suzuki with right-hand steering was taking him back to Chihuahua the same way he'd come, almost automatic pilot, a vehicle with a 660cc engine that knew its way, the air coming through the open window no longer cold, almost warm, and Rocket, summing it up for himself, the weather's changing back to what it should've been but wasn't up there at Pascuala Esparza and Little Pascuala's house, odd thing, and no weatherwoman or man could explain it, a climate of its own, don't fight it, don't ask questions, don't mull it over, why start now, you didn't when you were up there, and here, no snow no gray no half-frozen river, a seasonal day, and before he knew it, Rubén Arenal saw the mental hospital off Calle Apicultura, passed the Díaz building supply store in the Colonia Zootecnia, driving on Calle Apicultura, heading more or less north into Chihuahua, remembering what he was saying to himself just after he'd pulled the minitruck out of town: *La Pascualita*'s waiting for me, and I'm waiting for her, it's a special kind of love, and Rocket, it feels like years ago or was it the night before last? it doesn't matter, I am driving my neighbor's truck back into town, so Rubén Arenal, the morning after, or a couple of days later, always a little letdown after the buildup, a modest disappointment in love, and Rocket, otherwise it wouldn't be love, '*mano*, it's nobody's fault, I already miss her, my Little Pascuala, and now a few words from Nezahualcoyotl, "Hungry Coyote," *Coyote Hambriento*, or fasting coyote, King of Texcoco, my King, and to think of him, I'm as relaxed here in this Suzuki as if the seat was as soft as a feather bed, maybe this poem's words are out of context but they're in context with my heart, from "In chololiztli iciic," "Song of the Flight," just this much, no more: *Azomo ye nelli tipaqui ti ya nemi tlalticpac? Ah ca za tinemi ihuan ti hual paqui in tlalticpac. Ah ca mochi ihui titotolinia. Ah ca no chichic teopouhqui tenahuac ye nican. Ohuaya ohuaya*, "Is it true we take pleasure, we who live on earth? Is it certain that we live to enjoy ourselves on earth? But we are all so filled with grief. Are bitterness and anguish the destiny of the people of earth? *Ohuaya ohuaya*," yes, that's what I've got to say, *Ohuaya ohuaya*, and Nezahualcoyotl's words are mine, his feelings my own, O, *La Pascualita*, a dream? I can still taste her kisses in my mouth, O, Coyuco, a nightmare? as real as this road the Suzuki's driving on, suddenly this seat's as uncomfortable as the flat pad of a prickly pear, Nezahualcoyotl or no Nezahualcoyotl, and Coyuco's fate smashes my face, a lesson a warning: stick your neck out, chop! reach for a pencil, a pen, slice! voiceless, fingerless, no complaints because there's no voice to complain or disagree or say not this but that, just ask a question, bang! a bullet, dead on the spot because you haven't got a right to say a word, just comply, be silent, any objections? no no shut up! that's what I told you, not a word, written or spoken, and no tears, don't cry, anyway, true tears are wept for the sake of oneself, *I wasn't weeping for him but for myself, for what I'd lost,* quoting that out of a book I read, and I'm telling you now, we lost a lot when those students disappeared, they're probably dead, so we can weep for ourselves, for where we're headed, we're off the starting blocks like greased lightning bound for a brick wall, and where's the room for Little Pascuala when my heart's breaking for our country of ghosts, check your watch, citizen, there's no time for love, and you might argue our pain is our humanity, well, I'm feeling just about as human as I can stand, and that goes for a lot of us, any proportion or share in relation to a whole, and I'll bet pesos from El Banco de Guerrero, El Banco de Nuevo León, El Banco de Santa Eulalia, El Banco de Durango, and whatever's in my pocket, that the percentage of people feeling just about as human as they can stand is pretty high, personal suffering, not suffering *the way a star or storm suffers,* which is shit compared to really suffering, *like dogs, like men broken by their fate,* words blown through the Suzuki's open window by a warm breeze because they're light as a feather and don't mean a thing, just words, like *pain's only real for the person who suffers it as a fatality*—incident accident chance event—*by giving it citizenship, allowing it into his soul,* nods and a wink to Julio Cortázar's ghost standing by the side of the road, playing cat and mouse with poetry and suffering, and in Coyuco's case, a hundred percent agony, no choice, the decision was made elsewhere, police, army, Guerreros Unidos, Los Caballeros Templarios, CJNG, the civil government of our country offering up another corpse to the inventory, *El mar los descubrió sin mirarlos siquiera, con su contacto frío los derribó y los anotó al pasar en su libro de agua,* "The sea discovered them without even looking at them; with its cold contact it knocked them down and listed them, in passing, in its book of water," from *House in the Sand,* by Pablo Neruda, and I, Rubén Arenal, driving a borrowed Carry Truck with right-hand steering, a man in love with *La Pascualita,* and I bet she's in love with me—first days of love, we've got to start somewhere—a world of its own where I'm so close to what I'd call happiness, if that happiness is a forest, I'm in the center of it, breathing its freshness, the smell of earth and trees, but there's another smell, it's Coyuco decomposing or burning on a pyre of other students, pure horror, wracking sadness and anger deep as a well reaching all the way down to hell, and the result, psychological stress, exhilaration frustration, two for the price of God knows how much because it costs a lot to put two sentiments up in a room under the same roof, so where does it leave me, let me look at the palms of my hands, maybe the answer's there, the Suzuki'll drive itself, besides, I'm almost home, ready to return this truck to my neighbor, Rubén Arenal glancing at the palms of his hands, focusing his bright black eyes, the Suzuki making each turn, or following a straightaway with its own power, and Rocket, let's see what the dried clay under my nails and in the creases of my palms has got to say, although I'd swear my hands were clean when I left Pascuala Esparza and Little Pascuala's house, so it's clay reminding me of my source, like a river, Rubén Arenal rolling up his sleeves, not looking through the windshield, the Suzuki was doing fine on its own, and Rocket, what the fuck! my arms are covered with clay-drawn lines and figures, Rubén Arenal thinking of the "first foundation of the world," many thousands of years ago, so many that four distinct ages, called Suns, with their four different universes, existed prior to the present epoch, a spiral evolution of progressively better, more complex forms of inhabitants, plants, and food, the four primordial forces, water, earth, fire, and wind, successively reigning over those ages, until the fifth epoch, our Sun, right here right now, and Rocket, reciting part of the *Anales de Cuauhtitlán,* according to Miguel-León Portilla:

Then the second Sun [age] was founded.
Its sign was 4-Tiger.
It was called the Sun of the Tiger.
In it it happened
that the sky sunk,
the Sun did not continue its course.
When the sun arrived at midday,
then nightfall came
and when it became dark,
the tigers devoured the people.
And the giants lived during this Sun.
The old men said
that the giants greeted one another thusly:
"do not fall down,"
because he who fell down,
fell forever.

Rubén Arenal trying to rub the lines and figures from his hands and arms, nothing came off, no redness, imperturbable impermeable skin, and no pain either, rubbing as hard as he could, the Suzuki making its way home, and Rocket, ancient words might be a cure, now I'll try a few lines from "Legend of the Suns" in *Codex Chimalpopoca,* a translation by John Bierhorst, first the preamble, to spark my memory, which needs a light, "Here are wisdom tales made long ago, of how the earth was established, how everything was established, how whatever is known started, how all the suns that there were began," and now the second sun again, but this time from Bierhorst, that'll work, "The sun is named 4 wind. These people, who lived in the second age, were blown away by the wind in the time of the sun 4 wind. And when they were blown away and destroyed, they turned into monkeys. All their houses and trees were blown away. And the sun also was blown away. And what they ate was 12 Snake. That was their food. It was 364 years that they lived, and only one day that they were blown by the wind, destroyed in a day sign 4 Wind. And their year was 1 Flint," the Suzuki pulled up in front of Rubén Arenal's neighbor's house, Rubén Arenal parked the Carry Truck, his trembling fingers switched off the ignition, then he started searching his skin for lines figures symbols signs, now there was nothing there, the tigers had devoured them, the wind had blown them away, and Rocket, "In the perspective of the Great Time every existence is precarious, evanescent and illusory. Seen in the light of the major cosmic rhythms ... not only is human existence, and history itself with all its countless empires, dynasties, revolutions and counter-revolutions, manifestly ephemeral and in a sense unreal; the Universe itself vanishes into unreality," that's Mircea Eliade, a really smart guy, one of the best expositors of the psychology of religion, mythology and magic, I wonder if I've vanished with the Universe into unreality, an inquiry is in order, an official iinvestigation, there *was* dried clay under my nails and in the creases of my palms, my arms *were* covered with clay-drawn lines and figures—what it tells me is that I've got to live with two sentiments occupying the same place in my heart, the lines and figures, they're the directions open to me, plenty of north south east west, part of my evolution, the question now is which way do I go if I haven't vanished, because I'm still here, Rubén Arenal getting out of the Carry Truck, wiping his face with a handkerchief, stomping his feet on the ground, his not-too-fleshy jowls bouncing, and Rocket, solid earth beneath my feet, I can feel the impact, Rubén Arenal jangling the keys, walking to his neighbor's door, no one home, leaving the keys under a potted plant, turning around and following the sidewalk taking him home, and Rocket, a meaningful dialogue: Where are you going? Right now, home, Not now, *tonto,* who do you think's walking with you, Ramón Navarro? where are you going? Just outside, not into the street, but outside, past the husk skin shell pod, Did you bring any money today? Yes, I brought some, How much? Does it matter? where I'm going, it isn't money that counts, Now you're talking, *'mano,* but what're you going to do when you get there, outside the husk skin shell pod? I'm going to live, feel everything, *¡no seas tonto!* don't be a fool! with what I've learned about myself today there's enough for me to do for a life-time, short or long, whether I'm killed by the police or soldiers or live to be an old man, whether I penetrated *La Pascualita,* got into her heart, and love her—she's part of me and I'm part of her—or I never see her again, that's life, And you can leave it at that? What's "that"? you talk as if that isn't enough, living with disappointment, rage, and that loving feeling for someone, all at the same time—the opposite of the Righteous Brothers—I call that plenty, We can't choose the birth we'd like to have, it's always others who decide what sort of birth we're going to get, and when we're old enough to think about our life, we're already condemned to the life we've been given, accept it or refuse it, We can change, *cabrón,* you think you're a tough guy because of living by the credo life's what it is, maybe it's true, but only to the extent that we've got a lot of things going on and they're going on at the same time, simultaneously single-minded, enough to make a rat scream, that's the part I'll grant you, but it's more than accept or refuse, and Rocket, a short conversa-tion, as usual, back and forth, not the first time, not the last, and don't ask who I'm talking to, it's between me and myself, like most things, but let's say that it's straightened me out, what's standing up ahead of me isn't a matter of buying this or selling that or what can I have or get out of it, it goes deeper, I don't know what I'm going to do, but I know there're high and low roads, paths, alleyways, turn-pikes, lanes and highways to take, and they're real, not made of clay, the lines figures symbols signs that were written all over me just told me to open my eyes and take a good look around.

Two friends two friends, how close could they get without being one man, Ernesto behind the wheel of Rubén Arenal's pickup, and outside the Ford Lobo, red and white or cream and faded green, nature's drama continued: the wind, the moon, the sky, plants, animals, clouds, and Ernesto Cisneros, listen to the sounds, don't listen to what your mind's telling you, and the return of the *cuervo tamaulipeco,* a Tamaulipas crow, a companion, from Matamoros in Tamaulipas or from the town of General Bravo, it used to be called Rancho del Toro, in the state of Nuevo León, and the Tamaulipas crow, that's good advice you're giving yourself, a crow's voice loud enough to hear with the windows open, and then a soft-voiced *gar-lik,* barely audible, a bird speaking to itself, and Ernesto Cisneros, it's nice to have you back, *compañero,* come on in, don't just stand there balancing on the edge of the window, it's night and plenty lonely on this road, not a headlight in sight, my *cuervo tamaulip-eco,* wherever you've come from you're welcome, I'd embrace you warmly but I'm driving, the crow, fourteen inches long, sleek, handsome, with glossy dark, bluish feathers, hopping into the truck, standing on the bench of a standard cab, looking past the dash out the windshield at the cloudy night sky above the highway, nodding its head, a slender and black beak in the dashboard light, a Tamaulipas crow, *gar-lik,* croaking like a frog, a few more things to say to itself, then turning its head, taking a good look at Ernesto and the mask he was wearing, recognizing the wrestler, the face of Mil Máscaras, Aarón Rodríguez, "The Man of a Thousand Masks," and Ernesto Cisneros, that's it, make yourself comfortable, the bird snuggling up to him, tucking its head into his ribcage, Ernesto taking a long hard look at the empty road ahead, then down at the crow looking up at him, a crow making short sharp movements with its head and beak, indicating Ernesto's hands on the wheel, Ernesto looking at them, loosening his grip, holding one hand in front of his face, his conversation with Aarón far behind him, remnants of it hanging in the air not far from Bodega Aurrerá, but here in the Ford pickup, wearing the mask of Mil Máscaras, and now his hand marked with figures and lines, symbols and signs written in charcoal, not clay, but two friends, how close could they get without being one man, Ernesto putting his hand back on the wheel, taking the other off and looking at it, more figures signs symbols lines, holding the wheel straight with his upraised knees, rolling up his sleeves, arms covered with the same charcoal drawings, including ordinal and cardinal numbers, the *cuervo tamaulipeco,* handsome and sleek, a fount of wisdom, and the Tamaulipas crow, you need a cigarette, and Ernesto Cisneros, what's all this with the drawings on my skin, they weren't there when I left Iguala, and now, even though they're written with charcoal, they won't come off even if I spit on them and rub with my fingers as hard as I can, and the Tamaulipas crow, repeating itself, you need a cigarette, and Ernesto Cisneros, if it's a curse, I ask myself, what've I done to deserve this? I don't feel any different than I felt before, when I found this mask and it became part of me, my skin, my soul, in the name of the *Virgen del Sagrado Corazón,* Our Lady of Guadalupe, and the saints, what've I done? then Ernesto remembering his murderous behavior in Iguala de la Independencia, a convenient amnesia, and Ernesto Cisneros, I guess I've forgiven myself but my body hasn't, and the Tamaulipas crow, a cigarette, 'mano, Ernesto showing signs of panic behind the wheel, not on his face, but hidden behind one of Mil Máscaras' thousand masks, trembling hands, jerking knees, a spasmodic twitch of the muscles, alternately braking and accelerating, the crow watching all of it, offering a pragmatic prod with its compact head against Ernesto's right side as a distraction, and the Tamaulipas crow, not a single *gar-lik,* but a loud and clear shout: cigarette! Ernesto hearing the voice, fumbling with his shirt pocket, and Ernesto Cisneros, you remind me, I need a smoke, and the Tamaulipas crow, shaking its head, that's what I've been saying for a couple of miles, and slow down, get off the road, you're going to have an accident, 'mano, and Ernesto Cisneros, but I left Rocket's Faros in the bathroom at the hotel, and the Tamaulipas crow, a patient calming voice, the glovebox, check it, and slow down, Ernesto taking the first exit he saw, gliding slowly toward an intersection, then pulling off the road, nothing in sight, but fumbling now with trouser pockets, there wasn't a chance he kept a soft pack of cigarettes in them, but he kept on shoving his hands in his pockets almost separating stitches, no rice-paper cigarettes, not a pack of Delicados or Fiesta, not a white and green and black pack of Aros, a gold, red and white pack of Capri, no, until the crow, a screech, bringing Ernesto to a halt, and Ernesto Cisneros, what would I do without you, my Tamaulipas crow, Ernesto, reaching past the crow and opening the glove compartment, finding two unopened packs of Faros, thanking Rubén Arenal for his supply of coffin nails at hand, Ernesto exhaling a sigh, opening a pack, inhaling a lungful of smoke, coughing, and the night wind carried tobacco smoke out the window.

With Ernesto calm but wearing the face of another, the Tamaulipas crow hopped up onto the dashboard, ducking its head, stretching its neck out and leaning away from the windshield, a crow fourteen inches long with not a lot of room for its tail feathers that were brushing against the glass, bending forward over the speedometer to speak directly to Ernesto, and the Tamaulipas crow, you have a friend who owns this truck, I think you should see him right away, so when you get to town don't stop to change your clothes or wash your mask and scrub your hands but go directly to see him, and remember, November is the month for *cempasúchiles,* the Mexican marigold, flowers for the Day of the Dead, and alfalfa, too, but it's the flowers that concern you and Lupe, your Guadalupe, not the alfalfa, a pea-family plant with cloverlike leaves, food for a beast is food for man, but you can't eat when you're dead, the marigolds are a tribute to your son, Ernesto putting out the cigarette by pinching the burning end of it between his second finger and thumb, not feeling the heat, but plainly feeling the words pronounced by the crow, a tear dropping out of his right eye, running down the face of the mask he was wearing, leopard-skin and gold, Ernesto tossing the butt out the window, the crow hopping back to the edge of the open window on the passenger side, body half in tail half out, and Ernesto Cisneros, you mean to tell me—the crow interrupting him, and the Tamaulipas crow, the more human you are the more human you feel, don't get mad, don't be angry, no bending out of shape, you've already got a mask for a face, but no foaming at the mouth, that's not for you anymore, not after what you've done and been through, may God protect you from more suffering, the bird turning around, facing the night and the open sky, more tears flowing from Ernesto's blinking eyes, the Tamaulipas crow taking off, a wide spread of black wings lost in darkness, the headlights were switched off to preserve the battery, the crow making several passes over the Ford, Ernesto didn't see it, he was busy wiping the tears from his face, now wearing a blue-and-red mask with white shark's teeth, Ernesto feeling the mask covering his face, tilting the rearview mirror, looking at himself, the mask changing color before his eyes, now green and red with white shark's teeth, and Ernesto Cisneros, the masks are as changeful as spring, a moment for Lewis Morris, a Welsh academic, politician and popular poet, but quoting the poet didn't make him feel better, Ernesto turned the rearview mirror back to its place, leaned out the open window and searched the black sky for the crow, a companion, no sign of it, the clouds, hurrying away, followed by others, giving pursuit, clouds chasing clouds, Ernesto starting the engine, hearing a song in his head and heart, a lonely kind of song sung by Vicente "Chente" Fernández Gómez, the Sinatra of *ranchera* music, "Voy a navegar," "I'm Going On A Voyage," by Chucho Martínez Gil:

> Ya me voy muy lejos, vine a despedirme,
> solamente Dios sabe si algún día tenga que volver.
> Ahí te dejo todo, no me llevo nada
> ¿Pa' qué quiero cosas que al final del tiempo
> me hagan padecer?
>
> Si alguien te pregunta que pa' dónde me dirijo,
> dile que me fui sin saber siquiera,
> para dónde ir.
>
> Voy a caminar, voy a navegar,
> para ver si así, para ver si así
> te puedo yo olvidar.

Puede ser que el tiempo
borre para siempre tu amor traicionero,
puede ser que un día llegue hasta mi vida
un amor verdadero.

Si alguien te pregunta que pa' dónde me dirijo
dile que me fui sin saber siquiera,
para dónde ir.

Voy a caminar, voy a navegar,
para ver si así, para ver si así
te puedo te puedo yo olvidar.

I'm going far away, I came to say farewell,
only God knows if one day I'll return.
I leave everything there, I take nothing with me.
Why would I want things that in the end
may make me suffer?

If someone asks you where I'm going,
say that I left without even knowing
where to go.

I'm going away on a journey, on a voyage,
to see if by doing so, if in this way
I manage to forget you.

It may be that time
will erase your faithless love forever,
it may be that one day in my life,
a true love will come.

If someone asks you where I'm going,
say that I left without even knowing
where to go.

I'm going away on a journey, on a voyage,
to see if by doing so, if in this way
I manage to forget you.

And with this song, Ernesto put the truck in reverse, then into first
gear, heading for the highway, rejoining MEX-49 toward Gomez
Palacio/Cuencame and crossing into Durango, then 55.87 miles,
staying straight to go onto MEX-49/Carretera Entronque La
Chicharrona-Cuencamé, continuing to follow MEX-49, then 42.42
miles, merging onto MEX-40D toward Gomez Palacio/MEX-40/
MEX-49D/Chihuahua/Monterrey/Torreón, in the direction of
Torreón in Coahuila, La Perla de La Laguna, three lagoons long ago,
Mayrán, Tlahualilo and Viesca, now dry, and the city of Gómez
Palacio in northeastern Durango, a fine line separating two geo-
graphical areas, Ernesto traveling 55.48 miles, then merging onto
MEX-49/Carretera Comarca Lagunera-Ciudad Jiménez via the exit
on the left toward Chihuahua, 17.85 miles, and merging again onto
MEX-49D via the exit on the left toward Jiménez, crossing into
Chihuahua, accompanied by silence, no song, just the sound of
wind passing through the open windows, the night almost becoming early morning, no crow, but what stayed the same for the rest of
his journey was the flow of his tears, an echo of the words pronounced by the Tamaulipas crow, Ernesto feeling the tears falling
against his chest, moistening his shirt, damp and sticking to his
skin, Ernesto's eyes red and swollen behind the mask, but he could
see the highway clearly, tears coming and going, soaking his clothes,
Ernesto, afraid he'd flood the cab, looking down at his neatly polished boots, damp laces from falling tears, the accelerator and brake
pedal, salty water gathering there, a pond, sloshing forward or back
when he braked or put his foot down on the accelerator, Ernesto
Cisneros speaking to no one but himself, and Ernesto Cisneros, the
Tamaulipas crow, my companion, no *gar-lik*s, but the bird was right,
I've got to get myself to Rocket, and then to have a face to face, I
mean mask to face, my son my son, Ernesto seeing light in a spike

of fire, an aurora of fire that seemed to be pricking the sky, while the charcoal signs symbols figures lines still covered his hands and arms, he was covered from neck to toe, and the aurora, an omen like one of the presages Moctezuma II, Moctezuma Xocoyotzin, saw in 1517, but just one of the many omens, it was Ernesto after all, not the ninth ruler of Tenochtitlan, a city-state located on an island near the western shore of Lake Texcoco, but Ernesto driving Rubén Arenal's Ford pickup, just a vehicle, an F-150, not behind the wheel of a city or a state, and the light of dawn, sunlight on the horizon chased away the spike of fire, and Ernesto Cisneros, the first thing I'll show him after he's seen my face, one of the masks of Mil Máscaras, who knows which one, they keep on changing, the first thing I'll show him will be these things written on my arms and hands, he'll know what it means, all of it, mask and charcoal writing, because I've got to include what my face looks like now, and before Ernesto could get beyond a couple of the other presages and omens that Moctezuma II had seen, a list that wasn't very long—the temple of Huitzilopochtli burning, or seeing a strange type of lightning, a thunderbolt without thunder, that struck the temple of Xiuhteuctli, the god of fire—he arrived on the outskirts of Chihuahua, the pond of tears at his feet had dried up leaving a salty residue on the floor mat and the soles of his boots, Ernesto taking a glance at the floor of the cab, and Ernesto Cisneros, "Cry! Cry! Cry!" again that song, it's the message I sent to Mariano, Rosalía, Ignacio, I didn't know it then, but now I do, because it takes a while and a lot of tears, and a few of the lyrics, *Todo el mundo sabe a donde vas, cuando se pone el sol. / Creo que vives tan sólo para ver las luces de la ciudad. / Gasté todo mi tiempo intentádolo una y otra vez. / Porque cuando las luces pierdan su brillo, llorarás, y llorarás,* "Everybody knows where you go when the sun goes down, / I think you only live to see the lights uptown, / I wasted my time when I would try, try, try, / 'Cause when the lights have lost their glow, you'll cry, cry, cry," and that reminds me, as if it was a year ago and I can't figure out where I put it, my mind isn't adding things up, there's Ignacio, my second father, he should've hit me with his hand-painted wooden stick, knocked some sense into me, I don't hold it against him but it didn't happen, I didn't give him the chance, so once I've spoken to Rocket, as the crow said, I'll turn to Ignacio, a full confession if he doesn't already know it, then maybe he'll go to Mariano and Rosalía, an extended family, a family that extends beyond the nuclear family, including grandparents, aunts, uncles, and other relatives, who all live nearby, but not exactly a family, in this case they're neighbors, but more than friends, Mariano and Rosalía, I want somebody to tell me what to do, it's not their questions now but mine, and if Ignacio's like a second father to me, that makes him a father, first or second one isn't important, children don't usually tell everything they do think feel to their fathers, not me, not even my father, but Ignacio, that's another story, so whoever's thinking up there, "Yakety Yak," Leiber and Stoller for the Coasters, my brain's talking at length but not about trivial or boring subjects, a flow of words in a rush like an express train, no tricks! I won't stand for it, not now, not any more, it's time to limit the damaging effects, Aarón said it, I'm wearing a thousand layers of faces to protect myself, representing the faces of the families of the disappeared, I've got to set an example through ethical, righteous, worthy-of-the-mask behavior, and Egon Kisch, a journalist: "the Man-automaton—" that's me! "—working ever for the welfare of strangers and unconditionally subject to an extraneous will … " my fate is absolutely my own, but I've got to know how to do it, what to do, and we're still mourning, Lupita and I, whether Coyuco turns up or not, it's grief sorrowing parents lamentation no matter which way it goes, remember what I said, there's nothing she can do right now but cry, and weeping won't get us any closer to knowing anything, only wrenching our guts, and for Irma, too, named by her parents after Irma Serrano, La Tigresa, broken hearts all around, a few more turns and I'm there, this Ford's an inspiration, giving me the urge to do something, especially to do something creative, I can almost see the street entrance that leads to the foyer lit by an electric bulb hanging from the ceiling, a foyer separating Rocket's apartment and pottery studio from the street entrance, time flies when you aren't thinking out loud, and who needs a watch, Ernesto looking at his wrist, holding the steering wheel steady with his other hand, the watch his father gave him, a Timex, and Ernesto Cisneros, with a mechanical voice, "Ladies and gentlemen, this is John Cameron Swayze reporting for Timex in Acapulco, Mexico, just behind me you can see the rugged face of the famous La Perla cliffs, that gorge goes up up up to the height of a twelve-story building, and there, climbing barefoot to the top of the cliff, is one of the bravest men I know, that man is Raúl García, high diving champion of the world, take a good look at his hand, notice there's a Timex waterproof watch strapped around it, that watch will bear the full shock of impact as García hurtles down to the bottom of that narrow gorge and hits that water at more than eighty-five miles an hour," Ernesto admiring his wristwatch, remembering his father, long gone, not Ignacio, the other father, then another tear tumbling, and Ernesto Cisneros, he gave it to me in '62, and look at that, it's still going, still ticking away smoothly, see that sweep hand go! that's the amazing Timex waterproof, dustproof, shock resistant—interrupting himself, taking John Cameron Swayze's lead, but looking past the wristwatch at his hands, checking his arms, and Ernesto Cisneros, hold on, wait a minute, the figures signs symbols lines, they've all disappeared, carried out the window on the wings of the crow and the words of the song by Chente Fernández, that bird's my good luck charm, and the Timex might be shock resistant, but I'm as fragile as a strand of rain, James Whitcomb Riley, writer, poet, and I'm not even the same Ernesto that left Chihuahua a couple of days ago, how many, it's hard to tell, I don't know what I look like because my face, this mask that's my face, keeps changing, hang on hang on, eyes on the road, no accidents in a borrowed car or truck, not even if it was my own, and not a parking place, so once more around the block, Ernesto turning the steering wheel, making a corner with common sense, no speeding, keeping his eyes on the road ahead of him, a glance in the rearview mirror, Ernesto seeing another change in the mask, a shiny silver lamé Mount Fuji mask with white and blue vinyl, a presentation mask, not by Don Ranulfo López, 84 Calle San Antonio Tomatlán, Colonia Morelos in Mexico City, but his son, Leopoldo, or Alejandro, Ranulfo's grandson, a mask worn for press conferences, movies, or thrown to the crowd, Ernesto touched the zipper at the back of his head, but not a single strip of metal or plastic, straightening the wheel, squinting at the sunlight and the road with tired eyes and no sunglasses, it was still early, but the streets weren't quite empty, Ernesto's eyes following a cart drawn by a horse, out of the corner of his eye a bus idling at a bus stop, then a glance at a silver 1995 Lincoln Town Car, a white Nissan Versa with tinted windows, and finally, before turning the corner, admiring a 1972 white Dodge Dart two-door hardtop with a vinyl-padded black roof, and Ernesto Cisneros, there's a spot and it's right in front, like the old proverb, a poor man without patience is like a lamp without oil, Ernesto pulling the truck to the curb to park the Ford Lobo in the empty space a few steps from the entrance to Rubén Arenal's home, his pottery studio, the engine was switched off, Ernesto reaching behind the bench seat for a rag to dust off the seat and dry the sweat off the steering wheel, then shaking out the floor mats, and Ernesto Cisneros, talking to himself, I'll gather the things I took with me, but there was nothing to take out of the truck, his own body, and the clothes he was wearing, that's it, he'd gotten rid of the rest, and so he climbed down, locked the door, and stood wiping his hands on his trouser legs as the yellowish air feathered against a blue sky.

Now what? what're you going to do about yourself, I'm fed up with not knowing, but remember the poor man without patience, a minute gone by and you're already forgetting a useful proverb, yes, I'm getting a late start—true as the gospel, in the words of Francis Beaumont and John Fletcher, dramatists during the reign of James

I of England—but a start just the same, and with my face, masks
changing at a rate of I-don't-know-how-many an hour, it won't be
easy, but wrestlers in my country are held in high esteem, admired
and revered, and without being aware of it, I've changed more
than my face, and thanks to Aarón, a surprise witness, a guide, no
meddler, a spontaneous referee, and a compassionate linesman—
definitely not a judge—we all know protests aren't going to do any
good, it's been tried, we line up, we make signs with fat indelible
markers, marching marching, but what good does it do? the fol-
low-up's always a cover-up from beginning to end, that's the way it
works, protect yourself from the powerful impossible professors of
whitewash camouflage disguise, but I've got a decent hand despite
murdering three cops, and losing my son, our son, our Coyuco, not
finding him in Iguala, and I'll bet the same amount of pesos Rocket
is used to betting that when they use the Lidar system, which stands
for Light Detection and Ranging, and they *will* use it, at a cost of
around 600,000 pesos, and a satellite navigation-powered image
processing system called GrafNav, they won't find a fucking thing,
no trace, Coyuco, dead and ten to one not even buried, and the
other forty-three *normalistas,* like I said before, gone gone gone,
it's Coyuco's life, our son, Lupita's and mine, but in order to get myself going, I'll need a few friendly down-to-earth tips suggestions
pointers, solid advice, Ernesto tasting the almost fresh morning air,
looking at the street, a few pedestrians, then up at the sky again,
and Ernesto Cisneros, it's morning one hundred percent, I don't
consider it morning until the entire sky is lit, and now it's not very
bright but full of light, a swift silence landing on the street like a
settling bird, Ernesto, eyes tilting down, scanning the road ahead
of him, catching sight of a man coming from a side street, cutting
across the intersection without traffic, the man didn't turn his head
left or right, intent on moving forward, there wasn't a car to look out
for, dead calm, a calm that settled on Ernesto, too, recognizing the
man wearing a smile, his untidy long hair falling onto his rounded
cheeks, languid, sad eyes, and Ernesto Cisneros, a little tired after a

long drive, but that's for later, for now I'll give my dearest friend, my brother, a hug, Ernesto spreading his arms wide in wait for Rubén Arenal, Rubén Arenal walking in his direction, long strides, with open arms to greet his dearest friend, his brother, not rubbing any calluses, a habit put off for later, until a later time, not now, maybe never again, a man and potter at arm's length with tension disquiet fear, out of touch for the moment, Rubén Arenal identifying his friend's features behind one of the many masks of Mil Máscaras, Ernesto taking a few steps forward, a red, green and gold Aztec eagle warrior mask on his face, and a white letter M in center of the forehead, and Rocket, to himself, Guerrero Águila, that's him, after all he's been through, and Lupe, too, because somewhere someone's digging a hole to make a Hawaiian-style large pit pig roast for human beings, scooping the ashes and gathering the bones, filling plastic bags with them and dumping the contents in the river, the frightening reality that's the world, this world we live in, "Let us not stain the river with our blood," and the two men, Rubén Arenal and Ernesto, bearing the scars of the life they led that couldn't be anyone else's, fell into each others arms.

Coyuco's dream or *One last time*

Nothing will be out-and-out boring again, not that it really was, not for me, there was always plenty to do, or not do, and many who did just that, nothing, were at peace with themselves, no matter what other people said, and those who couldn't do anything but work, didn't have a choice, would keep on with what they knew how to do until they retired or dropped dead, beggars, taxi drivers, car salesmen, cowboys, mechanics, electricians and plumbers, hair dressers, bookkeepers, lawyers, waitresses, actresses, bakers, opticians, assembly line workers, gymnasts, refrigerator repairmen, adobe bricklayers, retired military, or those still in service, it's our right to do something or nothing if we could afford to do it, but from my perspective, here, on a heap of rotting student teachers—not quite rotting but beginning to smell—you can call us *normalistas,* students that left the Raúl Isidro Burgos Normal Rural School of Ayotzinapa, a *Escuela Normal,* a teacher-training college, at around five-thirty or six in the afternoon, I can't remember what time exactly, on September 26, 2014, with the idea of getting our hands on as many buses as we could find in Iguala, not Chilpo, because Chilpancingo was too dangerous, and now, here we are, after a longish or short period as students learning how to teach, most of us new, others a couple of years down the road of education, with politics, a desire to help, a solid indignation at injustice, a position point of view policy, an approach to this world, and with no harm to others, you can call us what you like, rebellious, intelligent, practical, but today we're a heap of dead student teachers, mangled, cut, torn to shreds, beaten to a pulp, shot, strangled, here we are and we aren't here for long, they've got plans for us, you can't leave what's left of forty-three bodies, and mine, just lying around for some journalist or honest policeman to find, I can't say what their plans are but the worst of it is over for us, lying here in pieces like stacked wood, more than a cord, it's as if I'm a bird flying over my own body looking down at the remains of forty-three lives, and my own, we didn't get far, I hope our deaths will mean something, but that depends on what you do with how you feel about what happened, parents brothers sisters wives girlfriends, it's like we've committed a sin, punished, dead, and in horrible ways, tortured and killed, what kind of sin could it be that's punished like they've punished us? no, I don't believe it, sins are punished by God, or forgiven, we didn't commit an immoral act considered to be a transgression against divine law, and what's coming next isn't for anyone to see, gruesome vile unspeakable, you'd better shut your eyes, I have to look, my eyes're open for eternity, I see what nobody else can see, except for the others lying here with me, they're dead but they aren't blind, I wonder if we'll be able see when there's nothing in the sockets of our eyes, eyes melted by the intense heat of flames, or in a tub of acid to dissolve everything that's left of us, even the bones, if that's what's in store for us then it's a sin added to the one they committed already by killing us, *que Dios tenga misericordia de nuestras almas,* May God have mercy on our souls, you can see that I haven't lost my faith, now and then a moment of sadness, not a rush of mental strain, exhaustion or difficulty breathing, if you aren't alive no one can force you to breathe no matter how many times they jump up and down on your chest, a few words from James 1:6, and I'll lower my voice, a whisper, *Pero pida con fe, no dudando nada; porque el que duda es semejante a la onda del mar, que es arrastrada por el viento y echada de una parte a otra,* "But let him ask in faith, with no doubting, for the one who doubts is like a wave of the sea that is driven and tossed by the wind," yes, *Santiago 1:6,* and all that because I've asked Him for wisdom, not for me, it's too late, and in His generosity He's given me plenty, when I was alive, but for my father and mother, and Irma, their friends and families, and the friends and families of my fellow students, that they may live with what's happened to me, to their sons, without too much bitterness or a fatal desire for revenge because there're other ways to fight, and since I'm no longer of this life, it's up to them to find their way, I can't help no matter how much I'd like to, what's done is done and can't be undone, says the corpse to the wind, but you don't have my ashes to scatter on the river or blow across the fields, it's so quiet now, why isn't there music here when there's been music everywhere else, it's playing and I can't hear it with ears that aren't operating normally or properly, out of order, *Porque como el cuerpo sin espíritu está muerto, así también la fe sin obras está muerta,* "For as the body apart from the spirit is dead, so also faith apart from works is dead," *Santiago 2:26,* yes, a fatal desire for revenge would be a life-threatening thing for my family, a thing I couldn't live with—I know, I know, I'm dead already, so what's there to worry about—but I can't think of my mother and father, and poor Irma, even if she was named by her parents after a singer and actress from Comitán de Domínguez in Chiapas, I can't think of them going through hell because of me, not when I was alive, and not now, but who can control the behavior of others, and when you have no voice, you can't comfort anyone, God knows I'd like to comfort them, children get old enough and they can be a mother or a father to their parents, take them by the arm, separately or together, sitting down face to face, a conversation, soothing words comforting words, removing their doubts or fears, with Irma it's a different story, she's a woman and I'm the man who loves her, a comfort of equals—there's nothing wrong with a world where you can get love with or without a few hairs—and besides, she's got her own mother and father, and since all of us are lying here, let the others be witnesses, hear ye, hear ye! Irma and I, hand in hand, visiting the colonial aqueduct, begun in 1751 to replace an earlier one built in 1706, that brought water from Río Chuviscar in the west to the town of San Felipe el Real de Chihuahua—Chihuahua before it was called Chihuahua in 1824—what I know about life could fill a thimble, so here we are, Irma and I, deciding to stretch our legs after a cold drink at Cafetería Lerdo, Avenida Melchor Ocampo, slowly reaching Paseo Simón Bolívar, our snail-paced steps, what's the hurry when you're in love! rounding the corner, a sharp one, passing Calle 12a, Calle 10a, then Octava, looking left looking right, who knows where we entered the park, maybe Calle Sexta, we're stretching our legs, but enough is enough, sitting together on a bench under a tree in the Parque Lerdo, the central part of the city, not far from Quinta Luz, the Museo de la Revolución, a ten-minute walk heading southeast from the park, but we're staying where we are, sitting on a bench in the shade not saying a word, feeling the things we aren't saying, things that warm us from the inside out while staring at a palm tree, a beautiful sky, a few people taking a stroll, others on park benches, too, reading El Heraldo or El Diario, or reading a book, but we don't see them, they're invisible like I'll be in a couple of hours, and it isn't dark yet, our eyes, Irma's and mine, they're open wide on a dazzling afternoon sun not losing its color, reddish-orange light staining the skin on the back of our hands, fingers entwined, the sun throwing its light at an angle of less than forty-five degrees, don't ask me how I can measure it, I just know, skimming the tops of roofs and trees, not falling off the edge of the city, not yet, but in no time it'll be dark, nightmarish night when there aren't any stars, no moon either, our blood soaking into the ground, because that's how I see it from here, lying on a heap of disfigured bodies, but in my dream with Irma, that kind of night never shows up, a caressing darkness floating on a gentle breeze, stillness and peace, a dream that begins and ends here, on this pile of human refuse, people thrown away, rejected as worthless, our flesh beginning to nourish the earth, "I don't know how much time's gone by, aside from this awareness of my motionless body I feel nothing," my empty sockets searching for what I'll never see, but what a lucky day! my dream's in my head, there's no having to look for it, it's here, tap tap tap with a forefinger I don't have, "the voices come and go, like the images I evoke," while my goal, as long as I can prolong this moment, is "to remember in order to survive," not my body, that's for sure, too late too late, but for all the details of the life I've had until now, who knows what the next chapter will be, life after death, the hereafter, eternity, motherfucking nothing? there's only so much my brain, a human brain, can grasp, where is my dream? that's what I need, I've got to get back to it, I'd search my pockets but I don't have hands that move or pockets to turn inside out, my clothes aren't where they're supposed to be, maybe I don't have hands or fingers, I can't see them or feel them, but I know I won't find a dream in my pocket, it's safe and sound, sheltered in my heart, deep as sleep, remember, we're on the bench in Lerdo Park, Irma and I, accompaniments to a setting sun that's taking its time, and we're grateful for it, nothing settles the spirit like a burning amber streak of light warming the back of your hand, we both swear to it, using the same words coming out of our mouths at the same time, but we can't go on sitting here forever, Irma says, and me, I just tell her to be patient, it's the sun we're waiting for, when it's stumbled over the edge of the earth and disappeared we can move on, but what I want to tell her is that one day she'll begin to search in herself for the other who's disappeared, has died, and is lost forever, an upside-down story of Narcissus, a search of the possible double, the possible other, meaning me, a premonition? a hunch? a suspicion that my days are numbered? who can say, but that's what's on my mind, not the sun setting and the shadows falling over the park, and she doesn't let go of my hand when we stand up, moving together, one person, indivisible, but without liberty and justice, part of a pledge *en el Norte,* a country more interested in the possession of the soul than that of the body, as my father says, a pledge that isn't my own, not now not ever, but the same words are found in the oath to our flag, our *Juramento a la Bandera:*

> *¡Bandera de México!*
> *Legado de nuestros héroes,*
> *símbolo de la unidad*
> *de nuestros padres y nuestros hermanos.*
> *Te prometemos ser siempre fieles*
> *a los principios de libertad y de justicia*
> *que hacen de nuestra Patria la nación independiente,*
> *humana y generosa*
> *a la que entregamos nuestra existencia.*

> Flag of Mexico!
> Legacy of our heroes,
> symbol of the unity
> of our parents and our brothers.
> We promise to always be loyal
> to the principles of liberty and justice
> that make our fatherland
> the independent, human and generous nation
> to which we give our existence.

But who's going to wave a flag? not one of us, no matter how much we love our country, look ma! hands that can't hold, fingers that can't grasp, and they scooped our eyes out with a spoon, we all know empty sockets aren't worth a thing, and our fathers mothers sisters brothers, too depressed and miserable to wave anything but torn bed sheets with slogans written on them, banners, placards, painted posters asking for news of their children husbands brothers, demanding justice, the least they could ask for, *compañeros,* so who's got the right to wave the flag if they don't believe in what it stands for, not the ministerial police or the federal police, not the police from Iguala, three units from Cocula, municipal police forces, together, badges guns boots uniforms, they stand behind little flags sewn on their sleeves but don't pay any attention to what it means, I know I know, you can't tar them with the same brush, but right now that's what I'm doing because I didn't see a police uniform on a human being that was trying to look after us, not one, Irma nodding her head, agreeing with me as we leave Lerdo Park, hand in hand, walking away from the bench, Irma and I, and voices come from the park behind us, they're like echoes, a shout is a shout, sometimes I can't tell them apart from those that arise in my dream, one foot in and one foot out, as you can tell, maybe there're people playing soccer and the voices and shouts aren't meant for us, but Irma turns her head to look back, just to make sure, in this life you've got to stay awake, keep your eyes peeled, be wise to what goes on around you, and a confirmation, she tells me it's a group of engineering students from the campus of Universidad Tecmilenio or lab technicians from Christus Muguerza Hospital del Parque, young men kicking around a ball, cutting through the park, playing off the tension of higher education or long working hours, and we start to laugh, we both know I don't have much of an education and not many hours to live, playing behind us while we're taking Calle Octava, heading toward Calle Francisco Xavier Mina, walking past the back of a modern rough-textured cement church with barred windows, Immaculada Concepción, we're making headway faster than our feet could really take us, but it's my dream and I see it the way I want to see it, you can't deny me a little pleasure under the circumstances—Christ! what's that smell? please don't tell me my corpse's begun to stink—Irma and I, our feet following the same path in the same direction, we're staring at an empty lot with a wire fence protecting wild grass and patches of earth, taking a right on Privada Jiménez, past Telmex, and before we know it, a couple of seconds, remember it's my dream, we're standing at the intersection of Calle 12a and Privada Jiménez looking at a Pemex filling station and a bright yellow Pirelli tire store, then we're entering the Bar Pacífico, hotel and restaurant, at the corner of Ocampo and Calle Jiménez, everything happens so fast when you're happy, when you want something to happen, not like a slow death, and mine was slow, painful, and far from tedious, the first thing, a couple of soft drinks, Coca-Cola, plenty of ice, I don't know if we're standing at the bar or sitting at a table, just my imagination, and if I stick to the right setting, we're drinking a Jarritos Mexican cola, or Jarritos Tamarindo, and drinking from a straw, I admire your olive skin, my Irma of the Tigress, a fierce woman, a passionate woman, your long dark hair falling past your shoulders, so exquisite I want to eat you, extremely beautiful and, typically, delicate, that's the definition, but you've got meat on your bones, muscle, too, deltoid biceps triceps, your sleeves aren't rolled up but I've seen them, an elastic and narrow body with red-carpet hips, not too wide, just right, and I'd never run away from you, *mi* Tigresa, because "to flee is the privilege of the selfish," which isn't part of my personality, ask mother and father, they'll tell you, embarrassed but truthful, and in the uncertainty of the days that go by, I love you more and more, shadows are the exclusive territory, not always of the damned, but often of the unlucky, making people suspicious of the present and afraid of the future, and I don't want you to fall under their spell, *mi* Tigresa, you live in broad daylight, not shadows, smoking a Capa Flor by Puros Santa Clara, or another brand, a Te-Amo Clásico, what's it matter? a river of blue smoke spilling from your lips, a symbol of independence for lives submerged by anxiety in the search for satisfaction and freedom, I lean forward, whispering, you're Mexico's reward, with the greater part of its dreams broken in pieces, shattered porcelain plates, crushed plastic dishes smeared with *mole negro, mole*

259

rojo, mole verde, mole coloradito, prieto, chichilo, stains wiped clean
with tortillas, in my dream I hear Rosalía saying, *nuestro México,* a
country of ghosts, it might've come from Rocket, I'll call him Rocket
because my father does, otherwise it's Rubén Arenal, too formal under the circumstances, considering that I'm starting to smell my
own rotten flesh, I'm looking at Irma, my Tigress, and we're finishing our drinks at the bar or sitting at a table, let's say at a table, it's
more comfortable, and like that, sitting across from each other,
Irma and I are holding hands, sleeves positioned discreetly between
folded napkins and cutlery, and I say, yes, a serpent and an eagle are
symbols of *nuestro México,* but what kind of bird speaks to a jaguar?
that's what I'd like to know, a *cenzontle norteño?* dusty gray-brown
with white wing bars and sides of tail, a male *zanate mexicano?* iridescent black with yellow eyes and a long tail, keel-shaped, or a
male *mirlo azteca?* boldly blackish-brown and white, upper parts
obscurely brown-streaked, and with these detailed descriptions
straight out of a guide to birds of Mexico, do you have the answer?
and Irma tells me she's never seen a bird speak to a jaguar, a serpent
and an eagle, yes, it's possible, one curled up in a tree, the other on
a branch above it, a perfect opportunity for a conversation, but what
kind of bird speaks to a jaguar? I can't tell you, why do you want to
know? and I shrug my shoulders, thinking, then asking myself the
same question, why the fuck do I want to know what kind of bird
speaks to a jaguar, don't tell me I'm tripping over the branches of the
sacred, divine and ridiculous, interested in the use of symbols to
represent ideas or qualities, creating my own myths to explain some
natural or social phenomenon, not at this stage of my life, which has
already ended, all our efforts to last are useless, too late for creation,
too soon for death, because of all the buffeting winds, but that's
what she asks me, and I let go of her hand, waving mine at the
waiter, asking for two Mexican colas with plenty of ice, straws, two
menus, but we don't look at them right away, she's intrigued by the
question concerning the large, heavily built cat, its yellowish-brown
coat with black spots, and a bird that's native to our part of the

world, our region, maybe even our hometown, is it the jaguar of our ancestors? or a bobcat? is it the Blue Hummingbird, Huitzilopochtli, the patron of the Aztecs? the whole of Aztec history reflects the people's dependence on the tribal god Huitzilopochtli, who was a form of Smoking Mirror, Tezcatlipoca, the Prince of this World, I imagine something larger than a hummingbird, in real life, more like an iridescent black male *zanate mexicano* with yellow eyes, and a real-life conversation, you might consider that funny coming from a half-baked dead man, it's not my fault and I doubt you're laughing, what makes me dead? my complexion turning from green to purple? my crumpled body? not a breath showing on the surface of a mirror? I just don't have the right to be any place on earth, my permission's been revoked, without forewarning, no red flag, no alarm bells, no judicial order, just kidnapped, tortured and killed, and Irma and I, deciding it'd be a good idea to eat something, not wanting the sugar to be the only thing in our bloodstream, we look at the menu, choosing something right away, and the waiter's standing next to us before we've waved him over to the table, and minutes later, we're sharing a beef *discada,* a kind of stew from here, and warm corn tortillas, two bottles of Modelo Especial, it's early evening, and while we're eating we decide on the *zanate mexicano,* and if it's up to me, I'll always pick a bird that looks like a crow, so it's a great-tailed grackle, a large and lanky blackbird, that's going to have a heart-to-heart with the jaguar that's waiting for us when we're through with our meal and leave the restaurant, but that's for later, after we've had coffee, and even if Bar Pacífico's a hotel and restaurant, no hotel room for us, we don't need one, our love is made wherever we go, Irma and I, each reaching out for the other's hand once the dishes are cleared, glasses of beer nearly empty, we've ordered our coffee, and there're only hours years eons, and forever, waiting for us, I can tell by the way she's looking at me that that's what she's thinking, too, twins of love, and now twins of pain, disappearance privation forfeiture, all forms of loss, there's no colder wind than that, the selfishness of death, you're mine and no one

else's, and in the street again, at the corner of Ocampo and Calle
Jiménez in front of Bar Pacífico where the jaguar is waiting for us,
Irma lights a natural flavor Santa Clara Chicos, a blend of San
Andrés short filler, or *picadura*, putting the tin back in her handbag,
offering me a drag straight from her lips, I take it when she hands it
to me, but I don't taste anything, not even a desire to cough when I
inhale the smoke deep into my lungs, and now that there's a moon,
neither waxing nor waning, just there staring at us, the jaguar getting impatient, roaring, so where's the bird you promised I could
talk to because I've been waiting out here with nothing to do but
gaze at the evening sky while you're filling your bellies with drink
and food and love, such is the impatience of a creature in the *Pantera*
genus, and unlike most big cats that're solitary except for mother-
cub groups, our jaguar is showing signs of feeling abandoned
rejected unwanted unloved, La Tigresa notices a kind of feline
frown on the jaguar's face and jabs her elbow into my ribs until I see
what she's trying to point out to me, slow as a dead man, I guess, no
other excuse, I give the jaguar a sincere smile, a few words of reas-
surance, come with us, it won't be long, and the three of us cross
Avenida Melchor Ocampo heading back in the direction from
which we'd come when we were on our way to Bar Pacífico, Irma
smoking her cigar, searching the night sky for a great-tailed grackle
willing to take time before going to sleep to speak to the jaguar
walking beside us, and slowing down, with the Pemex station on
our left, the three of us stand still thinking which road to take, and
the jaguar is the first to turn his head, a nose and ears like magnets
for smells and sounds, a singular standard of perception, Irma and
I taking each other's hand without looking down, a grip as firm as a
vise, we're staring open-mouthed at what the jaguar sensed before
we could see it, the Pemex station emitting a kind of night mist rolling out from behind its walls, a mist slowly separating into more
than forty individual spheres, at first their glow appears round, then
each of the vaporous spheres is elongated north to south, like the
mystifying cloudy appearance of open cluster M44, the Praesepe or

Beehive Cluster in the constellation of Cancer, a 3rd-magnitude glow that to my naked eye looks like the bearded head of a tailless comet passing between the 4th-magnitude stars Gamma and Delta Cancri—the nature of the cloud was a mystery until Galileo saw what he described as "not one only but a mass of more than forty small stars"—and in ancient China that misty glow was seen as *Tseih She Ke,* "exhalation of piled-up corpses," proof before my eyes, I didn't need more, the Chinese were right, the faces I recognize as they come out of the unstable mist, more than forty of them, forty-three to be exact, are the details of an emanation of dead bodies from the Pemex gas station, it's my dream, and one by one they make their identity known to me, there they are across the street, and moving solemnly in a column toward Calle 12a, a convoy of corpses, I speak in a whisper so I don't disturb them, Irma and the jaguar, tactful and well-mannered, both listening with humble submission and respect to the names of the disappeared, Miguel Ángel Hernández Martínez, Jesús Jovany Rodríguez Tlatempa, Abelardo Vásquez Penitén, Alexander Mora Venancio, Luis Ángel Abarca Carrillo, Jorge Álvarez Nava, Adán Abraján de la Cruz, Cristian Tomás Colón Garnica, Luis Ángel Francisco Arzola, José Ángel Navarrete González, Jorge Aníbal Cruz Mendoza, Giovanni Galindes Guerrero, Jhosivani Guerrero de la Cruz, Carlos Lorenzo Hernández Muñoz, Israel Jacinto Lugardo, my head's starting to spin, my stomach's sick, but I don't let go of Irma's hand, I squeeze it until it hurts both of us, an involuntary contraction of her facial features at the pain she hears in my voice, don't go on, she says, and I tell her I can't go on, it's killing me, but what am I saying, I know I'm already dead! the more-than-forty small stars pass single file before our eyes, I can't bear to look at them, afraid I'll see myself amongst the star-corpses marching in a straight line that bends at the corner, turning down Calle 12a, a glimpse at the jaguar tells me the animal isn't insensitive to what's happening, wiping away tears with a raised paw, and the names coming out of my mouth, clutching Irma's hand or lying here in a heap with my *compañeros,* no boundary or limit's fixed between my dream and reality, no dividing line, not now, but I'm still here, lying on top of my comrades, and I ask myself who, living or dead, can look through a stack of bodies, not my eyes, human eyes, maybe eyes looking down from Heaven, the names spill softly out of my mouth thanks to the free and unmerited favor of God telling me who's here in this human stack of wood, José Ángel Campos Cantor, Julio César López Patolzín, Everardo Rodríguez Bello, Cutberto Ortiz Ramos, Felipe Arnulfo Rosas Rosas, Christian Alfonso Rodríguez Telumbre, Martín Getsemany Sánchez García, César Manuel González Hernández, Jonás Trujillo González, Jorge Luis González Parral, Israel Caballero Sánchez, now it's not just my head that's spinning, the street's in a whirlpool, and I'm drawn in to its rapidly rotating mass, physically as well as psychologically, a turbulent situation from which it's hard to escape, I'm passing out, fainting, my fingers loosening their grip on Irma's hand, moving downward, dropping, falling into a black pit, before I lose consciousness I'll finish giving names to the faces I see whether mine's one of them or not: José Eduardo Bartolo Tlatempa, Abel García Hernández, Doriam González Parral, Miguel Ángel Mendoza Zacarías, Bernardo Flórez Alcaraz, Carlos Iván Ramírez Villareal, Magdaleno Rubén Lauro Villegas, Leonel Castro Abarca, José Luis Luna Torres, Mauricio Ortega Valerio, Jorge Antonio Tizapa Legideño, Antonio Santana Maestro, Emiliano Alen Gaspar de la Cruz, Marco Antonio Gómez Molina, Marcial Pablo Baranda, Saúl Bruno García, Benjamín Ascencio Bautista, and yours truly, an honorary dead, not on the list, that makes more than forty-three, I know, but it's the truth, all the star-corpses disappear going who knows where on Calle 12a, and so I fall into a deep sleep that isn't sleep at all but a kind of stepping aside out of the flow of traffic, observing what transpires there on byways and highways with passionate indifference since as interested as I am in what's happening before my eyes I can't do anything to affect or influence any of it, the physical side of life is out of reach, but since it's my dream, I won't let that stop me, so out of my way!

clear off! can't you see that I'm walking here, my legs don't move my eyes don't see, but I've got places to go, my body's left me behind, but my soul won't rot, I'm determined to keep it fresh, Irma and I continue our stroll, we're holding hands, the jaguar padding along-side us, its sway discreet, the night caressing our skin, all three of us, with a warm breeze, the jaguar's fur unruffled and soft to the touch, we're walking along Privada Jiménez, leaving the misty star-corpses, including my own, forty-three plus one, to continue on their jour-ney, wherever they're going, while we pass Calle Octava, Calle Sexta, Calle 4a, Calle Segunda, rough fragments of stone, concrete debris at the corner of Privada Jiménez and Avenida Independencia, we're following Privada Jiménez on into the night, arriving at Calle Tercera, "To my knowledge, English observer John Herschel was the first to call M44 the Beehive. In his 1833 *Treatise on Astronomy*, Herschel writes, 'In the constellation Cancer, there is … a luminous spot, called Praesepe, or the Beehive, which a very moderate tele-scope—an ordinary night glass, for instance—resolves entirely into stars,'" and using a very moderate telescope, in this case a pair of intelligent bright eyes, Irma again jabbing me in the ribs, not trying to point out an unloved unwanted jaguar, but the presence of the bird the jaguar's been waiting for that's flying high above us, I let go of Irma's hand, she let go of mine, now the three of us can each take our own way to follow the bird, we have to do it by sight because the sun isn't out, the bird throws no shadow, we follow it, turn left at Calle Tercera, and go quickly past a white wall painted with pale blue letters spelling, "FUT BOL RAPIDO," and below it, "REVO," Irma's eyes spot the bird sailing into the recreation area on our right, where lights illuminate an open space with two basketball courts, a double court for two simultaneous games, four hoops altogether, located beneath the gaze of a nearby mountain and foothills, the bird lands on one of the four white basketball hoops, none of them have a net, and the three of us stand in a semicircle under the hoop looking up at the yellow eyes of a *zanate mexicano*, the exact bird we've been searching for, the jaguar stretches itself out comfortably on the ground within the four-foot NBA standard radius outside the hoop, its huge yellow eyes with round pupils meeting the yellow eyes of the male bird, a jaguar's eyes are six times better than ours at night, and it's the great-tailed grackle that's got the first thing to say, *paraísos duros de roer,* heaven's a tough nut to crack, and we all laugh, me out of nervousness, the others for reasons I don't know, but I admit to Irma, whispering, that that's the best introduction to an informal exchange of ideas between creatures I've heard in a long time, and the jaguar clears its throat, a signal for Irma and me to leave them alone for a conversation that'll be fortified with the kinds of truths only animals are privy to, our fingers interlaced once more, leaving the basketball courts and heading automatically for the playground on the other side of the fence, walking past the sign that reads, Parque Revolución, which in my dream is empty, heading in the general direction of El Panteón de la Regla, on Calle Nicolás Bravo, where Francisco Villa isn't buried, but it's the children's rec-reation area we're going to, and since it's my dream, I decide to sit with Irma in the sandbox where little children play, she didn't want to sit in the sand at first, she's wearing a dress that she doesn't want to spoil with sand or anything else, but I convince her, patting the sand next to me, cool and moist in the night, removing my light-weight jacket, laying it out for her to sit on, Irma tucks her dress under her legs as she gets comfortable, I put my arm around her waist, drawing her as close to me as she can be, our hips touch, I can feel the warmth of her skin, and smell her sweat mixed with the perfume I gave her before I left for Ayotzinapa in the municipality of Tixtla, never once thinking I wouldn't see her again, and but for this dream, which has brought us together, it would've been true, lying here now on top of my dead schoolmates, in a state of decay, I remember that I traveled from Guerrero to Chihuahua just to be with Irma, even if it was only to see her for a couple of days, that's before I gave her the bottle of perfume, the night of the perfume was the last time, on my second visit, then it was back to Ayotzinapa, and you know the rest of what happened, up to the point that we've disappeared, and nobody's going to find us, not our bodies, not our flesh or bones, up in smoke, like I said, where we're sitting, the sand's a bit hard, not too hard, and a little moist, but that's because it's night, the sand's cooled off, I lean forward, still right next to Irma, and start digging in the sand with my fingers, not looking for anything but making a pile of sand like I was going to start a sandcastle or something, the jaguar and the great-tailed grackle are busy talking, I can't hear the bird, but now and then the jaguar's repetitive cough, or grunting *uh*s, increasing in tone and power, while decreasing in frequency between grunts, typically seven to a dozen grunts, but I don't understand a word, neither does Irma even if she's known as La Tigresa—the Yanomami call the jaguar the "Eater of Souls," consuming the spirits of the dead—Irma puts her cigar out in the sand, she's wearing a frustrated look on her face, but it isn't time for holding hands or doing anything else, no chance of intimacy at the moment of the greatest intimacy, it's time to say goodbye, she knows it, and that's why she's looking sad, my pile of sand isn't the point, the point is the hole I dug, Irma drops her cigar butt into the hole, starts filling in the hole with the sand piled up next to it, once finished, she pats it down gently, spreading wide the fingers of her hand, pressing it into the sand where she leaves her hand's impression for all the world to see.

Rubén Arenal, before cutting across the intersection, recognizing Ernesto as he himself came out of a side street, Ernesto's way of standing with more weight on the right leg than the left, approaching Ernesto's outstretched arms, admiring the red, green and gold Aztec eagle warrior mask on Ernesto's face, a white letter *M* in center of the forehead, and Rocket, I'll give him a taste of his own style, Mil Máscaras-style, a monkey flip, one of Mil Máscaras' signature moves, but I better lay off, he's been through a lot, I can tell just by looking at him, and I love him like a brother, Luz Elena loves him, too, she's told me a hundred times, *Xihuitl*, my comet, listen,

Ernesto's like a brother to both of us, Rubén Arenal falling into
Ernesto's arms, an embrace, and Rocket, to himself, in Conrad's
words, like a ship, we're as tight as a bottle, no water seeping in,
nothing coming out, our friendship's sound, in good condition, for
keeps no matter what's happened, and Ernesto's mask was changing, not right before his eyes, Rubén Arenal couldn't see it because
they were still in each other's arms, no macho hang-up, Mexican
Spanish from the 1920s, from the Latin, *masculus,* masculine or
vigorous, and the eagle warrior mask now a two-toned blue mask
with flying doves on each side, a jaggy red *M* on the forehead,
Rubén Arenal stepping back, giving Ernesto the once-over, stepping forward, gripping Ernesto's shoulders, which appeared
somehow more massive than Rubén Arenal remembered them,
and Rocket, you don't even have to tell me, 'mano, I know it's something big, and I've got news for you, too, but first, where'd you park
my truck? Rubén Arenal concentrating only on Ernesto, seeing
only his changing face, and not the truck parked a few steps away
from the entrance, the yellowish air turning slightly green with the
exhaust of a passing pickup, Ernesto covering the opening in the
mask for his mouth, impurity impurity, turning his head, making a
sign with a jerk of his head that said, there's the truck, brother,
don't worry, Rubén Arenal, a smile, then heading for the entrance
of his apartment, opening the front door, the foyer lit by an electric
bulb hanging from the ceiling, the door closing behind them,
opening the door to his ground-floor apartment, letting Ernesto in
first, and Rocket, I'm thirsty as a dry road, in the words of Cyril
Harcourt, Rubén Arenal heading straight to the refrigerator, a note
stuck to the refrigerator door, Luz Elena's handwriting, Rubén
Arenal reading, with respect to the thirst you might have when you
get home, *Xihuitl,* my comet, my brother, I've made you something
to drink, a fresh *agua de Jamaica,* and there are leftovers, too, what
I made for Avelina, Perla and Cirilo, we couldn't finish it all, and we
don't eat more than our share, with respect, of course, to your fore-
seeable appetite and not wanting to waste a bite, a mouthful, a

single crumb, Rubén Arenal, a broad smile, it was just what he needed and it'd be his sister's love in each mouthful of food and swallow of homemade hibiscus flower juice, showing what he found in the refrigerator to Ernesto, Ernesto shaking his head no for the food, but nodding yes for a drink, then sitting on one of the two wooden chairs, wicker seats, at the table in the kitchen area, part of Rubén Arenal's medium-sized studio, Ernesto's elbows resting on the rough wooden surface, a shiny gold lamé mask with red vinyl or leather *antifaz,* and the golden arms of a red sun with a gold letter *M* in the center of it, in the middle of his forehead, a mask covering his entire head, Rubén Arenal shaking his head left to right right to left, and Rocket, it's hard to keep track of your face, 'mano, your mask keeps changing, and Ernesto Cisneros, his first words, that's the way it's been and that's the way it's going to be, I've returned to the world where time slips away as a different man than the one who left here in your Ford pickup, my face keeps revising itself, an update but essentially the same, and it's the least important of the changes I've gone through as it's a kind of reshaping on the outside, but the improvements within are of an entirely different nature, and the worst of it is that despite my inconsistent appearance, a chameleonic mask that doesn't settle for a single outward show, things couldn't have changed more for the better, no matter my crimes, and there's a short list I'm really not proud of because when you add them up it amounts to murder, Rubén Arenal stopping in the middle of unwrapping what Luz Elena had so nicely wrapped in aluminum foil, narrowing his eyes, and Rocket, murder? and Ernesto Cisneros, I'm afraid it's true, not my intention, not what I set out to do when I borrowed your truck, and Rocket, your face, the mask it's wearing that won't come off, it's the face of a good man, not a murderer, and Ernesto Cisneros, that's the good I've been imbued with after the bad thing I've done, a fine wrestler's endlessly changing features, and a change of heart, I suffer from the loss of my child, mine and Lupita's, our Coyuco, a voice for the voiceless and a fact, but I learned my lesson, revenge isn't the way out, no matter how angry I am, and Rocket, you don't have to tell me a thing, I know it without having to hear it because I know you, 'mano, and I know the Fates, the weird sisters, and I've had an experience along those lines, not three and not sisters but a mother and daughter, buyers, too, supporters of my pottery, the Fates are white-robed incarnations of destiny, according to an average source of popular information, or the other way around, but mine weren't dressed in white, and their clothes, both mother and daughter, changed on their bodies like your mask changes on your face, when I first saw them they were dressed in black, and the mother wore a *rebozo* draped over her shoulders, I've even lost the need and desire to rub the calluses on the palm of my hand, at least for right now, a result? who can say, Esto, and a big sale went with the experience which included falling in love, and not down a couple of stairs but the whole flight, maybe two, three flights, that's how far I fell for a woman who looks a lot like Little Pascuala, but where I landed I can't say, it's a mystery, the two women disappeared, mother and daughter, and the bills they paid me aren't currency anymore, I told myself I won't try to trade in the money of the past for the legal tender of the present, maybe the end is in them, the bills and coins themselves, cash of no value, or it's the beginning, our future together, the young woman and I, a couple bound by threads stronger than yarn and in a single rich color, royal purple lake, like Old Holland-brand oil paint, or royal red, a symbol of our passion, and what I call progress is the energy I'll come up with for another search, the Reconquest of Desire, I'll look for them again, and always, here in our city, and I'll take on the puzzling drive to their house where there's snow where there shouldn't be snow, and a partly frozen river, the altitude doesn't justify such cold, they cooked for me, I ate like a king, maybe Axayacatl, the sixth tlatoani, *el que habla*, of Tenochtitlan, and my love for *La Pascualita*'s double was reciprocated, their house is a lot like the one you showed me in a photo, remember? a house in the high desert at the foot of the Sierra Nevada, the mountains outside of Reno, Nevada, and Ernesto Cisneros, I haven't lost my memory, it's better than ever, and Rocket, I can afford to believe or not to believe in my experience—a dead ringer for *La Pascualita,* ah, the darkness of chance!—my dinner, our lovemaking, and my financial gain that amounts to nothing, anyway, a voice told me I wasn't there for profit, at least not to sell my pottery but to trade it for something, I don't know what, but on my way home—I borrowed a two-wheel drive Suzuki Carry Truck from a neighbor who'd brought it down from Texas—my memories of what happened that night stopped being real as they lost their substance and became ethereal atmospheres, *San Lucas 12:23,* Luke 12:23, *La vida es más que la comida, y el cuerpo que el vestido,* "For life is more than food, and the body more than clothing," now it feels like I'm reeling on my own two feet, longing for the quiet of the starry nights and the scent of the wildflowers, or more realistically, the smell of damp clay, its smoothness in the palms of my hands, what's the use of longing? waiting for the evening to enter the city and darken it slowly, it gets dark sooner or later without having to wait for it, yearning hungry thirsty, waiting feels like that, and Ernesto Cisneros, I wanted revenge without knowing it after I figured out that I'd never find Coyuco, and look where it got me, my false face more real than my own and a tarnished heart, a cross like the one He carried on the way to Calvary burned into the center of it, that day my hope ended, and Rocket, you're ahead of me, Esto, as far as no hope goes, in advance by more than days, maybe I'll get there, where you are, or I won't, because I've got to go on looking for her, get up the nerve, and when I find her I'll know if she's really here, part of the kingdom of the living, and her mother, too, because when I woke up that house was an outer form without substance, the hull of an empty ship, a phantom house where nothing resembled what I remembered seeing the night before, or it was two nights, I can't tell, and there was no sign of life except my own and a roomful of birds, and Ernesto Cisneros, you'll find her, I'm sure of it, and when you find her you'll have to decide if you want her, even if she isn't of this kingdom of the living, you'll have to make a choice and live with it, one way or the other, because you drank the water from the spring that's sweet and clean when you were in a house like the one I showed you in a photo long ago, and when you woke up she wasn't there, neither was her mother, anyone can leave a house, and come back later, it's not a big mystery, but you drank from the spring so you'll have to make a choice, and Rocket, I'm willing to make a decision, she's just like *La Pascualita,* and you know how I feel about her, in a store window or on the street, and Ernesto Cisneros, I don't think she's from our world, not the place where we live today, but there *is* life after death, brother, and when you find her, it'll be up to you, and Rocket, you're right, I've been thinking the same thing, *'mano,* but where did that old money come from, Rubén Arenal emptying a pouch with the coins and paper money on the table in front of him, and Rocket, why'd they leave it for me, they could've come back to the house, wherever they had to go, it wasn't money that I really wanted, and I would've waited for them, they only had to leave a note, but they didn't, they made sure I found the envelope in a house that looked like nobody'd lived in it for years, no fingerprints, just birds, our world's a strange place, and if they're from the underworld of the dead, then that's a strange place, too, and Ernesto Cisneros, that's where you'll have to be careful, brother, she might be a hummingbird, not a woman, whether she looks like Little Pascuala or not, or La Cihuacóatl, snake woman, La Llorona, La Planchada, the ghost of a nurse in a well-ironed uniform, Eulalia, or La Lechuza, "the witch owl," who bewitched her son-in-law, *yerno,* you remember the story, or the Wise Woman of Córdoba, "flying through the air above rooftops with bright sparks coming out of her eyes," or she's 'Mana Zorra, Sister Fox, in another form, or a *teixcuepani,* a deceiver, "who transforms someone's eyes," or *una de los espíritus chocarreros,* a kind of poltergeist, maybe she's Santa Muerte, La Hermana Blanca, an intermediary between God and earth, or a member of *mometzco-pinque,* "a malevolent sect of female sorceresses who can remove their legs or enchant by taking apart or disarticulating the bones of their foot," more than a dozen possibilities, plenty of options, brother, take your pick, and Rocket, your wisdom goes with your face, the masks you're wearing, Esto, and it's a white spider web mask you're wearing now with a big black spider on the front, and an *M* just above your nose, you can't see it but I like it, and a tough looker isn't necessarily a tough fighter, but in your case, *mi hermano,* life's trials and tribulations have made you a strong man, if it wasn't true then you wouldn't have received the gift of a thousand masks, and Ernesto Cisneros, now I'm as tough as my namesake, brother, but what about atonement for knocking a cop out with a Glock, or killing three members of the *Policía Municipal,* and Rocket, you know why they call the cops Smurfs now instead of Night Owls, *'mano,* because they're blue and motherless, and Ernesto Cisneros, killing's no joke, and Rocket, I'm not making a joke, only a point, they're motherless motherfuckers, so they've never been born, *sin pecado original, no es posible para cualquiera, pero la Virgen,* without original sin it just isn't possible, not for anybody, nobody but the Mother of all Mexico, *Nuestra Señora de Guadalupe,* and Ernesto Cisneros, that's an excuse I can't make, dead is dead and I killed them, wounding another, and Rocket, I can't judge you, Esto, you have enough with your own conscience, where do we come from? the same time the same place, heading in the same direction, so how in this life or the next could I *possibly* judge you, no trial no verdict, an opinion, that's what I can offer you, *no hay pedo*—excuse the slang—okay, ready steady: it wasn't the best thing you could've done, but in a hot-blooded hard-to-control instant anything can happen and it did, you're the proof, and the witness, and what they did to Coyuco isn't your fault, here I go again, because of this because of that, justification reason mitigating circumstances, *damas y caballeros del jurado,* in mitigation he said his client had been deeply depressed, and rightly pissed off, and like I said when we were nine, you're intelligent, Esto, advanced for your age—we're the same age, you and I, but I feel like I'm your older brother—the limit of your endurance, your capacity for suffering has been established, and it goes far beyond the wrestling ring whether you're Mr. Personalidad, La Saeta Azul, El Manotas, El Galeno del Mal, El Guapo, El Profesor, El Látigo Lagunero, or anybody else, and Ernesto Cisneros, hope is the luxury of the reborn, the only thing that's keeping me from being an old man returning home a failure is the mask on my face and the soul that it's sharing with me, and Rocket, you aren't drinking, come on, it'll do you good, and Ernesto Cisneros, I need a straw, this mask makes it hard to drink without spilling all over myself, there's *antifaz,* as you can see, around the openings for my eyes, nose and mouth, an additional layer to my skin that isn't the usual thin layer of tissue forming the natural outer covering of my face, the skin's taut, touch it, and it feels like pro-grade Lycra, Rubén Arenal getting up from the table, reaching into a cabinet where he found an open package of straws, putting the straw in the glass of Ernesto's hibiscus flower drink, Ernesto taking the glass in his hand, raising it just until the tip of the straw passed between the *antifaz* around his lips, a forced smile of stretched Lycra, drinking avidly, the straw acting like the primary tubing of an IV, then putting down the glass, what's left of a feigned smile becoming a grimace, the mask of that joyous, inward cry that now entered the confused dimension of a sorrow coming forth from the deep well of his memory, and Ernesto Cisneros, my son my son, Ernesto raising the glass once more, the straw between his lips, in a hurry to quench his thirst and extinguish the embers of his thoughts, Rubén Arenal reading his thoughts, and Rocket, I offer you a song to go with your melancholy, 'mano, just listen, and drink my sister's homemade hibiscus liquid refreshment, it's "La Misma," "The Same," sung by Vicente Fernández, written by Isidro Coronel, who was born at the hacienda Techague, in the municipality of Atoyac—from the Nahuatl, Atoyac, meaning "place of the river," Lugar del Río—in the southern region of the state of Jalisco, in 1935, a song only two minutes, fifty-seven seconds long, a heavy-hearted but beautiful song:

Con el alma herida por un mal cariño
Que sin condiciones le entregué mi amor
Llevo ya dos días en esta cantina
Dos días, encerrado tomando licor.

Un mariachi toca, yo sigo tomando
Y vuelvo a pedirles la misma canción
Esto que me pasa no es nada envidiable
Ni al peor enemigo se lo deseo yo.

Tóquenme mariachis otra vez la misma
Esa que me llega hasta el corazón
'El Abandonado,' tóquenla de nuevo
Tóquenme diez veces la misma canción.

Aquí esta su cuenta, me dice un mesero
Ya me debe mucho, pégueme señor,
El mariachi dice, ya estamos cansados
Y yo sólo contesto, háganme un favor.

Pa' variar un poco tóquenme la misma
Esa que me llega hasta el corazón,
El Abandonado, tóquenla de nuevo
Tóquenme diez veces la misma canción.

With my soul wounded by a failed love
To whom I unconditionally gave my heart
I have been drinking in this cantina for two days now
Two days holed up drinking liquor.

A mariachi group plays, I keep drinking
And I ask them again to play the same song.
What's happening to me is nothing enviable
I don't wish this on my worst enemy.

Mariachis, play the same song again
The one that reaches deep into my heart
Play 'El abandonado' again
Play the same song ten times for me.

'Here's your tab,' a waiter says to me.
'You already owe me a lot, sir.'
The mariachi says, 'We're already tired.'
And I just answer, 'Do me a favor.'

'For a change, play the same song.'
The one that grabs my heart.
Play 'El abandonado' again,
Play the same song ten times for me.

Vicente Fernández's voice fading, but the words of the song tallying so well with Rubén Arenal's experience of an evaporating *La Pascualita* and Ernesto's image of Coyuco gone up in flames, no smoke, a perfect synchronicity, two men in a bath of empathy, an extraordinary episode in the otherwise and previously quiet lives led by two childhood friends, one in love with a ghost, the other who, along with his wife, Guadalupe, and a brokenhearted Irma, Coyuco's fiancée, longed for the son and future husband, respectively, who'd more than likely already become a ghost, parallel worlds crossing paths in Rubén Arenal's pottery studio and ground-floor apartment, and Rocket, drink drink, and what about Coyuco's disappearance, who on this earth could've benefited from the missing forty-three? and Ernesto Cisneros, when I'm not thinking about myself, the change I've gone through, that's what's on my mind, questions about the role of multinational companies in economic plunder, political domination—because political domination requires other kinds of domination, other accomplices and victims—asking myself what part was played by which parties in the disappearance of Coyuco and the other student teachers, the

Alacrán and the first lady, the Queen of Iguala, for example, at a thinly veiled pre-campaign party for the woman hoping to succeed her husband in office, yes, they're responsible, but they're not the only ones, an individual carries his or her own responsibility even if the orders come from a higher authority, a boss, a gang, an institution, an officer, the government, or just a sick fucking brain, María of the Angels and the mayor of Iguala didn't carry the shovels, but one way or another the city and state government provided them, spades and shovels in the hands of the ministerial police, the *Policía Federal,* the municipal police, the 27th Battalion, maybe the Guerreros Unidos, who's digging whose grave and who'll end up being the landfill, murder, torture, persecution, prison, successive hells, brother, if I had a map of the world in front of me I'd draw red circles around almost every place I could see, houses neighborhoods cities countries, it'd look worse than measles, chickenpox, smallpox, a world with a fever and a red rash, itchy inflamed blisters, or pustules leaving permanent scars, that'd be one lousy landscape, and if you look out the window you'll see we're already living there, and Rocket, your face is at it again, I mean the mask, always almost transparent and still plenty colorful, Esto, you've got your own case of magic skin, and Ernesto Cisneros, you're telling me? so what's its latest incarnation? I can't see it and don't feel a thing, and Rocket, you're stretch silver and blue lamé with red and white applications, a strange model representing a volcano in Japan with a red sun above a snowy peak, and on one side the word "Fuji," the other "Japan," not bad at all, I like it, Mil Máscaras is big in Japan, and Ernesto Cisneros, I know it, and you know I know it, I've got Noboru Ohkawa's photo book, and Rocket, now you're telling *me?* who do you think gave it to you, and Ernesto Cisneros, the power of memory is formidable and mysterious, but what I see right now is an image of my son, our Coyuco, Lupita's and mine, just as plainly as the last time I saw him, hand in hand with Irma, we weren't far from the city university, heading for Teatro de los Héroes on Avenida División del Norte, standing near the statue of Manuel

Gómez Morín, founding member of the Partido Acción Nacional, a party that's not my favorite not my choice, you remember, don't you, brother, because you almost drove past us, but you pulled over, no accident no traffic, got out of the truck, and shook hands with Coyuco like you hadn't seen him in years, Rubén Arenal nodding his head, taking a couple of swallows of hibiscus drink, Ernesto sipping from his straw, and Rocket, sure I remember, 'mano, the world is wrong, and we don't accept it, not you, not I, and not a lot of others, when you lose your son and can't find him, who'll help you, not the same people who made him disappear, and "for every man who has money there are a hundred who have nothing, it shouldn't be that way," and Ernesto Cisneros, "you're right, it shouldn't be that way, but that's the way it is," and Rocket, "why can't the one who has it give some to the other hundred now and then?" and Ernesto Cisneros, "yes, why can't he?" but let's stop quoting from a book, my eyes are drained of tears, my unexpected resurrection of memory is a desperate act of the will to live, a final gesture in the face of the inescapable, which brings me to the question of what I'm going to do, there's a kind of reparation to be made for the wrong I've done, not to the victims, but help for those who need it, the sum of my actions in this and previous states of existence, deciding my fate in future existences, and Rocket, following as effect from cause, it's good deeds that must be done for the living, but what about me, what am I going to do about Little Pascuala? and Ernesto Cisneros, you're going to look for her, and when you find her you're going to ask her to marry you, because that's what you want, isn't it? to have a wife and make pottery and live from what you earn by selling your tea cups, coffee mugs, sets of bowls, plates, *hidrias,* vases for flowers, and now and then an urn, an ashtray, with the insomnious passion of a craftsman, a creator of exquisite objects, sublime handiwork, yes, Little Pascuala, she'll raise you from artisan to artist, it's been said before but we know it's true, Rubén Arenal nodding his head, a little embarrassed, a smile with a hint of pride on his lips, and fueled by self-respect, a delight in dignity, Rubén Arenal swallowed the contents of what remained in his glass, set it down with a thump, and Rocket, Centro Comunitario Vistas del Cerro Grande, proposed in 2011, a community center near Parque Revolución between Calle Tercera and Calle Séptima, and if it isn't finished—who knows what's there or one day will be at that location—there's a social center on Calle Zubiran, east of Barrio de Londres, between Calle 33 and Calle 35, and Centro Comunitario Niños Alegres in Colonia Las Granjas, another in Colonia Ponce de León, Centro Comunitario Nombre de Dios on Avenida Heroico Colegio Militar, Triunfo Centro Comunitario Los Pinos on Avenida Buenavista, there's División del Norte, El Saucito, Todo por Chihuahua, San Jorge, Quédate Amigo, Mi Familia es Todo, Tierra y Libertad, take your pick, you can work at one of them, 'mano, and it'll do the trick, Rubén Arenal clapping his hands not more than once, Ernesto's eyes in his masked face rising from the surface of the table, a pair of peaceful eyes, a mild-mannered mouth, each neatly defined by strips of matte-blue *antifaz,* Ernesto looking straight at Rubén Arenal, having found something valuable in his words, an effectual suggestion, and Ernesto Cisneros, it's not our fault that life is shorter than we expect, that not even pain stops it from being ordinary and opaque, and Rocket, don't look at it like that, this is a second chance, can you smoke with that face of yours? and Ernesto Cisneros, just light 'em up, a cigarette's not wider than this straw, Rubén Arenal getting up from the table, opening a drawer, taking out a white and green and black pack of Aros, and Rocket, I'm out of Faros, Rubén Arenal lighting two cigarettes, passing one to Ernesto, who put it between *antifaz* lips, his face suddenly illuminated, revealing a bemused gaze caused more by the light of a thought than the cigarette's glow, and Ernesto Cisneros, a social center, what'll I do? and Rocket, they've got workshops for boxing, why not wrestling, too, you look like a wrestler of considerable renown, teach wrestling to kids who've got nothing to do and nowhere to go when they aren't in school or don't bother to go, kids who end up on the streets, living to the beat of agonizing violence, with the smell of roasted rats, with fear in their eyes and the reek of narcotic solvents permanently stuck to their noses and palates, searching for victims whose wallets full of plastic squares they steal, dreaming of guessing the four secret code numbers in a stolen card and straightening out their lives at an automatic teller machine, those are the kids that you can help, it's our future if we're going to have one, residents, inhabitants and the yet unborn of our Mexico, Mil Máscaras is a folk hero, like Blue Demon and El Santo, El Enmascarado de Plata, symbols of justice symbols of hope, and Ernesto Cisneros, I haven't got a *Tope Suicida* or *La Plancha* up my sleeve, not a double underhook suplex, and I never revolutionized a flying cross chop, and Rocket, you're never too old to learn, Esto, let your unexpected behavior in Iguala guide you reassure you confirm for you that you're capable of unpredictable almost operatic conduct, you can learn to wrestle, then show them some moves, or teach the routinely ragged, sometimes sniveling, and through-no-fault-of-their-own hungry but bright-as-stars victims of the life they've been born into to climb out of their difficult situations, make strides, and grow up with at least a handful of values and an earful of the kind of advice—that's all it'll take—held sacred by the likes of Mil Máscaras, El Santo, Blue Demon, the best revenge you could ask for, and Coyuco'd be proud of you, he'll speak to you at night, a faraway voice but clear as a bell telling you to stick with it keep going soldier on, Ernesto standing up, stretching, sure of himself now, a changed man with a changed face, and Ernesto Cisneros, your enthusiasm's electrifying, a wonder, urging me to move forward long before I'm behind the wheel, more than I hoped for and just what I need, fill my glass, will you, brother, and give me another cigarette, I won't be spending more time here today, my heart's full of hope, I'll start right away, it'll be one of the centers that you pointed out, they'll accept my face and lack of wrestling experience, but it'll take all of my clout, I'm wearing an adapting mask of Mil Máscaras, that's got to help, there was a long silence, followed by the sound of Ernesto sipping from his straw, and Rocket, the things that used to be true aren't true anymore, 'mano, that's all finished, "if all of us don't find a way forward, and when I say *us* I'm not talking about the slick intellectuals the elites admire so much, I'm talking about you and me and millions of men and women all over the planet," we won't forget what they did to the forty-three—not including our Coyuco—that'll never change, we'll keep on fighting to find out what happened to them, mourning and a decent burial's our goal, but your sorrow and crime are going to turn to good deeds, Ernesto felt like floating clear through the ceiling, Rubén Arenal, perceiving at the same moment the voice of *La Pascualita* calling him from a thousand miles away, thought he heard the phone ringing, or it might've been the doorbell.

The next sound you hear will come from the combined vocal folds, or vocal cords—composed of twin infoldings of mucus membrane projecting into the cavity of the larynx—wound together into a single bundle, even now with twin infoldings, otherwise it doesn't work, and speaking as one voice on behalf of the ghosts of Iguala, and your girlfriend and her mother, are you paying attention? Ernesto listening, Rubén Arenal listening, attentive allies, a moment of monologic magic before Ernesto left Rubén Arenal's ground-floor apartment and pottery studio, neither big nor small, more than adequate, and before Rubén Arenal precipitously launched himself into a city-wide search including the picturesque environs of Chihuahua for Little Pascuala and her mother, Pascuala Esparza, how strategically synchronous were the feathery voices of the dead:

> Using our tee-nie wee-nie lungs, reduced to ash in some cases, forty-three to be exact, and bloodless in the case of two, a woman and her daughter, pushing with all our might, projecting our voices past as-white-as-a-sheet lips, if we've got lips, to express the shared sentiment of our vast unified souls, spread out like a fingery fog fanning out over all of Mexico, don't deny us a little playfulness, after all,

we're dead, lively language is our only contrivance, good
natured but with sad shriveled roots reaching deep into
the earth in which we're buried or adhering to the riverbed
where they've thrown our ashes—forty-three and a pair,
with roots that're supposed to be attached to the ground,
conveying water and nourishment, but that never took because they're the roots of two wandering souls—you know
perfectly well who we're talking about, having good inten-
tions, but not always the ability to carry them out, a voice
speaking for all of us, speaking as one, a combined forty-
three and two, together, listen listen, and with one vibrant
voice, we want to thank you for not forgetting us, it's early
still to forget the forty-three, not six months or a year has
passed by, but for the mother and daughter, it's another
story, they've been wandering this earth of mankind for a
long time, some of you might not remember them, well,
it's never too soon or too late to say thank you, to remind
you, too, that we're still here, innocents in the eyes of God,
what did we do wrong? nothing, but forty-three mon-
strously murdered, and a daughter who died from the bite
of a black widow spider—who's fault is that!—accompanied in the afterlife by her mother, and by the way, who
would condemn a mother for wanting to find long-lasting
love for her daughter—yes, a mother, and for my part, I'd
like to say a few words, an unprecedented moment for the
living dead, I'd like to say that the forty-three are right,
don't blame me for wanting my daughter to be happy even
if we're permanent residents of a territory between life and
death, neither part of one nor the other, what I mean is do
you know a mother of a child, or a father and mother, for
that matter, who doesn't want the best for her offspring,
and as a single mother, no longer of this earth, I want my
child, a grown woman, to have a man of her own, and
I'll do anything to get her one, to find someone for her
with an abundance of insight, a wagonload of warmth, a

ton of talent that thrills, and a true heart, what I mean is
that I'll do whatever's in my power, and those of you who
aren't here with us, the forty-three, and my daughter and
I, well, you don't have a clue what we're capable of accom-
plishing, power that shocks, a stupendous strength of an
unearthly energy, we're life members of the dead, not yet
buried and some of us still walking around, not as aim-
lessly as you might imagine, we've all got our purpose, the
forty-three will soon have theirs, having left their world
under lamentable circumstances, today they're new to the
game, but let's get back to the single voice of the forty-
three *normalistas* and two women, mother and daughter,
I've had my say, so it's all together now, we can't shed tears,
our ducts are dry, but our tee-nie wee-nie lungs, reduced
to ash or bloodless, forcing out our feelings of gratitude,
showing a heartfelt and powerful intensity, with a voice of
cautionary conscience, a sense of right and wrong, saying
watch out! don't fail to appreciate someone or something
that's very familiar or obvious, don't assume that something's true without questioning it—straight out of the
dictionary—and we offer you a genuine bona fide enthusiastic expression of our thanks, our ardent appreciation
and an unaffected acknowledgment for the fact that you
haven't forgotten us, and never will, when the details of
our faces are no longer vivid in your mind, you'll taste our
former existence in every bite, you'll smell our skin with
every whiff, you'll feel our presence, not see it, with every
glance, okay, we know, you get the picture, we're long-
winded souls exercising our right, we've got the green light
because we control the traffic and the signals at the same
time, our luxury, our gift, after all, we're dead and you're
not, maybe you get the picture maybe you don't, but we
count on you to take what we've said, scratch your domes,
use your noggins, all you've got to do is add it all up, and
come to a conclusion.

Ernesto and Rubén Arenal, an unexpected earful that entirely made sense to them, considering the plans they'd formed, not written plans, no notes, no scribbling down with pen or pencil on paper, but a worked-out idea of what they're intending to do, spontaneously put together, between two men with one brain each, Ernesto would go to work for a community center, Rubén Arenal would head off in pursuit of *La Pascualita,* Ernesto and Rubén Arenal both hearing the voices of forty-three dead students and a pair of functioning ghosts, a mother and daughter, forty-five voices speaking as one voice, wisdom in numbers, and the gist of what they'd said penetrated with ease thanks to the receptive pair of friends with two sets of perfectly functioning ears, essential ingredients under many circumstances, more convinced than ever they'd made the right choice, and Ernesto Cisneros, I'm off to Niños Alegres, or Nombre de Dios, then El Saucito, after that Todo por Chihuahua, or Mi Familia es Todo, Los Pinos, Tierra y Libertad, División del Norte, Quédate Amigo, San Jorge, and the social center on Calle Zubirán, east of Barrio de Londres, each in the order I choose, I'll follow a natural or intuitive way, searching until I find a fan of Mil Máscaras, or a *centro comunitario* that'll agree to let me work for them, every man has to do this, find his place in the world, I'll tell them, and they'll take me on the payroll, but I'd do it for free, Lupita will understand, encourage my decision with eagerness, she knows what's important, she suffers like me, but with her own, natural born face, and if I earn a single centavo I'll turn around and put it into pockets that're empty, and Rocket, I see my future in your optimism, 'mano, your voice and commitment reflect my own, do we sound foolish light-headed not-at-all serious? maybe we do, but with tragedy there aren't a lot of options, we're drowning in our own sorrow, of course, excessive, self-absorbed unhappiness over our own troubles, naturally, but the fight hasn't gone out of us, either, logical or not, and since when is systematic pig-ignorant murder part of a procedure we human beings are supposed to understand much less condone or accept, no, nothing's changed, but we're going to keep on living, those motherfucking mother fuckers who killed Coyuco and forty-three others, it's not the first time it won't be the last—it wasn't long ago I said the same thing while having a little conversation between me and myself, but what's it matter, the whole world repeats itself, from beginning to end and back again—yes, we go on living more by an instinctive reflex, or at least that's how it seems, than by premeditated, carefully elaborated plans of action, just remember, Esto, as a culture hero, Mil Máscaras, you're a compact illustration of the limitations of individual heroism in making political change, but as far as our daily life is concerned, in this our somewhat insignificant city, you're on, you've accepted the challenge or bet, and Ernesto Cisneros, *¡adiós!* it's really something that we're defeated and victorious at the same time, as far as the forty-three *normalistas* are concerned, and Coyuco, one son one brother one husband's the same as all sons brothers husbands—that's our victory, Ernesto waving goodbye, Rubén Arenal following him to the door, into the foyer, unlocking the street door, watching Ernesto as he stepped into daylight.

Rubén Arenal, as drunk as he could get on the black juice of the night, rambling, but not for pleasure, in the city streets far from the countryside, not for pleasure because he was searching, and his eyes burned from concentrating on every shadow he saw moving in the faintly lit streets, no pleasure until he found *La Pascualita*, or her mother, Pascuala Esparza, or both of them together, Rubén Arenal bending at the waist, bracing himself with his hands on his knees, breathing in Chihuahua's swirling gusts of wind that blew his hair in front of his face, in this neighborhood, where he'd seen them walking, Little Pascuala dressed in black, walking next to her mother, also dressed in black, a *rebozo* draped over her shoulders, her mother's shoulders not *La Pascualita*'s, a black and deep-blue shawl with knotted fringe from Pátzcuaro in Michoacán, and Rocket, to himself, if it makes you sick to do this you can stop, you can get something to eat, or return home to lie down without your shoes on, but you know you aren't sick, there's nothing wrong with you but a case of suspense, a little anticipation, and a strand of fear that you won't find her that's tightening around your throat, that's why it's best to breathe as much of this night air as you can, no matter how drunk it makes you, and if you can't find them here you can head for their house, in the direction of Mápula, and the Hacienda of Mápula, a house that looks a lot like that damned photograph of a house in the mountains outside Reno, take your truck, Ernesto brought it back, it's parked on the street, you can't miss it, it's yours, isn't it? you *do* know what it looks like don't you? but let's drop the sarcasm, you're a lucky guy, not Ernesto, he's paid a price you can't imagine, you might find Pascuala Esparza and her daughter in the neighborhood if you relaunch the long-suffering act and—Rubén Arenal interrupting himself, two figures arm in arm passing beneath a streetlamp throwing long shadows at the intersection and disappearing from view on Calle Segunda.

Rubén Arenal standing up straight on Calle José María Morelos in the central zone, his heart pounding, not just beating, the two figures disappearing on Calle 10a, Rubén Arenal following discreetly behind them now, Calle 10a turning into a narrow Calle Décima, Rubén Arenal passing the Centros de Integración Juvenil, "Para vivir sin drogas," diagonally opposite the Cardiovascular Institute on Calle Ojinaga, the silhouettes of the two women elegantly dressed in black flitting in the night like a pair of bats, Rubén Arenal concentrating on them, almost stumbling on a cracked and broken cement curb in front of a metal fence, the streetlight above him was unlit then started flickering, it felt like somebody had put a hex on him, his concentration wavering, a boiling brain with warped perceptions, Rubén Arenal trying to focus his eyes on the blue eye-shaped Dr. Scholl's sign across the street, and Rocket, now that I've got them in sight, I can't afford to lose them, they've already crossed the street, better get a move on, *mi amigo,* no time for daydreaming, not even at night, Rubén Arenal making his way cautiously across the wide Calle Juan Aldama, safely reaching the other side, the yellowish electric Restaurant Gerónimo sign on his left, continuing on Calle Décima, then turning right on Calle Guadalupe Victoria, walking past Hotel San Juan, whose entrance lights glowed like throat lozenges, beckoning to him, a little wave of a pair of gloveless silky hands, or a baby's hands, so smooth so pink-and-white, like they'd never touched anything, or the still well-padded hands of a sexually precocious young girl, come here come here, but Rubén Arenal, tearing himself away, more enthralled than not, and plainly under a spell, squinting in the night, with every muscle in his face, to find Pascuala Esparza and Little Pascuala who were nowhere in sight, he was positive they were heading for No. 801, La Popular, "La Casa de Pascualita," right in the neighborhood, and Rocket, if I was strong enough and sure I wouldn't hit anyone I could throw a stone to the entrance of the shop from here, that's how close it is, and on foot it's only a minute away, but still there was no sign of them, Rubén Arenal moving with caution, almost lost in the dark, not wanting to miss even a speck of dirt whirling in the windy pools of blackness before his eyes in case it led him to Pascuala Esparza and her daughter, and Rocket, what's happened to the streetlights? they aren't lit here, and they haven't been lit since I started after them, Rubén Arenal, stopping to turn his head 180° and back again while standing before the entrance to a parking lot, across the street from a lingerie store, finally catching a glimpse of Little Pascuala and her mother in the reflection of a shop window thanks to a pair of headlights, Rubén Arenal hurrying in the direction of the two women, trying to get to them before they disappeared, but as he reached La Popular, a high-pitched sound, coming from a subtle point, remote and internal, accompanied by glittering bits of light like the ones that fly off a hand-held firework emitting sparks, stopped him in his tracks, Rubén Arenal seeing nothing but sparks, hearing the high-frequency sound that was worse than a ringing in his ears, sitting down on the sidewalk, leaning against a protruding stone worn smooth and set in a wall painted deep blue, or lighter, it wasn't easy to tell because there still wasn't a streetlamp lit nearby, no light from flickering votive candles, not a ray coming from the shop windows of La Popular, they weren't changing *La Pascualita*'s outfits behind curtains put up in the shop window, it was night and long after the store was shut, but Rubén Arenal smelling the scent of flowers mingled with recently extinguished fireworks, trying to figure out the date, a way to fix himself in time and place, it wasn't March 25th, 1930, the date of birth of his ardent attachment, his love for Little Pascuala, impassioned sincere, and he couldn't see his fingers in order to count, but the piercing noise was dying out, fading afterimages or the last reddish remnants of brilliant sparks of light played before his eyes, and Rocket, I'm under a spell that's come from these two women with their gift of infinite transformation, workers of wonders, performers of miracles, sorcery, what else could it be, either they don't want me to meet them again or they don't know that it's me and not some stranger who's searching for Little Pascuala because I'm in love with her, I'm not a threat, but maybe they don't know it, it's genuine love, unless they've tricked me with their magic, I can't think of that now, I've got to catch up with them first, my eyes will tell me what's up the minute they're laid on *La Pascualita* and Pascuala Esparza, I'm like that, you can't fool me if I get a chance to see into your eyes, so I'm telling myself to keep my peepers peeled for those two women, fugitive shadows of the night, Rubén Arenal getting up from the sidewalk, leaning against the blue wall to keep his balance, the searing pitch had sliced through his inner ear, the streetlights started to flicker, offering a little light in order to help him get his bearings, not find his way out of the spell, and to locate Little Pascuala and her mother, who were hidden in a doorway in the shadows cast from dancing lights thrown down at the sidewalk, an entrance in a red-brick building standing across the street, the lightless Café Reforma part of the same structure, nothing lit in Calle Guadalupe Victoria but the two streetlamps, the streetlamps going dark the minute he spotted them, not far away, but by the time he got to the entrance they weren't there anymore, Rubén Arenal, hearing a singsong voice calling his name, stepping back into the empty street, lifting his eyes to the roof of the red-brick building, and Pascuala Esparza, señor Arenal, if you don't mind I won't call you Rocket, reserved only for your friends, I know, but here we are, my daughter and I, come up come up, you can hear me, my voice makes up for the silence of my child, she's quiet, isn't she, silent as the foot of time, from "A Summer Evening's Meditation," by Anna Laetitia Aikin, a late contribution to the cosmic voyage genre of poetry, popular during the first half of the eighteenth century, don't be surprised at the things I know, so hear ye hear ye, what I mean is why don't you join us, there's room up here, just the three of us, and if you want, I can leave and it'll be just the two of you, seeing as though you're in love with my daughter, señor Arenal, what I mean is I don't believe in the world, there's another world where life is different, you'll be our guest, Rubén Arenal seeing a pair of beckoning waving ageless slender hands as if they were lit by a lamp projecting a narrow, intense beam of light, imploring hands with palms turned up toward the sky, black and filled with stars, then disappearing hands, retracted like cat's claws, and a solitary reappearing hand, no magic just shadows, Rubén Arenal taking a couple of steps backward, watching a weighted object fall from the roof, Pascuala Esparza dropping a key wrapped in a handkerchief that landed with a thump on the street at his feet, Rubén Arenal unfolding the handkerchief, finding the smooth key not cut to fit any lock, the shape of a key that looked like it wouldn't open anything, Rubén Arenal cautiously approaching the red-brick building, putting the key in the lock, the key fit the door, turning the key which opened the door, Pascuala Esparza's voice, faint and distant, accompanying him, but he didn't hear the words, Rubén Arenal entered the building, heading straight for the staircase that led to the roof.

It was a long climb but only a few flights of stairs, Rubén Arenal walking slowly, watching his step in a lightless stairwell, and Pascuala Esparza, just a few more steps, señor Arenal, and you'll be among friends, more than that if you consider *La Pascualita*'s affection, what I mean is you'll find us waiting for you at the top, her voice echoing in the stairwell, Rubén Arenal tilting his head back to look up but seeing nothing, his footsteps didn't make a sound, he felt his heart beating in his throat, and Rocket, down boy, go back where you belong, Rubén Arenal and his habit of rubbing the calluses on the palm of his right hand with his right thumb, and Rocket, a journey that's testing my nerves, one more flight, I'm almost there if I can find my way, suddenly a spark leaped out, falling into the deepest darkness, then all at once Rubén Arenal's clothes absorbing light of short wavelength and emitting light of longer wavelength, radiation leading the way, Rubén Arenal seeing his boots, the landing, the staircase and handrail, the stairwell shone transfigured, and Pascuala Esparza, whispering in his ear, exact correct accurate, señor Arenal, here you are where your clothes shine with such illumination while theirs are left in darkness, Rubén Arenal, at that moment feeling flattered, and Rocket, to himself, the light's chosen me from among the unknown occupants of the building, and I feel privileged, Rubén Arenal silently rejoicing to the point that he was sure the fantastic event was a good omen, forgetting what he was doing, where he was heading, who he was going to see, then a slight pressure on his skin, following the whisper, an icy breath on his face, an accidental contact, or it was intentional, the insistence of the pressure transporting him from a state of being elated at how he looked in his clothes to one of lust, but it wasn't Little Pascuala, it was her mother, the glow from his shirt showing him the features of Pascuala Esparza's face, her black clothes and a black and deep-blue *rebozo* hiding the rest of her, or there was only her face and no body, it was hard to tell, but it was a jolt, the shock throwing him into a swoon, Pascuala Esparza taking hold of his arm, holding him upright, and Pascuala Esparza, come here, my daughter, you must help me help him, you're a witness to our enchanter's, maestro's, wicked-wizard-of-stoneware-clay's condition, faint but again generating more than enough electricity to light our eyes and heart, now literally, Pascuala Esparza standing even closer to him, Rubén Arenal smelling something like a blend of the ocean and dead flowers, her face next to his, and Pascuala Esparza, and in the same way your work set us alight, ignited us really, and I'm not exaggerating, so we ask you once again to join us on the roof, Rubén Arenal embarrassed at the erection caused by the touch of Little Pascuala's mother, but accepting it was a case of like mother like daughter, and right now the daughter took his other arm, she didn't say a word, but used her strength with the aid of her mother to bring him to the balustrade, Rubén Arenal looking down the stairwell at where he'd entered the red-brick building, his head clearing, his clothes no longer glowing, all was right with the world in this building, and Rocket, it's all right, I can walk, gently getting himself free of their grasp, Pascuala Esparza, still as youthful as her daughter, a beautiful swaying of hands, her finger pointing the way, and he walked ahead of them with a firm adherence to his own goal and purpose right out the open door onto the roof.

From where he stood he could see more stars than he imagined were in the sky when he was standing on the street below, a roof's-eye view, the city he lived in seemed far away even if it was at his feet, Rubén Arenal looking over the edge of the roof, down down, the streetlights were back on, burning with a steady flow of electricity, not like when he was following Pascuala Esparza and her daughter and the lights either flickered or went out altogether, a Chihuahuan wind caressed his face, throwing specks of dirt in his eyes which he ignored, Rubén Arenal feeling a lightness he'd never felt before, not in his head, but a weightless body whose soul was without gravity, floating out into the sky above his head, not joining the stars but approaching them, and Rocket, if I'd known that I'd feel like this I wouldn't have waited a minute before climbing those stairs, and Pascuala Esparza, didn't I tell you? what I mean is that we were waiting for you, and here we are, all together, we're here to offer you this special event, a real treat, which comes from standing with my daughter and me under the night sky, not Huitzilopochtli, representing the blue sky, or the sky of the day, because what we're standing

under now is Mixcoatl, "the cloud serpent," the Milky Way, god of
Cuauhtitlán, or in its permanent duplication, a divine transfiguration, Camaxtle, god of the Huexotzinca and Tlaxcalteca, Camaxtle
Mixcoatl, that's how it was, depending on when and where, and
there's Tlahuizcalpanteuctli, the Lord of the Dawn, or morning star,
we're standing under him, too—it's early so he's still asleep—these
are our stars! high high above us, conceived of as gods, and thought
to be divided into two large groups, Centzon Mimixcoa, "the unnumbered ones from the North," four hundred northern stars, and
Centzon Huitznahuac, "the unnumbered ones from the South,"
four hundred southern stars, both living in Ilhuicatl-Tetlaliloc, the
second celestial stratum of the vertical universe, but we aren't here
to give you an astronomy lesson or a history lesson, it's our past,
my daughter's and mine, and yours, too, but not our present, and
Rocket, turning to face them, you ought to talk to my sister, and instead of laughing there was silence, *La Pascualita* reaching her arm
around his waist, Pascuala Esparza turning away, a little privacy in
public, all the stars in Ilhuicatl-Tetaliloc watching them kiss, but no
one saw the length of her tongue, long slender forked like a serpent's
tongue with its complex receptor system, split so it knew which way
to move based on the preponderance of chemical particles on one
side of its forked tongue in relation to a lesser degree of particles on
the other, and together they made a whole story, 3-D glasses for the
tongue passing through a small notch in her lip, the rostral groove,
which explained why her mouth wasn't open when she kissed him,
the tips of the tongue fitting neatly into two tubes in her version of
the Jacobson's organ, Rubén Arenal with a tickling sensation, but
entirely mesmerized, in her grip and it wasn't just her arm pulling
him against her, Little Pascuala, once she got her tongue out of the
inner recesses of his mouth, relying on her vomeronasal system to
give her information coming straight from Rubén Arenal's brain,
registering everything his heart felt, the receptors on her tongue
having gathered miniscule chemical particles, perceived as scent,
then retracting into its sheath, sending the chemical information

to her own brain in order to process and analyze it, Little Pascuala, knowing for sure that Rubén Arenal loved her and would keep on loving her no matter what, sending her tongue back into his mouth, this time seeking out the flavor of desire, a confident Y-shaped organ, *La Pascualita* giving Rubén Arenal a feeling of happy satisfaction and enjoyment, straight out of the book, Pascuala Esparza didn't have to see what her daughter was doing to know what she was up to, and Pascuala Esparza, to herself, my daughter's grown up, one of us, a first-degree ghost, what I mean is I'm proud of her, this dance is a dance we can all dance to, and in the words of Percy Bysshe Shelley, it's a "dance like white plumes upon a hearse," only señor Arenal doesn't know it yet, what I mean is it's not a question, ladies and gentlemen, friends, of a foolish little number that fills the repertory of a musical group like Los Cócteles Latinos, the Latin Cocktails, or referring to musical groups a lot closer to home, the Sin Almas, the Without Souls, or Las Sensaciones Fantasmales, the Ghostly Sensations, what I mean is it's not a question of dancing to some little chocolate-candy tune to persuade the palate of an average hombre who doesn't know the meaning of the rhythm and the beat, our natural treat he'll know and appreciate, for señor Arenal, it'll be a dance that's pungent peppery penetrating provocative, what I mean is, what we're going to give señor Arenal is the tremendous ecstasy of being the first on his block to join us in the next life, there but not there, a party that doesn't stop, you live and you live, and you continue to live even when you're pushing up daisies, that's our motto, but enough of me, there's plenty of live action to witness, no joke intended just facts.

La Pascualita, having finished testing and tasting with her tongue, acquiring the knowledge, learning by heart to recite Rubén Arenal's deepest desires, probing his soul, and satisfied with what she'd learned from her receptors, lively as they were in her lamented mouth, but her full lips as full of life as her lover wanted them to be, another turn of magic, a sincere self-congratulatory grin on Rubén

Arenal's face, still under the spell, always under the spell when they were together, and a surplus of the spell in his heart even when he wasn't in their company, *La Pascualita*'s and her mother's, how else do you explain that he's been haunted distracted preoccupied ever since he met them, and Little Pascuala, a little dab'll do ya, Brylcreem 1950s, and Pascuala Esparza, a little residue of sorcery will do the trick, an indirect or passing reference, isn't that right, *niña*, my child? and Rocket, you're inside my head and right in front of my body, you think I need Brylcreem? my hair's untidy, but it's heading straight toward my shoulders with a smooth, shiny appearance, as you can see, Pascuala Esparza and Little Pascuala nodding their heads, and Rocket, but you can't see it growing unless you can see into the future, Rubén Arenal brushing back his long hair with his hand, and Pascuala Esparza and Little Pascuala, a single voice at the same time, don't talk to us about the future, señor Arenal, you're our virtuoso of today and right now, a bright spark, our brainiac and boy wonder—so many hundreds of years younger than us— we'll never cease to praise you, Pascuala Esparza and Little Pascuala lifting their eyes to the starry sky, and *La Pascualita* and her mother, together, ladies and gentlemen, friends, all together, we sing the praises of Rubén Arenal, and to praise your fascinating fingers forming shapes out of clay, praiseworthy person that you are, we humbly thank you for the pottery you produced from your skillful hands, works echoing with the sounds of Paquimé, a ruin northwest of Chihuahua, echoing from the ruins of Casas Grandes, no, it's not a penny, or small-change talent, it isn't an ounce or lightweight skill, but genius artistry brilliance, and so we thank you, again, Rubén Arenal grinning from ear to ear, their compliments running like the blood in his veins, his bewitched being filled to the brim, polite expressions of praise taking his mind off the quick move Pascuala Esparza was making, in a flash she gave him a little push, a shove in the right direction, meaning they wanted him to join them through death, and not a pretty one, making a huge splat on the sidewalk be- low, and the rest would work itself out, the afterlife putting his pieces back together again, making marriageable material out of him just so *La Pascualita* could spend the rest of her long life, hundreds, thousands of years, with Rubén Arenal in another bodily form, more spirit than corporeal, but at the instant he felt himself moving to the side, tipping over and close to the edge at an unnatural angle that left him nothing but a fall, compared to standing up straight and solid on the roof, Ernesto came out of nowhere, swooping in like an eagle, or Fantômas, La Amenaza Elegante, not the Fantômas of Pierre Souvestre and Marcel Allain, the Emperor of Crime, but the Fantômas of the Mexican comics publisher Organización Editorial Novaro, a justice avenger, a hero wearing a white skin-tight mask, or a variety of disguises, his true face never shown to his nemeses, a thief committing spectacular robberies just for the thrill of it, equipped with advanced technology created by Professor Semo, and pursued by Inspector Gerard, Fantômas, a millionaire owning several corporations under assumed identities, with hidden headquarters outside Paris, assisted by several secret agents, including twelve tantalizingly dressed "Zodiac Girls," known only by their code names, the signs of the zodiac, but our Ernesto, a solo effort for tonight, wearing a lavender lamé mask with white leather markings and *antifaz,* a black cape with a lot of gold fringe and a wide gold collar, and just like Mil Máscaras before the match against Misawa Mitsuhara as Tiger Mask in 1986, Ernesto removed the lavender mask, throwing it to the public—in this case it flew past Little Pascuala's face and brushed against Pascuala Esparza's nose—landing out in the middle of the roof, a gesture revealing his gold lamé and shiny black latex mask tied with laces, and a purple letter *M* on the forehead, his real face, Ernesto, quick as a stab, reaching out to catch Rubén Arenal as he was about to go over the edge into the void before hitting the street below, the bold and daring feat taking everyone's breath away, now mother and daughter sucking in air, Rubén Arenal exhaling between pursed lips, held in the arms of his best friend, named after the football midfielder, and Rocket to himself, so it was so it was, and so it is right now, a miracle, if only he could've saved his own son, too, but sometimes through sacrifice and suffering we're forced to learn more than we expect to learn, and then we begin to live a more charitable life.

Pascuala Esparza and her daughter were speechless, despite being spirits and not of this earth they didn't see it coming, nor did they expect anyone to save Rubén Arenal from his fate which, as far as they were concerned, was to join them in life after death, the two women, mother and daughter, each wearing black, backing away from La Amenaza Elegante in the guise of Mil Máscaras, Ernesto still holding tightly on to his friend, and Ernesto Cisneros, I bestow upon you now the modification of a few famous words:

>"Mil Máscaras."
>"What did you say?"
>"I said: Mil Máscaras."
>"And what does that mean?"
>"Nothing … Everything!"
>"But what is it?"
>"Nobody … And yet, yes, it is somebody!"
>"And what does the somebody do?"
>"Saves the world from terror!"

And Rocket, you've changed the name but I know the source, they won't be disappointed, 'mano, not those two Frenchmen, alive or dead, and they're long gone, it's in the spirit of things, if you'll excuse the joke exploiting the different possible meanings of the word, I've been saved from falling, awakened from a form of induced sleep, Rubén Arenal looking straight at the two women, then turning his head, giving Ernesto a grin, and Rocket, but not an induced love, that's my responsibility, it's coming directly from the corner of Avenida Melchor Ocampo and Calle Guadalupe Victoria, the corner right below us, exactly where La Popular stands, it's my love for Little Pascuala that's brought us here, putting me in danger and forcing your hand to save me, Ernesto letting go of Rubén Arenal, who took a few steps towards the center of the roof and the two women standing in front of the door to the stairwell, a menacing look on his face, and Ernesto Cisneros, I've completed my first act of something resembling virtue in the process of my reform, having recently committed the crime of murder, not one but three, don't get yourself into the same boat, brother! Rubén Arenal continuing toward Pascuala Esparza and her daughter, hearing the words, heeding the words, the muscles in his face relaxed, Rubén Arenal standing an arm's length from *La Pascualita* and her mother, and Rocket, looking from one to the other, forgiveness forgiveness, you wanted a husband, Little Pascuala, and you wanted your daughter to be happy, Pascuala Esparza, and happiness has its role in this world and the next, I forgive you, and Pascuala Esparza, you've read us like you know us, señor Arenal, and that's because we let you come too close, out of appreciation for your talent, no doubt, what I mean is we could've got hold of you with a simple series of words said as a magic spell or charm, what I'm saying is straight out of the book, and honest, too, because we owe you that much, don't we, *niña*, my child? but love is love, whether in this life or the next, between us we're a bridge, señor Arenal, what I mean is all we have to do is reach out and take each other's extended hands to create a coupling, you've been more than willing and we didn't do much to twist your arm, did we, *niña*, my child? and our interest in your pottery is as genuine as the sun is warm and bright—although to be truly honest we prefer the night—splendid handsome proud pottery made from your skillful hands, señor Arenal, and we paid cash in rare bills and coins, to our credit, and giving you credit where credit is due, payment in full, justified by your virtuosity and big-heartedness, so I offer you a little mystery story, as magnificent as your work, by Alberto Blanco, born in Mexico City, another maestro, almost your contemporary, "La estatua y el globero," "The Statue and the Balloon Man," with a translation by Edgardo Moctezuma for those who prefer to hear it in English:

Voy caminando de noche por el Paseo de la Reforma. A lo lejos veo venir a un globero, solo, en el magnífico escenario. Las luces de neón le dan un aire helado a la vista. Al aproximarnos veo que se le suelta un globo de color rojo. Escapa y queda atrapado entre las altas ramas de los árboles, justo encima de la estatua de un general. Éste sostiene en la mano derecha un sable que brilla. Comienza a extender el brazo lentamente, lentamente, hasta que logra pinchar el globo. En vez de estallar, el globo se quiebra como si fuera de vidrio. El globero recoge los pedacitos luminosos. Me muestra un puñado: me veo reflejado con un rostro distinto en cada uno de ellos.

I am walking at night in the Paseo de la Reforma Avenue. From afar I see a balloon man approaching, alone, in the magnificent scenery. The neon lights give a frozen air to the sight. As we draw closer I see that a red balloon slips away from him. It escapes and ends up trapped in the high branches of the trees just above the statue of a general. He holds in his right hand a saber that glitters. He slowly begins to extend his arm, very slowly, until he succeeds in puncturing the balloon. Instead of exploding, the balloon shatters as if made of glass. The balloon man picks up the luminous little pieces. He shows me a handful: I see myself reflected with a different countenance in every one of them.

And Pascuala Esparza, there you have it, señor Arenal, and you can interpret these beautiful words in whatever way you wish, and once we're gone you can share your thoughts with your friend, I'll give you a clue, maybe we're *los pedacitos luminosos,* the luminous little pieces, maybe we aren't, we don't want to give anything away, do we, *niña,* my child? it's not a question, not for us, we won't reveal what's behind the mystery, the night opens up before you, like when you were children, for us that was long, long ago, but for you and your friend, not more than sixty years, maybe less, who's counting? you don't look your age, either of you, so we bid you farewell with an expression of regret, Pascuala Esparza and Little Pascuala backing out the door, no more words, floating backward into the darkness of the stairwell, the emptiness breathing out a puff of smoke, an unworldly belch, a noisy emission of gas through the mouth of heaven, Rubén Arenal turned to face Ernesto, who shrugged his shoulders.

The two friends, standing a short distance from each other, not far away because the roof wasn't that big, but far enough for facial expressions to be lost in shadows cast by fanned-out street lights and trickling starlight, and Ernesto Cisneros, in Iguala de la Independencia, I met a man who's named after the wrestler whose mask I'm wearing, Aarón, but not Rodríguez—no last name and a first name that always changes—and he told me that in order to perform the tasks I'll carry out to put right what I've done, I must have faith in my transformation, and that the *M* on my forehead is my *Emeth,* or Truth, and Rocket, straight out of *The Golem,* we've read the same books and know the same things, and in your case, Esto, he's right, you're wearing the letter like it's branded on your face, and Ernesto Cisneros, so it is, brother, and only God knows how long I'll wear it, but I've come to terms with it and what it comes with as far as my duty's concerned, Ernesto folding his arms across his chest, expecting a reply, but seeing Rubén Arenal looking down at his feet, and from where he was standing, Ernesto could tell there was a gloomy expression on his friend's face, and Ernesto Cisneros, your Little Pascualita and her mother, they are who they are, brother, not of this world, and you've got to believe it, our Coyuco, Lupita's and mine, he's where he is, burned to ashes that're scattered on a river, and that's the truth, we believe it, but it doesn't make it any easier to swallow, so I know how you feel, a loss is a loss, I'll carry the sorrow for the rest of my days, only I'll do what I can to right the wrong I've done, and Lupita will weep on my shoulder until she's dry of tears, maybe she'll work with me at the community center, Vistas del Cerro Grande gave me a job, did I tell you? and I won't have to convince her, no know-how or cunning, and she won't have to commit a crime she'll regret, a volunteer all the way, what do we have left, memories of our son, and his things that're still in the house, touch them hold them in your hands smell them, no scent of the dead but a pleasant, sweet smell of Coyuco when he was alive, breathing the same air we breathe today, right now, brother, in this night, Rubén Arenal, a smile breaking on his face, blinking his eyes free from staring out into infinity, not within, motioning Ernesto to join him, the two men sitting down on the rooftop, looking up at the constellations revolving above their heads, not that their eyes could see them rotating, the groups of stars forming recognizable patterns were still, remaining where they were, where they always were and always would be, from one day to the next, one night to another, it was the earth that traveled in the sky, none of it mattered, there was only one truth they bothered to understand, and with it, nothing else mattered, it wasn't the kind of truth that went with facts, but something bigger they couldn't define like an armful of mist and clouds—hold on hold on it's slipping away—that's what they decided between them, sitting side by side, without words, but with memories, how simple it was understanding things that got lost and things that remain, complete with tears and gut-wrenching sadness, and Rocket, I'd kill for a *changuirongo,* an ounce and a half of Patrón Tequila, *hecho totalmente de agave azul,* silver's good enough for me, ginger beer, lots of crushed ice, or a drink prescribed by José Manuel Di Bella, born in Mexicali, with lemons, plenty of crushed ice, mineral water, Coca-Cola and Enrique Partida's *reposado,* "... tequila, little brother. The 'Neutronic' we called it from then on. Devastation, ghostbody. Later, at dawn the hearty *menudo* with Consuelo. Sometimes several sleepless mornings"—tripe stew after the *Neutrónico,* that's the ticket, we only need the ingredients, Esto, and a Consuelo who'll make us *menudo,* but here we are on a rooftop near La Popular, I lost love that'd only just started and we don't even know if you can eat a tripe stew with that face of yours, and Ernesto Cisneros, it's an additional layer that isn't my skin, there's trim around my eyes, nose and mouth, nothing more, and in Aarón's words, it's "a wrestler's mask that's no longer a mask," yes, brother, all in all I've had my good dances, right up 'til they took our son, Lupita's and mine, our Coyuco, and if we had a bottle of Patrón's silver or Partida's *reposado,* with a mix or without, and a tripe stew thrown into the bargain, I'd join you and you couldn't stop me until I was drunk and ready to bust with all the tequila and *menudo* I'd put in my belly, mask or no mask, and Rocket, from where we're sitting, all we can do is count the stars, Ernesto inched over to Rubén Arenal until he was right up against him, Rubén Arenal raised his arm and dropped it over Ernesto's shoulders, broader than he remembered them, shoulders carrying the weight of all he'd been through, the Chihuahuan wind blew through their hair, flowing locks falling in front of their eyes, which they brushed away with a flick of their hands, not a single star reached down out of one of the constellations to comfort them, they consoled each other, love lost and death weren't far apart, separately and together they watched the sky, the wind didn't chill them, the night was warm, Ernesto and Rubén Arenal, impatient with the night that offered them no relief, standing up at the same time, each using the other to lean against until they got firmly on their feet, Rubén Arenal using his index finger to follow the lines of the purple letter *M* on Ernesto's gold lamé and shiny black latex mask, and Ernesto Cisneros, what about that drink? and Rocket, right this way, *'mano,* indicating the door he'd gone through ahead of Pascuala Esparza and her daughter, leaving the lavender lamé presentation mask with white leather markings and *antifaz* where it'd landed, Rubén Arenal leading the way down the dark stairwell holding on to the handrail, hearing Ernesto's footsteps behind him, and Rocket, without turning his head, not flying down the stairs, Esto? you came out of nowhere like a red-shouldered hawk, or showing off Mil Máscaras' *Tope Suicida,* I didn't see you coming, I guess nobody did, but you really pulled my nuts out of the fire, 'mano, I was already hearing "Rescue Me," by Fontella Bass, and Rubén Arenal heard Ernesto laughing for the first time since he'd returned from Iguala, the two friends standing on the sidewalk, a gust of wind carrying the smell of pork rinds and gasoline, and Rocket, let's go this way, I don't have the courage to walk past the windows of La Popular, not now, and never again, Ernesto shrugging his shoulders, a new habit he could afford with his new face and build, wearing both confidence and doubt, only the echo of Coyuco's disappearance and death brought a razor to his throat leaving a grimace outlined by *antifaz*.

Rubén Arenal and Ernesto, turning right on Calle Guadalupe Victoria, heading at a fast clip past Calle 12a toward Gustavo Díaz Ordaz, Ernesto moving at the speed of La Amenaza Elegante, Rubén Arenal keeping up with him, taking a left on Gustavo Díaz Ordaz, a wide boulevard with almost no traffic at night, a bus passing them, two friends following the curve of the boulevard past Juan Aldama, displaying the agility of La Amenaza Elegante, Rubén Arenal and Ernesto holding to the wide curve to the left past Calle Ojinaga, at the corner were chairs, bicycles and tires for sale, and one street after Morelos Nueva, it was a small world they traveled in, separately or together, with the same name for more than one street, they turned right on José María Morelos y Pavón in Cuauhtémoc, past number 1801, past a law firm, and after 1805, the two friends slowing down, and Ernesto Cisneros, I've always liked this street, streets named after men in history remind me how much I love our Mexico, José María Morelos, Servant of the Nation, a priest, military insurgent, a Mexican patriot, organizer and architect of the second stage of the war of independence, Morelos was captured in Temalaca by Colonel Manuel de la Concha, tried by the Inquisition, executed by firing squad in 1815 in San Cristóbal Ecatepec, there're ghosts everywhere, brother, but his lieutenant, Vicente Guerrero, a living hero at the time, *Un Estado Libre protégé las Artas, la Industria, las Ciencias y Comercio; y no premia más que la Virtud y el Mérito*, "A free state protects the arts, industry, science and trade; and it rewards only virtue and merit," Guerrero went on fighting in the southern states during the *Resistencia*, and you know the rest, everything's connected in our country's history, and we better not forget it, and Rocket, I haven't and I won't, depending on how much energy or curiosity, temptation or responsibility we've got left, Esto, *mi enciclopedia gigante*, but what're you up to and where are we going? and Ernesto Cisneros, hang on, brother, we're almost there, it's a private watering hole, a retreat from the known world, and Rocket, you never told me about it, *mi mapa del mundo y explorador*, my world map and explorer, and Ernesto Cisneros, trust me, trust me, we'll drink and face the world tomorrow, the wind that was neither warm nor cold kept up with their Fantômas–like comic book swiftness, pushing them even faster and farther with an occasional gusty shove, until Rubén Arenal and his best friend with Mil Máscaras' face got to a wooden paneled door in a wooden paneled wall.

Guadalupe taking off a lightweight blue nylon jacket, Irma in her shirt sleeves, and Luz Elena wearing a T-shirt, a sweatshirt's sleeves tied loosely around her neck, the three women heading straight for the kitchen, Guadalupe carrying a rolled-up banner under her arm, Irma with a placard of cover stock on a wooden stick, Luz Elena holding a bright orange heavyweight paper, with a slogan written in indelible pen, Irma leaning the stick against the wall next to the refrigerator, Luz Elena doing the same with the handmade poster, Guadalupe putting the rolled-up banner between them, Guadalupe, Irma, Luz Elena, together, their skin glowed with perspiration, and Guadalupe Muñoz, I figured I'd take my jacket along in case it got cold when the sun went down, no such thing, still hot and more sweaty than when we were standing there shouting until we got hoarse, nobody listening to us but each other, the members of a group of relatives, friends, and the three of us, not many but a lot

more than a few, and Luz Elena, everyone take a seat, we'll have
something cool to drink, Luz Elena reaching for a pitcher in the
refrigerator, pouring three glasses of *licuado de fresa,* a thick, homemade smoothie, milk, fresh strawberries, ice and sugar, then leaving
the pitcher in the center of the table, and Irma Payno, I've got to
have a smoke, and Guadalupe Muñoz and Luz Elena, in one voice
and at the same time, if we've heard it once, we'll hear it forever,
your famous last words, *'mana,* and Irma Payno, I'm not dead yet,
chavas, so don't count me out, Guadalupe and Luz Elena, despite
their sadness, clapping their hands, raising their glasses, Irma taking a 5x50 La Casta Robusto by Santa Clara from her handbag,
lighting it, not inhaling but taking a deep drag, exhaling a perfumed
cloud that hovered above them, and Guadalupe Muñoz, wiping her
mouth, we aren't winning, and Luz Elena, it's only been a couple of
days since we organized, and Irma Payno, we're listening, but I get
the feeling nobody else is, Guadalupe shaking her head yes, and
Guadalupe Muñoz, they aren't giving us more than the time of day,
De Narco Políticos a Narco Estado ¡Ya Basta! From Narco Politicians
to Narco State—Enough Already! *¡Basta Ya! Queremos un México
Sin PRI,* Enough Already! We Want a Mexico Without PRI—*la
dictadura perfecta,* the "perfect dictatorship," Mario Vargas Llosa
was right, and Irma Payno, *¡Vivos Se Los Llevaron! ¡Vivos Los
Queremos!* They Took Them Alive We Want Them Alive! our slogans, I'll swear they did it, the army, the federal police, the municipal
police, they turned them over to the Guerreros Unidos, or they did
it themselves, and don't tell me nobody knew what was going on,
there's the Iguala C-4—locked up murdered disappeared, may God
protect our sons brothers husbands future husbands wherever they
are, Irma exhaling another cloud of bluish smoke, and Luz Elena,
with respect to nobody listening, and I'm not talking about earshot,
the range within which sounds may be heard, but with respect to
really paying close attention, taking into consideration what this
means, not only for us but for our Mexico, taking into consideration
that our country's sinking lower and lower, this tragedy drags us

down so low that in order for anybody in the world to look us in the eyes they'd have to get on their knees and search the earth for what's left of our dignity, dig where you're standing, sisters and brothers, our pride's lying in the dirt! and Irma Payno, it's an investigation we want, and Guadalupe Muñoz, and who's going to give us one? they aren't handing them out with tortillas, and Luz Elena, an investigation, but one that isn't connected to Alacrán or the Queen of Iguala, and Guadalupe Muñoz, keep dreaming, in the words of Little Richard, they're "Slippin' and a-slidin', / Peepin' and a-hidin'," and as for us, we can't behave as if everything were normal, not ever again—normal, I mean, and Irma Payno, I was going to marry him, and Luz Elena, I was going to pour him a glass of this strawberry smoothie, and Guadalupe Muñoz, I was going to hold him in my arms, like he was a young boy, and Irma Payno, we could've offered him a cigarette, or one of my cigars, he isn't a child, Irma tilting her head back, running her hand through her hair, exhaling another cloud that rolled above the table heading toward the ceiling, and Luz Elena, with respect to where people go when they're dead, who knows the truth? maybe they're walking around without bumping into us on the street, maybe sitting right here, at the table, without asking for a drink, not even wanting a smoke, but what I do know is they're inside us, always and forever, and Guadalupe Muñoz, we aren't living in a time capsule where everything stays as it is, a kind of storage for a selection of objects that're picked because they're typical of the present time, buried for discovery in the future, the days keep on changing, and our emotions are like the days, transformed by this assault on our children, and Luz Elena, with respect to time and the indefinite continued progress of existence, and in Coyuco's case it doesn't apply, the Aztecs had an unusual way of counting time, each month had twenty days, named after things or animals, and Guadalupe Muñoz, that's right, *m'hija*, there were eighteen months in a year, with five "unlucky days," or *nemontemi*, left over, I've seen it in the *Codex Mendoza*, and Luz Elena, each year was named after its first day, and the year, having 365 days,

305

could only begin with four day-names: House, Rabbit, Reed and Flint Knife, that's the way it was, and it's not like that today, not for us, and Guadalupe Muñoz, let's play with math, *m'hijas,* the Aztecs used two major calendrical cycles, the *tonalpohualli,* or "count of days," a sacred almanac of 260 days, and the *xiuhpohualli,* an annual calendar of 365 days, the *tonalpohualli,* was put together from a sequence of numbers from one to thirteen paired with a sequence of twenty day-names, the two calendars were combined so that each day was identified clearly and definitely by both a sacred date and an annual date, now here comes the math, since the least common multiple of 260 and 365 is 18,980, which equals 52 x 365, the combined cycle of the two calendars repeats after 52 years of 365 days each, and this 52-year period, known as the *xiuhmolpilli,* or "sacred bundle," played a significant role in Aztec religious life, Irma taking the Casta Robusto from her mouth, setting it in an ashtray, and Irma Payno, just to tell you I know something about it even if I'm younger than you are, *chavas,* in the second chapter "Which treats of the months of the year and of the symbols by which the days of the month were known," of my copy of *The Ancient Calendar* by Fray Diego Durán, he writes, "In ancient times the year was composed of eighteen months, and thus it was observed by the Indian people. Since their months were made of no more than twenty days, these were all the days contained in a month, because they were not guided by the moon but by the days; therefore, the year has eighteen months. The days of the year were counted twenty by twenty," Guadalupe and Luz Elena clapped their hands and raised their glasses again, Irma took up her cigar, drew on it, not inhaling, and Guadalupe Muñoz, my son would've been a lucky man to have you as his wife, *niña mía,* and Luz Elena, everything's upside down, the world is always the wrong way around, if you do somebody a good turn, they blame you for it, and if you try to ruin people, they say you're right, and Guadalupe Muñoz, what we're doing is right, and in the end the man or woman who does right is happy, I'm only waiting for Ernesto to come back safe and sound from where he's gone, then we can try to go on living, and Luz Elena, we'll do our best, never let go, and hold out for the truth, and Guadalupe Muñoz, Coyuco's our son, Ernesto's and mine, and you don't leave your son to rot in the earth or float away as ashes on the river without saying goodbye to him, and Luz Elena, wishing him a good life in the next world, and asking God to bless him, and Irma Payno, what more can we do but insist on knowing what happened to every one of them? we won't take no for an answer, and Guadalupe Muñoz, while we're living we'll make good use of the days, in God's eyes and our own, following our calendar, or the combination of the ancients' sacred almanac and the annual calendar, the *tonalpohualli* and the *xiuhpohualli,* Guadalupe lowering her voice, whispering, and Guadalupe Muñoz, because changing or not changing, it isn't the same to me, some people can take it or leave it, not me, the birds change, they lose their feathers, and so we can shed our own, let's take the path that's been dropped in our lap, besides, it's already happened, it isn't a question, *m'hijas,* not really, we've had our eyelids cut off, too, our eyes are open day and night, there's nothing that we can't see for what it is, it's a miraculous change, and we aren't alone, we're all grieving Coyuco and the forty-three who've disappeared, parents brothers sisters wives friends girlfriends, without knowing it, I'm pretty sure Ernesto's changed, too, let's wait and see, he'll be home soon, I can feel it in my bones, there's a lot ahead of us that we've got to do, we've just started, and if we don't find our sons brothers husbands boyfriends friends, if we never find out what happened to them, there'll be no mercy for those who're to blame, I'm not saying we ought to kill them, even if they deserve it, I won't do it, but someone else will, there'll be no compassion or forgiveness for whoever they are, and as Ignacio would remind us, a few words from the sixth book in the New Testament, *La Epístola del Apóstol San Pablo a Los Romanos, 1:18, 1:19,* the Letter to the Romans, chapter one, verses eighteen and nineteen: *Porque la ira de Dios se revela desde el cielo contra toda impiedad e injusticia de los hombres que detienen con injusticia la verdad; / porque lo que de*

Dios se conoce les es manifiesto, pues Dios se lo manifestó, "For the wrath of God is revealed from heaven against all ungodliness and unrighteousness of men, who by their unrighteousness suppress the truth. / For what can be known about God is plain to them, because God has shown it to them," and Luz Elena, so we're supposed to leave it up to Him? and Irma Payno, is that what you're saying? and Guadalupe Muñoz, that's why, when I've got nothing to say, I say nothing, words speak for themselves, silence says it all, and Luz Elena, faith is the beginning of healing, *'manas,* Irma shutting her eyes, opening them, nodding her head at Guadalupe and Luz Elena, and Irma Payno, I guess your Ignacio Pardiñas would've quoted *Hebreos 11:1, Es, pues, la fe la certeza de lo que se espera, la convicción de lo que no se ve,* "Now faith is the assurance of things hoped for, the conviction of things not seen," and Guadalupe Muñoz, *¡le felicitamos!* my compliments, he would've recited the same words, *m'hija,* and I've got a few more for both of you, not my own, they belong to Brenda Lozano, maybe you've read her, maybe not, but they're words that fit the subject, *No saber dónde están los que queremos es no saber dónde está uno,* "To not know where your loved ones are is to not know where you are," and Irma Payno, words that go straight to my heart, and Luz Elena, mine, too *'mana,* it's our truth, and not only ours, and Irma Payno, *Tal vez porque quedan las palabras para quien deja que otro se vaya. Porque dejamos que alguien se vaya para recordarlo, como nos vamos para ser recordados. Acaso porque amamos para que nos amen como abandonamos para que nos abandonen,* "Maybe because words are what's left for someone who lets another go, because we let someone go so as to remember them, just as we go to be remembered, perhaps because we love so that we are loved, just as we abandon others so that they might abandon us," it was Brenda Lozano who wrote that, too, I'm young, but I've got more than one book up my sleeve, *chavas,* and Luz Elena, with respect to Lupe and her wishes, an earnest or humble request, when I'm here I want to be there, and the other way around, if you get my meaning, I'm not always so clear, but what's

He going to do for us? how can we count on Him? there's our slice
of obligation, the course of action to which we're morally bound, it's
up to all of us, with God's blessing and our bodies on the street, Luz
Elena and Irma looked at Guadalupe, who didn't reply, but a beatific
radiance shone on her face as the sun fell off the edge of the horizon,
spreading its last reddish-yellow glow in silence over the spotless
windowpane in the kitchen.

E rnesto pushed open the wooden paneled door of the cantina
on José María Morelos y Pavón, a street named after José María
Morelos, Servant of the Nation, Rubén Arenal right behind him,
the door closing silently behind them, the two friends no longer
moving at the speed of La Amenaza Elegante, but heading straight
for the bar before taking the time to look around the room for an
empty table, the cantina lighted by low-watt bulbs in wall sconces
with ornamental brackets, and Ernesto Cisneros, not only have I
always liked this street, but I've always liked this place, and Rocket,
I can't see a thing, there's not much light and plenty of smoke, the
man behind the bar appearing out of nowhere in the glow of one
of the small shaded lamps at each end of the bar, asking them what
they'd like to drink, recognizing Ernesto behind his mask, a thinly
veiled partially concealed Mil Máscaras combined with Ernesto's
familiar features, and Rocket, you must be a regular, 'mano, no
matter what you look like, ¡Dos, dos, dos hombres en uno! Ernesto
turning his head to look at Rubén Arenal, and Ernesto Cisneros,
that's right, then shaking the owner's hand, but they didn't order
anything, leaning instead with their backs against the bar, their eyes
getting used to the light in the room as conversations cut their way
through the cigarette and cigar smoke, Rubén Arenal looking this
way and that in order to see where the voices were coming from,
at first finding nothing and no one, until his eyes settled on a large
painting of Xtabay, a supernatural creature with the torso of a goddess and the legs of an allegorical creature, a demon seductress who

lured men to their doom with her captivating voice, a figure from
Mayan mythology, the painting covering almost an entire wall of
the underlit bar, Xtabay walking along the bank of a river at night,
and right behind her, a large five-leaved kapok, or ceiba tree, *Ceiba
pentandra,* set in a lush jungle landscape vibrating with terrible colors, a large bat with a screwy expression on its face flying through
the sky strangely lit by a distant fire, the bat appearing to circle the
river and the tall tropical tree, and Ernesto Cisneros, what do you
think, she's a knockout, isn't she, not just the painting, and when
you've had enough to drink of what they serve here she'll start to
look a lot less dangerous than she really is, the owner's from Ticul,
almost nineteen miles east of Uxmal, in Yucatán, which explains
the presence of this masterly portrait of frightening folklore, don't
look too long, brother, don't stare, she'll ask to sit at our table if she
gets the idea into her head that you're interested, and Rocket, there's
a table over there, let's take a chair, let's take a chance, and the two
friends crossed the short distance to a vacant table shrouded in cigar smoke.

In a corner under a wall sconce where the smoke cleared because
someone walked past it stood a jukebox with muted colored lights,
the figure put a coin into it, selecting a song, and to the accompaniment of a joyful version of "Libertad y Olvido," not by David
Záizar, which was in a more *campirano* style, accompanied by guitar and harmonica, one of his trademarks, but performed by Los
Pavos Reales, with vocals by Salvador and Eddie Torres-Gómez,
and Carlos Miranda, in a *conjunto* or *norteño* style, accompanied
by accordion, *bajo sexto, tololoche,* and in a faster tempo, Rubén
Arenal and Ernesto sitting down, hearing the bitterness in the lyrics of a song whose meaning they transposed from romantic love
to another kind of love, a universal love, and speaking with voices
reminding them of their feelings for Coyuco, with love, compassion
and honor for the forty-three *normalistas* who'd disappeared, and
for the many citizens of Mexico never to be heard from again:

A nadie le digas que yo fui tu amante,
A nadie le digas que fui tu querer,
No manches mi nombre con esas palabras
Déjame tranquilo, déjame vivir.

Una vez te quise yo nunca lo niego
Y a ti te entregaba todo mi querer,
Y hubo ocasiones que creí amarte
Creí que en el mundo no habría otra mujer.

Hoy no me arrepiento de haberte querido
Guardo tus amores en mi corazón
Pero para darnos libertad y olvido,
A nadie le digas que yo fui tu amor.

Do not tell anyone that I was your lover,
Do not tell anyone that I was your love,
Do not stain my name with those words,
Leave me in peace, allow me to live.

I loved you once and I never deny it,
And I handed you all of my love,
And there were times I believed that I loved you
I thought that there would be no other woman on earth

Today I do not regret having loved you
I keep your affection in my heart
So that we may give each other freedom and oblivion,
Do not tell anyone that I was your love.

It didn't take much to bring their thoughts to Coyuco, a *canción ranchera*, a polka, a *corrido, son jarocho, son huasteco,* nor to turn to thoughts of any other of the disappeared, and in the cantina, cigarettes and cigars burning tobacco, Ernesto and Rubén Arenal removing the lid that covered their hearts, music always linking them to their emotions, their emotions to music, a fair deal, an automatic response for sensitive women and men, the owner coming to the table, noting nothing different about Ernesto's face, as if he'd seen it all before, the changes life brought on everyone, holding a circular serving tray with two mixed drinks, placing them on the table, one for Ernesto, one for Rubén Arenal, and before lifting the glass, Rubén Arenal wondering what the owner had made for them, about to open his mouth to repeat part of the question he'd asked while walking down José María Morelos y Pavón before they got to the cantina, something like, Esto, *mi experto en bebidas mixtas,* what're you up to, and what're we drinking? but nothing came out of his mouth, Rubén Arenal watched as Ernesto lifted the glass to the *antifaz* around his lips and downed the contents in a single gulp, no time for questions, then, and Rocket, down the hatch, *'mano,* whatever it is, and it burned going down, a gulp as complete as his friend's that swallowed everything the owner had mixed in the glass, but it wasn't bitter or unpleasant in any way, the two men sitting across from each other at the table under a cloud of cigarette and cigar smoke that came from every direction and nowhere at the same time because they couldn't make out the faces of the other clients in the cantina, who was smoking what, not with the light that came from the wall sconces and the two small lamps at each end of the bar, not from what seemed like the never-ending string of tiny warm lights strung where the ceiling met the walls that might've come from a permanent Christmas celebrated in the cantina for as long the owner had run it, a seasonal decoration becoming a local institution, the owner arriving after they put their empty glasses down, retrieving the glasses, putting them on a tray he balanced with one hand, a professional in every sense, wiping the surface of the table to eliminate any sign of the rings the two glasses might've left, then leaving a large circular ceramic ashtray and a box of matches between them, Rubén Arenal searching his pockets for cigarettes, finding a pack of Faros, offering Ernesto a smile at what looked like an unending supply of coffin nails, the beacon of the lighthouse on the pack lighting the tabletop and ashtray, Rubén Arenal tapping out a cigarette, offering the pack with the protruding cigarette to Ernesto, who pinched it between wrestler's fingers, then Rubén Arenal put one between his own lips, lit them both off a single match which he tossed nonchalantly into the center of the ashtray the owner'd provided them.

The first drink hit Rubén Arenal as he took the first drag off his cigarette, he wasn't visibly trembling, but his thoughts were shaken up by the sudden change of perspective the owner's cocktail triggered in a mind as vulnerable as his was after the attempt Pascuala Esparza and *La Pascualita* had made to toss him off the roof, a menace he now realized hadn't been digested at the time, then the experience of being saved by Ernesto in the form of the Fantômas of the comics publisher Organización Editorial Novaro, an unexpected intervention, Rubén Arenal taking another drag off his cigarette, his face and the back of his hands burning with a wave of heat as the drink made its way through his bloodstream, causing a sensation like a rash but without the texture or inconvenience, more on the order of a profound warming of the soul, steady nerves, Rubén Arenal sitting in unfamiliar comfort, free from worry, filling his lungs with smoke, exhaling into the dense cloud above them, and Ernesto Cisneros, I guess you see what I mean, swell drinks that guy makes, aren't they, and that isn't a question, and Rocket, I'm in a state so serene I don't want to leave it for anything in the world, and Ernesto Cisneros, look out, brother, he's bringing us another, and you'll never get drunk, I never do, it's the magic of what's in the potion that brings me back here every time, the owner setting two glasses down on the table, carrying the same tray, receding like the tide, leaving the two friends with full glasses, Rubén Arenal raising his glass, and Rocket, what's in it? and Ernesto Cisneros, I never asked, and I never will, I don't want to know, it's the effect I'm after, a harmonious state of high-spiritedness without hurtful hallucinations,

---

a vision or two, but nothing to throw us off the track, just what every customer in the place is after, Ruben Arenal and Ernesto, their eyes fully adjusted to the light, turning their heads to look at the customers seated at the tables and at the three men standing at the bar, Ernesto taking a drink, and Ernesto Cisneros, it isn't sweet as nectar, but a pleasant taste, leaves seeds flowers, we'll never know, oh, what dreams! what possibilities! and Rocket, I suppose you're trying to tell me anything's likely to happen now, well, I'm starting to believe you, Rubén Arenal finishing his second cocktail, a potion leading to an earnest and industrious effort, the drinks the owner made for them, for everyone in the cantina, a concoction not meant to encourage a woman or a man to forget their suffering and sadness, but to carry them all from uneasiness to tranquility and a desire to continue with their lives.

And Ernesto Cisneros, what do you see when you look around you, here, in this bar? I'll tell you what you see, you're seeing a lot of people with problems, real not imagined, unwelcome or harmful and needing-to-be-dealt-with problems, death disappearance desecration, who, instead of giving up, lying down, come here to take advantage of what we're drinking, following the voice of this elixir in order to put things right or settle the score, industrial-strength adjustments made to the unsettled inner being, and Rocket, do you hear what's playing now? an instrumental version of Cuco Sánchez's "Anoche estuve llorando," "Last Night I Was Crying," by Antonio Bribiesca, and Ernesto Cisneros, we're listening to señor Bribiesca now, just like Coyuco and Irma used to listened to him together, among other musicians, 'mano, so you're in accordance with the truth, it isn't the first time, and won't be the last, and Rocket, I wonder if she'll go on listening to him, and Ernesto Cisneros, don't make me cry, but I'll say this much: I hope that she does, and Rocket, the supernatural beings that live on the surface of the earth are identified with specific natural phenomena, and in this sense they're represented in an anthropomorphic way, they aren't only owners of natural phenomena, but in a certain sense they're the phenomena themselves, as the *kiyauhtiomeh* are the rays, the *mixtimeh* are the cloud ones, the *ehecameh* are the wind ones, which can cause disease, disease-causing spirits that infest all four realms of the cosmos, and Ernesto Cisneros, for the Nahua, an *ehecatl*'s responsible not only for disease, but also for any misfortune, including drought, barrenness, and death, and they lurk about trails, houses, bathing areas, or any place that people might frequent, then at the most unsuspecting moment, they enter a victim's body and cause it to fester until the person's too sick to move, they're particularly fond of attacking children, the aged, and anyone who's been weakened in any way, and Rocket, emotionally, like us? and Ernesto Cisneros, don't worry, there isn't a gust in the place, but now you're talking, and so's the cocktail, a vision or two and we're all set, and Rocket, so far all I see is Xtabay, and Ernesto Cisneros, give it until after the third glass, patience patience, *Porque los bellos seres que transitan por el sopor añoso de la tierra,* "For the beautiful things that journey through the ancient slumber of the earth," and Rocket, but there's more to it:— *¡trasgos de sangre, libres, en la pantalla de su sueño impuro!—todos se dan a un frenesí de muerte,* "—ghosts of flesh and blood straying on the screen of its impure dream—all surrender to a frenzy of death," and Ernesto Cisneros, José Gorostiza's words are a perfect fit, but we aren't dead and in heaven yet, and when we do kick the bucket it doesn't have to be because we've been tortured, murdered, and chopped into pieces in order to get to the other side, I prefer to travel in one piece, and Rocket, your faith's grown in leaps and bounds since you're wearing one of the many faces of Mil Máscaras, the expression on Rubén Arenal's face was sincere, steadfast and staunch, showing the light of a strong belief in God, no more and no less, the words themselves were spoken with the intonation of complete trust or confidence in Ernesto, Guadalupe, and Coyuco, a missing person but present every moment in his heart, and any relatives Ernesto had whether he knew them or not, so boundless was his belief in friendship and family.

Rubén Arenal reaching for the pack of Faros, another cigarette
to unite them, and Rocket, what magic is this? our Faros have
dwindled to two cigarettes, with no sign of breeding, and Ernesto
Cisneros, in this bar cigarettes don't last long and when they're gone,
it's the cigars that count, remember the story of the twins Hunahpú
and Xbalanqué, born of the maiden, Xquic, Little Blood or Blood
of a Woman, and the spittle from the mouth of the skull of Hun-
Hunahpú—sounds familiar doesn't it? reminding us of the myth of
the birth of Huitzilopochtli, our Aztec god of war—Hun-Hunahpú's
head hanging in the calabash tree that instantly bore fruit the moment it was put there by the Lords of Xibalba, Hun-Hunahpú and
Vucub-Hunahpú, as two are often one, tricked by the Lords of
Xibalba, and Rocket, I've read the story in the *Popol Vuh*, the sacred
book of the Quiché Maya, and Ernesto Cisneros, then you remember the fate of the hero twins, how the Lords of Xibalba tried to
get the better of them but didn't succeed, not like Hun-Hunahpú
and Vucub-Hunahpú, who went before them, entering the House
of Gloom, Quequma-ha, in which there's only darkness, the place
where Hun-Hunahpú and Vucub-Hunahpú were defeated, the test
with sticks of fat pine, called *zaquitoc,* and the lighted cigars, it was
the undoing of Hun-Hunahpú and Vucub-Hunahpú, you know it if
you've read it, brother, the Lords of Xibalba saying to them, "Each
of you light your pine sticks and your cigars; come and bring them
back at dawn, you must not burn them up, but you must return them
whole," Hun-Hunahpú and Vucub-Hunahpú returning without
their pine sticks and cigars, burned to the last ash, and in this manner they were defeated, slaughtered right away, but before burying
them, the Lords of Xibalba cut off the head of Hun-Hunahpú, burying the older brother together with the younger brother in the place
of sacrifice of the ball game, Rubén Arenal with a worried expression on his face, and Ernesto Cisneros, but Hunahpú and Xbalanqué
defeated the Lords of Xibalba, so we'll smoke the cigars provided by
the owner of this bar once we've finished our last Faros, that's how it
works here, we're supposed to finish our cigars, smoke them to the

very end, and Rocket, but *'mano*—Ernesto interrupting him, and Ernesto Cisneros, no, don't waste your time wondering, our cigars are simply for smoking, and these matches are our tiny pine sticks meant to be lit and blown out, and together with our third glass of the owner's potion we'll dream, and in our dream we'll see our way clear, with a sincere and intense conviction, to do our work or duty well, there are no real, unwelcome or harmful problems that can't be overcome, just look at Hunahpú and Xbalanqué, we'll get the better of those who killed Coyuco, and the others, the wholehearted and tireless campaign begins in a place like this, a one-of-a-kind cantina, the owner and bartender coming to the table with his circular serving tray with two more mixed drinks, replacing the empty glasses with a couple of full ones, laying a pair of cigars on a cloth napkin between them on the table, the bartender backing up and turning around, without making a sound, there were plenty of conversations, a couple nodding their heads to the music of a *son jarocho*, "El Siquisirí," an instrumental by Los Utrera, members of the Cobos and Utrera families forming a group of musicians and dancers from the flat, hot, humid lands of Los Tuxtlas, the *son jarocho* playing on the jukebox, a machine with limitless resources, a musical selection greater than the gigantic estate of Francisco Villa in Parral, Ernesto raising his glass, taking a sip, barely a swallow, wanting to savor the elixir, then setting his glass down, Rubén Arenal offering him a cigarette, Ernesto gently rolling it between his thumb and index finger before putting it in his mouth, Rubén Arenal planting one between his own lips, then using a single wooden match to light them both, leaning back in his chair, exhaling smoke, Ernesto leaning forward, looking Rubén Arenal in the eye, and Ernesto Cisneros, your eyes are already dilated, and Rocket, then it's beginning? and Ernesto Cisneros, it's begun, and long before this moment, the two friends, like brothers, sitting silently, smoking their Faros, taking a swallow now and then of the potion, keeping their eyes on the two cigars that lay on the napkin on the tabletop waiting for them.

They weren't alone in the cantina, the place was full to overflowing, or they were the only customers, that's how it seemed to Ernesto and Rubén Arenal, blind and seeing, the smoke gathered like low-hanging clouds above them, the burning gaze of Xtabay, a demon seductress, coming from the wall opposite their table, cut through the haze to reach them, and as beautiful as Xtabay was, a true temptation, her spellbinding stare savagely penetrated their skulls, splitting them open so the sky beyond the ceiling might read their thoughts, the empty glasses of the third dose of the potion lit by the glowing ends of their cigars, whether they were inhaling them or not, the tips shone bright red, day or night, night or day, and a white and delicate flower, *xtabentun,* or *ololiuqui* in Nahuatl, from the snake-plant, or *coaxihuitl,* lay on the napkin where their cigars had been, resting on a hand-stitched piece of cloth now stained with nectar from a flower picked fresh off the vine, a reflection of the legend of Xtabay, wandering the long-forgotten roads of Mayab, standing beneath the arms of a ceiba tree, waiting to seduce men and travelers, Ernesto reading Rubén Arenal's thoughts, and Ernesto Cisneros, she's a danger to them all, a danger to us, *'mano,* her eyes are drilling into our heads, reminding me that we're in the same world but at a different time with modern dangers that owe nothing to ancient perils, we haven't made a lot of progress, our reality's a lot uglier and more threatening than the beauty of legends, don't ignore the past, we won't get anywhere if we don't learn from history, and Rocket, don't look now but Xtabay's off the canvas and heading our way, and Ernesto Cisneros, ignore her, she's magnificent, but look the other way, no eye contact, or she'll grab you, fuck you, and gobble you up—we aren't here to disappear, traveling from mouth to stomach by way of her gullet, it's encouraging visions we're after, the two friends drawing long and hard on their cigars, the ash at the end of each cigar growing into a fat grainy gray bottle cap, the cantina quiet and loud, Ernesto and Rubén Arenal, hearing and deaf, ignoring Xtabay, the evil spirit in the form of a beautiful woman floating past them, Rubén Arenal and Ernesto detecting a slight trembling in the earth, all at once, their table rising off the floor along with the chairs they were sitting on, two chairs and one table tilting up and moving closer to the wall where the large painting, now without Xtabay, covered most of the wall, and what was left on the canvas was the image of a beautifully rendered kapok set in a lush jungle landscape at night vibrating with delightful colors, rich, dark and ardent now that the evil spirit wasn't there, a large bat with a kind-hearted smile instead of a crazy expression on its face, flying through the distant fire-lit sky above their heads, as if they were closer to Mérida than Chihuahua, the bat circling the nearby river and tall tropical trees of the artist's imagination, then passing over them on its way out over the water, circling circling, Ernesto and Rubén Arenal, still smoking cigars, still seated at their table that was now part of the painting on the wall, with everything turned right side up from their perspective on the canvas, no longer looking backward at the receding floor, seeing the cantina in front of them through a kind of picture window that was the frame of the painting, without hearing the music from the jukebox or the customers' conversations, recognizing the cigarette and cigar smoke they'd left behind, identifying Xtabay at one of the tables, seated with a solitary man, Ernesto and Rubén Arenal observing the movements in the bar from the safety of the landscape surrounding them, an almost silent swish of the bat's wings worrying the warm still air, Rubén Arenal taking the cigar from between his lips, wiping moisture from his forehead with a handkerchief, Ernesto's mask damp with the humidity of the painting's night, a full-face white pro-grade Lycra mask, a second, semitransparent skin, with black *antifaz* and an application in the form of a bat, but no red *M,* and Rocket, you've invented your own mask, señor Rodríguez might've worn the same one, it's a suitable selection, brother, the attribute of an old hand at this early stage of transformation, and with a splendid specimen flying over our heads, look out! here he comes, Rubén Arenal and Ernesto, with the cigars between their lips, ducked their heads at the same time as the bat swooped low and then out over the slow-moving river whose current carried no debris, no bodies, but a scattering of leaves, a broken branch, a flower, nothing more.

Rubén Arenal and Ernesto sitting upright at their table in the painted landscape, where everything looked real, tasting the moisture in the air, breathing the smell of vegetation, the odor of the earth, the stubs of their cigars having dropped off when they ducked their heads, but the tips still glowing, no dust or dirt kicked up on the road a stone's throw away because there wasn't a single passerby, Ernesto and Rubén Arenal, smoking, their hands folded in front of them, the flames of the distant fire growing brighter, reflected on the irises of their eyes, Rubén Arenal inspecting Ernesto's face, a closer look at his friend in the primitive nighttime, and Rocket, now the red *M*'s where it's supposed to be, Ernesto reaching up to touch the Lycra letter on his forehead, then a sigh of relief, and Ernesto Cisneros, to make the picture complete, the bat must've painted it in passing, so instrumental is my connection to Mr. Personalidad, El Hombre de las Mil Máscaras, a puzzling partnership understood by few, not even myself, but since it happened, I always appraise it with ample appreciation because I don't know who I'd be if it weren't for him, not after committing murder, what I've got is another shot, *perdone,* my apologies for saying it! and Rocket, no one will see us cry for what you did on the empty soccer field in Iguala, the tears we've got left are reserved for your son, and the others, Ernesto looking down at his feet, a serpent, the symbol of lightning, the divine type of warlike might, circling his boot, gathering itself snugly around the ankle, no biting, no squeezing, a friendly serpent to keep them company during their stay in the painting without Xtabay, she was busy in the bar, a landscape without threats, not even the flaming sky approaching them was dangerous, it was just the color and light of an impenetrable night, not easy to understand but a result of the potion they'd been served by the owner of the cantina, who came from Ticul, belonging to the chiefdom of Tutul Xiú in pre-Hispanic times, a town nineteen miles east of Uxmal, Yucatán, and Rocket, what're you looking at? and Ernesto Cisneros, a snake that's a warrior, brother, and she's come to join us, and Rocket, and you didn't call her to come to you, didn't do a thing, you're more than a model of Mil Máscaras, snake charming's thought of as the highest test of proficiency in magic, and magic brings victory in war, and Ernesto Cisneros, Huitzilopochtli's mother is Cihuacoatl, Woman Serpent, one of the guises of Coatlicue, Robe of Serpents, and Our Great Mother, the most dreaded and powerful of all the goddesses, this potent potion's more than magic, and this snake's more evidence in our favor, Our Lady, the Serpent Woman, mythical mother of the human race, wound around the ankle of my boot, a favorable forecast into our future, *La Epístola Universal de Santiago,* James 4:15, *En lugar de lo cual deberíais decir: Si el Señor quiere, viviremos y haremos esto o aquello,* "Instead you ought to say, 'If the Lord wills, we will live and do this or that,'" because it isn't up to us, you know it and I know it but the municipal police, the federal police, the ministerial police don't know it, they think it's up to them or it's up to nobody, and whoever gets in their way gets stepped on stamped out erased from earth, no grasp of the will of God, Rubén Arenal watching the serpent make herself comfortable, gradually inflating her body using the warmth emanating from Ernesto's leg to increase in size, the marriage of human and snake, two different organisms living in close physical and spiritual association, Ernesto and Rubén Arenal persuaded the painting on the wall of the cantina was a pleasant place to live, but knowing it was temporary, a blessing of the owner's elixir, all at once, the music and conversations from the bar, still foggy with cigarette and cigar smoke, coming in loud and clear, in particular, a *son jarocho* from Veracruz, written by Arcadio Hidalgo, "El Fandanguito," "The Little Party," sung by Ixya Herrera, played by Conjunto Hueyapan with Moche Herrera on *jarana jarocho,* Xocoyotzin Herrera on *requinto jarocho,* and Fermín Herrera on *arpa jarocho:*

¿Señores, qué son es éste?
¿Señores, qué son es éste?
Señores El Fandanguito
Señores El Fandanguito
¿Señores, qué son es éste?

La primera vez que lo oigo
¡Válgame Dios! pero qué bonito
¿Señores, qué son es éste?
Señores El Fandanguito

Y este jarro, y este jarro me huele a vino
Vuelta le doy, que me desatino
Y este jarro, y este jarro me huele a coco
Vuelta le doy, que me vuelvo loco

Fandanguito marinero
De la costa pescador
De la costa pescador
Fandanguito marinero
De la costa pescador

Al cantarte soy primero
Pues me gusta tu sabor,
Y al bailarte sólo quiero,
Que me acompañe mi amor

Currutí
Currutí currutí currutá
Cantando se viene
Contando se va

¡Ay! currutí
Currutí currutí currutá
La madre abadesa
De la catedral

Fandanguito, Fandanguito
Vuela veloz como el viento
Vuela veloz como el viento
Fandanguito, Fandanguito
Vuela veloz como el viento

Con tu cantar exquisito
Alegras cualquier momento
Fandanguito, Fandanguito
Tú vienes de Sotavento

¡Ay! que me voy
Que me voy
Me voy prendecita
Lucero hermoso de mañanita

Que me voy
Que me voy
Me voy prenda amada
Lucero hermoso de madrugada

¿Señores, qué son es éste?
Señores El Fandanguito

Gentlemen, what *son* is this?
Gentlemen, what *son* is this?
Gentlemen, it is El Fandanguito
Gentlemen, it is El Fandanguito
Gentlemen, what *son* is this?

It is the first time that I hear it
Oh, my God! How beautiful!
Gentlemen, what *son* is this?
Gentlemen, it is El Fandanguito

And this jug, and this jug smells like wine
I spin it because I'm acting foolish
And this jug, and this jug smells like coconut
I spin it because I'm going crazy

Sea-going Fandanguito
Fisherman from the coast
Fisherman from the coast
Sea-going Fandanguito
Fisherman from the coast

I'm the first to sing your verses
Because I love your feeling
And when I dance to your rhythm
I want only to have my darling by my side

Currutí
Currutí, currutí, currutá
Singing she comes
Singing she goes

Oh, currutí
Currutí, currutí, currutá
The mother superior
Of the cathedral

Fandanguito, Fandanguito
Fly swiftly like the wind
Fly swiftly like the wind
Fandanguito, Fandanguito
Fly swiftly like the wind

With your exquisite singing
You bring joy to every moment

Fandanguito, Fandanguito
You come from Sotavento

Oh, I'm leaving,
I'm leaving,
I'm leaving, my little darling
Oh, beautiful bright morning star

Oh, I'm leaving,
I'm leaving
I'm leaving, my beloved
Beautiful bright star of the dawn

Gentlemen, what *son* is this?
Gentlemen, it is El Fandanguito

And before their eyes, the dance of the *puhuy*, or owl, the dance of
the *cux*, or weasel, the dance of the *iboy*, or armadillo, the dance of
the *xtzul*, or centipede, and the *chitic*, or walking-on-stilts dance,
Rubén Arenal and Ernesto setting their eyes first on the customers
dancing the centipede dance, each wearing small masks, and bearing the tails of the macaw on the napes of their necks, then on those
dancing the *chitic*, expertly dancing on very tall stilts, each customer working many miracles with the things and people at hand in
the cantina, burning furniture as though they were really burning,
that's how it appeared to Ernesto and Rubén Arenal, and instantly
the furniture was as it'd been before, not burned but whole, and
the dancers cut themselves into small pieces, too, killing each other,
and the first one they'd killed was stretched out on the cantina's floor
as though he were dead, but instantly he was brought back to life,
Rubén Arenal and Ernesto hearing one customer saying to another:
a piece of advice, 'mano, first, when you go to die, cry, and use any
means necessary to shed a tear, even if it's only one, because that's
the path the soul takes, and second, do everything you can to push

your soul out of your body, because if you don't, you'll suffer the most severe and insufferable pain that's given to man, and Rocket, words straight out of a story by Juan Rulfo, and Ernesto Cisneros, I heard them, and they mean everything, let's remember them, and Rocket, in the words of Ana Gloria Álvarez Pedrajo, "Generally, I pray for the poor souls in purgatory. Their cries during the night are not bothersome to hear, but their exile is what saddens me," and Ernesto Cisneros, so do we all, *nosotros los creyentes,* we the believers, dancers have the code in the movement of their bodies, birds in magnetizing the air with their beaks—more sorcery and less science! the visions provided by the elixir drawing Ernesto and Rubén Arenal closer to the scene beyond the canvas, leaning forward from their chairs toward the fascinating dances and magic taking place in the cantina, the elixir beginning to wear off, and with these displays of magic, Rubén Arenal and Ernesto, without being tired at all, more energized than enervated by their experience, putting their cigars in the large ashtray, a piece of sculpted clay hardened by heat resembling the pottery Rubén Arenal made in his studio, Rubén Arenal looking at it but without an impulse to inspect it closely, Ernesto and Rubén Arenal, getting up from their chairs, climbing down out of the painting, leaving their table and two nearly extinguished smoldering cigars behind them on the canvas, righting themselves on the floor, first one foot then the other, their eyes sweeping the marvels of the dancing cantina, catching sight of Xtabay, who'd returned to the painting after seducing a customer who was no longer in the cantina, a large kapok behind her, and their table and chairs still standing in the jungle where they'd left them, Rubén Arenal and Ernesto moving through the impassioned customers beneath a layer of cigar and cigarette smoke, the two friends ambling rhythmically to the music, rolling their shoulders to the beat, making their way through the crowd toward the exit, the last scene of Howard Hawk's *To Have and Have Not,* Humphrey Bogart, Lauren Bacall, Walter Brennan, but there were only two of them, Ernesto and Rubén Arenal, heading for daylight, reaching for the handle of the wood paneled door, the elixir entirely worn off after they'd seen and felt what they were meant to see and feel, nothing forgotten, not ever, not today or tomorrow, memories fresh as the dawn awaiting them after another nudge in the right direction.

And Ignacio Pardiñas, since you tell me you enjoyed hearing a quote from Alberto Blanco, according to your story it was Pascuala Esparza, *La Pascualita*'s mother, who said the words to both of you—I'll go with it, a theme, and for right now I won't quote from the Bible, not until it's necessary, here we go, my son, and you, Rubén Arenal, Rocket, a name reserved for your friends—who hasn't said it!—a few lines from Alberto Blanco's poem, "Mi tribu," "My Tribe":

> *La tierra es la misma*
> *el cielo es otra.*
> *El cielo es el mismo*
> *la tierra es otro.*
>
> *De lago en lago,*
> *de bosque en bosque:*
> *¿cuál es mi tribu?*
> *—me pregunto—*
> *¿cuál es mi lugar?*
>
> Earth is the same
> sky another.
> Sky is the same
> earth another.
>
> From lake to lake,
> forest to forest:
> which tribe is mine?
> —I ask myself—
> where's my place?

And Ignacio Pardiñas, hoping that you'll see its significance, my young men—one who's like my son, the other like his brother—speaking loosely, of course, with cards on the table, completely open and honest, Rocket, you're my second son, apparently but not actually valid, but good enough for me, so I'll call you Segundo henceforth as of now from this day forward, and adding it up *m'hijos,* you're my family, if you throw in Mariano and Rosalía, and Lupe, too, of course, Ignacio sitting straight in his armchair, holding his hardwood walking stick painted with a serpent and an eagle, the skin on his knuckles taut with the firm grip of a strong old man, Ernesto and Rubén Arenal sitting side by side on the sofa in the living room of Ignacio's house on Barrancas del Cobre, music coming from the radio in the kitchen, an instrumental, and Ignacio Pardiñas, "Rosita," a waltz by Beto Villa, saxophonist and father of the *orquesta tejana* style, born in Falfurrias, Texas in 1915, and as far as your Coyuco goes, our Coyuco, excuse my temporary lack of sophistication or good taste, it's anger and frustration speaking out, you can't replace a burst tire with a spare, there's no substituting him, and none of the others, not now not ever.

Ernesto and Rubén Arenal, sitting quietly, listening to him, the three of them waiting for Ignacio's friends, Mariano and his wife, Rosalía, who'd left their house and were heading on foot for Ignacio's place on Barrancas del Cobre, according to Ignacio, who'd made the call, speaking to them on the telephone, inviting them along with the others, Guadalupe and Irma and Luz Elena, with a couple of words of warning in advance on Ernesto's appearance, explaining that he's exhibiting a face that wasn't his own but a face they'd recognize right away, in one form or another, it was still his voice when you listened to him speaking, don't be afraid don't be afraid, we know him and we'll always love him, Ignacio spelling out just enough but not too much on the telephone, you never know who's listening and why give away the whole thing with a handful of words, you'll have to see it to believe it, a miracle to one's liking, that's what Ernesto and

Rubén Arenal heard him say, more or less, Rubén Arenal looking at his friend, a change taking place before his eyes, right now it was an Aztec-style mask, right side green, left side red, a jagged white *M* on the forehead, golden eagle applications, and gold Aztec-style *antifaz*, really a second, semitransparent skin with the power and skill of Mil Máscaras behind it, and Rocket, never underestimate the energy, strength and artistry of a face like that, but he was speaking to no one, speaking under his breath, while thinking how Ernesto had saved him from going over the edge of the roof, and Rocket, a little louder so they could hear him, think what you'll do for Centro Comunitario Vistas del Cerro Grande, and Ignacio Pardiñas, it'll be the right place for you, *m'hijo,* then tapped his walking stick on the floor three times, as if he were calling the court to attention, or a servant to his side, but nobody moved, Ernesto, motionless with his hands flat on his knees, eyes bright behind the mask, facing straight ahead, Ignacio and Rubén Arenal perspiring, no moisture showing on the Aztec mask, a water-resistant skin, Ignacio wiping his face with a handkerchief, looking at Ernesto, tapping three times on the floor with his wooden stick, and Ignacio Pardiñas, you're dry as sand, *m'hijo,* in the words of Charles Godfrey Leland, humorist, folklorist, and journalist, Ignacio turning to Rubén Arenal, what do you make of it, my son doesn't sweat, but we're soaking wet, turn on the fan, Segundo, before we lose consciousness while we're waiting, not enough oxygen to go around, Rubén Arenal crossing the room, switching on the fan standing on a small table with a single drawer, and Ignacio Pardiñas, open it, you'll find a nice Bible lying where it's supposed to be, Rubén Arenal opening the drawer, finding a clean copy of an old Bible looking up at him, and Ignacio Pardiñas, talking about breathing, *m'hijos,* there's *Génesis 2:7, Entonces Jehová Dios formó al hombre del polvo de la tierra, y sopló en su nariz aliento de vida, y fue el hombre un ser viviente,* "Then the Lord God formed the man of dust from the ground and breathed into his nostrils the breath of life, and the man became a living creature," you see it doesn't take long to find a reference in our Bible to anything that's on my mind, and Ernesto Cisneros, speaking at last, *Salmo 104:29-30, Escondes tu rostro, se turban; / Les quitas el hálito, dejan de ser, / Y vuelven al polvo. / Envías tu Espíritu, son creados, / Y renuevas la faz de la tierra,* "When you hide your face, they are dismayed; when you take away their breath, they die and return to their dust. When you send forth your Spirit, they are created, and you renew the face of the ground," Ignacio tapping loudly three times on the floor with his cane, and Ignacio Pardiñas, just like my exchanges with Mariano and Rosalía, and there was a knock at the door, Rubén Arenal, standing up, volunteering to answer it, Ignacio nodding his head, and Ignacio Pardiñas, thank you thank you, Rubén Arenal opening the front door, Mariano and Rosalía standing in front of Rubén Arenal, standing so close to each other that it looked like one person sharing legs, arms, and hands, with two heads, Rubén Arenal rubbing his eyes, ignoring the desire to go for the calluses on the palm of his right hand, Rubén Arenal waving them in, kissing Rosalía on the cheek, shaking hands with Mariano, and the three of them headed for the living room.

And Mariano Alcalá, don't get up, señor Pardiñas, El Fuerte, *mi Fuerte, nuestro* Pardiñas, *el fuerte viento,* Ignacio standing anyway, leaning on his stick, giving Mariano a hug, resting against him for a second, then kissing Rosalía, a single kiss, and settling back in his armchair, Rosalía heading straight for the kitchen with a large plastic bag in her hand, and Mariano Alcalá, something cool to drink, she'll whip it up in a couple of minutes, brought the ingredients herself, Mariano getting comfortable in an armchair facing Ignacio, Rosalía already in the kitchen with what it took to make fresh *agua de guayaba,* including a couple of limes, altogether plenty of vitamin C, high in fiber, searching Ignacio's cabinets for sugar, a half-gallon pitcher, checking for ice in the freezer, getting down to slicing the guavas in half to blend, seven of them, putting them in the blender jar, adding sugar, not a lot, less than half a cup, squeezing in the juice from one lime, filling the blender jar with

water, switching the machine on for a minute, pouring the contents
into the pitcher, adding a couple of cups of water, stirring it with a
wooden spoon, Rosalía tasting a drop from the spoon, not adding
any more sugar, and Rosalía Calderón, Mariano! *mi Jícama Gigante*,
my large but tender turnip, I need your help in the kitchen, a window of opportunity for a refreshing drink, and Mariano Alcalá,
excuse me, getting up from the armchair facing Ignacio, heading for
the kitchen, once there, standing beside his wife, Rosalía pointing to
the cabinet with the drinking glasses, Mariano taking them down,
and Mariano Alcalá, how many? and Rosalía Calderón, there're five
now, and we're expecting three more, and then there's one for the
ghost of Coyuco, if he shows up, Mariano bowing his head, wiping
a tear from the corner of his eye, Rosalía turning to face him, taking
him by his shoulders, and Rosalía Calderón, be strong, we've got to
be strong, and Mariano Alcalá, and if all forty-three of them come
to visit? plus Coyuco's ghost? and Rosalía Calderón, we don't have
enough glasses, Ignacio doesn't, I'd have to go home and get all the
glasses we've got and still there won't be enough.

Another knock at the door, Rubén Arenal didn't hesitate to get up
from the sofa to open Ignacio's door to whoever he'd invited, knowing it was Guadalupe, Irma, and his sister, Luz Elena, and Ignacio
Pardiñas, in a calm and respectful way, thank you, Segundo, gripping his wooden stick to help himself get out of the chair, the serpent
and eagle giving him a lift, encouraging him, Rubén Arenal opening
Ignacio's door, and Rocket, welcome welcome, a kiss is in order for
each of you, and more, Rubén Arenal embracing Guadalupe, Irma,
and an extra squeeze for Luz Elena, folded against him, and Luz
Elena, with respect to your grip in this world, *Xihuitl*, my comet, it's
tighter than ever, Luz Elena walking alongside her brother, following Guadalupe and Irma into the living room, Ignacio standing in
front of his chair, arms sticking out at his sides, the cane hanging
straight down from a closed fist, Ernesto walking hesitantly toward
Guadalupe, a look of surprise on her face that vanished in a second,

a whistle like a sigh from Irma's lips, Luz Elena moving ahead of her brother, coming up behind Guadalupe, who was kissing and caressing Ernesto's face with her hands, Luz Elena waiting her turn to give Ernesto a hug, Ernesto with the face of another, and it was in this atmosphere that his transformation was greeted by those who knew him well, welcoming it at once, each in turn taking a moment to hold him close to their breast and biologically warm heart, not a single what-the-fuck! no what-happened-to-you-my-God-what-a-shock, and then turning to Ignacio, still standing with outspread arms, Guadalupe, Luz Elena, Irma taking turns kissing him on the cheek, then helping him back into the comfort of worn cushions in the armchair, Rosalía and Mariano coming out of the kitchen with a tray of glasses and a pitcher of ice-cold *agua de guayaba,* and the greetings and embraces extended from the lips and arms of Guadalupe, Luz Elena, Irma to Rosalía and Mariano.

Eight glasses of *agua de guayaba,* guayaba juice and water, some full, some half empty, standing on the low table in front of the sofa, one untouched glass alone in the center, Rubén Arenal sitting cross-legged on the floor, the others sitting in chairs, including four from the kitchen, with one chair unoccupied, Guadalupe and Ernesto on the sofa, and Ernesto Cisneros, here, take my place, brother, please, waving his hand at Rubén Arenal, indicating the spot on the sofa next to his wife, and Ignacio Pardiñas, it isn't the time to be polite, *m'hijo,* we've all got birds inside our heads, *tener pájaros en la cabeza,* we've been thrown off course, to one degree or another, and the time will come when we'll find our way again, it looks like sooner than later, what do you say, Segundo? and Rocket, I could've been sitting in that chair, but let's leave it for a guest, I'd rather stay where I am, as close to the earth as possible under the circumstances, grounded, and Luz Elena, with respect to where we belong, our location, my brother's right, we ought to be sitting naked on the bare earth just to get a little closer to the source, our skin a kind of connector, keeping two parts of an electric circuit in contact and our lives going strong, but we're here in your living room, Ignacio, and it's here we'll stay, Guadalupe taking Ernesto's hand in hers, and Guadalupe Muñoz, absence of our loved ones is enough, with its anxiety of doubt that leads to anger, because anger's our vital engine, a driving force, our greater-than-ever electricity, look what magic it's performed, my Ernesto's a version of Mil Máscaras, angry but ready to work for justice, no matter how much levity we've tossed around in our story—that's the treatment of a serious matter with humor or in a manner lacking due respect—how fond we are of humor and foolishness, whoever's listening, whether in this world or the next, don't be fooled, things aren't always how they appear, our hearts are broken and we're going to do something about it, we're ready to fight, and the fighting's begun, Irma and Luz Elena nodding their heads, and Irma Payno, hold on hold on! who're you speaking to 'mana? we're all here and we know what's happened, and Guadalupe Muñoz, the occupants of the world outside, that's who, the listeners, m'hija, because almost everybody's got eyes and ears and some of them are going to watch and listen in an attentive manner, they aren't all ignorant scaredy-cats trembling with their eyes shut locked up in their houses easily frightened by authority, sirens, and gunfire, not willing to risk their lives, and Ignacio Pardiñas, Lupe's got it right, you might think it isn't fair, the way we've told our story, you might even think it's vulgar, and not too serious, but there's magic where there's death, especially the unexplained, things guiding us that we don't know and won't ever figure out, you might call it supernatural, but it's as real as the glasses of *agua de guayaba* on the table in front of us, where are we in our lives when those who ought to be living here with us aren't living here anymore and are nowhere to be found? the skewed vision you've encountered is out of respect for the missing and the dead, whose voices, like our own, are full of fury and confusion, two mirrors facing each other, and Irma Payno, we've organized our first protest march, a small demonstration, and it's the start, and Rosalía Calderón, of course you have, it's what we expected, and we'll be there, all of us, the next time you're on the streets, which better be tomorrow and every day after that until we get some answers, and Mariano Alcalá, a few words from Eduardo Ruíz Sosa, born in 1983 in Culiacán, Sinaloa, "the chief weapon of all regimes (both political and criminal) is that eternal combination of absence and ignorance: not knowing where the disappeared have gone is both weapon and wound; there can be no shrine to their memory until their bodies turn up (perhaps because we deny that they really are dead and grant them a kind of suspended life that would cease were we to erect a monument to them), and then the very thing that drives us on to look for them instills in us a terrible anxiety that leads us to believe they will come back of their own accord, that we must wait for them, that we cannot leave the house because they forgot to take their keys when they left," and Irma Payno, I think I'm going to be sick, Luz Elena reaching for Irma's nearly full glass of guayaba juice and water, and Luz Elena, here, 'mana, take a drink, Irma taking a few gulps, catching her breath, and Irma Payno, I've got to have a smoke, Guadalupe and Luz Elena turning their heads, nodding to each other, and Ignacio Pardiñas, you're welcome, go right ahead, m'hija, a smoke'll be good for most of us, Irma ran her hands through her hair, reached for her bag, opened it, and removed an Aromas de San Andrés Robusto by Puros Santa Clara from a turquoise leather holder.

Rubén Arenal offering Ernesto a cigarette, not out of a white and green and black pack of Aros, but a crumpled pack of Faros, tobacco rolled in rice paper, a reddish man at sunset on the pack pinching the brim or tipping his hat, looking out at a lighthouse, Rubén Arenal lighting it for him, then his own, then sitting back down on the floor, Irma taking a draw on the cigar but not swallowing smoke, blowing a cloud into the air, Rosalía turning toward Luz Elena, and Rosalía Calderón, who's looking after the kids, and Luz Elena, they're at the neighbor's, and Guadalupe Muñoz, can I try one of your cigars, niña mía? Irma setting her cigar in an ashtray, opening her leather case and taking out another cigar, clipping it, handing the Aromas de San Andrés Robusto to Guadalupe, and Irma Payno, go slow, Lupe, or you'll knock yourself out, behind the *antifaz* Ernesto was smiling, and Ernesto Cisneros, it's what we all need, Lupita, taking a long pull on the Faros, his mask changing before their eyes, left side gold, right side red, red feathery applications on the gold, gold on the red, and a lime-green *M* on his forehead, the mask worn by Mil Máscaras in *Mil Máscaras vs. the Aztec Mummy*, Luz Elena leaning toward Rosalía, and Rosalía Calderón, almost a whisper, we saw everything in a vision, the voice of *pipiltzintzintli* spoke to us through our señor Pardiñas, *nuestro Fuerte,* and we understood everything, the voice put us in the picture, Ignacio smiling, tapping three times on the floor with his cane, and Ignacio Pardiñas, we heard it, didn't we, Mari? and Mariano Alcalá, that's for sure, El Fuerte, *mi Fuerte,* we were there, and *el pipiltzintzintli* spoke to us, and Ignacio Pardiñas, and there was a poem by Octavio Paz, and Rosalía Calderón, a little something from *Cantares Mexicanos, mi Jícama Gigante,* my giant but tender turnip, large as you are, and Mariano Alcalá, don't forget the words of Nezahualcoyotl, *jazmín mío,* my flower, we were all there, the three of us, you, me and our señor Pardiñas, and Irma Payno, just listening to you, hearing the names you've given each other, El Fuerte, Mari, *Jícama Gigante,* and *jazmín mío,* an expression of affection, makes me want to cry for Coyuco, my hands are empty and my heart is cold, and if there was a deep well nearby, I think I'd throw myself into it and look for Coyuco on the other side of this life, Irma set her cigar down in the ashtray, Ernesto, leaving his Faros behind, stood up from the sofa, affected by her sadness and desperation, wringing his hands, taking deep breaths through the opening in the mask that was his mouth, lips like Lycra, approaching Irma with confident strides, not a long journey, but an important one, Guadalupe taking the San Andrés Robusto from between her lips, a look of pride on her face, Ernesto lifting Irma straight out of the chair, holding her in his new-found wrestler's arms, all at once the room lost daylight but wasn't too dark, a spotlight shone down on Ernesto and Irma, separating them from the others, sketching a wrestling ring in the middle of Ignacio's living room, Rosalía looking up from where she was sitting, speaking to Irma, and Rosalía Calderón, according to Adela Fernández, Piltzintecuhtli, Señor Niño, *hijo de Oxomoco y de Cipactonal, identificado con el Sol Joven, protector de los niños,* "Child Lord," son of Oxomoco and Cipactonal, identified with the Young Sun, the protector of children, a god of the rising sun, a god of healing, *m'hija,* my child, so let him keep you in his arms, our Ernesto can help you, and Mariano Alcalá, that's right, my flower, you said it just before we went up to the roof, and Ignacio Pardiñas, up to the roof as usual in situations like this, Irma looking up at Ernesto's face, now a white Lycra mask with a cutaway mouth and chin, shiny black applications on the upper forehead, one under the nose, feathered applications around the eyes, including black heart-shaped pieces with three small holes for the ears, a red *M* in the middle of the forehead, a presentation mask, and Irma Payno, what I feel is your strength, and tears started running down her cheeks, and Ernesto Cisneros, from now on my role is action, not words, his arms were a hundred arms like branches reaching out to envelop Irma, and the intertwined fingers of his hands were a thousand fingers like long twigs spread out to form a net that supported her, keeping her from falling.

Ernesto raising her above his head, she weighed almost nothing, a feather in his hands lifted by wrestler's arms, Irma held so safe so tight she couldn't even run her hands through her hair, Ignacio tapping his cane three times on the floor in approval, the spotlight following Ernesto as he walked in a circle carrying Irma clasped by a thousand fingers, a murmuring from the onlookers, and Irma Payno, who're Oxomoco and Cipactonal? and Rosalía Calderón, the first man and woman that were created, and Mariano Alcalá, once, long long ago, they were high gods, no different from the Lord and Lady of Sustenance, rightfully belonging in paradise, residents of the uppermost heaven, and Rosalía Calderón, but they were so antiquated by the time of the Aztecs and so overlaid by later levels of myth, they were brought down to earth to almost human height, and Mariano Alcalá, as first forebears, our ancestors, they took on the role of culture innovators, creating the world of civilized man, giving him knowledge of many things, but they were celebrated as lords of the *tonalpohualli*, the count of the days was their great work, in the words of Burr Brundage, and *Anales de Cuauhtitlán*, and Rosalía Calderón, according to John Bierhorst's free translation of the *Annals of Cuauhtitlán*, or Year Count, which in Nahuatl is *xiuh-pohualli*, "The year count, the day sign count, and the count of each twenty-day period were made the responsibility of those known as Oxomoco and Cipactonal. Oxomoco means the man, Cipactonal means the woman. Both were very old. And from then on, old men and old women were called by those names," and Ignacio Pardiñas, what they're telling you, *hija*, is that time can heal the pain of our grief, our suffering won't last forever, the first man and woman that were created, created our days, months, years, and Rocket, maybe the words betray a lack of original thought, maybe not, but we can get hold of a cliché by its handles, let's all look at our fingers, it's no joke, Ignacio tapping three times with his cane, admitting his use of a platitude, and Rocket, "Time Is On My Side," yes, it is, by Jerry Ragovoy—Kai Winding did it first, then Irma Thomas recorded it with additional lyrics by Jimmy Norman, and you know the rest, Guadalupe hauling in smoke from her cigar, blowing a cloud of smoke above her head, Mariano pouring himself another glass of *agua de guayaba*, Rosalía smoothing her dress with the palm of her hand, tugging gently at the hem, and Rocket, continuing, as for the ancient progenitors and first cultivators of maize, Oxomoco and Cipactonal, they "invented the count of the destinies, / the annals and the count of years, / the book of dreams, / they set it in order as it has been kept, / and as it has been followed," an example for us to follow of the determination of a people not to lose the memory of their past, and Ignacio Pardiñas, *El tiempo está de mi lado, sí así es*, and Guadalupe Muñoz, like I said, we've tossed around plenty of levity in our story, you might call us empty-headed, but we aren't, we've got to breathe, stay full of life, because if we don't breathe and aren't full of life we'll never find a way to soften the sharp edges of pain or know how to live with what's happened to those kids, our children, and God doesn't want us to shrivel up from weeping tears until we haven't got any, not a drop of salty water in our bodies, not our God, and not the ancient Gods either, if they created the days, months, years, we're supposed to live them, sorrow or no sorrow, and Ignacio Pardiñas, cry until we've cried enough, that's what I say, but not until there's nothing left of us, Ignacio tapped three times on the floor with his stick, the hand-painted eagle and snake moved swiftly down the length of it and back again.

Ernesto circling the circle sent down to earth as a spotlight, carrying Irma in his arms, the others watching them, the sudden denseness of the air leaving them dizzy, and through their eyes, as Ernesto walked in circles with Irma, raised up as an offering to something that wasn't there, the life and movement in the circle took on the bright, luminous, grotesque colors of the circus, a whirling lively gathering of hues striking the pinpoint precise pupils of Mariano, Rosalía, Ignacio, Guadalupe, Rubén Arenal, Luz Elena, who hadn't said a word for several minutes, Luz Elena sitting up straight, and Luz Elena, with respect to traveling companies of acrobats, trained animals, clowns, this is something special, it's our own Ernesto's big top under your roof, señor Pardiñas, our Pardiñas, leaving all of us wondering what'll be next, and Mariano Alcalá, such magic! but it isn't the third hour of the night, and Guadalupe Muñoz, no, it isn't Piltzintecuhtli, Señor Niño, it's too early, and Rosalía Calderón, shh! don't break the spell, let's wait and see, but there was no spell, no state of enchantment by words or motion on Ernesto's part, he was a hard-working workhorse, a rookie wrestler without controlling or influencing Mariano, Rosalía, Ignacio, Guadalupe, Rubén Arenal, Luz Elena, his friends, by availing himself of maneuvering magical powers, and the climax was almost anti-climactic, a sawed-off pinnacle for the performance, it wasn't a wrestling match, the spotlight went out, the daylight came in, Ernesto setting Irma back on her chair, a beatific smile on her face, no tears no trembling, and Irma Payno, earth is a great thing to help you see, but it's even better when you're just above it, thank you Ernesto, I'm calm now, not withered and dying, and Luz Elena, with respect for a true understanding of the relative importance of things, or a particular attitude toward something, a bird's-eye view gives us a picture we can't have sitting in a chair, a wrestler's arms are good for more than a submission hold, like Gory Guerrero's Special, a hanging, back-to-back backbreaker, or *La Mecedora,* The Rocking Chair, or *La Campana,* The Bell, or *La Torre,* The Tower, a transitional hold, and Guadalupe Muñoz, taking a pull on her cigar, my Ernesto's an instrument for things not in this world, no words but acts, and a man of courage, and Luz Elena, with respect for that which is true or in accordance with fact or reality, "Tell me and I'll tell you. Hear me and I hear you," and Rosalía Calderón, "If you even think, I'll hear you. Or if I think, you'll know what I'm thinking," Ignacio tapping loudly three times with his cane, and Ignacio Pardiñas, in the words of the English poet and politician Edmund Waller, from *Divine Poems,* "Could we forebear dispute, and practice love, / We should agree as angels do above," and we do! then a voice coming out of nowhere, it was Coyuco, and Coyuco Cisneros, summoned! Ignacio's walking stick called me, I'm not an echo of your past, but a precise presence of the here and now, Ernesto staggering, Guadalupe getting up to help him sit down, everyone blinking their eyes, fingers wiggling and pressing against the small pointed projection of their ears trying to clear the tube leading to the eardrum, jaws opening and closing, a voice in each of their heads saying, what we're hearing we can't be hearing, Coyuco standing at the entrance to the kitchen, not entirely there, but more than an unfilled-in outline, what looked to each of them like Coyuco taking on color and shade in the space within the outline, and Ignacio Pardiñas, ah, what a marvel! this presence is presence itself, and it gives a true pleasure, Coyuco's completely there, shimmering like silver, studded with all manner of gems like the golden throne "hard by a hillock of green jasper and on the hill top"—that's *One Thousand and One Nights*— take him in from head to toe, Coyuco's shape was adorned with a purple variety of quartz, blue beryls, rubies, emeralds, and a few rare gems: Alexandrites, with their effects, depending on the nature of ambient lighting, Musgravites, red beryls, and his black eyes were Serendibite, an extremely rare gemstone and mineral from Sri Lanka, Mariano, Rosalía, Ignacio, Guadalupe, Ernesto, Rubén Arenal, Luz Elena, their own eyes blazing like live coals, a voice in each of their heads saying, what we're seeing we can't be seeing, but it's him, no real arms and legs but the semblance of them, no face but it's his face, and nothing like skin, a bejeweled body from head to toe, and Coyuco Cisneros, I'm far away, alone, and a stranger, I go and come back, and I've forgotten, and Guadalupe Muñoz, you're still my son, no matter what form you take, and Coyuco Cisneros, there are things in the sky, men, women and children, everything is white, and their happiness is in the middle of whiteness, and at night, there are stars and a moon to light our way, nothing evil can happen to us there, and Rocket, many went upward and got to the sky, and the city is great and full of strange things, our Chihuahua, Courage, Loyalty, Hospitality, *en nuestro México,* country of ghosts, I've said it before, I might say it again, and Mariano Alcalá, yes, this is the world and this is life, it's not good, I know, but it sharpens our minds and fills them with thoughts, and Luz Elena, with respect to visions and sounds, what I see and what I hear, *queridos amigos,* "If you say it, I must believe it. If I see it, I'll say: Yes, I have seen it. If I hear it, I'll say: Yes, I've heard it. All you need do is speak," and Rosalía Calderón, "In the end whatever is going to happen will happen, because it must," Irma running her hands through her hair, in no doubt, self-possessed, and Irma Payno, *Salmo 73:23-24, Con todo, yo siempre estuve contigo; / Me tomaste de la mano derecha. / Me has guiado según tu consejo, / Y después me recibirás en gloria,* "Nevertheless, I am continually with you; / you hold my right hand. / You guide me with your counsel, and afterward you will receive me to glory," Ignacio tapping three times with his walking stick, and Ignacio Pardiñas, with those words, Irma, you're my daughter, too, along with my son Ernesto, and Segundo, my second son, then everyone turning to look at Coyuco, or what appeared to be him, it was his body, skin covered with gems, his face, precious stones, and a chorus of their voices, Mariano, Rosalía, Ignacio, Guadalupe, Rubén Arenal, Luz Elena, everyone's voice except Ernesto's, even the light and air in the room joined them, and the wind outside, they could see it and feel it, and Mariano Alcalá, Rosalía Calderón, Ignacio Pardiñas, Guadalupe Muñoz, Rocket, Luz Elena, all together, saying, we can't live without you, and you can't live without us, we're together, our eyes weep, our hearts ache, our eyes empty themselves, the deepest cut is the one that doesn't break the skin, and then silence, until Ignacio used his cane to tap three times on the floor, looking down at where he'd struck it, then up at Coyuco, and Ignacio Pardiñas, do you have something to say? and Coyuco Cisneros, not much because I'm not here, and Mariano Alcalá, you're here as far as we can tell, and Ignacio Pardiñas, *Mas vosotros no vivís según la carne, sino según el Espíritu, si es que el Espíritu de Dios mora en vosotros. Y si alguno no tiene el Espíritu de Cristo, no es de Él,* "You, however, are not in the flesh but in the Spirit, if in fact the Spirit of God dwells in you. Anyone who does not have the Spirit of Christ does not belong to him," Romans 8:9, and Irma Payno, I know what's next, *Pero si Cristo está en vosotros, el cuerpo en verdad está muerto a causa del pecado, mas el espíritu vive a causa de la justicia,* "But if Christ is in you, although the body is dead because of sin, the Spirit is life because of righteousness," Romans 8:10, and it wasn't your sin but another's, you're a virtuous man, killed by criminals, destroyed by transgressors, and you'll forever be my saintly spirit, an upright ghost living in my heart, Irma began to cry, wiping her tears with a handkerchief Guadalupe handed her, and Coyuco Cisneros, my eyes are in the heavens and my ears are in the air, following the words of the one who is dear to me, and Irma Payno, yes, listen, and believe, and Coyuco Cisneros, I was born, I lived, I died, those are three things, Ignacio tapping three times on the floor with his walking stick, Irma releasing a muffled sob through the handkerchief, and Ignacio Pardiñas, someone's calling, and he's called out three things, I recognize your voice, Coyuco, and I know those words are true, and Coyuco Cisneros, I'm tired of going without having anywhere to go, and I'm tired of coming back and bringing nothing with me, my hands are empty because they can't hold anything, my head isn't really my head and it isn't part of my body, my legs and arms aren't attached to me, they're here and somewhere else, what you're looking at is what I'm letting you see so that the state of things as they actually exist doesn't cause you more harm than has already been done, Mariano, Rosalía, Ignacio, Guadalupe, Rubén Arenal, Luz Elena offering a chorus of sighs, a simultaneous utterance, Ernesto wringing his wrestler's hands, and Coyuco Cisneros, I know what your heart's telling you, I hear it when it speaks, and your tears and anguish are my own, and Guadalupe Muñoz, you're free to go, and we thank you for coming, we weren't expecting you or any gifts, what could you possibly carry, my son, our Coyuco, your father's and mine, and Coyuco Cisneros, there or not there, but there nevertheless, and Guadalupe Muñoz, when we raise our eyes to the sky, we'll look for you, thinking of you sitting on the clouds, or when we lower them, looking at the earth beneath our feet, we'll think of you, for all one knows you'll be residing for eternity in Mictlan Opochcalocan, and Coyuco Cisneros, I can't tell you where I'll be, but I'll call to you, shouting, "Look at me, I'm here!" you might feel the wild wind, *Mictlanpaehecatl*, the wind which comes from Mictlan, and Mariano Alcalá, Rosalía Calderón, Ignacio Pardiñas, Guadalupe Muñoz, Rocket, Luz Elena, together, another chorus, *¡qué así sea!* so be it!

There wasn't a shadow, shape or glow that resembled Coyuco in Ignacio's living room, not a body covered with gems, or a face with precious stones, but Coyuco had been there, Ignacio's living room was bathed in calm, Mariano, Rosalía, Ignacio, Guadalupe, Ernesto, Rubén Arenal, Luz Elena were deep in thought, then suddenly Rubén Arenal jumped up from where he was sitting, his bottom sore from the floor, and Rocket, my hands, look at them! Rubén Arenal pushing up his sleeves, and Rocket, what do you see? do you see what I see, or am I under a spell? no dried clay under my nails, nothing in the creases of my palms, but take a look, the return of the "first foundation of the world," clay-drawn lines and figures on my hands, clay you can't rub off, making their way north, look out elbows here they come! Mariano, Rosalía, Guadalupe, Irma, Luz Elena getting up to look at him, Ignacio didn't move, not a single tap on the floor with his cane, but he leaned forward, perilously close to falling out of his armchair, Guadalupe and Irma keeping their cigars behind their backs, no smoke in the eyes, a clear view of Rubén Arenal's hands and forearms, Ernesto quiet as a statue without birds, and Rocket, a translation from Bierhorst worked the last time, wisdom tales made long ago, but I can't find anything in my memory to help me out, Ernesto thinking of his hands marked with figures and lines symbols and signs written in charcoal while driving the F-150 Lobo, his arms covered with charcoal drawings, including ordinal and cardinal numbers—two friends, how close could they get!—and remembering with pleasure the presence of the fount of wisdom, handsome and sleek, the Tamaulipas crow, out of nowhere, silent as snow falling on the earth, but with the vision of a bird, the *cuervo tamaulipeco,* and Rosalía Calderón, I'll get a little water from the kitchen, Rosalía hurrying from the room, returning with a wet kitchen towel, Ernesto not forgetting the charcoal drawings and the Tamaulipas crow, Rosalía using all her strength trying to remove the markings on Rubén Arenal's hands and arms, Rubén Arenal hoping the tigers were nearby to devour them, or the wind to blow them away, if only he could invoke the tigers, the wind, Rosalía busy with the towel, Ernesto keeping his eyes on Rubén Arenal, the wet towel did nothing but make his skin red from rubbing, the drawings were all still there on his hands and arms, and Ernesto Cisneros to himself, what's happened to him is what happened to me, but for me it was charcoal, his lines and figures are drawn in clay, they're back as a sign or warning that something momentous or calamitous is going to happen, there's something he's left undone, only God knows what it is, and only God can take him through it, good or bad, Ernesto, a man of action and no words, not now anyway, saving them all for the community center near Parque Revolución between Calle Tercera and Calle Séptima, Ernesto didn't say anything but searched his mind for something Rubén Arenal might've said in the bar that was a clue to how he could help him, and Ernesto Cisneros, God never said no to a helping hand.

And Ignacio Pardiñas, that's no spell, it's a message, Ignacio looked at Ernesto, and Ignacio Pardiñas, I can read your mind, my son, take another look, they're forming into letters, Ignacio turning to Rubén Arenal, and Ignacio Pardiñas, I'd bet the money in my pocket, not a lot, eight hundred pesos, that you're hearing from *La Pascualita*, and Rosalía Calderón, from La Popular, Calle Victoria and Avenida Ocampo? Mariano nodding his head, and Mariano Alcalá, there's only one, my flower, and Irma Payno, bursting with curiosity, what what what? and Luz Elena, fixing her eyes on her brother, *Xihuitl*, my comet, my brother, with respect to what we know and what we don't have to know, maybe you don't want to talk about it now and with everyone here, maybe you do, so with respect to freedom, and more precisely with respect to liberty, it's up to you, and Ignacio Pardiñas, let's leave it to Rocket to decide if he wants to tell you what I already know, it's Segundo's secret, Ignacio settling back into the cushions of his armchair, Mariano and Ernesto putting Rubén Arenal in a chair with a lamp beside it so he could keep watch on the writing on his skin, Guadalupe went on smoking the cigar Irma'd given her, Irma smoked, now and then running her hands through her hair, Rosalía pacing back and forth behind Rubén Arenal, who sat with a worried expression on his face as the signs and figures and symbols continued changing into letters spelling words everyone was afraid to look at closely for fear of what they'd find written there, but it wasn't long before Rosalía stopped pacing, her hands behind her back looking intently over Rubén Arenal's shoulder at his arms covered in writing, and Rosalía Calderón, come here, everyone, look at what's written on Rocket, his neck, shoulders—she pulled back the collar of his shirt—and you, Luz Elena, you're his sister, unbutton his shirt to see what's on his chest, he can't do it, he's too busy trembling, and besides, his eyes are shut, Guadalupe stroking the hair on Rubén Arenal's head while Luz Elena checked on the state of his chest, finding writing there, too, all the way to his waist, including the tattoo of a maguey on his stomach, Luz Elena asking permission to go further, Rubén Arenal nodding yes, Luz Elena unbuckling his belt, peeking past the elastic waistband of his boxer shorts, Mariano, Rosalía, Guadalupe, Irma, Ignacio, Ernesto, in deference to privacy, turning away with a sense of embarrassment at the thought of seeing something that was none of their business, Luz Elena inspecting her brother's skin, confirm-ing that the writing ended below his navel as if an invisible hand had neatly trimmed the bottom of the page that was his upper torso, then making him stand up, tugging gently at his trousers, Mariano, Rosalía, Guadalupe, Irma, Ignacio, Ernesto, each with their back turned toward Rubén Arenal while his sister found the southern half of his body unblemished, blank except for the pubic hair and hairs on his thighs, and Luz Elena, with respect for what my eyes have seen, and it isn't the first time and won't be the last, I'll leave my inspection at that, you're free and clear where it counts, you can open your eyes, my comet, my brother, and don't forget to zip your zipper and buckle your belt, the others turning around, Luz Elena standing up, Rubén Arenal surrounded by family and friends, and Guadalupe Muñoz, don't be shy, take off your shirt, *m'hijo*, let's read what your skin has to say, Ignacio, sitting in his chair, tapped three times on the floor with the tip of his walking stick.

*W*hat was written

A woman with too much beauty could either keep a man
alive or kill him, and these words will either keep you
alive or kill you, what I mean is they'll be your guide, it'll
be your choice, once and for all, and the beauty I speak
of is my daughter's, you've witnessed that beauty, tasted
it, her migrant flesh has rubbed right against your own,
I've said it before and I'll say it again: how beautiful is
beauty, but you were saved from joining us once before,
your masked friend, a brother to you, wearing all the
faces of Mil Máscaras, kept you from entering our circle
by invitation, from our welcoming arms outstretched,
La Pascualita's and mine, and thousands of others, the
numbers are many and can't be counted, each traveling
in a world beyond reach of life, a world populated by
what all of you would call ghosts, the unsettled spirits of
the dead, what we're offering is a state of intense excitement and happiness, eternal delight in mint condition,
and the achievement of something desired, promised,
or predicted—just look it up, that's what it says—and
we aren't expecting a centavo of compensation, no re-
payment's necessary, your presence is all that matters,
for my daughter's sake, but we make no emotional ap-
peal, no entreaty, it sounds like an offer right out of a
comic book like your cherished Fantômas, La Amenaza
Elegante, or more on the order of Kryptonite rocks, X-ray
Specs, a miniature monkey, or Charles Atlas' Dynamic-
Tension, "*Just fifteen minutes each day* in the privacy of
your room is all it takes to make your chest and shoulder
muscles swell so big they almost split your coat seams …
turn your fists into sledge-hammers … build mighty legs
that never tire!"—leave it to *el Norte*, crazy as loons, but

nobody's perfect—once you're dead you've read it all and remember it, but it isn't Kryptonite or Charles Atlas, what we've got is nothing you'll ever find at the back of a comic book—yours not mine, I wouldn't buy one—it's the genuine article, what I mean is you'll enjoy being in Heaven, where you can do as you like as long as you're side by side close together in solidarity and in love with *La Pascualita*, a wrong move and it's over, not a threat, what I mean is it's just a fact, indisputably the case, now you've all had a chance to read these words, some out loud, some to themselves, and señor Arenal, Rocket to your friends, you've heard what's written on your skin, so what do you say, and at the risk of repeating myself, remember, you're our maestro, expert, genius, wizard and pro.

They were all sitting around Ignacio, waiting for his first words after they'd read the writing on Rubén Arenal's skin, early afternoon light spreading itself out at their feet, and Ignacio Pardiñas, a last ditch effort, that's what I'd call it, reminding me of a paragraph in *El pueblo del Sol, The Aztecs, People of the Sun,* by Alfonso Caso, the Mexican archaeologist who, like his older brother, Antonio, was a rector of the National Autonomous University, and a founding member of the Mexican Academy of History, "The people of the sun, led by the priests of the god, settled in the middle of the Lake of the Moon. Then they began to fulfill their mission by collaborating in the cosmic function through human sacrifice, a symbolic representation of the assistance that man must give to the sun so that the latter can continue his struggle against the moon and the stars and vanquish them every day," but let's get one thing straight, we're far from our past and our present is strewn with different kinds of obstacles, so here and now, in our circumstances, we can't let ourselves be sacrificed, whether it's to corrupt violence or to a false form of love, the disappearance of forty-three student teachers and Coyuco, or to misleadingly attractive ghost-love, too many of us die, and there's work to do where we live and breathe, Ignacio tapping the floor with his hardwood walking stick, hand painted with the design of an eagle and snake, and Ignacio Pardiñas, that's right, take a good close look at it, an eagle represents the sun, and the sun's a symbol of Huitzilopochtli, Blue Hummingbird of the Left, or of the South, it was Huitzilopochtli who, in the year One Flint, encouraged the leaders of the Aztec tribe to migrate, leaving their mythical homeland, Aztlan—it was in the middle of a lake—and beginning their long wanderings, hundreds of years roaming through the north and central parts of Mexico, and during those years, Huitzilopochtli, guiding the priests, his spokesmen, carrying his statue—that's why their name was *teomama*—the priests giving the people instructions on their journey, centuries centuries, and at last the priests saw the eagle land on a spiny cactus whose red tunas were like human hearts—you can see them if you close your eyes, just concentrate—the eagle poised on the cactus was the omen Huitzilopochtli had given them, a cactus in the middle of the island in the Lake of the Moon, Lake Texcoco, the trees turning white, the waters becoming white, a sign that there, in the land of the sun, the Aztecs were to stay and found a city, to build a life in Tenochtitlan, Ignacio tapped the tip of his cane three times on the floor, and Ignacio Pardiñas, the chosen people of Huitzilopochtli arrived at last at the place where they were to grow great and become the masters of the world, instruments through which the god would accomplish great deeds, an eagle just like the one on my walking stick revealed their home to them, Guadalupe putting her face in her hands, releasing a sob, then looking up at Mariano, Rosalía, Irma, Luz Elena, Rubén Arenal, Ernesto, Ignacio, and Guadalupe Muñoz, well, things change and time passes, whatever's conceived is born, and whatever's born dies, nothing stays behind, Ernesto reaching for her hand, caressing it, and Mariano Alcalá, what our El Fuerte, *mi Fuerte*, is saying is that here's where we'll stay because this Mexico is our home, and it's from our home that we'll

fight, for better or for worse, and Ignacio Pardiñas, we aren't relying on chance, not a game of *Siete y Medio,* getting seven and a half
points, the cards worth as many points as their face value, except
the figures, which we all know are worth half a point, and we aren't
playing a sure thing either, we'll do what we've got to do, that's that
that's all, Rubén Arenal, not saying a word, concentrating on the
marks on his skin, Luz Elena raising her head to look at Ignacio,
and Luz Elena, with respect to respect itself, or simple courtesy,
my brother's silent as the growth of flowers, in the words of Aphra
Behn, seventeenth-century dramatist, poet, novelist, translator,
woman and short-lived spy—you couldn't ask for more accom-
plishments, and Ignacio Pardiñas, we haven't had far to travel, not
physically, with the exception of our Ernesto who, alone in the arms
of the night, went to Iguala and back, now a changed man, though
we've all gone a long way in a short time since Coyuco and the others disappeared, worn the treads off our souls, but consider well the
words of *Salmo 25:14,* Psalm 25:14, *La comunión íntima de Jehová
es con los que le temen, / Y a ellos hará conocer su pacto,* "The friendship of the Lord is for those who fear him, / and he makes known
to them his covenant," and we do fear him, or love him, it's about
the same, so this is where we stay, grow great like our ancestors
in Tenochtitlan, "dedicated to maintaining cosmic order and strug-
gling against the powers of darkness," no, you can't knock us for
trying, we're God's coworkers, it's our pride, that's why you can't let
La Pascualita take you away, Segundo, we'll need as many hands as
we can get, Mariano, Rosalía, Irma, Luz Elena, Ernesto, Guadalupe,
each with their eyes fixed on Ignacio, their ears tuned to his words,
no one paying attention to Rubén Arenal, until he jumped up from
his chair, knocking it over, and Rocket, they're gone, look look look!
nothing's written on me but the hairs and brown birthmark of my
skin, and the maguey tattoo, Rubén Arenal smiling from ear to ear,
his hands on his hips, Irma the first to look at his arms, hands, chest
and back, the others followed, then a common joyful murmuring, and Luz Elena, with respect to a signal that the danger's over

for now, he's all clear, Ernesto reaching out with his bare hands to lift Rubén Arenal off the floor, the strength of the muscles in his shoulders and arms holding him in the air before his masked face, the mask known as The Cyclops, handmade by maestro Ranulfo López, a red leather mask with silk threads, olive green leather applications around the eyes, nose, and mouth, and the center eye, red and black on white leather trimmed with green, and a plush black quarter moon above it, Ernesto's mask inches from Rubén Arenal's grin, only Ignacio remaining where he was sitting comfortably in his chair, knowing the words of the Bible had done the trick, and Rocket, I'm convinced, Esto, "good rewards for good deeds, evil returns for evil deeds," Ernesto lowering Rubén Arenal until his feet touched the ground, and Rocket, it's too bad criminal anthropology doesn't include police uniforms and politicians' neckties, look out Lombroso there's work to do if you weren't already dead and disapproved, not just sloping foreheads, really long arms, funny ears, a fucked-up mandible or maxilla, just take a gander at the uniforms of the municipal police, the ministerial police, federal police, or the soldiers of the 27th Battalion, it's the clothes that make the man, maybe I'm exaggerating, they can't all be bad, not like Alacrán and his reptile Queen, my brothers and sisters, there's a wide river between the few honest ones and out-and-out evil, let's pray it's a river whose waters we won't cross, not ever, not one of us.

Ignacio tapped his wooden walking stick three times on the floor, Mariano, Rosalía, Irma, Luz Elena, Ernesto, Guadalupe nodding their heads in accord with Ignacio's agreement with what Rubén Arenal had just said, and when the nodding stopped their clothes began to change, gradually and without lifting a finger, a fade-out of the old and a fade-in of the new, everyone's clothes but Ernesto's, and each face, bit by bit and inch by inch, altering according to some unknown formula, transforming itself from its original anatomical form, once familiar faces evolving in an unheard-of but outwardly natural process, changing completely in form, as far as each of them

could tell, except Ernesto's face, an overhaul he'd had in Iguala de
la Independencia, and Ernesto Cisneros, without moving his lips,
a little Alexandre Dumas right before my eyes, "All for one, and
one for all," or *One For All-All For One* by Galneryus, the Japanese
power metal band, and Rocket, you didn't speak out loud, 'mano,
but I heard you anyway, in order to stand up for our disappeared
brothers, sons, husbands, and to try to make a better here and now,
which makes me think of Blue Demon's movie, *Los campeones jus-
ticieros* by Federico Curiel, 1971, *The Champions of Justice* battling
the forces of evil with El Médico Asesino, Tinieblas, Black Shadow,
La Sombra Vengadora, we're becoming like you, man and woman
alike, all of us, on the face of it, no pun intended, Rubén Arenal
looked at each of the others in Ignacio's living room, Guadalupe
admiring the transparent black sleeves of her wrestler's costume, a
modern touch of Martha Villalobos, María del Ángel, La Diabólica,
or La Diabólica without the mask, and Guadalupe Muñoz, reaching
back to the last earthquake, in our time, we're beginning to look like
our own versions of Superbarrio Gómez—"We can see it! We can
feel it! Superbarrio is in the house!" "The people united will never be
defeated!"—wearing masks with the faces of animals, gods, and ancient heroes, or no masks at all, but wrestlers in our own right, look
at Luz Elena, no mask, but a black opaque bodysuit and calf-high
black-and-white lace-up boots, reminding us of Pantera Sureña,
the Orquídea Negra, and Luz Elena, you aren't wearing a mask either, Lupe, you're looking more on the order of Lola "Dinamita"
González, when she was young and on the cover of *Lucha Libre*
magazine, Guadalupe's true face blushing beneath the thin layer of
someone else's skin, and Mariano Alcalá, for my age, I'm feeling
fit as a falcon, his dark blue wrestler's tights molded to a pair of
muscular legs, a hint in his masklike face of Aníbal, Ignacio Carlos
Carillo, when he fought against El Solitario, Rosalía, in a rose-colored sleeveless bodysuit with a single strap around her neck going
from shoulder to shoulder, two gold flowers printed on the hips,
a bodysuit cut high on her thighs, Rosalía with a full head of hair

and resembling Zuleyma, Elvia Fragoso Alonso, a *luchadora* in the 1980s, Rosalía running to the bathroom for a bath towel to cover her embarrassment, returning to Ignacio's living room with a towel wrapped around her waist, and Rosalía Calderón, I've got the figure of La Princesa Hindu, and now God's given me a face with the mask of La Dama Enmascarada, Magdalena Caballero, may God rest her soul, a pioneer of women's wrestling and first national champion, first cousin of Irma González, I'm a younger but not better or worse self, proud but a little embarrassed, and now that my face's hidden, I can go outside wearing Elvia's revealing outfit without anyone knowing who I am, La Dama Enmascarada's face-covering mask with white *antifaz,* not made of pig skin but comfortable fabric—my skin's got to breathe, after all—they won't know me unless they've seen a picture of her, now let's inspect Irma, the youngest of us all, already transformed, looking lovely and powerful, it's her turn, Mariano, Rosalía, Luz Elena, Rubén Arenal, Ernesto, Guadalupe gathering around her, everyone except for Ignacio, completely re-conditioned but still sitting in his chair, gripping his hand-painted wooden walking stick, everyone admiring Irma's shapely figure in a two-piece costume, and Luz Elena, with respect to what's sexy and what's not, you've got us all beat, you really are La Tigresa, and a sort of Irma Serrano, but you look an awful lot like Sexi Star, Dulce María García Rivas, trained by Humberto Garza Jr., Mr. Lince, Gran Apache, and Abismo Negro, may he rest in peace, and you're hair's turned blonde, take a good look in the mirror, you'll like what you see, who wouldn't? Irma looked at herself in the mirror, a silver mask with tiny silver horns and a sparkling silver star above her forehead, a mask covering most of her face, Irma using her index finger to tap twice on her exposed chin, approving of the color of the lipstick she saw in the reflection, Irma drew an invisible line around her lips without touching her face.

A circle slowly formed around Ignacio, sitting in his chair, the warm light of the afternoon showing hints of dusk and throwing early shadows on the floor, seven pairs of hands respectfully folded before him as he looked slowly up the lengths of their bodies from the floor to heads not bowed but aimed nobly at him, and as many pairs of eyes searching, probing and shrewd, accurately accessing the oldest man in the room, by months not years, Mariano only slightly younger, and Rocket, but it can't be Santo, it isn't possible! and Mariano Alcalá, of course it's possible, in this situation there're only miracles, and Luz Elena, he isn't even El Hijo del Santo, with due respect to fathers and sons, but the original, one and only El Santo wearing his silver mask, that's our Ignacio, a kind of leader or senior figure in our group, if only by the calculation of years months days hours, Luz Elena, Rubén Arenal, Mariano, Rosalía, Irma, Ernesto, Guadalupe, each rubbing their hands together in preparation for what they didn't know but flourishing in faith that it was going to be something exceptional, Ignacio getting to his feet unaided by his cane, a younger man at his age, and Mariano Alcalá, a little history if you haven't heard it, and a tip of the hat, if I was wearing one, to Salvador Lutteroth, our father of Mexican wrestling, former property inspector for the tax department, founder with Francisco Ahumado, his financial partner, of Empresa Mexicana de Lucha Libre, the Mexican Wrestling Enterprise, the two men incorporating themselves in 1933, promoting events in Arena Modelo—you know it now as Arena México—and Rodolfo Guzmán, our Santo, El Profe, because they called him professor, wrestled for the first time as El Santo in the old Arena Modelo in 1942, getting his first title ever in February 1943, defeating Ciclón Veloz, Fausto Nicolas Veloz Gallardo, winning the Mexican National Welterweight Championship, and then in April 1943, Lutteroth opened Arena Coliseo, just northwest of the Zócalo, at the southern edge of Tepito—in Nahuatl, Teocaltepiton—a barrio of Mexico City, and for its first card ever, Lutteroth booked a Santo vs. Tarzán López main event, El Santo lost the match, but the rest is history—I said it, a dumb thing to say—but history it is, without an ounce of myth, only truth, the whole truth, and nothing but the truth, El Enmascarado de Plata's a folk hero and symbol of justice, you can call me lazy, 'manos y 'manas, because I'm leaving out plenty, Jesús Lomelí's part, for example, and how Santo got his name, come closer come closer, it's more than history, and it's fun, what I've heard, what I've read, Jesús Lomelí was the Mexican Wrestling Enterprise's main talent scout, and a referee, too, so one fine day, or night, the superstar wrestler "Roughhouse" Jack O'Brien, whose real name was Marcelo Andreani, noticed Rodolfo Guzmán and his brother Miguel "Black" Guzmán's talent—Miguel Guzmán trained his younger brother, our Santo—and Jack O'Brien recommended them to Jesús Lomelí, and señor Lomelí took the brothers to Mexico City, got them signed to contracts with Empresa Mexicana de Lucha Libre—those who didn't work for them, you could count them on one hand—and it was the start of something big, Rodolfo Guzmán was wrestling un- masked as El Hombre Rojo, but it didn't last long, our Santo left La Empresa, and so did señor Lomelí, who started promoting on his own—Frontón México, if my memory's still up and running—so the clock's ticking and days go by, our Santo wrestling for señor Lomelí as El Murciélago Enmascarado II, because Jesús Lomelí didn't want him to be Hombre Rojo anymore, but here's the catch, there's an original El Murciélago Enmascarado, Jesús Velázquez— you're following me, aren't you—and this Murciélago Velázquez didn't like the rookie using his name without permission, so he complained to the boxing and wrestling commission, and the up- shot, the payoff, Rodolfo Guzmán dropped the name, so now it's time Jesús Lomelí used his ingenuity to invent something, and he came up with El Santo, El Diablo, El Ángel, take your pick, that's what he said, they're brawny irresistible spirited names, or he didn't say anything at all, just reciting the list, a few suggestions, take it or leave it, wiping the sweat off his face with a towel, giving our Santo a look straight in the eyes, maybe throwing in a few more words, never say die, mi amigo, you've got an appetite and plenty of tal- ent, I can hear his words like he was whispering them in my ear, so what happened? Rodolfo Guzmán fixed on El Santo, considering he was a relentless *rudo*, maybe tongue-in-cheek, maybe not, but you've got to figure there was a hint of ironic intent, and that *rudo*, our Santo, El Profe, because they called him professor—I know and you know there's no harm in repeating it—became a great *técnico* in 1962—it can happen just like that! *rudo* to *técnico*—but now my tour through history's over folks, you can get out of the bus, and I hope I haven't made you dizzy, facts facts, Mariano taking a bow in his dark blue wrestler's tights, with a touch of Aníbal on his face when Aníbal fought El Solitario, Aníbal, the Carthaginian Warrior, and his spinning headscissors takedown, a big grin stretching the thin layer of Mariano's masklike skin, altogether animated by his new role, rejuvenated by his wrestler's outfit, trim appearance, and undeniable ability to recite.

And Ignacio Pardiñas, thank you, my brother, my partner, Ignacio making a formal gesture waving his arm out in front of him with an open hand, and Ignacio Pardiñas, thank you to my companions in the ring, I bow to you, without absurdity I claim my role in the name of fate and a promise to fight with each of you for the truth we're owed and the rights we deserve, Ignacio raising his hand-painted cane, whirling it over his head, a champion of enthusiasm, and Ignacio Pardiñas, whether or not we're really wearing these costumes and masks—it might be a figment of our communal imagination—it's of little consequence because we're engaged, and I turn with honor to Segundo, let's see his splendor after a narrow escape from danger, a close brush with ghosts right out of *Ugetsu monogatari*, or "Tales of Moonlight and Rain," by Ueda Akinari—tales as beautiful as beauty itself, read them and dream, you'll see what I mean, and all eyes turned to Rubén Arenal now sporting a trim little mustache, shirtless in normal size trunks, arms at his sides with fists loosely closed, thumbs touching his bare upper thighs in a typical pose by and a dead ringer for Enrique Juan Yañez González, or Enrique Llanes, and Ignacio Pardiñas, don't be shy, give Segundo a healthy look up and down, our Rubén Arenal—Rocket to his friends—has taken the shape of Enrique Llanes, known as El Sol de Otumba, born on August 24, 1919, in Otumba, a municipality in the state of Mexico, a handsome wrestler who wrestled without a mask, making his debut in the Arena Modelo in June 1942, he's one of the greats! working for the Mexican Wrestling Enterprise, Enrique Llanes, the inventor of the submission hold called *La Cerrajera*, The Locksmith, a finishing move, a modified abdominal stretch, and the *Quebradora con Giro*, a Tilt-a-whirl backbreaker, was his signature move, during his career he held both El Campeonato Mundial Peso Medio de NWA, the National Wrestling Alliance World Middleweight Championship, and El Campeonato Nacional Semicompleto, the Mexican National Light Heavyweight Championship, and just to make the circle complete, Enrique Llanes was trained by the celebrated champion, Carlos López Tovar, known as Tarzán López, the Tarzán that made his professional debut as Carlos López in April 1934 at the Arena Peralvillo-Cozumel in Tepito, Mexico City, Rubén Arenal, his ears tuned in to every word, more proud than ever, standing as straight as he could, not used to the exceptional level of firmness in the resting muscles of his legs despite all that running around Chihuahua, first in one direction, then another, to find himself beneath the unforgiving sun in front of the plate glass window of La Popular, with its wood-paneled shop floor, arriving there to look with admiration and love at the tall, slender figure of *La Pascualita* in a bridal gown he couldn't afford, and Rocket, you're a fascinating fact machine, señor Pardiñas, like señor Alcalá, and more lively than I've ever seen you, and Mariano Alcalá, that's why he's El Fuerte, *mi Fuerte, el fuerte viento,* our strong wind, Ignacio tapping three times on the floor with his walking stick, but with his recently acquired strength it almost snapped in half, and Ignacio Pardiñas, you can be proud of who you are, Segundo, more than a duplicate of the son of José Yañez López, a telegraphist aligned with the Mexican revolutionaries, and María González Moreno, a direct descendant of Pedro Moreno González, a famous insurgent in our war of independence, Ignacio sat down in his chair with his back as straight as a pine, resting his now powerful hands on the top of the cane, indicating with his chin hidden by a silver mask that everyone should relax and return to where they'd been sitting before he continued with what he had to say about Enrique Llanes.

And Ignacio Pardiñas, Enrique Llanes was trained to be a locksmith by his cousin, and there's a story that goes with it, one day on the bus, coming back from a job, Enrique Llanes saw his idol Tarzán López sitting there, that's right, Carlos López Tovar, and he went to shake his hand, Tarzán López asked him if he was a locksmith, saying something on the order of you look like a locksmith and you've got a locksmith's tools with you, well, as you can plainly see, 'mano, I'm a plumber, but I'd love to learn the locksmith trade, and Enrique Llanes, wearing a smile, answered him, it's true, señor López, I'm a locksmith, and he offered to teach the locksmith trade to Tarzán López in exchange for *lucha libre* training—at the time, Tarzán López was the biggest star and draw in the country—Tarzán López accepted the deal and taught Enrique Llanes amateur, submission and pro-style wrestling at the Gimnasio San José, and later, in the mid-forties, they even formed a tag team, *La Pareja Ideal*, "The Ideal Team," becoming the most popular babyface, or *técnico*, team of the era, masters of both *llaves*, you know the rest, it's the tale of the rise of wrestler Enrique Llanes, one of the finest technicians in the country, and Mariano Alcalá, you see what kind of man you are! and Rosalía Calderón, he retired from the ring in 1963, but worked for years in radio and TV, and Luz Elena, with respect for a title that isn't only the position of being the champion of a major sports competition, in the eighties, he was a commissioner within the Comisión de Box y Lucha Libre Mexico D.F., the Mexico City Boxing and Wrestling Commission, and Guadalupe Muñoz, he died of natural causes on September 18, 2004, and Ignacio Pardiñas, a lesson to us all, there's life after death, we're proof of that—except for Irma, in her two-piece costume, looking a lot like the living Sexi Star, I'm sure Dulce García wouldn't mind, Rosalía in a rose-colored sleeveless bodysuit resembling the alive-and-well Zuleyma, I'm sure La Princesa Hindu, Elvia Fragoso, wouldn't mind, Luz Elena in a black opaque bodysuit, reminding us of the ever-present Pantera Sureña, I'm sure Lidia Rangel wouldn't mind, Lupe, wearing a black and gold bodysuit, with La Dinamita's face for a mask, I'm sure María Dolores González wouldn't mind, and of course, our Ernesto as the eternal Mil Máscaras, I'm sure Aarón Rodríguez wouldn't mind either, we're representing the living and the dead, which makes us twice as strong, Luz Elena, Rubén Arenal, Mariano, Rosalía, Irma, Ernesto, Guadalupe believing in the words spoken by Ignacio, each of them represented a formidable force in the form of a wrestler, Luz Elena proud in Pantera Sureña's bodysuit, Rubén Arenal as Enrique Llanes puffing out his chest, Mariano's neat Air Force blue Aníbal-like face with white *antifaz*, Rosalía with Zully's beautiful head of hair beneath the mask of Magdalena Caballero, Irma's silver star and tiny silver horns on her silver mask glinting in the last golden rays of sunlight, Ernesto's face wearing a thin skin that was Mil Máscaras' leopard-skin mask with red trim around the eyes, nose, and mouth, and a white *M* on the forehead, Guadalupe ready with her signature moves: Lola González's powerbomb, a flying legdrop, or a senton splash—instead of landing stomach first across her opponent, it was a simple back splash—Ignacio as El Santo, leaving his walking stick where it was leaning against the chair, he'd use his hands, the strength in his arms, the purity in his heart, Ignacio getting up again, spreading his arms to embrace them all, eight warriors moving to the front door of Ignacio's home on Barrancas del Cobre, the door opening of its own accord, no human intervention, the breath of Coyuco propelling them, or a stupendous effort of Coyuco's otherworldly will, they felt he was at the center of things, walking with them, arms linked once they'd got out of the house, turning left, then a sort of V formation, but on the earth, their feet on the ground, walking slightly downhill away from the cement staircase with approximately nine steps and a railing on the left-hand side, not going to Mariano and Rosalía's

house, but continuing on Barrancas del Cobre in the opposite direction past Calle 34a, Ignacio as El Santo leading the way, Barrancas
del Cobre leveling off, a lemon-yellow house beside a pale orange
house on their right, passing a pale green single-story house, one
on each side of the road, not a wrestler out of breath, eight pairs of
lungs in tip-top shape, proceeding quickly and with determination,
Mariano, Rosalía, Luz Elena, Rubén Arenal, Ignacio, Irma, Ernesto,
Guadalupe, shoulder to shoulder, a row eight wrestlers wide, each
the escort of the other, the sun heading for the horizon, no longer
throwing shadows, and on their left, a metallic maroon Chevy 4x4
pickup parked at the side of the street with its hood up, the wrestlers arriving at the end of Barrancas del Cobre, taking a right on
Calle Trigésima, then a left into Hacienda Agua Nueva, a road with
a tree-lined median strip between single lanes of opposing traffic,
a few pedestrians, plenty of parked cars, at last coming to a long
cement whitewashed brick wall with razor wire running along the
top, and a couple of palm trees, a wall concealing one side of a cemetery, Panteón Municipal 2, that lay spread out behind it, they took
a right on to Calle 20A, carrying on in twilight, more shapes than
distinct figures with faces, Panteón Municipal 1, across the street on
their left, a large cemetery with a white painted façade and a slate-
gray stone arch, a bicycle parking rack, a single stone bench, and
a man selling flowers under a blue plastic canopy on the left side
of the entrance, a bicycle parking rack with two stone benches on
the right side, Mariano, Rosalía, Luz Elena, Rubén Arenal, Ignacio,
Irma, Ernesto, Guadalupe huddling together under a mild evening
sky for an informal, private conversation, and Ignacio Pardiñas, all
wrestlers are tied together by more than their *funciones,* or their
programas, and Mariano Alcalá, *en el Norte,* up north, it's called a
card, five matches played out over the course of about two hours,
and Guadalupe Muñoz, maybe life'll be less complicated now that
we're *luchadores* and *luchadoras,* their heads were bent, their masklike faces almost touching, as they stood there in a circle until the
refraction and scattering of the sun's rays from the atmosphere drew

their attention to the soft glowing light in the sky, each raising his or her eyes, admiring the twilight, and then they heard a song, "Al pie de la tumba," "By Your Tomb," a *ranchera* written by Alfredo García, played and sung by Conjunto Tamaulipas, Rafael Ramírez and Tono Borrego, the music and words entering their ears, one wrestler after the other, until they were all looking around to see where it was coming from, at first thinking it might be the flower seller's radio, but it was switched off, then perhaps from a small loudspeaker attached to a wall near the entrance to the cemetery, but it wasn't a loudspeaker, it was a bird or shadow trying to get a foothold at dusk in a crack in the wall, the apparent form of something when the reality was different, so much like life, and without finding the source, under the watchful gaze of a bird, or the stain of a shadow, the music surrounding them, hearing the heartbreaking lyrics, they breathed in each verse like an absent mist which filled their hearts with a renewed sense of loss, of unjust treatment, not much melancholy, and more than a hint of anger at the government, the police, the army, and authority in general:

> *Me fui al cementerio*
> *A soltar el llanto*
> *A ver si llorando*
> *Te puedo olvidar;*
> *Ahora comprendo*
> *Que es imposible,*
> *Porque ya ni muerta*
> *Te dejo de amar.*
>
> *Al pie de la tumba,*
> *Mirando hacia el cielo*
> *Quisiera escuchar tu voz*
> *Quisiera abrazarte*
> *Quisiera besarte*
> *Pero no es imposible*
> *Tu ya estás con Dios.*

Dormido te sueño
Despierto te miro,
Muy dentro de mi alma
Siempre vivirás
No puedo olvidarte
Yo quiero seguirte
Que me llevan lejos
Adonde tú estás.

I went to the cemetery
To pour out my sorrow
To see if by crying
My heart could forget;
But now I can see
That it just can't be done,
For even in death
I can't stop loving you.

I sit by your tombstone,
Look up to the heavens
I wish I could hear your voice
I wish I could kiss you
I wish I could hold you
But there is no way,
You're now with God.

At night I dream of you,
By day I can see you,
You always will live
In the depths of my heart.
I just can't forget you
I wish I were with you
They might as well take me
Away where you are.

Mariano, Rosalía, Luz Elena, Rubén Arenal, Ignacio, Irma, Ernesto, Guadalupe trying to shake off the paralyzing significance of the song, there was a lot to be done down the road, and they understood it was going to be more than they could imagine, they couldn't afford to become rooted to the spot, no place for feeling sorry for themselves, and Rocket, let's have a smoke before we go in, Rubén Arenal taking a pack of Faros from his pocket, not Delicados or Fiesta, cigarettes were passed around to those who smoked, and the pack wasn't a white and green and black pack of Aros that he extended toward Ernesto, having tapped out a Faros to make it easier to reach, Ernesto remembering Aarón's gold, red and white pack of Capri as he put the cigarette between lips surrounded by *antifaz,* Ignacio shaking his head no, putting a Chiclets in his mouth, Rosalía holding her hand out for one of Ignacio's Chiclets, Irma offering Guadalupe a La Casta Toro 6x50 by Santa Clara, with a Viso filler from Estelí Nicaragua, San Andrés Morron and Habano, wrapped in San Andrés Maduro, the right size for the occasion, Mariano thinking twice, asking Rubén Arenal for a Faros, the rules had changed since they'd undergone something on the order of a terrific transformation, inside and out, Luz Elena didn't dare because it reminded her of El Güero, she'd quit smoking when he left her with three kids to raise, until then she'd always had something in her mouth not counting her tongue and a toothpick, the group moved a couple of feet away from the entrance in the direction of the two stone benches, the song went right on playing, the trembling sun hanging for an instant on the ledge of the horizon before letting go, falling out of sight, Ernesto, Guadalupe, Rubén Arenal, Luz Elena, Mariano, Rosalía, Irma, Ignacio finding themselves in the dark, in more ways than one, none of them knowing what they were going to see and do once they went into Panteón Municipal 1, but they prayed the dead would rise up and offer them their strength, not in numbers, or physical power and energy, but a boost a lift a shot in the arm with a solemn promise to stay with them, going the distance, and beyond, and hoping for more than a few words of advice when they asked the souls walking the earth outside of death, turning round and round with too much time on their hands, to point out the way, maybe you can walk with us for a couple of miles, or whatever it takes to get there, the beginning not the end, because that's where we're headed, we've got to move fast, the end might come before we know it, we're prepared, we swear up and down, just ask any one of us, we've got patience, and endurance, too, but the end can come a lot sooner than expected if we're caught, killed, carved up into little pieces, buried or burned to a crisp, our ashes scattered like the others, or thrown in jail to rot for eternity, so just lead the way, we'll fight them, we're recognized wrestlers, widely known, with limitless skills in the ring, flesh and blood endowed with extraordinary know-how, we've got our faith, and you to guide us, along with God, according to *Isaías 30:21,* Isaiah 30:21, *Entonces tus oídos oirán a tus espaldas palabra que diga: Este es el camino, andad por él; y no echéis a la mano derecha, ni tampoco torzáis a la mano izquierda,* "And your ears shall hear a word behind you, saying, 'This is the way, walk in it,' when you turn to the right or when you turn to the left," what do you say? no compass required, and if you can't join forces with the living, you can use your fingers, bony as they are, to show us the spot, more than an indication, the exact point in time or space at which we'll begin our work, north south east west? you might say we've already begun, then don't hold back! ride with us to our destination, Rosalía and Ignacio getting rid of their Chiclets, Irma and Guadalupe finishing their cigars, Rubén Arenal, Ernesto, and Mariano grinding out the Faros that'd burned their throats by using the heel of their wrestling boots, Luz Elena patiently watching them, together they turned away from Calle 20A, walked beneath the arch of the entrance to Panteón Municipal 1, past the iron gates that were open like welcoming arms, the early stars lighting their way, Ernesto, Guadalupe, Rubén Arenal, Luz Elena, Mariano, Rosalía, Irma, Ignacio entering the cemetery, greeting the first bleached white tombs on their left, a sea of graves lying ahead of them, outlines of crypts and vaults, junipers and pines against the darkening blue sky, their eyes adjusting to the night-time, while indistinct shapes came up out of the dry earth through prickly scrambling wild shrubs, a face peering around a statue, another materializing next to a mausoleum, friendly branches of trees beckoned them from afar, here we are here we are, volunteers one and all, with this encouragement, Ernesto, Guadalupe, Rubén Arenal, Luz Elena, Mariano, Rosalía, Irma, Ignacio moved forward, their masklike faces displaying more than a hint of the hallmarks of reputable wrestlers past and present, and as they made their way farther into Panteón Municipal 1, reacquainting themselves with their surroundings, blending in with the arrangement of the natural and artificial physical features of the graveyard, they swore once more to stick to their pledge, counting on the wonders of the spirits of the dead.

ACKNOWLEDGMENTS

I want to thank Claudia Paz y Paz, former Attorney General of Guatemala and member of GIEI, Grupo Interdisciplinario de Expertos Independientes, a committee which investigated the disappearance in Mexico of forty-three student teachers from Ayotzinapa; Almudena Bernabeu, international attorney, co-founder and director of Guernica 37 International Justice Chambers; Salvador Saso Torres, poet, novelist and friend. My special thanks to Fermín Herrera, professor of Chicana/o Studies at California State University, Northridge, for his inestimable knowledge of the Nahuatl language and Mexican music, for his talent as a musician, and for his friendship.

ABOUT THE AUTHOR

Born in Milwaukee, Wisconsin, Mark Fishman has lived and worked in Paris since 1995. His novels, *The Magic Dogs of San Vicente,* and *No. 22 Pleasure City,* were published by Guernica in 2016 and 2018 respectively. His short stories have appeared in a number of literary reviews, such as the *Chicago Review*, the *Carolina Quarterly*, the *Black Warrior Review*, the *Mississippi Review, Frank* (Paris), and *The Literary Review.* A short story earned a first prize for fiction in *Glimmer Train*, issue 100. He was the English-language editor of *The Purple Journal* (Paris) and *Les Cahiers Purple* (Lisbon).

MIX
Paper from
responsible sources

FSC
www.fsc.org   FSC® C100212

Printed in March 2020
by Gauvin Press,
Gatineau, Québec